Reunion

Another Story from the Adventures of Harry and Paul
A sequel to, *The Night Always Comes*

Paul John Hausleben

Photographs of the author by Paul John Hausleben
Cover design and concept by Paul John Hausleben

ISBN: 978-0-9886336-2-9

DEDICATION

To Binky wherever the hell she is now

CONTENTS

"Someday, the present days will be the days that you talk about fondly, not the days of old memories."

Paul John Hausleben, April 2013

ACKNOWLEDGMENTS

This time around, I will thank Harry M. Rogers Jr., my family, and friends. I need to single out a special thank you to my grandfather. Thank you for sitting together on the front porch at 182 Belmont, white tee shirts, cold beer, warm nights, watching the world go by and learning tidbits for these stories. This story was inside of me for a long time, I just needed to find it, and for that I thank you Gramps, I really do.

Preface

Reunion is a very different work from anything else I have ever written. This book certainly has a great deal of fun, spoofs and humor within the pages, but more so than anything else I have written to this point, it has an abundance of hidden messages of what I feel are very important aspects of life. I will not identify those aspects or hidden meanings, or expound upon them, instead, I will leave it to you as the reader to uncover them.

Perhaps you will interpret your own hidden meanings, and apply them to your own life. The book also contains a strong element of religious undertones. There was no intention for *Reunion* to be a religious book by any means, but I felt that the main characters required a strong faith to be fully developed. In my opinion, religion in America was very different during the time and setting of this story, and because of my belief, I strongly felt that I needed to depict my own view within the pages of *Reunion.*

Reunion is the direct result of some ideas in which I had developed at the very end of *The Night Always Comes.* I wrote *The Night Always Comes,* at a very dark and frankly, depressed time in my life. I wrote the book; start to finish, within a feverish four-week period. *The Night Always Comes,* flowed along very quickly, and at times, it felt as if I could not type it quickly enough. The humorous sections of that novel depict, for the most part, actual events that occurred for Harry and me, and that made it flow a bit stronger. Even I, recognizing my own eccentric tendencies, was surprised at the humor that comes out of such darkness.

Laughter is indeed the best medicine!

At the conclusion of *The Night Always Comes,* I actually did not intend to write any more about, "The Adventures of Harry and Paul." However, certain ideas, characters, and elements of a framework for new adventures came into my mind, including some inspiration from our actual, real-life, adventures.

I felt it would leave a great deal of, "their stories" incomplete if I chose not to continue. I pondered it for a bit and came up with the rest of this story. I knew right from the very first word that I wrote that I would choose the title of this book to be *Reunion.*

I feel that reunion within an individual is one of the most important aspects of life. All of us in some way, shape or form, tend to "fall apart" in various ways during our life, and then require a reunion of sorts to put ourselves back together. It could be reunion with your spouse, your religious beliefs, your career, your children, or perhaps your own inner soul. It is part of life, and on occasion, we all require it.

It is my hope that this book captures some of that.

Utilizing Harry and Paul, I wrote to display how a lifelong bond never really can be broken by time or by space, and reunion can be a glorious event.

I enjoyed the experience of writing, *Reunion.* I hope you enjoy reading it as much as I enjoyed writing it! I hope you enjoy reading it as much as I enjoyed writing it! Come along once more with Paul John Henson, Harry M. Redmond Jr., their family, and friends to see where it takes all of us.

It is my wish that this book, in a roundabout way, will help you with some type of reunion that you might be seeking in your own life.

Paul John Hausleben

April 2013

Prologue

"Paulie boy," my grandfather said to me one summer in the early evening, "life is always full of twists and turns. It, at times, can be so painful, tearing your very soul apart with what seems is a piece-by-piece, slow dissection. At other times, it can be full of joy, laughter, and euphoric moments that stir your inner being, and restore you to new heights."

He took a long sip of Big Boulder beer from a can and looked at me, as we sat together on the steps of the front porch of 182 Belmont Avenue watching as the cars, and life went by on the busy city street in front of us. My grandfather had become accustomed to American beers, but he much preferred the stronger ales of his homeland in England. Oftentimes, he would drink the beer warmer than my father enjoyed it. I can still remember the case of beer sitting in a cardboard lid outside of his apartment door. He was, "Warming it up," as he would say.

It was the summer of 1970, and I was about ten or eleven years old, with long blonde hair that hung down to about my shoulders, and was always in my eyes. I reached up, pushed the hair from my face, and my grandfather looked at me and laughed.

"Are you ever going to cut that hair off, Paulie boy?"

I shook my head emphatically back and forth to indicate no.

He took another swig of beer and asked me, "Do you not worry about being made fun of or being called a girl by the other boys? Or will you bloody well beat them to a pulp if they laugh? I bet you would beat them to a pulp, even if they are a bit bigger or older, eh?"

"I do not worry about them, Gramps. I am not afraid of them, even the older and bigger kids."

"You and that lad from a few blocks over, what is his name? Harry? He is a big lad. I bet you two will not back down from anyone, eh?"

"That is right, Gramps. Harry and I can take on any of them."

"Good for you, Paulie boy. Never allow people to judge you, Paulie boy, for how you look, or how you talk or how you walk. Make them judge you for what you do, how you treat others, and for the person whom you really are. Never change for anyone, Paulie boy, always be who you are. If they think you are different, or you do not fit in, then prove them wrong, for you will be the better man for it. God made all of us the way he decided to make us. So be who you are and always be proud of it."

My grandfather gave me a little playful push in the shoulder and I smiled at him.

We sat in silence for a little longer until he spoke once more. Looking back, my grandfather was giving me credit for being smarter than I should have been at that age, or he was just speaking his thoughts out into the air.

"Keep a positive attitude despite adversity and obstacles, Paulie boy. It is the single most important frame of mind that a person can have. Always recognize and then unite yourself with others who think and act the same as you do. Choose and pick people who are similar to you, and then together, you will love and care for each other, smile every day, cry when you need to, laugh more than you cry, dance to the music that you enjoy the most, and admire the sunrise and sunsets."

My grandfather pointed over to the sun sinking low in the sky over the old apartment house across the street from us. I noticed how breathtaking the sky was as the heat of the day faded and the night was becoming cooler.

"Pretty nice, eh?" he asked me.

I nodded my head to indicate that I agreed. It was beautiful.

Between sips of his beer, he spoke once more, "Once you have a circle of support, combined with the correct frame of mind, as well as loving friends and family, you will have all the power that you need to succeed at anything in life. Then you and your loved ones and friends can charge off into life's battles with your battle flags unfurled, ready to take on anything that this old world can throw at you. Believe me, Paulie boy. I have done it in my life, and you will do it in yours. You are going to grow up and be an important chap in an awful lot of people's lives. You are going to do special things. I can tell."

He looked down at me and took a long swig of his beer.

"You are a good one, Paulie boy. You are tall, strong, and tough. Sometimes, when I look at your mum, Aunt Lois, your sister, and all of your cousins, I cannot believe what your grandmother and I started here in America with this family."

He leaned in close and I could smell the beer on his breath as he whispered to me, "Rwy'n dy garu di, and do not tell your mum or grandmother that I spoke the word bloody in front of you, eh?"

I smiled at him and put my arm around his shoulders, "I won't, Gramps."

My grandfather was a really cool guy, and I loved him too.

We sat in silence together, until it became dark, and then we went into the house for the night.

Reunion

1

A New Life

Through many experiences in my life and many instances, I have learned that one single, slight moment in time can change everything. Like a flash, both good or bad incidents and events can occur at any time, and I always found that to be a profound, mysterious, and sometimes chilling aspect of life. Recounting events in my own life is a complicated process for me. It very often invokes memories of times of great highs and great lows. I often sit in idle times, and wonder how I could have ever arrived at the point in time that I am in right now, and what transpired throughout the years to bring me to this point.

I really thought for a while that I was just an ordinary guy, just someone who grew up with a lot of friends and a wonderful family, who actually was very lucky. Then again, I have long since given up on classifying my friends, my adventures, and myself or the people I love or associate with, for being ordinary. Most of all, the significant events in my life could never be classified as commonplace. In fact, if I were to sit down over a few beers and tell the story of my life to someone who never knew me, then that person would have a hard time not dismissing the stories as simply being the wild ramblings of a drunkard!

One of the things that is a blessing for me is that I can remember everything. Actually, being honest, I am not sure if it is a gift or a curse. I sit when I am alone sometimes, and it is very strange. I hear a song on the radio; I see something on the television or a person speaks a random word or thought to me, and it triggers my memories.

The memories instantly transport me back to a time or place and I can see faces, hear voices, and remember the events or incidents word for word. There are always some ghosts of the past that follow me around, they float around here and there, and at times, I can see them and hear them very clearly.

Now, do not get me wrong, I do enjoy the reflections and I do not dwell upon the past or fret about it, in fact, I think it enriches my life. Some of these events were joyful, and some were very painful, but nonetheless, I journey back. It seems as if inside of my head, God gave me a little book of time and memories that I keep on a shelf. On occasion, I can open it and read it.

Sometimes, it makes me laugh, and sometimes, it makes me feel like crying.

Today was a day when my book of time easily opened. I was sitting alone in my chair in my office at work and it was becoming late in the day. I had been very busy earlier in the day, with a meeting with an unusual person. I was used to unusual meetings, and in fact, I seem to attract strange and eccentric persons, but this one had been a real winner. It had drained me a bit more than I thought and after the meeting had ended; I had lost track of time. For no real reason, I looked out the window next to me, and I spotted the sun creeping down in the west. It lit up the horizon with that fantastic blue clear sky that just seems to be there every once in a while, in my life. It appears from time to time and invokes some of the most powerful of my memories. Off I went, back in time once more, to when a number of these sunsets and clear horizons came along for me, and many of the other people whom I love the most in my life.

"I am really hoping that your parents like me, Binky."

"Oh please, you will do fine, I just checked the statistics for a first-time meeting of my future in laws, and the success rate is very high. Besides, you already have met my father, the night when you broke his hand, so that should go fine . . . he knows you already."

I had a quick flashback to the first time I ever met Mr. William T. Hobnobber, and I shook it off very quickly. There is no doubt that it had been one of the strangest and most bizarre experiences of my life. Mr. Hobnobber certainly was a unique and overwhelming personality.

We were driving over for dinner to meet Binky's parents and tell them that we planned to get married. Three days ago, Binky had returned from her time away caused by, as she described it, "Her flawed research." On that night, we had enjoyed a wonderful, yet tearful reunion.

It had indeed been, as our old friend Howard Pailet, would have said, "A magical time."

I knew in my heart that I could no longer stand to be apart from Binky, and on that incredible night, we had both decided to begin a new life together. I had proposed to her on the night Binky had returned and she had accepted.

"I think Father will be upset that you did not discuss your intentions to marry me beforehand, but given the circumstances of my flawed research, as well as my ill-advised decision to leave, and my surprising return with no advance notice, I think he will understand."

Binky and her endless research and statistical gathering, it was part of her quirky personality, but I loved it!

"Well, I am still not exactly sure how to act, or what to say, but I will do my best. I sure hope they like me."

I pulled my old jeep into the long, winding driveway of the Hobnobber home and made our way up to the garage.

Binky reached over, smiled, and hugged me as I shut the ignition off. "What is there not to love? After all, I picked out the best, long-haired, hippie, professional hockey goalie that was available."

"Correction. I am now a retired, professional hockey goalie. We will see. I sure hope you are right, Binky."

Any slight element of confidence that remained inside of me had waned when I had recalled my previous meeting with Mr. Hobnobber way back in the winter of 1980. I thought how silly it was for me to be lacking confidence and to be so anxious. After all, I did have a long career, standing calmly in front of one hundred miles per hour slap shots for many years as a professional ice hockey goalie, but I guess we all have our level of anxiety at times. This was just different; the young lady next to me had just agreed to be my wife. Believe it or not, now that I had experienced both instances for an accurate comparison, my engagement had a lot more impact than getting knocked in the head with a hockey puck!

We walked hand in hand up to the front door, and Binky was reaching in her purse for the key, when the front door suddenly burst open. We both were a little startled. I looked into the home and saw that standing in front of us was a tall, statuesque woman, with shoulder-length blonde hair. She smiled broadly with perfect, white teeth and sparkling blue eyes. She was stunning. No, to be quite accurate, she was gorgeous! Her hair was perfect, and her figure was a perfect hourglass. She wore a black dress with a gold necklace, gold dangling earrings, and a huge diamond engagement ring surrounded by an immense wedding band, displayed proudly upon her ring finger.

"Dear Binky, come in, come in!"

Oh boy, Binky's mom! I now knew where Binky obtained her own gorgeous looks.

"Hello, Mother, it is so nice to see you, we are so excited." Binky gave her mother a hug, and I walked in behind her as they embraced.

I gazed around at the sprawling home. Correction, it

was more like a mansion that was the Hobnobber family home. The center entrance to the home had a sprawling, center staircase that curled majestically up towards the second floor of the mansion. Above the polished marble floors that lined the grand entrance area was a large, sparkling, hanging, gold trimmed chandelier. The glowing lights of the fixture twinkled behind illuminated crystal tips, broadcasting a prism of color around the entrance of the home.

Fish out of water, Paul; you are a true fish out of water. Poor kid from Paterson meets fabulously wealthy and gorgeous chick, they get married and live happily ever after. Oh brother, what a story!

It was like some tearjerker soap opera plot.

In a few short years, I had sure put myself in a lot of different places and situations, from hockey rinks all over the country, to fancy mansions. I am sure a long way from 182 Belmont Ave and 20 John Street in good old Paterson, New Jersey.

"Dear Mother, I would like you to meet, Paul!" Binky introduced us and turned towards me, smiling broadly, as she grabbed my hand to pull me closer to her and her mother.

Mrs. Hobnobber stood back as I reached out to shake her hand and say hello.

"Oh boy, stop right there, mister. Let me have a good look at you there, Paul! After all this time, incredible drama, tears, flawed research, and all of what I have heard about you! I need to check you out in person and see who has my little Binky twisted up tighter than an afternoon of intense research."

I felt even more awkward while Mrs. Hobnobber stood back and she began intensely gazing me up and down. Binky stood there smiling as if she had just won the lottery.

"Spin around, please."

Mrs. Hobnobber made a spinning motion in the air with

her left hand. Binky grabbed me and turned me as if I was some kind of display model on a rotating pedestal. This was ridiculous. I was now really feeling like I was some kind of prize fish they caught, and they were measuring me for stuffing and mounting on a wall for a trophy.

"You selected a winner, dear. I am so proud of you! Oh my, what a male specimen, dear Binky!"

Specimen? Now, I am a specimen.

"He is so tall! Much taller than I had imagined. After all, Binky, the only picture I ever saw of him was that one from the newspaper in Kansas City that you sent me. You know dear Binky, the one where he was coming off the ice and the young girl was taking off her brassiere for him to sign. Did you ever go out there and find that young lady, dear? I know you wanted to go out there and break her in half." Mrs. Hobnobber stood and looked at Binky, awaiting her answer.

Binky nodded her head rapidly back and forth to indicate no. I thought how the poor hockey fan back there in Kansas City would never realize what fate she had narrowly escaped! There was the famous incident way back when at the Black Bear Club involving one of them, as Binky called her, "Scantily clad little flirts," that displayed just how tough Binky could be!

"He is positively striking, all that hair, that beard, and oh boy, you can tell by that body he was, and still is, an athlete! Your lovemaking sessions must be incredible! I agree with you that he should never tie all that hair up."

Binky nodded her head up and down, this time in her rapid agreement nod.

I was hoping that she did not get dizzy from all this multi-directional nodding.

This was rapidly turning into a second-place ranking of weird encounters, right behind the current front-runner, which was, of course, meeting Mr. Hobnobber. Where was Harry to rescue me now?

"Forget a handshake there, big guy. I like my hands the way that they are without any broken bones. Now come on over here Paul and give me a big hug. I need to feel you for myself."

With that, Mrs. Hobnobber reached out and grabbed me for a hug that felt like she was clamping me in a vise. After almost breaking my body in half, she stood back, fluffed her hair out as Binky does, and then planted a big lip, lock, type kiss on me, taking me completely by surprise. I now knew from where Binky inherited her superhuman strength!

My old hockey nemesis, Jim O'Malley, would have met his match with Mrs. Hobnobber. She would have taken him apart with one hand tied behind her back. I did not know what to say, I just stood there like an absolutely horrified, tongue-tied imbecile. I felt like a little puppy that someone just brought home from the pet shop for the first time to a new family. All the time, Binky just stood on the sideline beaming at her perceived good fortune by selecting, "a winner" in the men's selection lottery.

I finally managed to say, "It is so nice to meet you, Mrs. Hobnobber, it is my pleasure."

"Oh, don't call me Mrs. Hobnobber, call me, Sarah."

She smiled broadly, shifted her feet, dabbed at her lipstick with a tissue, and fixed her hair. The lip lock kiss had caused a slight fluster in her appearance and required some correction. I detected that she also could shift back and forth from a prim and proper mode, to a wild woman at the flip of a switch. Let us see, hmmm, the picture is becoming clearer now, research, and wild stares inherited from her father, and the normally prim and proper mode that could include split second transformations into a wild woman from Mom!

I sure loved my Binky; she was one of a kind, that was for sure, but it appeared that her mother was almost as eccentric as her father was.

When Mrs. Hobnobber had told me that her name was Sarah, my mind went back in time to the first night I had met Binky on that famous blind date at Lord Crudley's bar. I had actually seen Binky at the end of that now famous playoff game when I shut out the New York Colonials and my team; the Long Island Roosters had won the championship, with a last-minute goal in the seventh game of the playoffs. Binky was sitting with Harry and Rose in the stands. I glanced up at them on my way up the runway into the locker room. It was a wild crowd scene, but I know our eyes had very briefly met. It was not until Harry introduced us and a few years after that, did the fleeting memory come back into my mind.

That, however, is a whole other story.

On that fateful night at the gin joint, it was when Harry planted incorrectly in my head that Binky was merely a nickname, and that her real name was, Sarah. That created a firestorm at our first meeting when I made the mistake of asking Binky her *real* name and ignited her wild side. It turned out that my old buddy had received the wrong information, but in light of this tidbit of information, I felt I should forgive Harry for the slight mix-up in the names.

Mrs. Hobnobber then smiled at us and she gathered us gently together for a group type hug.

She then spoke in a low whisper, "I have a feeling by the glow on my dear Binky's face though that Paul will be calling me, dear Mother before very long."

Mrs. Hobnobber winked at both of us.

"Binky, I hate to break up this fantastic meeting, but your father requested that as soon as Paul arrived, that he would meet with him in his private study. I have not seen him for hours. He locked himself behind closed doors, but he rang me on the intercom a while ago to give me those instructions. I am afraid I have kept Paul too long already, and your father will have already calculated some type of odds of this adversely affecting the evening we have planned. So, let's make haste, and steer Paul to the study room, while we go check on dinner, see where Tinky is, prepare some snacks, and mix us some drinks."

Hmm, so this is what Mrs. Hobnobber considers a fantastic meeting, eh? I guess I agree with that, but perhaps not quite in the same context as Binky and Mrs. Hobnobber would. Now, I have a one-on-one meeting with the great man himself, Mr. Hobnobber, in his own private study!

It keeps getting better all the time.

"Now Paul, please do not be nervous. Father, in all probability, has conducted some research, and decided that meeting you face to face, man to man, in his study is the proper way for you both to reunite after your last meeting so long ago."

Mrs. Hobnobber chimed in, "Binky is correct, my dear Paul, my husband's hand healed in six months. I am sure there are no real hard feelings, or lingering repercussions."

That made me feel better. After all, it was not as if we had a hockey brawl and beat each other over the heads with our sticks. I had only shaken the poor man's hand. Binky gave me a hug and a kiss and pointed towards a long hallway that was off to the side of the grand entrance foyer. I peered down a long, foreboding hallway, which was dressed with fabulous artwork on the walls and trimmed in oak moldings, as well as lit by ornate, but dim, light fixtures. I wondered what terrible trap or fate awaited me on the other end of this hallway.

"Father's private study is the last door on the right side of the hallway. Remember, I love you dearly, twenty-seven. Mother and I will be in the kitchen. Please come find us when you two men have finished your man-to-man discussion. We need to find Tinky, so that you may meet him as well."

"Go get him, twenty-seven!"

Mrs. Hobnobber gave me a slap on the backside and I jumped in the air. I felt like now all that I needed was to be wearing my goalie equipment, and for O'Malley to be staring me down, and I would be all set for battle.

I set off on the long trek towards the door to Mr. Hobnobber's study.

In my mind, as I walked down the hallway, I also could not help but try to figure out whom, or what, is a Tinky? Both Mrs. Hobnobber and Binky had mentioned the name, but for the life of me, I could not imagine what a Tinky was, or is. Must be the family dog or some other pet, I thought to myself.

I set off down the hallway, thinking about how my old man also had a study, years ago, in our old home in Paterson. It was a little different, as it also saw double duty as a bathroom, but nonetheless, according to my old man, it was his study. I am sure that I will find Mr. Hobnobber's room, just a hairpin different from the old man's room.

I made my way down the long hallway which seemed as if it ended somewhere near Fargo, North Dakota. Now, my mind circled back to the famous climb to our torture chamber on the Flipper amusement ride years ago, when Rose, Binky, and I climbed halfway to the moon to meet the Grim Reaper and his faithful, toothless, assistant. It was now a draw as to which place that I would rather be, this hallway, or on the staircase to Hades in Seashore Heights, New Jersey.

I decided that the best decision was to face one great Hobnobber challenge at a time as I climbed to the top of Mount Weirdness to speak with the ancient and wise sage who dwells on the top of the peak.

I finally reached the correct door, breathed in deep, and gently knocked on it.

From deep within the confines of behind the door, I heard Mr. Hobnobber's voice.

"Is that you, Paul?"

"Yes, sir. It is."

"Are you alone?"

"Yes. I am, sir."

"Wait!"

I heard him moving around inside the room. Then, I saw the door handle turn and heard the lock snap open on the door.

"Please come in quickly and close the door behind you. Turn the lock behind you once you are inside to lock the door once more."

This is going to be fun.

Does he have a gun or some other device to confront me with on the other side of the door? Perhaps he had hired O'Malley for a side job, and they were both going to jump me once I was in the room, to even the score for his broken hand and all the times I shut down O'Malley on the rink. I spun various scenarios around in my mind. It seemed so ominous, as if perhaps he had somehow gotten wind of our announcement of our pending marriage. I thought oh well, I am prepared to fight for my lady, after all the battles I had with O'Malley; this should be mere children's play. Therefore, like Sir Galahad, I bravely opened the door and walked in.

"Come in, Paul, close the door there, and lock it."

I walked in, quickly shut the door, and turned the lock on the handle. The room was huge, and it was spectacular. It was wall to wall with oak bookcases, filled from floor to ceiling with rows upon rows of books. I had never seen so many books in a person's private home!

The vast resources of Binky as well as Mr. Hobnobber's endless quests of research finally revealed!

The walls had maps, pictures, and various works of art hung over all of them. There was a large, impressive oak desk at one end with a picture window behind it. Piles of books, newspapers, and papers littered the desk.

Mr. Hobnobber still had not looked up from his desk. He had kept his head down, and he was resting his head on his right hand and arm while covering his right ear. He appeared to be studying a pile of papers on his desk.

"It is very nice to see you again, sir. It has been a long time. I will not offer to shake your hand since I know that did not go over well last time. I am sorry about that. I really want to apologize."

"Oh, do not worry about that, drivel! I healed fine in a few months. What do you think I am, some kind of wimp or something? We have a matter of much more dire importance to handle here, son. What took you so long? I have been waiting for you for hours."

"Oh, I am sorry. Binky took a while to research some news that she heard of, and then we were delayed by my first meeting with Mrs. Hobnobber."

"Oh, stop all that endless babble and twaddle. Stop your mindless explaining and come on over here will you."

Mr. Hobnobber still had not looked up at me, and he continued to hold his hand and arm over his ear, while he held his head. It was obvious that he was upset, and my assumption was that he had been studying some type of disturbing document on his desk.

I walked over and was prepared to sit down in one of the guest chairs in front of his desk.

"Now, this is a serious matter, and I expect some type of explanation and plan from you, Paul. You just cannot come waltzing in here like some hot shot, long-haired, hippie, goaltender, without offering a solution. You have a reputation as a problem solver. Therefore, we need to come to some type of agreement as far as a plan goes."

Oh, boy, I was in some serious trouble for not speaking to him before proposing and he was extremely upset with me. Somehow, he had gotten wind of it before we could tell anyone.

"I am sorry sir, but it all happened so fast, Binky came back, we reunited, we both were caught up in the moment, and I asked her. . .."

"WHAT ON EARTH ARE YOU TALKING ABOUT? I

am not talking about that you have most likely proposed to my lovely, smart and gorgeous little girl, and that she, for some outlandish reason, decided to accept. I anticipated years ago that when that time came, you would not have the common decency to speak with me beforehand, because you are some thickheaded, brutish, goalie who must have taken too many headshots! In your defense, though, my research-crazed daughter left you with little choice, while she pulled that west coast stunt and left us all because of flawed research. I had warned her about that years and years ago."

Mr. Hobnobber was letting me have it with full barrels, and I stood there and took it like a man. He continued blasting me while still not looking up from his desk. He then began a long-winded, confusing, diatribe prefaced by a small element of sympathy as to the situation.

"I do understand to some degree, if you needed to take advantage of the romantic moment and all that emotional nonsense, but that is not what I am talking about. You most likely have picked up some kind of lovebird, half-crazed idea from all that whacked out music you listen to so often. You should listen to another progressive rock band rather than, No Way, because your music selection proves that you do not think very clearly from all those hockey puck shots to the head. You have so many love stars in your eyes that you cannot think straight."

"I am sorry, sir, but I have lost you in this conversation. I have to admit that I am not quite following you. What plan do you need us to work on?"

"Why, this of course!"

He finally picked his head up and looked at me, and his eyes spun like a kaleidoscope as he stared at me. I looked at him, but it was still not quite clear what I was exactly looking at.

"You still cannot see it, what are you, blind? Come over here. How did you almost make it into the big league, and not the Grudley's Book of World Records for being the first blind ice hockey goalie?"

I walked closer to Mr. Hobnobber, and he pointed at his right ear.

"Look here! Now, can you see the trouble that I am in?"

I stared in close, and to my surprise, there was a faint trickle of blood coming out of his right ear. I now saw the trouble that he had mentioned. There was a large paperclip stuck inside his right ear!

"This is unbelievable, sir. I can now see that you have a paper clip stuck in your ear."

I decided the best course of action was to present the facts.

"Now, I can see that your half breed, traitor to the American way English heritage, has made you a resident of 221B Baker Street, in London, but I already knew that, Paul. What are you, some kind of doofus? I did not need you to advise me of that fact! I need your help in getting it out!"

I stood up and really, really, could not believe that this was happening to me. In all the great adventures, with Harry and without Flippers, Mr. Bug, diseased stuffed animals, bar room brawls, O'Malley's . . . all of it, not to mention the millions of long lines of clouds of black weirdness and strange occurrences; this has to be the epitome of them all. I gathered myself; after all, I was a goaltender who had faced an awful lot of tough situations. I just was not expecting one of them to be extracting a paper clip from my future father-in-law's right ear.

"I do not know, sir. Why do we not just go get the ladies and take you to the emergency room? I am not really qualified for a paper clip extraction from an ear canal. It is not exactly my area of expertise."

"It has to be, son. You are my last hope. That is why I waited for hours for you to arrive and I locked myself here in my study. I was sitting here studying this legal document, and the inside of my ear was itching, so I mindlessly took the paper clip, straightened it out, and stuck it in my ear to itch it. I must have pushed it into the skin inside because it hurt and try as I could, I cannot remove it from my ear. If I went and met with Mrs. Hobnobber, she would have freaked out and forcibly taken me to the hospital. Let me tell you that she is quite strong, and there would be no way for me to resist." Mr. Hobnobber violently shook his head back and forth.

"I cannot go to the hospital for this! Not only do I have an ego the size of Manhattan Island, if it ever got into the local press that the great, Mr. William T. Hobnobber ESQ., New Jersey state senator, longtime councilman, a legendary courtroom attorney, and onetime mayor of this town, had to have a paper clip pulled out of his ear in the emergency room, I have to say that I would be ruined."

"I see your point and predicament sir, I really do."

In reality, I was suddenly forcing back, bursting out into rollicking laughter, but a sense of self-preservation held me steady.

"Therefore, when faced with this adversity, I decided to wait for you to arrive. I was sure you rough and tough hockey players stitched each other up a few times here and there during games, so I am sure you can handle a little paper clip stuck in someone's ear."

When presented with that dumb-downed, type of logic, I decided to take a peek and see what was going on inside of his ear canal.

"Yes sir, we did have to resort to some interesting medical practices here and there. I just do not want to be sued for malpractice."

I smiled a little, hoping that a touch of humor that poked fun at Mr. Hobnobber's profession may help to break the tension. It was, of course, in the grand scheme of things, a rather ill-advised attempt at humor.

"Quit making stupid jokes, twenty-seven, and take a look in there!"

I peered in and sure enough, the end of the clip had gone through the skin on the inside of the ear, and there was a hooked end preventing it from pulling out. Mr. Hobnobber must have been tugging at it for a while, and that only made it worse and caused it to bleed.

I was indeed a problem solver, and I had a plan.

"Sir, this is similar to another incident I had once before."

"I knew it! You weird, strange, and whacked out goaltenders deal with everything! What is the plan?"

"Actually sir, this is not hockey related, but one time, Harry, his brother-in-law Ronzo, and I went fishing together, and Harry, on a back cast, got his fish hook stuck in Ronzo's backside. The hook went really deep in his butt, past the barb, but when he dropped his drawers, I managed to push it past the barb and then cut it and pull it clean out the other way."

Mr. Hobnobber looked up at me, and I could tell he was processing the information. "Ronzo, Ronzo, hmm, Binky told me about him. He has a massive ass too, like the size of Texas."

"That is true, sir, so I think I can do the same thing here. It will hurt for a second, but if I can push it in and then clip it, I can pull it out backwards."

"Go for it twenty-seven, get in the game. I am ready."

Now, being an electrician in my new life after hockey, I always carried with me, a little pocket tool that had multi-functions on it. This one folded up into a little tool, but it had wire cutters and needle-nose pliers on it. I spotted a whiskey decanter on a table in the study and found a tissue. I soaked the tissue with some whiskey and dabbed it in his ear.

"Now look, sir, this will hurt, because I need to push it in first, and then clip it."

"Do it, I can take it, I am not a wimp, after all, I withstood you crushing my hand like some evil bully. First, give me that whiskey bottle."

I handed Mr. Hobnobber the bottle, and he took a long swig of it.

"I am now ready."

He gripped the arms of his desk chair as if he was preparing for a takeoff to the moon in a rocket ship.

How dramatic, I thought.

I reached in, pushed the clip forward, and he let out a bloodcurdling scream which caused me to fall backwards and drop the tool.

He was a wimp!

I quickly recovered, and before he could scream again, I gave it a quick snip and one, two, three, I pulled it out. I had both ends of the paperclip in my hand and I dropped them on the desk. Immediately, the intercom buzzed on Mr. Hobnobber's desk and he recovered enough to hit the talk button.

"Yes, dear."

I heard Mrs. Hobnobber's voice come over the small speaker, "Did you just shake hands with Paul, honey?"

"No, no, no, everything is all right; we are just comparing cheers from his old hockey days with my old team cheers."

Mr. Hobnobber was making frantic motions with his arms and hands for me to scream something, so I yelled out the first thing that came to mind, which was the old Long Island Roosters fan club cheer from my days playing on the island.

"ROOSTERS! ROOSTERS! ROOSTERS! COCKLE DOODLE DOO! COCKLE DOODLE DOO! COCKLE DOODLE DOO!"

Mrs. Hobnobber's voice returned to spout at us over the speaker.

"Oh, I am so glad that you two are getting along so well and having such fun, please come out for drinks now."

"Yes, dear, please, one minute."

I breathed in deeply and exhaled. Wow, beginning this new life of mine, sure was exhausting. I did not have this much stress in the net while dodging headshots.

"Good work, son, I underestimated your intelligence, skills and ability to think on your feet."

He patted me on the back while hiding his right hand behind his back.

"Thank you, Paul. I am sure I can trust you to keep this in the utmost confidence, just between us. I can then, of course, work a deal, and see what I can do to overlook certain breaches of your behavior and inconsiderate indiscretions on your part. One of which I am sure, will be not consulting with me before proposing to my wonderful, smart, and gorgeous daughter."

I could see how Mr. Hobnobber was a successful politician; he could work a back-door deal, as most New Jersey politicians could.

"Of course, sir, I will never say a word. I was glad I could help."

Mr. Hobnobber smiled, and he seemed satisfied.

"I suppose that we all should actually thank you for rescuing us, if Binky had called home one more time to speak to all of us, and take turns crying in our ears for an hour and not saying another word other than your name, then we would have changed our telephone number. It was brutal, and besides, she always called collect. It cost me a fortune to hear her cry for an hour every night for four years, so thank you for saving us and my wallet."

"You are welcome, but that is what I do sir, I make saves."

Mr. Hobnobber screwed his mouth up like a corkscrew as he looked at me.

"Well, sure you do there, son, whatever it was that you said. I would offer you a cigar, but I know you will want to swap spits with my daughter later and she hates the smell of them, so I will have one and you will have to take a rain check."

He lit up a big cigar and took a few puffs.

"Let's go join the ladies and see what they have cooked up for us, son." He led me out of the study and we walked back up the big hallway.

"You know, sir . . . you should check your ear out and put some antibiotic ointment on it, just to make sure it does not get infected."

"Thank you, son, you know, there may be hope for you yet, maybe, you should become a doctor, rather than some loser, retired, former professional, hippie, goaltender that fell short of making it to the big league by a week or so."

He put his arm around me while puffing on his cigar. I knew by now not to take him too seriously. After all, I was merely the victim of cold, stark, and bleak factual research once more. I could see how Mr. Hobnobber was indeed ruthless in the courtroom, pummeling his poor victims with verbal darts loaded with researched facts.

We made our way back to a huge kitchen that looked like a restaurant kitchen. It had a huge, stone covered, center-serving island that dominated the large kitchen. The center island alone was bigger than my entire kitchen in the house I grew up in on Belmont Avenue in Paterson! On the outside wall was a large, stainless steel stove, a wall oven, and a cook top grille. The kitchen was fabulous; it was like nothing I had ever seen.

Binky came running over to me and gave me a hug.

"I am so glad to hear that your talk with Father went so well, you guys are as if you are best friends now."

"Sure, we are Binky, we really shared a lot."

"Hello, Father. It is so nice to see you."

Binky walked over and gave her father a hug and a kiss. The cigar did not seem to bother her, I guess she really was Daddy's little girl.

"Paul is wonderful, isn't he?"

"I must say that, he seemed to have arrived at the right

time, that is for sure." Mr. Hobnobber turned and winked at me. "Now son, one of the first things I need to break you of, is drinking that wretched Big Boulder beer, that stuff is the reason your hair's so long, my drinks will correct that trouble."

I looked up at his baldhead and wondered where that one came from.

"Tonight, I will endeavor to introduce you to fine, single malt Scotches."

He handed me a glass filled full of Scotch whiskey with some ice.

"Just a splash of water there, Paul. There is no sense ruining a good Scotch with water. Dear Binky, would you like a Martini, shaken, not stirred?"

"Oh yes, please Father, that would be perfect!" Binky always stuck with her traditional drink selection.

"Let's go into the living room and have some, snacks, sit, chat, and enjoy our drinks," Mrs. Hobnobber offered the suggestion, while holding open the door and motioning with her arm for us to follow her. Binky had a Martini, as did Mrs. Hobnobber.

I took Binky's drink for her and Mr. Hobnobber took his wife's drink while we walked to the living room. I had learned that proper, fancy procedure, long ago from Howard at the Black Bear Club. As we began to walk out, I lifted the glass of Scotch to my lips to take a sip of the drink.

"Say, where on earth is that crazy son of ours? Have any of you seen, Tinky?"

I had just taken a sip of my drink, and when I heard Mr. Hobnobber say, "Tinky," I coughed, choked, and spit up some Scotch.

"Oh, twenty-seven, are you all, right? Is that drink unusually strong for you? Father, Paul is not used to such strong drinks! He usually just has a few Big Boulder beers."

I was coughing and choking, but it was not because of

the drink. Harry and I had stolen many sips of whiskey from Ronzo and Harry's old man since we were sixteen years old. We sucked down many strong drinks on top of High Mountain in North Haledon, while lamenting together some Harry related drama. I knew that I could handle some strong whiskey.

"Big tough, rough goalie, a little sippy-whippy of Scotch, was too much for you there."

Mr. Hobnobber was laughing, and he came over to pat me on the back as well as taunt me a little.

"Be nice now, Father. Paul will get used to it. Won't you, Paul?"

I shook my head to indicate that I was all right as Binky checked on me and hugged my neck. I could not even believe my ears—nonetheless speak. First off, I didn't even know that Binky had a brother, and to think that his name was Tinky was even more than I could handle.

Then again, Binky and Tinky!

Why would I think it would have been any other way to be honest with you?

I leaned into Binky as we walked through the grand center, foyer area of the home, "You never mentioned that you had a brother."

Binky looked at me and smiled.

"No, I guess I never did. We have had such a whirlwind romance. I must have skipped him."

Skipped him, eh? It was as if she was talking about a pet parakeet and not her brother.

"Yes, Tinky is about a year and a half younger than I am. He is a musician. He is around here somewhere. I know he really wants to meet you."

Binky reached up and gave me a kiss on the cheek. I handed her back her Martini while everyone sat down in the living room.

"I am so happy, Paul. I cannot even imagine that things can go from being so gloomy and horrible, to being so wonderful in such a few short moments. When are you going to tell everyone our news?"

"I guess, I will tell everyone right before dinner, once your brother is here."

Binky nodded and squeezed my waist. I chugged the rest of the Scotch. I needed it!

"How about a refill, anyone?" I held my glass up to indicate that I would go to the kitchen and get them another drink. The reality was that I needed to escape for a moment to catch my breath and let the Scotch work some inner magic.

"Wow, you sure adapted quickly on that Scotch whiskey. You went from a lightweight, to a lush, in five minutes." Mr. Hobnobber downed his drink and handed me his glass.

"Do you know where it is, Paul?"

Mrs. Hobnobber pointed while handing me her empty glass. I nodded to Mrs. Hobnobber, picked up the empty glasses, and made my way to the kitchen. I walked into the kitchen and sighed, while scanning for the location of the Scotch bottle on the counter, when I heard a deep growling voice behind me.

"Hey, what's going on? You must be the world famous, Paul John Henson."

I had a startling flashback to a long time ago. I recognized that it was the long-lost gangster voice that I had spoken to one time on the telephone, when I first called Binky! I turned around to see a short young man with long, flaming red hair, a red mustache, beard, and a red face. In fact, he was red all over.

He was one big red advertisement.

"I am Tinky Hobnobber, Binky's brother. I would shake your hand, but hell no, because I play the bass guitar and keyboards and I cannot afford to have my hand in a cast for six months."

I laughed, and he smiled at me. He had a friendly

manner to him, and I could immediately tell that he was very easygoing and likable.

"Nice to meet you, Tinky. Word sure spreads fast around here. I am Paul John Henson."

"Yeah, yeah, yeah, well, you broke my old man's hand a long time ago there, Paul. We have been waiting for and praying for you and my sister to get back together for a long time. Before you ask, my name is really, Tinky. I have been traumatized for life and shouldered with a huge lack of self-confidence, because my parents must have sucked down some cheap Scotch or smoked some bad weed when they were younger, and thought it would be cool to name their two children with rhyming names, like some kind of stupid, fairy tale."

Tinky walked closer to the counter and placed a glass on the counter next to the Scotch bottle. I assumed that he was going to join us for cocktails.

"It is cool though, I have accepted it, and talk like a mobster with this low voice, so everyone thinks twice before making fun of my name. It is kind of like that country song, you know, 'A Boy Named Betty.' To top it all off, I am red like a fire engine, so it all wraps up into one big, tidy Tinky bow."

He smiled at me and I chuckled, as I realized that he had a great sense of humor, and while there may have been a great element of truth to his speech, he was primarily being tongue in cheek with me. I thought how speaking, as if he was a gangster, would not really help him. I would guess Tinky to be around five-feet-five and one-hundred-and thirty-pounds or thereabouts. He was a little guy for sure!

Tinky continued to tell me about himself.

"I was also very traumatized by those crazy toilet bowl commercials on television when I was a little kid. You know . . . the one where there is a little dude in a rowboat inside the tank. I would sit on the toilet bowl and wonder if he was inside the tank rowing around. Even to this day, it kind of freaks me out to think that a little guy lives in our toilet bowl tank." Tinky smiled at me, but he did not lean in for the famous Hobnobber stare. He must have not inherited that trait.

I realized that his sense of humor was quite eccentric, and in between laughs, I asked, "Hey, can I also pour you a Scotch? Your dad and I are having one."

"Sure, thanks. Hey, I am not into sports, but I think it is cool that you played professional hockey. Did chicks really take off their brassieres and ask you to sign them?"

"Well yes, they did Tinky, not that much, but yes, it happened."

"Wow, they never do that for us at gigs, I guess I should have been a goalie. Binky must have freaked when she heard that, she is pretty tough, you know. She used to take me out all the time when we were little kids. She took out a lot of other guys in high school when they made lewd comments about her body and stuff like that."

I laughed as I have experienced and witnessed her attitude and super strength. I handed him the drink, and we raised our glasses for a toast. We toasted, touched our glasses together, and each took a sip.

"I hear that you love music, and are into, No Way."

"That is correct, I am, what kind of music do you play Tinky?"

"All kinds, I like No Way a lot, I just can never figure out the lyrics, especially, 'Close to the Crevice.'"

It seemed to be a common malady for everyone for many years now, all of them trying to figure out that recording.

"I have played the organ at our church for years now and I am in a band. I am sure glad you and my sister are back together."

Tinky laughed, and he waved his hand in the air.

"It got a little rough with her phone calls and all that weeping every night. I was ready to go find you myself. I guess you know by now that my parents are pretty weird and Binky, well, I know you dig her and all, but she is a little bizarre. I can say that, since she is my sister, I do not want you getting mad at me and shaking my hand or something like that. I had no idea you were as big as you are. What are you like, six-foot bazillion or something?"

I laughed and Tinky smiled. I could not help but notice that Tinky just had a tendency to ramble on and on with his thoughts.

I patted him on the shoulder and said, "Hey, let's go in the living room, I have to talk to the whole entire Hobnobber family together."

"I know my name is Tinky and all that, but, you know, I am really the only normal one in the family. I am not into all that research stuff and those wild mood changes from one minute to the next, from quiet and reserved, to a mad barbarian. I think it is cool that you have all kinds of long hair and the beard and stuff going on."

Tinky could sure talk. He was like one long run-on-sentence. However, I really liked him. He and I were going to get along fine; he was all right.

I could not help but think Harry M. Redmond Jr. would have thought the same of him as well.

I could see Harry standing there, laughing, and saying, "You know something, twenty-seven? This Tinky guy is all right, and he is our kind of guy."

It was true; Tinky was our kind of guy.

I finished making the drinks, and Tinky helped me carry them out to the living room. We sat around the living room, talked for a while, and enjoyed some appetizers. Binky sat on my lap and we enjoyed some pleasant conversation amongst us all.

I felt the time was right to make the announcement of our plans for our future together.

I tapped Binky on her leg so that she stood up. I was not really nervous, but I certainly doubted my timing. I guess it was really now or never. Binky looked at me and she seemed calm. I may have been interpreting her body language, but she seemed as if she was ready for the big moment.

I started to speak, "I want to thank everyone for being so kind to me, and for this great evening that we are all sharing. It is really wonderful to have finally met all of Binky's family after all this time."

I turned to Binky to confirm that fact.

"This is everyone, is that correct, Binky?"

Binky nodded her head with her rapid confirmation nod.

"I know this is really sudden, with Binky just returning, but I wanted to tell everyone together that I have asked Binky to marry me and she has accepted. Our engagement occurred the other night, but I had not yet had a chance to buy a ring, because well, all of this happened so fast. I would like to give her an engagement ring now, in front of her whole family."

Binky's mother started crying right away. She ran over to her husband and hugged Mr. Hobnobber.

Tinky was thrilled, "Maybe, I can finally turn Binky's bedroom into a recording studio!"

Mr. Hobnobber rubbed his right ear a little, checked for blood, and then yelled, "I knew it!" He then held his wife and fist pumped the air in victory.

I went down on my right knee in front of Binky and took the ring out of a little box that I had in my pocket. I held the ring out, gently grasped Binky's hand, and then I placed it on her ring finger. Binky looked at the ring. She started to cry, and she covered her mouth while she looked at it glowing upon her finger.

It was quite a ring. For once in my life, I did not skimp, it was a rock, and I was very proud of how I had picked it out by myself. I had a lot of money from my hockey days accumulated in the bank, my mum and I had saved it for many years and never touched it, so it had grown to be quite a large sum, if I do say so myself.

I only looked like a poor hippie freak from Paterson, but in this case, you did not want to judge a book by the cover! That money allowed me to purchase a ring that I could be proud of, and it capped the moment like nothing else I had ever done to this point in my life.

Binky stood up and hugged me tightly, she was sobbing tears of joy, and I felt some of them drip down upon my shoulder. It had been such a long road back to where we were tonight. It was finally the culmination of what God had intended for us. I firmly believed at this point that God had a plan for Binky and me. We may not have agreed with all the painful aspects of it, but who were we to doubt. I had read in scripture where it advises, that we all should never lose heart, so that we all could be reunited and renewed. I could testify to that fact. Sometimes, it is a test. A test for your blind faith as well as your stamina, I do not know why, but I knew it was true.

God's plan was now coming to fruition for Binky and me, the pain, the separation and then the joyous reunion.

I knew for certain, from experience, that life is not always fair. Tonight, I could not help but think that Sky Blu Redmond was smiling down at us from her lofty post in Heaven. I knew that it was her prediction fulfilled, and I felt my heart leap for joy at the mere thought of it.

It was a wonderful moment. We all gathered, and we shared hugs, kisses, and a toast. No one would shake my hand; I only ever received hugs from my new in-laws, as well as the occasional bonus of a long, lip-locked kiss from Mrs. Hobnobber. After some more tears and hugs, we walked into the dining room to enjoy our dinner.

Binky pulled me aside in the kitchen and we shared a special moment together.

"Paul, my goodness, this ring, it is beyond belief. Where did you get this kind of money to buy such a ring?

"It is fine, Binky. I need to have a chat with you about what you are getting into, but it is fine, I did not steal it, I actually have quite a bit of money saved for us from my hockey days."

She laughed and looked at me for a while, before she said, "You know, twenty-seven. You really are amazing, sometimes I cannot even guess at what you have going on in that mind of yours. It seems like you are always one step ahead of us all."

We had a wonderful time, and the meal was remarkable. We ate, then cleaned up, and talked until it was becoming quite late. The Hobnobber family was surely quirky, but I loved them all, it just took a little while to understand them all. After all the years of being with Harry and his family, I was very adaptable to strange and unusual behavior. I imagine that I had learned under the best weird preparation training available.

After dinner, Tinky excused himself for some bass guitar practice, and the ladies were in the kitchen cleaning up some dishes.

"Welcome to the family, Paul, you are a great guy and I know it is going to be a blast having you around."

"Thank you, Tinky, we will get to know each other, we can talk some music together really soon."

"That will be good, really good."

Tinky left us and I sat alone in the living room with Mr. Hobnobber after his son had left.

"Paul, in light of these evenings' events, I do forgive you for not consulting with me ahead of time, on marrying my lovely daughter. I understand that the events unfolded in your hockey puck hardened, thick skull, too quickly for you to remember to include a mere figure of such low importance, like Binky's father into the equation."

"I am glad you understand, sir."

"I was initially greatly concerned, though, at how you plan to provide for my dear Binky. The size of that ring you gave her, tells my investigative mind that there is much more to the story of this long-haired, hippie goaltender from Paterson. Perhaps, I have made an error, and greatly underestimated how lucrative playing professional hockey can be. I will venture a guess. You invested all the money that you earned playing that brutal sport and now it has accumulated into a huge nest egg, right?"

"Well sir, I have my dear English mum to thank for that. As I played, I simply sent my entire bonus and signing money back home and she banked it, managed it, and we never touched a penny. It turned out that my mum knows a bit about money, as well as, she makes the best roast beef and Yorkshire pudding that you have ever had."

Mr. Hobnobber looked at me and smiled, "I do look forward to meeting your mum as you call her, as well as your father. They seemed to have raised quite a young man, and in the meantime, I will research a bit about English style cooking. It sure has struck a chord within my taste buds, Paul. Say, have you figured out those obscure lyrics to 'Close to the Crevice' yet?"

"No sir, I am still working on it."

"Well, get with the research there, Paul, I have been waiting for years for you to come through."

"I will make it a top priority, sir."

"You do that, twenty-seven, please, get on that right away." Mr. Hobnobber leaned back in his leather chair, took a sip of his drink, looked at me, and he smiled.

2

Reflections

"Come on in here, Paul, and sit down, we can talk for a while."

My father-in-law waved to me as we walked from the dining room table to the large living room of the Hobnobber's sprawling mansion. Oh no. I thought about how a one-on-one discussion with my father-in-law is always an experience that sometimes takes me a week, or even more, to recover from. He placed his arm around my shoulders as we walked towards the living room together.

"You know, we really do not know each other all that well, even though you conned your way into our lives, entranced, and then married my daughter. We need to become better acquainted."

I shuddered at the thought and mere suggestion that we needed to become *more* acquainted.

"You had this whirlwind reunion with Binky, after she returned from her little jaunt propelled by flawed research. We then had a nice dinner planned, in order to get to know you better. It was one night shortly after Binky returned, and you ruined that night by presenting her with a giant ring, like some kind of show off."

Mr. Hobnobber leaned into me with the famous Hobnobber stare.

"Before we all knew it, I was spending a fortune on this big wedding. The truth is, you have not come through for me on some things, I am still waiting for you to interpret the words to, 'Close to the Crevice' for me. I am thankful though that at least my lifetime dream of shooting hockey pucks on a real goalie has come to fruition."

"I am sorry for the delay on the lyrics, I am working on the words but it is a little complex. I was glad to help with the dream fulfillment. In retrospect, we should have worked out at a rink rather than your back patio, that way you could have saved a lot of money on the window repairs."

Mr. Hobnobber ignored my retrospective suggestion, and instead, as we arrived in the living room, he pointed towards one of the large, black leather chairs in the room.

"Sit in the big chair there, son, like you did a few years ago, when we first met, and you broke my hand."

Mr. Hobnobber would never, ever let me forget that first time we met.

"Thank you, sir, I appreciate it. I do still feel bad about your hand, it was only meant to be a handshake."

Mr. Hobnobber ignored me once more, and we both sat down in identical chairs opposite one another in the living room.

"I sure enjoyed dinner. That was an outstanding meal that Binky and Mom prepared."

My father-in-law finally acknowledged my words, as he gave me a slight nod and smile when he heard me mention dinner.

"As you weird and eccentric goalies would say, you really notched a shutout Paul when you snagged Binky. I am not saying this just because she is my beloved daughter, but she is smart, gorgeous just like her mother, and due to her incredible research abilities, that young woman can cook!"

By now, I was very familiar with my father-in-law's forthright assessment of me and I had learned not to take it to heart, but what he said was indeed true about my wife. I did not know it at the time when we married, but Binky was a gourmet cook. I had made sure that I kept up with my workouts to stay my same old playing weight! I smiled at his comments, but I did not say anything.

I was indeed sitting in the same chair, in which I had sat in years ago, when I had first met Mr. Hobnobber. I had a flashback to that moment when we first met when I had come over to the Hobnobber home to pick up Binky for our famous weekend at the Black Bear Club. In self-defense, I shook off the memory rather quickly.

I had to admit that the first encounter revealed an awful lot to me about my future father-in-law and his unique personality. I had become used to him a little more, after about a year of being married to Binky, but it still was an overwhelming experience to meet or speak with him. I watched from my chair as my father-in-law walked over to a small table where he kept his after-dinner liquors. This was another fabulous room within the Hobnobber mansion. It was large, with a large stone fireplace, a stone chimney and a wide hearth in front of it. The room was dark, with oak paneling and dark trim. The furniture in this room alone was more furniture than we had in my entire home that I grew up in on Belmont Avenue! The room had ornate and interesting light sconces that hung on the wall and illuminated the room in a soft, warm glow.

"I am going to have an after-dinner brandy, Paul. Would you like to partake in one also? It settles out the stomach after a big meal like that."

"Yes sir, I would like that."

Mr. Hobnobber pulled out two brandy glasses and set them down upon the table, while he searched for a specific bottle from his collection.

"You know, I really enjoy this. We take off on the ladies and force them to do all the dishes and cleanup work after preparing the meal. It is as if we are kings!"

I thought about that statement for a moment before saying, "I did clear the entire table and then Binky told me to come in here and relax."

"Ah geez, don't be a doormat, son! Women try to guilt you into being a good guy. I thought you were a rough, tough, hockey goalie."

Mr. Hobnobber held the top of a glass decanter in his one hand while he waved towards me with the other hand. It seems, as though, Mr. Hobnobber was a subscriber to my best friend, Harry's famous theory from so long ago. However, that indeed was such a different time and place.

"Now, after you roped my daughter into marrying you with this big tough-guy image of a former professional hockey player, you come up with this crazy notion to become a Lutheran minister. I have heard of career changes in my life, but this one takes the cake. I am sure when you finally get to be a candidate for ordination, the examining bishops will realize all of your strange and unsettled behavior, is really due to the blows that you suffered to your head in your playing days and you will not make the cut."

"Thank you for the vote of confidence sir, I do appreciate it."

"Just stating the research results. Statistics show that only one or two, former professional goaltenders, ever made it to full ordination in the Lutheran denomination. Your career choice has little chance at success."

Mr. Hobnobber finished pouring our drinks, walked back over to the chairs, and he smiled at me. He handed me the drink and stared in at me with that wide-eyed stare that his daughter learned from him. Mr. Hobnobber's stare was just a lot more intense and wild-eyed than Binky's patented stare.

"I would like for us to plan some more family time for everyone. I think your mother-in-law, Tinky and I, would like to join you and Binky for more dinners, parties, you know what I mean, perhaps, we can get to know you better. I think that even your hollowed-out brain can follow my point here, son, you know . . . some quality time, family bonding and all that jazz. I am thinking about semi-retiring soon, and I will have a lot of extra time on my hands."

Mr. Hobnobber became very animated in making his point as he waved his hands in the air while taking small sips of his drink.

"We all have mentioned that we would like to spend a lot more time with you and my daughter. We could continue our training regimen and one of these days, I will be able to beat my professional athlete son-in-law at something."

Joy, joy, joy, I thought. In desperation, I decided to offer up an excuse as well as a compromise, "I am retired from hockey now sir, and not in that good a shape anymore. Why don't we try some board games? I am really bad at chess and checkers."

"Oh nonsense, Paul. I saw you play in the net, you were the real deal, and besides, I hate chess and checkers. You mean to tell me that you have become such a winky dink that you go from standing fearless, in front of blazing slap shots from the point in playing that stupid sport, to playing boring, board games!"

Mr. Hobnobber rolled his eyes at my suggestion. I guess he had not bought the idea.

"I am talking about some real quality time!"

Oh no, I thought.

I already had to allow him to take shots on me to fulfill his lifetime wish of scoring on a real goaltender. That went over poorly when I stopped about fifty shots, and then I allowed him to score one or two. He became angry and accused me of playing "soft" to allow him to score, and then he shot a puck right through his kitchen picture window. After that fiasco, we had to race in a one-hundred-yard dash that I went half speed on. I tried not to beat him badly, but he was still mad when I beat him by about twenty yards. We then shot basketballs, swam laps in a pool, did a pushup competition, sit-ups, weight lifting, pull ups and chin-ups, as well as many other athletic one-on-one competitions. All to no avail, as try as I could to lose without his detection, I beat him in all of them.

Binky told me that he just was having a hard time at facing his old age and would not admit that he no longer was a great athlete, as he once was, when he was young. She stressed that I should work with him through these anxiety issues. I was the one, however, that was suffering through the anxiety, as I had to deal with this insecure lunatic.

I was just about to answer him when the telephone rang and Mr. Hobnobber excused himself. He answered the telephone, then returned, and apologized as this call was going to be a long telephone conversation. I waved to him that I understood and secretly thanked the unknown caller for saving me.

I took a sip of my drink and thought back to all that had happened since that night when Binky and I were reunited. It had been a whirlwind romance, that was for sure, and that night when Binky returned to me, was certainly a night to remember.

In fact, that night changed my life forever.

I never did cut my long hair or shave my beard or mustache, even for our wedding. Binky would never allow it or even consider it. As a result, I still looked like the long-haired, hippie goalie from Paterson, New Jersey. My appearance had not changed much, but that was about the only thing in my life that was the same.

Mr. Hobnobber was indeed correct, about his description of Binky and me and our rapid progression toward marriage. Despite his gift of exaggeration, which I am sure served him well in the courtroom, as well as in the senate; he had not exaggerated the facts of my courtship of his daughter. I had known deep in my heart for a very long time that Binky Hobnobber was the gal that I wanted to marry, and even when she was gone, and out of my life, and her return was uncertain, I knew that would never change.

The joy of her return was actually a fulfillment of the prediction of Sky Blu Redmond of so many years before. Sky had told me that Binky would someday return. That prediction had always given me hope, and when it came to fruition, it was not only the greatest joy of my life but also one of my life's great mysteries.

After she returned, we both made it clear that we wanted to get married as soon as we could, and we did. We had the now famous dinner engagement at the Hobnobber mansion, where I gave her the engagement ring, and we announced to the entire family our plans. I had met her brother Tinky, as well as Mrs. Hobnobber that evening, as well as performed my first emergency surgery, when I extracted the errant paperclip from Mr. Hobnobber's ear. After such a strange start, things had come together nicely for us. Binky had secured a solid position in New York City, working for a financial firm on projecting futures, where she was in her glory utilizing her incessant research skills.

I was very happy in my position working for an electrical contractor as an operations manager, but I had also doubled up my part-time courses of study at a local college that I had begun a year or so earlier, as I continued the pursuit of going on to a career in the ministry. That deep-felt desire did give me an awful lot of apprehension, as I was not sure that I was doing the correct thing. At first, I did not mention it to Binky. I wondered what my future wife's reaction would be to my career change.

One night at my apartment, right after our engagement, Binky came over and saw me studying for an examination. Glancing through the books on the table, she finally asked what exactly it was that I was pursuing by going to college. I had told her the day after we reunited, that I now attended college part time, but I never really revealed what I was studying.

Looking back, I think Binky thought it was just some general study for some background for business.

She finally asked me after glancing at the books, and it was very difficult to tell her what my future goal was.

I had originally started this education as just a whim, and at the time I began studying, I did not know if I was really serious about it or not. Now, I was really enjoying the course work, and I had decided right before Binky had returned that this was now a concrete goal of mine to try to become a Lutheran minister. The reunion had all happened so fast that it was hard for us to share all that we had going on in our minds and in our dreams. That night in the apartment, when I finally had the courage to confess to Binky what my future career plans actually were, she was very supportive. I was very relieved at her reaction. She did not seem shocked at all, which was a great boost to my spirits. Being the wife of a minister may not have been exactly the life that she had dreamed of when she envisioned being married. Especially since I was shifting gears from being a rough, tough, professional ice hockey goalie to a Lutheran minister, which was really a bit north and south.

Upon hearing my answer, she had smiled, hugged me, and said, "I do not care what you do, as long as we are together and you are happy in your work, which is all that matters."

What a gal!

That is really all you could ask for in a wife. Support, caring and love. That is a winning formula. It was obvious to me that Binky, after all we had been through, just wanted to be together. She also agreed with a conversation that I had with Sky years ago that I would make a great religious leader. Time would tell, I had a very long road ahead of me, but it was wonderful to know that I had my wife's support.

We were never apart after our reunion and we shared so much together as we marched through a quick engagement towards marriage. I also explained in detail to Binky, how I had banked quite a bit of money from my professional hockey career. She agreed with me that we should just let it accumulate in the bank as I had over the years. I lived very modestly, still drove my old wreck of a jeep, and rented a very small apartment. I was not a materialistic guy, but really a minimalist in many ways. Financially we were fine; folks would never have imagined that this poor guy from Paterson had banked such a large amount of money from playing ice hockey. I had shared part of my financial situation with Mr. Hobnobber on the night I presented Binky with her ring. I wanted to emphasize, to both of her parents, exactly what my financial situation currently was, because I did not want her folks or anyone else to think that this previously poor, hippie guy from Paterson, was chasing this lovely young lady from an affluent family, "on the other side of the tracks," for all the wrong reasons.

We also shared with her family, why I was attending college and what I planned to do for a career in the future, if it all worked out.

The Hobnobber's were supportive of the idea and of my plans. I am sure that deep down, they were shocked, as were my parents, but they were all very encouraging.

Binky was all that I could have ever imagined in a woman, and all I ever wanted. I kept my hippie look, listened to my No Way records, wore the same old clothes and canvas sneakers, watched hockey and did not change very much. Binky encouraged me to stay the same as I had always been. She never wanted me to change. I was, as she proudly told me all the time, as she had so many years earlier on the fateful night we separated, "The man of her dreams."

Still, we both never forgot my best buddy, Harry M. Redmond Junior.

Binky knew how much it hurt me that he was gone from my life and now her life as well. It left a void for both of us, and we wondered where he was and what he was doing. Other than a postcard with no return address, we had not heard from him since he fled New Jersey; grief stricken after Sky had passed away.

I still could never shake the memory of his exit on that fateful day shortly after Christmas Day in 1980. I also could never forget his deceased wife Sky, (Binky never had met her) our mutual best friend Rose, and the great times that we had, before it all changed for us. Nevertheless, we put it all behind us, just as I had suggested the night when we reunited.

We did not dwell on the past mistakes, we only moved forward.

Binky and I saw Rose all the time, and the three of us spent quite a bit of time together. She was still Binky's best friend, and to be honest, next to Harry, she was my closest friend. It was wonderful to have the three of us reunited once more. Rose was thrilled when she heard that Binky and I had reunited, and that we were getting married. She was beside herself with excitement. The three of us had a tearful reunion the next week after Binky had returned and we were back together. Rose was still married to Daniel, but both Binky and I felt she was not as happy as she tried to pretend that she was. They had no children yet, and we both knew Rose well enough to tell that there was still an inner sadness inside of her.

Rose did not share details of the situation or of her marriage, even with Binky. My wife and I decided to support her, but we did not pry.

It felt so good for the three of us to be back together, but just as Binky and I had discussed, the three of us knew that it was not the same, while we were still missing that one large piece of the puzzle. The three of us discussed often how our mutual friend, Harry M. Redmond Jr. was still out there somewhere, and the fact that none of us still knew exactly where he was, or what he was up to in his life.

Binky and I decided on renting a small house out in a suburb of the city of Paterson, New Jersey, called Great Falls. Our house was not far from one of the ice hockey rinks that I cut my teeth on early in my career, and it was the rink where I nailed my first chance at a tryout with a local hockey club.

My old man always said, "The apple never falls far from the tree," and with my life, that sure was true.

Great Falls was a quiet little town, very well kept, and it was a nice place to live. We felt lucky to have found such a comfortable home for us to start out in. It was about ten miles from where Harry and I had grown up. It was very close to a commuter rail station that was red-eyed, straight into New York City, so that Binky did not have to drive her car into the city. We rented the house about two months before the wedding, and that gave me time to fix it all up, paint the colors and decorate the space in the way that Binky wanted.

We planned the wedding date for only two months after our engagement, so it turned Binky, Rose, and Mrs. Hobnobber and my mum into a virtual tidal wave of wedding planning, debate and organization. I will spare you the intricate details, but you can only imagine how Binky had kicked into a mega, super, intense, research mode for this one! Binky left no stone unturned as she researched and checked every detail of weddings going back to the early part of the eighteenth century until modern times. She was a hurricane of wedding planning, and we all held on tight for two months as she tore through the process.

One night at a dinner party, right after our engagement,

my parents had finally met the Hobnobber's and Tinky, and they all got along quite well. In fact, as far as Hobnobber meetings and dinner parties went, it was one of the most enjoyable of them that I had attended so far. Either Mr. Hobnobber was on his best behavior, or I was just becoming acclimated to him and his personality, but I actually found that I was enjoying his company.

That was indeed a frightening thought!

On this particular night, he was most entertaining. My sister and her husband visited from southern New Jersey to attend and to meet my new family. My sister is three years older than I am, and although we were close, she had a family already and a very busy life. She had moved away and been married long before Binky had arrived on the scene, so it was nice for all the families to meet.

My parents were used to me picking out unusual and eccentric people to collaborate with, having known the Redmonds for as long as we all had, so the Hobnobber's wild and crazy world did not faze them in the least, and they took it in stride. Mr. Hobnobber admired my old man and his street smart, tough guy approach, and he told him that he would have made a good attorney.

After dinner, while we were all relaxing and becoming more acquainted, I sat in a chair within an earshot of them, as the old man gave him a good lesson in street education from 182 Belmont Avenue in Paterson.

"I would have liked to spar in the courtroom with you, Henson. It would have made a good time of it. You have the kind of quick wit and reactions that you need for a good debate, you missed your calling." Mr. Hobnobber told him while the two of them shared an after-dinner brandy.

"Yeah, yeah, yeah, well, ya would have lost there, chief," my old man growled. "You would have met your match from this street educated, tough guy from Belmont Ave in Paterson. My diploma is not from any school, but it is stamped with 'B.S.' and it does not stand for a bachelor of science either there, pal."

Mr. Hobnobber howled with laughter, as he loved the old man and his tough guy, confidence.

"Say, Henson, as much as it pains me to admit it, that son of yours, when you overlook the obvious fact that he is a freaked out, eccentric, loudmouth, hippie goalie who is thick as a brick, is actually quite a young man."

I had warned the old man ahead of time of the sometimes painfully forthright, verbal analysis of people that defines William T. Hobnobber, so the old man was not rattled one bit by his verbal onslaught. The old man became a little introspective. I could not recall many times in my entire life that I actually saw this side of my father, but every once in a while, he put down his guard and allowed his inner spirit to shine.

"I appreciate that, Hobnobber. I never could get him to cut that hair or shave. Thank goodness, Binky came back, I swear Paul might have run off and joined up with some hockey club in Moscow, if she had not! We love Binky, she is wonderful, and we are thrilled that she is becoming part of our family, but as much as a fantastic catch she is for Paul, no doubt, Binky did all right with Paul too. I am so proud of that boy that sometimes, I get teary eyed thinking of all he has accomplished in such a short amount of time."

They both turned, looked at me sitting in the chair and I looked at them, but I did not say a word.

The old man continued, "But when you put aside his accomplishments, from having a professional hockey career, to now going to college, and all the other things that he has done, or is planning on doing, the thing that defines him the most, is his character."

Mr. Hobnobber stared in at the old man now, intrigued by my father's viewpoint.

"I am sure that you, just like me, have met our share of tough guys here and there. I did in the military, at my shop, I am sure you did in politics, and in the courtroom. I can guarantee you, Hobnobber, that you will never meet a tougher, more fearless man than our son. I do not just mean on the ice either, but in life, he is a big, giant, rock. Nothing dents him . . . the strangest situation, or the worst of times, does not bother him. He always takes it in stride and remains positive in his attitude. When his best buddy Harry's wife passed away, and it was one of the most awful times of all of our lives, he held us all up, me, his mum, the Redmonds and most of all . . . Harry."

The old man's voice cracked with a little emotion, and he took a sip of the brandy to steady his voice before he continued.

"I can tell you that he will defend his family, friends, and what he believes in, to his death, the good Lord help someone whoever messes with, Binky. He only seems calm and relaxed, but there is an inner fire inside that young man. I think he picked up a lot of it from his English Grandfather, you know, Mum's dad. Her father was quite the man, a real, life tough guy from England. The rest of his spirit, Hobnobber, I do not know where it came from or how he got it, but it burns deep and fast. I swear that he would stare down the Devil himself."

Mr. Hobnobber smiled; he walked over to him and put his arm around the old man. "I have a feeling I know where the rest of it came from there, Henson."

For one of the few times in my life, my father allowed me, or any other person, to hear or feel his true feelings towards me. It was very touching, to say the least.

Mr. Hobnobber as well as Mrs. Hobnobber loved my English Mum. Everyone always loved Mum, and they were interested in how she and my old man had become a couple, as they were such opposites in background and personality. They all chatted with her for hours, about her background, her English cooking, and what it was like raising a long-haired, hippie goaltender for a son who often came home bleeding and broken from street and ice hockey games since he was ten years old. She had some funny stories to tell of my early attempts at playing goalie, that was for sure. Mum had become quite the medic, and she became quite skilled at patching me up from some of my early efforts. Mr. Hobnobber even asked Mum for investment tips, since Mum had developed quite a lofty reputation for money management.

She quipped, "It is easy, William. There is no real secret. I am indeed, quite a bit on the thrifty side!"

The old man yelled from across the room, "Nah, we tell it like it is! We are just plain, old, cheap there, Hobnobber. After all, I drove the same car for over thirty years! Now today, if I wanted to, I could buy a joint like your mansion here, for cash on the barrelhead!"

Mr. and Mrs. Hobnobber loved them, and they both could not contain their laughter at the old man's honesty.

My sister also joined in on those conversations, as she had some of her own stories to add. She told of our adventures growing up in the old neighborhood along with Harry and her brother, always creating some type of turmoil.

It had been a wonderful party and night at the Hobnobber's home, and it gave us all a better understanding of just how special our families were.

The wedding, when it finally arrived, was grandeur and elegant. Binky had been United Methodist when we met, but we had been attending the local Lutheran church together. Binky decided that she wanted to be married in the Lutheran church. I asked her repeatedly to make sure she wanted this, but she sincerely seemed to be comfortable there, and Binky assured me that it was not just to satisfy me. The head pastor married us in a traditional ceremony that was very conservative, and for lack of a better description, it was wholly a Lutheran service.

Everyone came from far and wide to attend, well that was not quite true. Not everyone that we wanted to be there attended. Missing, of course, was Mr. Harry M. Redmond Junior. We still had not heard from him, nor had anyone in his family heard from him since the last postcard.

Binky and I felt terrible that he would miss the greatest and special moment of our lives together until this point. It sure would have been nice if Harry M. Redmond Jr. could have been standing there with me as my best man, just as I had stood next to him when he married Sky. Rose and I had spoken of it many times, as she felt the same way when Binky was missing from her wedding party, while she was out on the west coast and would not return for her wedding. It was not to be the case for Harry and me; we might be now forever separated.

It appeared that our lives had now gone in different directions.

However, many other folks came, and it was great to see them after quite a few years of us all being apart. Ronzo and Linny came, Mr. Redmond came up from Florida, even Patty, and the Big Spike flew all the way from California to attend. I think one of my biggest thrills was that a bunch of old teammates, opponents, coaches and friends from my hockey days came to the wedding. Even Jim O'Malley showed up in his pastor's collar! What a sight to see that one was.

I had tracked down through the Redmonds and the local Catholic parish, the contact information for Father Mark. We had sent him an invitation, and he provided Binky and me with a great thrill when he attended. He was so much older now, but he was still very sharp.

My family and Binky's family were very small in numbers. Many of my close relatives had passed away on my father's side, and they were across the pond in England on my mother's side, so our wedding invites were rather small as far as relatives went. Rose, of course, was Binky's maid of honor, and Binky also asked my sister to be in the wedding party. I had asked Ronzo to be my best man, and Tinky served as an usher. It was a small wedding party, but we sure all looked good.

It goes without saying that Binky was beyond beautiful for the wedding. Between her gown, her hair, and her smile, it was like a picture postcard. She was, and still is, in my mind, the most gorgeous woman that I have ever seen.

There I stood next to her. After all that had happened, all that went wrong, a long-haired, bearded, hippie goalie marrying this lovely woman.

A moment changed everything once more.

The reception was a rollicking time, held in a fancy private club that Mr. Hobnobber was a member of out in Bergen County. It had the best of everything, food, beer, booze, wine, desserts, music, strolling violinists, it had it all, with no expense spared. I could remember forever all that transpired that day, but suffice it to say, that when you have an eclectic mixture of Redmonds, Hensons, Hobnobbers, and mix in our friends and a bunch of wild, hockey players (including a certain Pastor James O'Malley!) then you sure had quite a time.

Usually, you have a music selection to dance to, for your first dance as man and wife, some teary eyed, weepy, romantic ballad that professes endless love between the man and woman.

Usually.

That was not the case with Mrs. Binky Hobnobber Henson. She, of course, picked "Living Love" and we tore the dance floor up once more, but this time we were man and wife. When we were finished dancing, the dance floor exploded, everyone ran out and danced as if there was no tomorrow. I, of course, then had to make the dance rounds with my mum, Ronzo, Linda, and then Patty.

Patty once more held me suggestively close just as she

had done at Harry's wedding and every other party that I could ever remember since I was about sixteen years old.

As usual, she rubbed and gyrated up against me, pulling my long hair and yelling out, "Are you jealous yet? Big Spike and Binky, are you jealous yet?"

Same old Patty!

Binky and I were shocked when a group of my old Long Island Rooster teammates, as well as Pastor O'Malley gathered in, and did the now famous Rooster fan club cheer together. I was hoping that O'Malley did not have a flashback, grab a hockey stick that he had smuggled in, and start one of his famous brawls. Looking back, I am sure a little excessive alcohol intake fueled the cheer.

We took many pictures; many tears were shed, people laughed, people hugged, and people cried. It was quite a day and quite a night.

Two other highlights came to my mind. Binky had asked my sister and me to dance together to a foxtrot. Now, we had not danced together since many, many years back, when she and I danced in and won some competitions. They cleared the floor and my sister and I did the best we could, I think it all came back to us after a few seconds. My sister is a fabulous dancer, much better than I ever was, and we pulled it off. The guests and our parents loved it, and my sister and I shared a very special moment together that brought us back to a wonderful time, which now seemed so very long ago.

The second highlight occurred when Tinky came up on the music stage along with Linda and the two of them, along with the house band, worked through the famous song by Big *Tex and Linny*. The makeshift band featured Tinky on the piano playing the melody and Linny singing. They beautifully played, "All Those Things I Used to Love about You Now Just Drive Me Crazy."

After the song had ended, we all became pensive because the rendition was so heartfelt. Binky and I noticed how Rose had become very upset when she heard the song. It struck a nerve with all of us knowing that, "Big Tex" was not here to strum and finger roll the famous melody on his banjo. It sure brought us all back to some very fond memories. Then Linda belted out her most famous tune, when she sang the ballad, "More Love than You Can Ever Imagine."

I can tell you that woman could really sing!

It was fantastic.

Binky and I managed to speak with everyone, but it was very difficult to do so, because the time passed so quickly. I did have a special moment to meet with Father Mark.

"Paul, I see that you still have not changed at all, the bedrock of the wild Redmonds and now the wild and crazy Hobnobbers. Good luck to you, it is so good to see you. Your wife is remarkable. She is a joy. Have you heard anything from, Harry?"

I shook his hand, and we embraced for a moment.

"Thank you, Father Mark, it is great to see you also, and no, not a word from him since the last card we all received."

"I see, I know the pain you have in your heart for him not being here, but keep the faith, Paul . . . and keep praying for him. His grief must still be strong. He is trying to disconnect from us to ease the pain of remembering."

"Oh, I do, Father Mark. You see, if you believe in it, then it will happen."

He smiled at me. I think he recognized the words as Sky's own.

"Father Mark, I have to tell you something. Because of you, your words, your influence, and your role in my life, I have made a profound decision on the course and direction of my life."

Father Mark stood back, obviously puzzled by my statement.

"I have decided to work through school and go on to a

seminary to be a Lutheran Pastor."

Father Mark looked astounded, and then he leaned in, shook my hand again, and smiled broadly.

"God bless you, Paul John Henson. I knew you had the call. I knew it since you were a little boy. Now, I would be remiss to my own calling, if I did not prefer it to be a Catholic calling, but if that were the case, then this great day would not have happened! Paul, you will make a special pastor, you are strong, because God gives you something special, an edge, a guiding light that includes an inner fire that burns bright and strong. The Lord Jesus has his hand on your heart and steers you where he feels that he needs you. He always has and always will, Paul. I am so happy for you."

I always found it so amazing that Father Mark held no prejudice with me being a Protestant or, specifically, a Lutheran. He was a special man and truly a man of God.

"Thank you, Father Mark, I do have you to thank as well as Sky. She told me once when we first met that I would be a great religious leader. I really think that the both of you started a fire within me, Father Mark. I think it all came to me that night at Harry's house when you explained to me why you felt God allowed Sky to become so sick and die. I understood that there are so many great things for us as men to explain to each other and God selects some of us to receive the power, knowledge, and in many cases, the courage, to explain his glory. I really do believe that, Father Mark."

The old priest with a heart of gold hugged me and thanked me, for all we had shared together, both good and bad over these many years.

I smiled at him and told him, "Who knows, Father Mark, maybe I will get to calm down one of my own wild and crazy parishioners who are full of road rage, working hard to impress some young ladies, while on his way to the Jersey shore in a sports car."

Father Mark laughed so hard that his side hurt, as he remembered the now famous Harry road rage incident.

"Good luck with that one, Paul!" He warned me.

Wedding days go by in a single flash, like a brilliant moment in time. All that planning, all that angst, all that working out the final intricate details so it all goes along perfectly and, "poof" in a blink of an eye, it is all gone. Much earlier than we all hoped, it was time for Binky and me to head out. We were visiting the White Mountains of New Hampshire, to a little place called North Conway. It was now February, and the cold, snowy weather up there fit both of our dreams for the perfect honeymoon getaway. It was a place to which I often retreated to while I was playing hockey up in Albany. In North Conway, I enjoyed some skiing, a little outdoor skating and other outdoor events. It was wonderful. Whenever I had free time, I would escape there. The view from Main Street looking at Mount Washington was something that this hippie from the gritty, urban streets of Paterson could only have dreamed of seeing. I always felt that God's hand was certainly on the White Mountains of New Hampshire.

Binky and I met with Rose as we were getting ready to leave. Rose still had not changed at all, she was so emotional, but she was, along with Harry, our oldest and dearest friend. She was having a very difficult time today, in addition to the high emotions of the wedding; she also had to deal with the fact that her husband had not attended the wedding. Rose simply reported to us that he had to work and could not get out of the commitment.

The situation was peculiar, and it seemed as though there was a lot more to the story than just that, but we did not ask any more about it.

"Oh guys, I could not even dream that this has finally happened. I am so happy for you both. That amazing chemistry you have together, I just knew in my heart that it would never die, or ever, ever go away. This day was so wonderful, I just wish that Harry. . .." Rose started to cry and her voice trailed off before she could finish it.

I finished it for her, "That Harry, was here. I know. Rose, we all do."

Binky was hugging her, and I walked over to them. I gently lifted Rose's head with my hands and looked at her eyes, which quickly filled with tears.

"Rose, I think that he is with us all wherever we are. Harry never leaves us. I have to say though, I often wonder if your mind misses him or is it your heart."

Rose looked at me, and she gently whispered, "Both. Paul, it is both."

"Then, Rose, believe it and it will happen. Always believe."

"Sorry, about that long phone call! I had to rake a pig-headed associate of mine over some hot coals to strong arm him into a deal or two! You know how it is when you are a big shot politician as I am. Business is business, you know!"

Mr. Hobnobber had returned to the living room, and I jumped in the chair when he shouted at me.

"A little jumpy, huh? I thought you used to be a fearless goaltender, not some little, quivering, and scared rabbit!"

"I am sorry, sir. I think you caught me daydreaming."

"No doubt, dreaming about what a great time we can all have together someday soon?"

"Well, not exactly, sir, but yes . . . that does sound like a grand time."

"Hey, if you are not scared out of the last remaining wits you have, let me show you a little something really fun which I just picked up, it is really something special. In addition, based upon that phone call, I need to change something. Come on down to my study and check it out, son."

I followed Mr. Hobnobber down the long hallway to his study, which, of course, was the scene of the now infamous, "paper clip incident."

We walked into the room and he pointed to the wall behind his desk. He was proudly smiling with a wide smile, exposing his perfect row of white, gleaming choppers. Despite his testimony to the contrary, with teeth like those that he still had at his age, I doubt he played very much ice hockey in his youth!

"It is one of those stress busters! You know a little gimmick to have fun with."

Mounted, there on the wall, was a little, black colored box. It was about eight inches high and about ten inches long. On the face of the meter, there was a red needle that had a gauge behind it. The markings on the gauge went from zero to one hundred in percentile. All the way past the one hundred mark, written in big red letters, were the words, "RUN FOR YOUR LIFE, THE METER IS GOING TO BLOW!" The needle was presently pointing to eighty percent.

I was puzzled as it made very little sense to me, "It is very nice sir, what exactly is it?"

William T. Hobnobber stood there, still smiling as if he had won the lottery.

"It is an Annoy-O-Meter," he answered.

"Oh, I see, it is very nice, sir."

I looked at it closely, and I could see the bottom corner of the gizmo had a slot cut in it, a slot in which you could slide a little paper tag inside of it. The paper had my name written on it, "Paul John Henson."

Mr. Hobnobber was still beaming proudly. I think the smile froze solid on his face.

"You see, you write the name of the person, place, or thing that is annoying the living hell out of you, and then you slide it into the slot on the bottom, and adjust the needle to the level of annoyance."

I now understood his big smile.

"I understand, sir, and I see I am currently on the meter at an eighty percent level."

"Why of course you are, son! You are my son-in-law and all of us, fathers-in-laws, have annoying, sons-in-laws. After all, you stole my little girl from me! What did you expect? To skate free with no repercussions at all? That is nothing! After you whipped me in the one-hundred-yard dash with no consideration at all to my advancing age. I had you up near the ninety-five percent or so mark."

"I feel better, sir, knowing that I have dropped so much as of late."

"Well—good news! You should really feel good now, as I need to replace you for the time being, based upon that phone call I just had."

I watched as Mr. Hobnobber went over to his desk, took a little paper tag, and wrote something down on it. He then slid my name out of the slot and replaced it with the new tag. On the new tag, he wrote, "Senator Riggs."

"There. I feel better already. What do you think, twenty-seven?"

"It is nice to know that our state government is such a finely tuned operation, sir."

"I tell you, the person that invented this gadget is a genius, pure genius. I will leave that loser, Senator Riggs up there for a day or two before I put you back up there, son. Say, let's go have another brandy or two."

I guess I had developed a very thick skin from being a professional goalie for all those years. After all, I was the single focus of every opponent I ever faced, to try to put a puck past me, through me, or around me, with no real concern to my physical well-being. I guess if I was stupid enough to stand there and let them pummel me, then I got what I deserved.

It never really bothered me. I guess all the pain and the

action numbed my emotions. Now, as I continued to study for the ministry, in a roundabout way, I will need to be just as I had been in the net, as people will confront me with troubles, delusions, anxiety, tragedy and other assorted aliments that I will need to provide a "save" for in their lives.

Senator William T. Hobnobber was certainly a fine proving ground for me, as he was a prime example of some of the weirdness that I was certain to face in my new career. Mr. Hobnobber helped to prepare me for what fate was going to deal me in the future. However, once, just once in my life, I would like to have a normal day, where strange, bizarre, and weird things did not occur. You know, where the sun is shining, the birds chirp happily in the trees, the breeze is gentle on my skin, my long hair blowing carelessly in the air, you know the "Mr. Bluebird chirping in my ear," type of thing. Someday.

"Oh, hi honey. I see you and Father are having a great time after dinner." My wife met me in the hallway, walked up, and gave me a big hug. "I love how great you two get along, he really loves that you are his son-in-law, you know!"

"Oh, I know that Binky, he lets me know all the time."

"I love you, twenty-seven, you are the best."

As I smiled and then kissed her, I wondered where I could get one of those Annoy-O-Meters.

God, please forgive me, but I could just see the words on the tag in my mind, "William T. Hobnobber."

We drove home and when we walked into the house; I noticed it was very cold. We had been over at the Hobnobber's mansion for most of the day, so I wondered when the heat had gone off. It was obvious that something had malfunctioned with the furnace. The old man had taught me from when I first could walk, how to repair old heating systems. Our heap of junk steam boiler at 182 Belmont Avenue was always malfunctioning on the coldest of winter days. We both could smell trouble in a boiler or furnace like old hound dogs. I grew up draining muddy water out of our old steam boiler on Belmont Ave, and that mission was as much a part of my childhood as playing in my backyard was.

"I better check the furnace, Binky. It seems like the heat has gone out."

"All right, twenty-seven, are you hungry?"

"No. I am still full from dinner, thanks."

I went down into the basement and sure enough, after some poking around, I found that the fan motor on the furnace fan had frozen up.

"Oh boy, I better see what I can do to get this going or it is going to be a long, cold night for, Binky and I." I said aloud as I had a shudder of fear that we might have to return to her parent's house if I could not get the heat on. We would need to spend the night there until I could get a new motor in the morning.

Utilizing the potential of spending the evening with the Hobnobbers as motivation, I was determined to attempt a repair. I lost track of the time while I pulled the motor out and brought it over to the workbench. It was not a lot of fun as it was being quite stubborn and uncooperative. I was working hard on it and doing my best to pull a frozen bolt out of the furnace blower housing so that I could even get to the motor.

It was not going really well when I heard my wife calling for me from high up in the house.

"Down here, Binky, I am still in the basement here."

I heard her come down the stairs and walk into the workshop.

"What are you doing, Paul?"

"Well, I can't seem to get this bolt out to replace this motor. Until I do, you will have no heat in the house."

"Oh, I see, well, you like it cold anyway. Do you want me to look up how to extract frozen and stubborn bolts?"

"No, I have it, I will let you know, say what is up, why were you calling?"

I had tied all my hair up behind my head to keep it out of my eyes while I worked on this stubborn contraption. Binky reached behind my head, pulled out the hair tie, and put it in her pocket.

"Oh, I almost forgot. How could I forget? The prospect of researching something diverted me. Look what came in the mail today."

Binky dropped a postcard on the bench in front of me, put her arm around me, and hugged me. I looked down and saw that the front of the card was printed with, "Thinking of you." I turned it over and the only thing written on the back was a signature that read, "Harry M. Redmond Jr." and a phone number with an area code that I did not recognize. The address on the envelope was, "To: Mr. and Mrs. Paul J. Henson."

This time, the card had a return address on it as well as a phone number. I put it down on the bench, folded my hands together, and smiled.

3

A Familiar Voice

"What are you going to do, Paul?"

Binky stared deeply into my eyes. I flipped the postcard over and over in my hand. My heart was racing a little, with the excitement and reality that Harry had finally reached out to us.

"Well, first, I am going to oil up this frozen fan motor, put it back in the furnace and get the heat on in this house, so my beautiful, gorgeous, and fabulous wife does not freeze. Then, I am going to go upstairs and call the number on this postcard."

"Oh, twenty-seven, is this really true? I cannot believe after all of this time that we have finally heard from him! Tell me that you think it is true, and that Harry is finally reaching out to us?"

"I think so, Binky. Otherwise, he would not have given us the contact information. I wonder if anyone else got a card with his telephone number. Hey, do me a favor, while I put this motor back in, and please call around to Linny and Ronzo, Mr. Redmond, Rose, Patty, Father Mark, Mum, please call everyone, and see if they received the same card. Can you do that, Binky?"

Binky gave me her famous rapid head nod to confirm that she was on the mission. She grabbed my hand and squeezed it. I could feel her excitement building.

"Sure, I will go upstairs right now and make the calls."

After some more work, I pulled out the frozen bolt, oiled up the motor, and determined that it seemed like it would work until I could purchase a new one. I put the motor in and said a quick prayer that it would operate. I clicked on the thermostat and heard the motor start to spin, the flame ignited and "boom" we had flame and heat!

Thank you, Lord, saved from the grips of William T. Hobnobber once more.

It was nice to know that if I bombed out as a minister, I could always go back to electrical or heating and cooling repairs.

I scrambled upstairs where Binky was feeling the heat coming out of the vents while giving me a thumb up signal. She was on the phone talking to someone, but she smiled at me.

"All right Linda, well, we will let you know then as soon as Paul calls him, thank you. Yes, tell everyone we love them too."

Binky hung up the telephone, and she explained, "Well that was Linny, and they did not receive anything. It appears after all my calls, that we are the only ones that he sent it to. Oh Paul, this is going to be so traumatic for you dear, do you want me to do some quick research on this type of situation? Reunions are so difficult, and you have had way too much experience as of the last few years with them."

I smiled at Binky's concern for my fragile frame of mind. "No, I am good, Binky. Look, it has to be good. Otherwise, he would not have sent me the number. Right? Don't you agree?"

Binky gave me her famous rapid up and down head nod as an indication that she agreed. She then walked over and hugged me tightly, and I could hear her begin to cry.

"Hey, why are you crying?"

"Oh, Paul, at times I am still so sorry at how I caused so much trouble by leaving all of you. I still cannot forgive myself for that. Perhaps if I had not been so selfish, then maybe Harry would have never left, Rose would be happier, and we would not have wasted all of that time between us. I could have provided some type of research that may have helped you."

"Hey, hey . . . stop it . . . will you? I thought we agreed, a long time ago to put all that past us. The main thing is now that we are here, we are together, and we will find out what is going on as Mr. and Mrs. Henson. I was there, Binky, there was nothing that anyone could have done, I tried, and Harry had made up his mind. Sometimes, people make decisions and they have to go where they think that life leads them. Some things are out of our control and you have to have faith and put it all in God's hands and not your own. Now, please stop crying, I need you, and I have you, and I am not going to let anything change that. I am ready to face this. That is what I do, and now we face these things together."

Binky nodded her head and composed herself. She walked over to the phone and handed it to me.

I took the postcard, looked at the number, took a deep breath, and dialed the number very slowly. The phone made the connection, and it started to ring.

One ring, then another and another.

He must not be home, I thought. Perhaps an answering machine will pick up and I can leave a message. Binky stood right next to me, looking at me with her hand over her mouth. Binky always did that when she was nervous, I think it was a habit, or her way of not shouting out spontaneously.

"Hello."

I heard that old familiar voice come on the other end of the phone and my heart leapt for joy in my chest. It had been so many years since I had heard his voice.

"Harry! Oh my . . . Harry, it is me, it is, Paul."

The line was quiet on the other end.

"Twenty-seven, it is so good to hear your voice."

He stopped speaking and I could hear him composing

himself on the other end of the line.

"I guess you received my card."

"I did, Harry, I did, how are you?"

"I am good, Paul. I am all right. I am so glad that you called. Damn, it has been so long, so, so, long. I am actually surprised that you even wanted to call me back, after all of this time, and not hearing from me." I could hear that he was starting to become upset on the other end of the line.

"Oh, c'mon, Harry, are you kidding? You know what we always said that we would be friends forever. Time has not changed that, you had to do what you had to do. I understand that."

Binky walked over behind me. She rested her head on my back as she put her arms around my waist and hugged me as tightly as she could.

"I hope you are doing well. You are married, I guess. I saw that the telephone book had you listed as a Mr. and Mrs. I only can hope that you married, Binky. I pray that she came back to you, Paul. Please tell me that you married, Binky, please Paul."

"I did, Harry. She did come back. Binky and I got married about one year ago."

I heard him sigh deeply on the phone and he whispered very softly, "Sky was right, I knew she would be right."

He was crying hard now.

"Binky is here with me right now. Harry, I am so glad you are all right, please tell me that you are all right. Where on Earth are you?"

He became a little more composed and at the first sign that he was still the same old Harry M. Redmond Jr., he said, "Stop being such an old lady, would you? I tell you I am all right. If I wasn't, then, I would tell you."

I could not help but to smile. That same old criticism of me sounded so good to hear.

"I am in Michigan, way up on the Upper Peninsula, near Canada. Hockey country, twenty-seven, hockey, and God's country. Tell Binky that I love her. I miss youse guys more than I can ever say."

He paused for a few moments and I heard him cough a little.

"I am coming home, Paul. I am finally ready to come home to New Jersey."

"That is wonderful! Great, great, great news! Binky loves you too. We all love you, Harry. We all miss you. Are you flying? Can I come get you at the airport in Newark?"

"No, I am going to be driving the old Wagon Bus, I still have it."

"Did you call your old man and tell him yet, or Linny or Patty? They have been so concerned for years now, Harry . . . we all have been so concerned."

"No, just you, Paul. I would always call you first. You know that. I will start to make the calls now that we have spoken. How are your old man and Mum? Are they doing all right, Paul?"

"Yeah, yeah, yeah, they are fine, older, but they are fine. The old man is finally retired. Get this Harry—he actually sold the 1964 Putter Classic model 200 and bought a Substantial Industries Rhino 400!"

Harry was laughing now, and it sounded so good to hear that famous laugh.

"No kidding, I can't wait to see that! Now that you have called, I can pack up and get out of here."

His voice grew quieter for a few seconds and he was speaking in almost a low whisper.

"It is just me now. Cocoa died a few weeks back."

I felt my heart sink. Another blow to his poor heart.

"I am so sorry, Harry. He was the greatest dog ever."

"He was, Paul, he sure was. You know he was eighteen. Eighteen years old is really a long time for a dog. Is Skippy gone now too, Paul?" Harry was crying once more; this was a difficult conversation to have for the both of us.

"Yes, old Skippy, passed around three years ago, Harry.

Hey, they both lived good lives, Harry. After all, they were both old. Please come home, Harry, we all need you home now."

Binky moved next to me and put her arm around my shoulders. She held me even a little tighter. I looked at the tears that she had rolling down her cheeks and she tried to wipe them away so that I would not see them.

He still wanted to talk; it was a magnificent outpouring, in which I could tell he needed to get off his heart and mind now.

"I was just waiting for you to get my card and I was praying that you would call. I almost dialed your number once or twice, but I thought that maybe after all this time, you would be so mad at me that you no longer wanted anything to do with crazy old Harry. I missed your wedding and I am sure a lot of other things too, so I sent the card to see if you would call."

"Of course, we would call you! You know that we are together forever."

"Then, I will be leaving in the morning. I will call you from the road. I will make some calls from here, but please call everyone and tell them the news. Will you do that, twenty-seven?"

"I will Harry, please drive carefully, you have our address. Hey, we are going to do it up big time, a big shindig, just like the old days at 20 John Street! We will invite everyone! Binky is a fabulous cook, and we will party like there is no tomorrow!"

Binky was now smiling and laughing. She felt that the tension had eased.

"Oh no! As 20 John Street, then you had better have some upside down, Christmas trees in your tree in the backyard, twenty-seven. I will be looking for them, along with a bottle of booze hidden in your cupboards! I hope you do not have any exploding swimming pools in your yard!"

"No pools, but I will do my best there, number thirty-five. I will do my best. We are over near Main Street on First Ave in Great Falls, close to Route Forty-Six. You would turn right by the tank in the park. Please call us and please take care."

"I will call you when I am close to New Jersey."

'Click,' the line went dead. Harry never did say goodbye when we spoke on the telephone. In fact, in all of our years together, that may have been the longest telephone conversation that we had ever had with each other.

I grabbed my wife and I could see that tears had filled her eyes. I smiled at her.

"It is going to be all right, Binky. He is coming back home. He is finally returning home."

We held each other in the kitchen, the two of us rocking together; just holding on to one another in the dark for what seemed like was hours. She cried in my arms and she held me, as she never did before. She smelled so good, her hair was soft, and her tears were gentle and warm. I felt as though I was able to absorb her pain and emotions. I could feel her breathing, her crying, and her chest moving as we held onto each other. She consumed my very soul, and we were one.

I prayed softly there in the stillness.

"Thank you, Lord. Thank you for this wonderful woman you gave me as a wife and thank you for steering our friend finally back home to us all. Believe it and it will happen. Amen."

Another reunion, it sure seemed my life was full of them over the last couple of years.

I listened and heard the heat cycle on once more. I had a quick thought of Mr. Hobnobber sitting alone in his fancy chair in the living room, and the chair next to him that I would usually be sitting in, was vacant. I smiled as I had escaped for a few more days! Good job, there on that fan motor twenty-seven, good job.

Binky started to make all the telephone calls to tell everyone the wonderful news. We had an extra room here at our house; it was small, and filled floors to ceiling, with Binky's books, files, and papers that enhanced and supported her research capabilities. Once we cleared it out, we could put Harry up here for a little while, until he found a place and got it together. Binky called them all; she spoke with my parents, her folks, Tinky, Linda and Ronzo, Patty and the Big Spike, Mr. Redmond, and Father Mark.

Harry M. Redmond Junior was a legend, and the news of his return would spread like wildfire. I am sure the New Jersey National Guard units all went back on full alert, knowing he was heading back to his home turf.

After Binky had finished making all the calls and spreading the great news, she grabbed a Big Boulder beer for me and she stood next to me in the living room. She smiled at me and I could tell she was feeling much better now as she handed me the beer.

"Thank you. Would you like me to fix you a Martini, Binky?"

"No, maybe in a few minutes. It has been such a day, twenty-seven, such a day. I would enjoy a Martini, but right for now, I have to obtain some direction."

"Direction, from me?"

"Yes, dear Paul, my wonderful husband. Since you are my great, smart and strong, pastor to be someday soon, I require your expert counseling services. I prefer your advice right now to my own, at times, flawed research. Since you have now successfully completed your first levels of school with excellence, and the seminary has approved your attendance, I think we should practice for your future career. What shall I do about our dear friend, Rose?" Binky asked, and then she came and sat next to me on the sofa.

"Before you answer that question, you need to know that everyone is attending. They are all heading here and everyone will wait for Harry to arrive at our house. Mr. Redmond is catching the first flight he can, as are Patty and George. Linny and Ronnie are driving. My parents are very excited to meet the legendary, Harry, as is my brother. Father Mark, Mum of course and your father, they are all attending. I will cook all the food and create the party of a lifetime! Our little home will never have had so many people in it!"

Binky was intense now; I could see the little research wheels spinning on party planning already. She then leaned into me for the famous, intense Binky stare and waited for my answer.

"Hmmm, it is as Mum would say a bit of a sticky wicket, eh? I may have to think and pray on this for a bit, but my goalie instincts tell me to move in close to the shooter."

"What? I have never heard that one before," Binky's eyes grew wide with her statement.

"You know Binky, when I had a shooter one on one, I would creep on my skates out of the net, and close in on him to cut down on how much of the net they could see, and remove the best shooting angles."

I jumped up from the sofa to demonstrate while my wife began laughing hysterically at me.

"It is basic geometry, Binky," I complained, as it seemed as if she was not following me.

Binky was laughing, and she waved her hand at me.

"I can see it now, Reverend Henson in his private office . . . while he counsels his parishioners in his goaltending equipment! I still have not heard that you are answering my question of what to do with telling Rose the wonderful news and inviting her to Harry's homecoming."

"Oh well, I admit I am still a weird, eccentric goalkeeper at heart, honey, but you know what I mean, the people I love are the net, and when it is becoming serious, I pull out all the stops to protect the net."

Binky laughed even more until she was holding her

sides.

"So now, we are all hockey nets! You still have not helped me with my question. You are failing on your counseling mission here, Pastor Paul."

I smiled and now I could not stop laughing. I thought how it was so good to have married a woman who could laugh at me like that. Couples, who never laugh together, in my opinion, are taking themselves excessively seriously.

"So now that you have confirmed my high level of eccentric hockey behavior still exists, and I have confused you with my analogy of protecting my loved ones. I will answer your question. I do admit that I need to work a bit on my analogies for my future career."

Binky finally stopped laughing and stared back in.

"Ah yes, you do, Paul," she agreed.

I made my best attempt to answer the question now, "Rose still cares about Harry, and I do not mean as just a friend. Deep down, I think she still loves him. She is not happy in her marriage, and it is going to be a very difficult situation when she hears of his return. I think it is up to us to protect her, and we can do so by. . .."

The front doorbell rang, and I stopped my sentence. I got up and placed my beer on a coaster on an end table. I walked towards the front door and held my finger up to Binky, to indicate that I would finish my sentence in a minute.

"It is getting awful late. I cannot imagine Linny and Ronzo made it that fast from the Pocono Mountains and stopped by to say hello."

I opened the door and to my utter surprise and shock, standing in front of me was Rose. She was holding two suitcases. She had obviously been crying, and she turned and hugged me. Binky came running over when she saw that it was, Rose.

"Oh guys, I need your help! I have left Daniel and I need a place to stay, I cannot take it anymore."

Oh, boy Lord, I can see that this is sort of like on-the-job training for me, but just once, could I have one of those, "Mr. Bluebird chirping in my ear" days?

Just one day, please.

I thought about what Father Mark had said to me at our wedding, "God has his hand on your heart and steers you where he feels you are needed."

It sure was strange that Rose showed up on our doorstep right at the very moment that we were discussing her situation. Then again, nothing really surprised me anymore.

Binky helped Rose into the kitchen and I carried her bags up to the spare bedroom. I had to move mountains of Binky's research books and information that she used in her research quests, out of the spare bedroom and into an extra closet as well as our attic storage loft. The work delayed me quite a bit longer than I wanted to be. When I finally returned to the first floor, Binky had made some coffee for us all and Binky and Rose were sitting around the kitchen table.

Binky pointed at my cup.

It was going to be a long night. There goes our plan to relax with some Big Boulder beer and a few Martinis. I stood next to the table as Rose began to speak.

She was a mess, and my wife was doing her best to comfort her and get through the conversation.

"Things have been awful for quite a while. We have been in Catholic counseling for a year or more. Daniel is just not a lot of fun, he has had trouble finding work as of late, and I have had to support us both. The pressure has been terrible on both of us. For lack of a better description, he has become mean, unstable, and abusive."

I crept in closer and put my hand on her shoulder.

"Has he hit you, Rose?" I asked, feeling that little fire that always burns inside of me rise up in my chest. As dumb as my analogy was, I certainly have all intentions of protecting my "net."

"No, Paul. Well, not yet at least. However, tonight he came close, he was very drunk, and he pulled me forcibly by the arm, and spun me around. When I told him that he needed to stop drinking so much whiskey, he put his fist up to me and went to swing at me. He stopped midway into his punch, but it scared me terribly. That is when I packed up and left."

Rose looked at me and then towards Binky.

"I do not trust him, he is an angry man, and I am not sure what he is really capable of. I am so sorry, I have nowhere else to go. My parents are so old now and they are in Florida. I have very little money right now either, just a few dollars, not too much."

Binky took her friend by the hands and told her, "You are safe now, Rose. You are always welcome here with Paul and me. It is going to be all right."

My wife hugged and comforted her friend. I thought, as my mum would say, what a bloomin' awful mess this one was. Harry is coming back, and Rose and her marriage has exploded. The timing of this one was sure intriguing, that was for sure. I provided some words of comfort and some advice as best as I could, but there was very little that I could say or do that would soften the blow of the situation. Binky also jumped into the discussion and Rose slowly started to settle down.

I knew that Rose was deeply religious, and she was Catholic, so we all prayed together and I did my best in my novice way to quote some common scripture to help her. When the time seemed right, I looked at my wife and I could tell by the look in her eyes, that she knew, as well as agreed with, what I was about to say.

"Look, ah, Rose, I know this is a tough night for you and that there is an awful lot going on here, but we need to let you know that tonight . . . I spoke to Harry on the phone."

Rose's expression changed to astonishment when she

heard the news, and she actually jumped right up out of her seat.

She stood right in front of us, as if she were in shock. She was now staggering and held onto the table for support. Rose wiped her face and dried her eyes with a napkin from the table.

"Paul, you did? How is he? Where is he?"

"He is all right, Rose. He sounded sad, but he sounded strong. He is driving here from Michigan. He has been there for all of these years. We expect him to arrive in a day or two. Everyone is coming. It will be a big reunion right here. We are going to throw him a welcome home party to remember."

Rose sighed, smiled, and then she sat down. This had been a day, and now a night to remember for all of us, and I could only imagine the range of emotions that Rose was experiencing.

Binky and I studied her face. I knew my gut instincts were correct about her inner feelings.

Rose spoke in a low whisper, "I am so glad, I cannot believe it. After all this time, Harry is returning home. What a night this has been."

"It sure has been something, Rose. We expect Father Mark in the next day or so. He wanted to be here for the homecoming for Harry too. Perhaps, it would be good if you spoke with him about your situation. He is retired now, but I am sure he will have solid advice as well as some resources for you. I know that between Binky, Father Mark, and me, we all will help you and we will support you no matter what happens."

Rose nodded her head in agreement, but you could tell that she was still in shock. I decided to see if Rose would be willing to call it a night now.

"Rose, it is getting awful late, you need to rest. Why don't you go upstairs, take a shower and get some sleep? It will be better in the morning. Binky will get you all situated."

Binky helped Rose up as they both agreed and headed upstairs. While my wife helped Rose, I sank in a chair in the living room. What a day this has been, it sure has been long. A moment changes everything once more; the pattern is surely challenging! What a roller coaster ride of emotions in one single day, from raw laughter to total sorrow. I looked at my watch and it was almost two in the morning. I had school today, and it was a long ride into New York City on the train to seminary classes. At least it would be Friday and we would have the weekend to prepare and to plan for Harry's return. I did not think this was going to be easy now, not for one minute.

Tomorrow, I needed to look for that old paper bag that is somewhere around here and find another smudge stick. I think we all need a good dose of a smudge-a-dub-dubber. Thank you, Sky.

We all tried to catch at least a few hours of sleep and all too soon, the dawn came for all of us. These days, we only had one vehicle, so Binky took me to and picked me up from the train station. My wife had decided to take the day off from work to make sure that she took good care of Rose. When I jumped off the train in the late afternoon, I had to admit that I was very tired. When Binky met me at the train station, we exchanged greetings, a quick kiss, and a hug.

"You look so tired, Paul. Are you doing all right?"

"I am a little beat, how are you?"

"Worried about you!"

"I am fine. How is Rose? I bet it was a tough day for her."

"A little rough, yes, she slept a lot of the day away, which was good to keep her mind from wandering. When she was awake, we did have a chance to talk a lot. She is actually better than I thought she would be at this point, twenty-seven."

"Has Harry called in?"

"Oh yes, Paul, and we had a wonderful chat. It was so exciting to speak with him! You would be so proud of me. I did not burst into tears until after we had hung up the telephone."

I was proud of her, and I worked very hard to suppress a chuckle or two.

"I feel that my research is correct on his journey, and I felt much better about my calculations, when Harry told me that he has made it to Pennsylvania. He is going to get some sleep tonight and set out early in the morning tomorrow. He should arrive right around one in the afternoon tomorrow. I think his actual time of arrival will be very close to my initial prediction of his arrival."

As Binky drove our old jeep, I could see her eyes going back and forth in her head. She was in her glory as she explained the details of her latest research and information.

"I knew that his older transportation would most likely not exceed sixty miles per hour during the trip and he would stop for rest, fuel, and food, so I based my calculations upon that. I think I am within thirty minutes or so, plus or minus a few minutes here and there, and this information has assisted me greatly in the party planning."

I just smiled. I loved my wife and her research obsession, and unlike other folks, I never wanted to stick a sock in her mouth when she went off on one of her famous research explanations.

"I cannot emphasize enough how it was so nice to speak with Harry. It was such a thrill! I did not tell him where you were. I thought that you could tell him tomorrow. He sounded excited. Tired, but excited. Everyone is coming into town and I have spoken with all the gang, the out-of-town folks are staying in hotels, but we should be all set for tomorrow."

Binky was really worked up now because she went on and on with the details of the day and her plans.

"I have cooked all day, and I ordered a cake from the Italian bakery on Main Street. You know, welcome back Harry written on it and such."

I finally had a little break in the action to slip a comment or two in there, "Wow, you have done a spectacular job, my dear! I can see how your superior research, cooking, and organization skills have come into play today. I feel guilty for not helping you at all."

Binky fluffed her long hair with her hands, as she often did when I complimented her and she continued, "Thank you, twenty-seven, but that is what a wife is for, besides, it is important for you now to concentrate on your studies."

I was indeed lucky, as Binky was now working and supporting us full time, as my schedule at school had forced me to leave the electrical company, so she was our sole source of income right now. We, of course, still had our savings in the bank which was still there from my hockey playing days, as well as some savings that Binky had, however, we had both decided not to touch the savings accounts, unless it was an emergency.

"Rose slept most of the day, eh?"

"Yes, she was not good at first when she awoke today, but when she did get up, she did have something to eat. We then sat for a bit and she was able to talk."

Binky took her eyes off the road for a moment and looked at me quickly.

"I have to be honest, dear Paul, that the majority of our conversations were about Harry and tomorrow. I think you were dead-on in your assessment yesterday on her feelings. As a result of our conversation, I decided to begin some new research on the subject today."

Binky pulled the jeep into the driveway and we got out.

"Hey, I will get changed and go for a quick run before we eat. I need to work out and clear my head."

Binky put her arms down at her side and dug her left foot into the ground. She wanted to make a point with me,

"Oh, don't you think you are too tired? You need to rest some, Paul! You are going to be a Lutheran pastor now, not a goaltender!"

"I am good. Please do not worry about me. I still need to stay in playing shape. I may be a very poor pastor, you know, so I need a backup plan!"

Binky shook her head, but she knew she was not going to win this debate.

I checked in with Rose, changed into my old Long Island Roosters warm up suit, with a now faded, number twenty-seven on the back of it, and hit the road. I still worked out a great deal, not the same regiment that I did of course, when I was playing, but I still was in good shape. The run loosened me up both in mind and body, and it felt good. I came back, showered, and the three of us sat and ate together.

Rose seemed better, and she did not eat too badly at all. In fact, she ate quite a bit! Binky was a marvelous cook, and she had made a pasta dish for us. In addition, we also had some salads, beer, and wine. The fridge overflowed with food for tomorrow, as well as snacks, desserts and all kinds of other food for the homecoming. After dinner, we all cleaned up the table, and Rose, Binky, and I worked to lay out everything in preparation for tomorrow.

By the end of dinnertime, Rose was feeling pretty good. She had switched from her usual Purple Pirate beers and instead, she had enjoyed a few glasses of wine. It was nice to see her so relaxed. We even had a chance to witness a few of her famous smiles and laughs. As easily as Rose could cry, she could also just as easily smile and laugh, so it was nice to see.

I remembered my pledge from the night before to find a smudge stick. I went poking around in some old bags that I had long ago stowed away in a hidden crevice somewhere. I did find a smudge stick up in one of my old storage boxes and Binky and Rose had a fun time taking turns making fun of me as I smudged the house and went from room-to-room and corner-to-corner of the entire house.

"Go ahead and laugh, you two, I have seen this in action and believe me it works."

I never did reveal to Binky that I had smudged my old apartment on the night that she had returned to me. I felt that some mysteries of my strange life, at this point at least, were better off left not advertised. Someday, I would share it with her, along with some other strange but true incidents of my life. It just was not going to be right now. As much as I loved my wife, I had to time some of her exhausting research missions!

After my little smudge mission, my body suddenly reminded me that I was exhausted. I had only slept an hour or two the previous night, and I had been up early to catch the train. As the girls chatted, I retreated to the living room and my favorite chair. I had some course work to do, but it would have to wait. I plugged in my headphones and placed my coveted vinyl record of "Close to the Crevice" on the record player. I settled in, and I am sure I did not make it more than five minutes into the record, before I was fast asleep.

I was very tired because I did not move from the chair. When I woke up, early morning light filled the entire room. I slowly cracked my eyes open, and I could see little streaks of light dancing through the window into the room. The headphones were off my head, and lying on the side of my chair, next to the record player. I knew that my wife must have been watching me carefully at some point. I adjusted my eyes to the bright light of the house. I could hear Binky banging pots and pans around in the kitchen and her and Rose talking. I also smelled the aroma of some coffee brewing, and it was enticing to me. I looked at the clock on the wall and I saw that it was nine in the morning. Oh boy, I had been tired! Binky had just left me in the chair last night. I guess she did not want to disturb me. It reminded me of a time so long ago when I finally fell asleep on the sofa in Sky and Harry's house and I woke up to Harry working in the kitchen.

Déjà vu, I suppose.

I sat in the chair for a bit of time, while working out of the deep sleep that I had been in, and suddenly, I realized the impact of what was going to occur today. After the passing of so much time, Harry was returning! It will be the reunion of the famous duo of Harry and Paul, but so much has changed. I wondered what he would be like or if time and the grief of the loss of his wife would be too much for him, and he would be bitter and cold. All the adventures of our past ran together, and I once more found it hard to fathom that he was finally returning. I knew that I would be ready. I hoped and then prayed that he would be the same old Harry.

I popped up out of the chair, went upstairs to wash up, shower, and get dressed.

I felt good. This was going to be some kind of special day. I could just feel it. I needed to hold on tight, Hurricane Harry was returning and deep down inside of me, I knew that this day was a culmination of an awful lot of hopes, prayers, and dreams by everyone who knew and loved Harry M. Redmond Junior.

I came down into the kitchen and greeted everyone.

"Well, if it isn't my long-lost, sleepy husband! I missed you last night, but you were sleeping so tightly, I just left you in the chair. You did not even move when I pulled the headphones off of your head."

I smiled at Binky and told her, "I was a bit on the tired side, Binky. I missed you too." I gave her a hug and a kiss and then said hello to Rose.

"Good Morning, twenty-seven. My, you look so handsome for it being so early in the morning!"

"Dear Rose, the flattering remarks are warmly appreciated!"

I gave her a quick hug as I passed by her on the way to a chair.

"Do you want some French toast and some tea? Or would you prefer strong coffee, twenty-seven?" Binky was standing in front of our cooker and she waited for my answer.

"Sure, thank you, Binky. Please, the coffee sounds and smells wonderful. I can enjoy some tea later. How are you, Rose? I am so sorry I sacked out last night, if you needed to chat a bit, I was a little rude to you and my wife for sure."

Binky came over and poured my coffee cup full of some piping hot coffee. My wife said to me, "Paul, please, you were not rude, but you were exhausted. I actually wish that you would take more time off, such as you did last night. You push your body and mind way too hard."

Rose moved over and sat down next to me, "I agree with Binky. Please Paul, after all we have been through, you never need to apologize to me! To answer your question, I am just needing Pastor Paul, I suppose."

Pastor Paul . . . that sounded pretty good, I will need to remember that one.

"Oh boy, I am a long way from that Rose, but let me try my best. Please keep in mind that it is early yet, my dear Rose, very early."

Rose sighed, and she sat back in her chair as she spoke, "Being here the last few days has made me think a lot, Paul. It really has. It has made me think about what true love really is. I think Daniel and I were a mistake right from the start. I hate to admit that, but I suppose, I can speak freely enough to you and Binky. I think it was not as much love between us as it was lust. He was handsome, intelligent, sexy, and charismatic. I was so hurt and lonely after Harry and I did not work out, and the four of us had split and gone off in separate ways that I really could not deal with all the pain. Until Daniel came along, I only ever had you, Paul, to talk to in confidence when you were in town and not off playing hockey somewhere. How I cherished those moments, when you and I could meet and speak, it was my link to our past and to . . . Harry."

Rose looked over at Binky to gauge her reaction because I am sure she was bringing back some painful moments for Binky as well. Binky was standing next to the cooker listening to her intently, but she did not say a word.

Rose then continued, "I was well, I do not know, I guess, I was vulnerable."

A long time ago, I had learned to listen before speaking, and for the most part in my life, it had served me very well. I sat there and listened intently. In my mind, I thought, I know you are testing me, Lord. I know you are. I thought back in time to that sacred kitchen table at 20 John Street and how many wonderful times, as well as profound discussions, we all had around that old table. Now, my own kitchen table was the center of a similar scene. It was amazing to me how life was a great circle, and we all were a part of it, as we all went around and around inside of it.

I vowed to ask Mr. Redmond where that wonderful table went after they sold the house at 20 John Street. How I would love to have it someday.

"In watching you and Binky the last few days, I can only hope to someday have what you two now have. After all that you have been through, the highs and the lows, being apart all those years, you playing hockey off by yourself in strange places, Binky pondering her future, and yet your love endured. In the end, you found each other, just like it was always meant to be."

Binky now wiped her hands on a towel, came in close to me, and put her arm around my shoulder as she sat upon my lap.

"Time and places could not divide the two of you. Your love closed the distance."

Rose was remarkably strong at this point. I had never seen this side of Rose; she was so intense and in control.

Generally, Rose would have broken down and cried uncontrollably by now.

"I watched as Binky last night, took the headphones off of your head, then, she gave you a kiss, put a blanket over you, and she made sure you were safe, secure and warm. A simple act, yet it was full of love. What the two of you have together, cannot be anything but true love, you have endured the tough times, the hard times, the separation, the pain, the loneliness. You have run the course. You two, have something so very special. I think it is love in its most pure form."

Rose then turned and looked directly at me, "So, my question is, Pastor Paul . . . how do I know when it is a real love? When can I ever have what the two of you have? I am not talking about loving a pet, or your mother, brother, aunt, uncle, or your father, I am talking about real love between a man and a woman, as God intended it to be."

Both my wife and Rose leaned in for the proverbial words of wisdom from me, a fledgling shadow of a pastor, in reality; I was just a long-haired hippie, and a retired hockey goaltender.

Nothing like an easy one to start with, Lord! Boy, oh boy, from O'Malley to broken toes, to stitches in the head, to dealing with William T. Hobnobber, to the tough questions. When does it ever get any easier? Remember our deal with one of those, "Mr. Bluebird days" someday soon!

I knew a hockey analogy would not work. That test run had been a bomb. Ah, why not just wing it there twenty-seven, you sure let a few people put a puck or two in back of you over the years, so failure is all part of the game?

I winged it like a big cornball. I decided that I needed to whip up some quick mumbo jumbo.

"You will know, because there are no obstacles to true love, there is only purpose. Rose, true love is like a freight train, pulling a full load steaming through the night on snow-covered tracks. Somewhere, before it set out on its journey, it was loaded up. It was loaded up with a lifetime of purpose and all the mysteries of love packed inside. Loaded with a purpose, its steam blows off through the smoke stack, its horn sounds off to warn people that it is coming . . . the lights of the train illuminate the night. This is a special train that is loaded with respect, sorrows, goals, fears, desires, laughs, tears, happiness, and most of all, understanding and compromise. Filled with all of that, the train then has what it needs to make it to the final destination. Nothing will stop it, not snow or ice, cold, rain, wind, heat, or heavy loads. In fact, the heavier the burden, and the steeper the tracks, the more the train pulls, until finally, after pulling and tugging, it arrives into a station and rests for a while. It then delivers the load that it needed to deliver, and then it starts all over again. Over and over, the train never stops. It always delivers every single day of you and your lover's lifetimes together. You will know. Believe me that you will know when the train finally arrives."

My voice became softer than it had been, and I spoke in almost a whisper, because my own words were having a profound meaning, even to me.

"You will prove your love and then lie next to your true love and feel your lover's heart beat in exact time to yours, and both of your chests will rise together in unison, as one. You then will become one, your souls will be consumed together, and there will be no loads that are too heavy, or any train tracks too steep to climb. Nothing will be impossible for the two of you when you are together, not kissing the sun, or touching the stars, or walking barefoot across some hot desert, nothing. It will be just as you described as God intended it to be."

There, I finished, and only the good Lord knew where on Earth that had all come from. I sat back and studied their eyes. A train analogy for true love, eh? I had a strange feeling that if I did make it to be a minister, I sure would be the most unusual one that has come along in a very long time.

Rose smiled at me and said, "Believe it and it will happen."

I smiled back as my wife kissed my cheek and hugged my neck.

I whispered into my wife's ear, "Was that better than the hockey net thingy from last night?"

I received a rapid Binky head nod in an up and down motion so that I knew that I had hit pay dirt. The three of us joined our hands together on the kitchen table and squeezed them. As so often happens in our lives, the front doorbell rang.

What is it with front doorbells and timing in my life? Oh well, I may never get that French toast, now, will I?

We stood up, went to the front door, and found it was my parents arriving. We all greeted them, and as soon as we had started to chat with them, another ring came at the door. This time it was Linda and Ronzo. After greeting them and exchanging handshakes, hugs, and talking about the excitement of the day, I remembered my breakfast.

I was suddenly very hungry.

On the way to the kitchen, I passed my mother, who had caught Rose, and she was consoling her about her situation. I smiled at Mum and she smiled back. She was doing her best to help dear Rose, and I appreciated Mum's efforts.

I strolled into the kitchen and found the old man eating my French toast at the table. He looked up at me and between chewing he said, "Hey, chief. Binky said you changed your mind and did not want this, so I did not want it to go to waste. It sure is great about Harry coming back. It is going to be some amazin' kind of day, Paulie! It sure has been a long time. Say, Binky sure can cook! This is the best French toast that I ever had."

I had to laugh at the old man. As he had grown older,

there was nothing wrong with his stomach or his appetite, that was for sure!

"Yes, she can, Dad, she is the best."

I sat at the table and watched as the old man wolfed down what was once my breakfast.

The old man nodded. He looked up and said, "So, ya doin' all right?"

"Yeah, yeah, yeah, really good, Dad. How is the new Rhino 400 running?"

"Great! Best thing that I ever did was to buy it and finally get rid of that old, 1964 Putter Classic model 200!"

Despite his enthusiasm, I am not quite sure that I wholly, or entirely, believed that testimony. The old man would always hold the Putter in deep respect and honor deep in his heart.

"I am going to trade them every two or three years or so until I get too old to drive. You should see the other cars flee in terror when I come down Route Twenty-Three now! I love it, I really do. Hey, are you ever going to get rid of that old jeep and buy something new?"

I shook my head to indicate, no.

"I do not think so, Dad. It is a Henson family tradition to keep vehicles until the wheels roll off, the floorboard's rot out and we have to push them down the road."

The old man smiled at me; no doubt, he recalled his beloved 1964 Putter Classic model 200.

"I have to admit, I understand, because in a strange sort of way, I miss that old Putter. I would give an awful lot to lay one more time under that car on a freezing, cold morning and knock the ice out from under the linkage rods to loosen up the push button dashboard transmission."

He smiled at me and pushed his breakfast around on the plate with his fork. It is amazing how the passage of time could create such strange but fond memories.

He looked up at me.

"That is a shame about Rose. Between you and me, that

guy she married, always seemed like a whacko to me, anyway. That jackass made Rose deal with a bunch of bullshit if ya ask me. I always thought that he had a bad attitude, and I wanted to knock him out and set 'em on his ass once or twice when I first met him. She is a great gal. I hope she is all right. Your mum and I love that young woman. Nuthin' against, Binky, cuz we love her, but I kinda always thought that Rose and you would have gotten together when Binky was gone. Anyway, I would not want to hear that her whack job husband had hurt Rose or hit her. I would have to hunt him down there, Paulie. You know that I would send him a calling card from the old neighborhood, if you know what I mean. I know that you would do the same."

He looked up at me and I nodded.

"Mum and Binky will talk with her and help her along," the old man said.

I nodded my head, but I did not comment.

The old man took another swallow of the French toast.

"I have my plan for the garden this year. It should be a good year, just waiting now for the weather to turn. Spring training and the garden. It is right around the corner now, Paulie. Hey, did I tell you that I beat old man Alto out on the first ripe tomatoes in the neighborhood this past gardening season?"

The old man was always competing with the neighbor across the street who was an older Italian guy who had a huge garden. Each season, the two of them would bet a six-pack of Big Boulder beer over who would have the first ripe tomatoes in the neighborhood.

"No kidding, that is great, Dad. What did you plant? Those Blobbee Big Giant varieties?"

The old man put down his fork and waved for me to come in a little closer.

"Where is Mum?" The old man whispered.

"She is with Binky, Rose, and Linny in the other room."

"Well, I have to confess, since you are an almost man of the cloth there, but I knew I was going to lose this past year, so I went down to the Foodworld supermarket and bought a couple of big red tomatoes. I took them home and then I tied them up inside one of my plants with this fine fishing line. I called old man Alto over and he was amazed. I was betting that he was too old these days for his eyeballs to see the fishing line. I was right! He just shook his head and did not suspect a thing. He brought the beer over that afternoon!" The old man beamed at how he had out maneuvered his gardening foe!

I shook my head and laughed; the old man was too much. He really was.

I asked him, "So, are you enjoying the new area and the new neighborhood?"

The old man finished the last of the French toast and he pushed the plate aside and wiped the syrup off his mouth. Putting his fork down, he pondered my question for a moment or two.

"It is a nice place. Nice house there, Paulie. But it will never be the same as Belmont Avenue. Nothin' evah will. There are far too many memories. It is what you say. How do you say it? All of those ghosts that are there. All these people here today, especially with Harry returning today, all of us would say the same thing, we would trade all of it in a heartbeat to go back there to that old neighborhood and have what we had. We just did not really know it at the time. It was special. It was home for us all. Go ahead and ask Ronzo, or Harry's old man, they will tell you the same thing. There was nothing like it, never will be, Paulie, never will be ever again."

I smiled, because I knew he was right. The old man was a smart guy, he really was. He looked at me, smiled, and leaned back in his chair.

"Hey, do you think that giant chief guy, who sold Christmas trees over at the church on Chamberlain

Avenue, would remember me? He was a great guy, what a great guy he was!"

"Sure Dad, yeah, yeah, yeah, you are unforgettable, he would remember you."

I stood up from the chair, reached over and I patted him on the back.

"Thanks, Dad, for the chat and for always being there for me. If I never say it enough, thanks for being my old man."

"Sure, sure, sure, Paulie, hey don't tell Mum or Binky about the tomato thing will ya? Do you think it is too early for a Big Boulder?"

"No sweat, Dad. I will not say a word. No, go ahead . . . grab one out of the fridge now. There are some Dingleberries in there too."

The old man waved his hand in the air and laughed as he spoke, "Nah, those Dingleberries are way too sweet. I am a Big Boulder man."

I smiled at my father and his spirit. I thought as I walked toward the living room that what defined him the most was his indomitable spirit.

I met Ronzo, Mum, Rose, and Linny in the living room and saw that Binky was working the front door. Before you knew it, the grand reunion was underway!

The Big Spike, Patty, Mr. Redmond, my in-laws and Tinky, they all were arriving. It was hard to tell, but I could not really detect any current phases that the Redmond family may have been embroiled in. Sometimes, it is not easy to detect and today may have been a day to be the regular Redmonds! Time would tell.

Our little house was full, and it was wonderful to see everyone once again. You could feel the joy in the air! Conversations started in every corner of our little house, and the excitement and joy at the arrival of Harry was building. It was even more special to see all of us together once again under these circumstances.

Father Mark arrived, and soon we all were ready for the return of the prodigal son. We just needed Harry to arrive.

I helped Binky in the kitchen as the early arrivals surprised us, but it seemed like food and drink were the last things on most of our guest's minds, (the old man being the sole exception) the excitement of Harry's return was way too much for everyone. It seemed as though we all just wanted to share the anticipation together and after all of this time, for us to be together once again.

Rose and my mother came in to help and we soon had coffee, tea and some snacks going around. Tinky and I put up a giant, "Welcome Home" banner over our dining room table, and we hung some balloons around here and there. Soon, the house was looking good, and it was party time!

It reminded me in so many ways of 20 John Street and all that we shared there together. We all had not been together since Binky and I were married, so this was wonderful to experience. The bakery delivered the cake right on time. Binky had picked out a spectacular cake. It was huge, and had layers and layers of cake covered in blue and yellow icing, with the words, "Welcome Home Harry" along the top.

We were all set.

It was right around one o'clock, maybe a few minutes after, when the doorbell rang. I was speaking to Mr. Redmond and Rose, when they both heard the bell ring; they stopped talking and intently looked at me.

Mr. Redmond looked at me, smiled, and said, "You go first Paul, it is your house. You always lead us all anyway, without you we all fall apart. You are our rock."

Rose looked at me; she grabbed my arm and squeezed it tightly.

"Believe it and it will happen," was all Rose said.

A quiet hush came over the entire house when the front bell had rung.

Binky came running over and grabbed my hand, "I

think my research is correct, twenty-seven and that is going to be Harry."

I acknowledged her accuracy with a smile, "I think you are correct, honey."

The whole house was silent while I walked through the living room and headed to the front door. I stopped when I realized that Binky was not walking along with me. My wife was just standing there, frozen in place with her hands covering her mouth. I turned and waved for her to join me.

"Binky, please, we always go together, I am nothing without you."

She smiled and ran up next to me. She put her hand in mine, and together, we opened the front door.

There in front of us stood, Mr. Harry M. Redmond Junior.

He smiled and said, "Hey there, twenty-seven, long time, no see, my friend! Hey, Mrs. Henson. I am home, I am finally home."

The three of us embraced, and we held onto each other for what seemed like forever. In the background, inside of the house, I could hear the tears of joy and the shouts of our families as they witnessed the reunion scene unfold. All I can say is that these were the most special collection of people that I have ever known, and they all remain near and dear to my heart even to this day. Not a single person held any of the slightest animosity towards Harry for his long absence; we only expressed joy upon his return!

I had not cried since that awful day when Harry and Cocoa had left me standing in the street, watching as his Wagon Bus disappeared from my sight. I did not cry at my wedding, or when my knee exploded, or when Binky returned, and said she would be my wife, or countless other times. It is just the way God made me . . . I guess. I did not cry right now, as Binky and Harry sobbed their eyes out, and we held each other in the doorway to our home.

The best I could muster up was that I simply said, "Welcome home, buddy. I think this is the beginning of another perfect Harry, Binky, and Paul day."

As we entered the house together, the joyful reunions began, as Harry's family rushed in and took turns one by one, hugging him and reuniting.

Oh my, the tears that flowed!

They all took turns welcoming him back, his father, then his sisters, Ronzo, and George, then my mother and the old man. On and on it went, Father Mark, even Mr. and Mrs. Hobnobber and Tinky, who had never met him before, were hugging him, and crying their eyes out.

I was proud of Harry, who despite the tears of joy and raw emotion of the situation, did not question or come back with one of his patented remarks when Tinky introduced himself by name. He looked at me over Tinky's shoulder as they hugged and our old face and hand signals worked. Harry played it cool! Same old Harry and Paul, even under extreme situational duress.

Binky and I held our breath, as the last person standing in line to greet him was, Rose. Rose had been standing next to my mother with tears pouring from her eyes while watching the entire scene unfold. When Harry finally spotted her, he just waved her to come by him with his arms wide open, and Rose rushed in. They held onto each other for a long time, and to be honest, it was at that moment that, if I could have cried . . . I would have.

I do seem to say this every few years or so as our lives all continued the same emotional roller coaster. However, these words seem to best describe these situations over and over; pictures were taken, tears were shed, people laughed, people hugged and people cried.

I stood next to Binky, put my arm around her, and pulled her close to me as we watched the incredible reunion. "Are you happy there, Bink-a-roo-ski?"

She looked at me and smiled, "Oh yes, as long as you

are always here. I think that number twenty-seven train of yours is always pulling into our backyard, dropping off whatever it was that you said was loaded up inside of it."

I laughed and my old man came by and caught us sharing a kiss.

"Hey, Bunky, sorry to interrupt such a tender moment, but do you have any more of that French toast?"

My wife shook her head at the old man and his feigned attempt at recalling how he chronically used to mispronounce her name. She smiled and pointed to the kitchen.

"Come along, dear Dad Henson, Bunky will make some more for you."

4

What Tomorrow Will Bring

The long tearful return of Harry ended as he had made the rounds of everyone. He looked good, a little heavier, and while he no longer dyed his hair, as he did when Sky was alive, he still wore his peace tee shirt and dungaree jeans with patches sewn on them.

Binky, Mrs. Hobnobber, Rose, and my mother, had retreated to the kitchen to start to prepare to bring the food out. My old man was eating more French toast at the table when Harry pulled me over to the side.

As he smiled, he shook my hand once more and held me for a second.

"Wow, a strong handshake there twenty-seven, man, you look great, like you have been still working out. You are like a superman or something. Did you grow while I was away or what? Your wife is radiant, she is more gorgeous than I ever remember, and Mrs. Hobnobber, wow, holy shit, she is a knockout! How did Binky's old man end up with such a hot chick?"

I laughed, same old Harry, still with his eyes on the ladies.

"It is easy to see where Binky got her looks from! It sure was not from her old man."

"I am good, Harry, I still could play, you look great also, and it is nice to see you smiling. The last time that I saw you, it was rough. Really rough. We have so much to catch up on, you and I."

"We sure do, we sure do. I cannot tell you how great it is

to be here. Let me tell you that I am on cloud nine. I missed you and my family more than I could ever say, and to come back to this, wow, it is something special . . . it really is. Thank you from the bottom of my heart. We need to talk and we will later. It has been quite a road, Paul, but we will catch up and it will be good. I think we will talk for hours."

"I am sure we will, Harry, I am quite sure we will."

He put his head back, pushed his hair off his forehead, and I spotted a slight quiver in his face, as his eyes rolled back in his head for a second.

I knew what was going on in his head.

I put my arm around him and pulled him over to me.

"You will never forget my friend, but you are here now and all these people here care, love and support you, never forget. Never, ever. However, I know that Sky wants you to move on now."

"Good advice as usual, twenty-seven, I will hold it together, I am good."

He breathed in deeply and looked at me. He lowered his voice and looked to see if anyone was watching or listening.

"Hey, I spotted your hand signal and our old face twitched to play it cool. I still remember all of our old hand signals. Are you for real, your brother-in-law's name is really Tinky? Binky and Tinky? To top it all off, the guy talks like some old Hollywood actor in one of those old gangster flicks."

"He is for real, but he is a great guy, we will hang out with him, I am telling you the five of us together will be great, he is our kind of guy."

Harry screwed his face up in his now famous corkscrew fashion and said, "He is awful red, Paul, everything about him is red. Beard, hair, skin, man alive, he sure is one red dude."

"I know, but take my word for it. You are going to love the guy. Hey, by the way, I smudged the house yesterday."

"Good idea there, buddy, we need all the help we can get. Hey, I noticed some kind of diploma thingy on the wall over there with your name on it. What have you been up to?"

"Well, like you said, we can catch up later, but really quick. After I retired from hockey, I decided even before Binky came back here, to go to college. It is a long story and I promise to give you the details, but the long and short of it is something that may be a little hard to believe. Hold on tight there, number thirty-five, but I am studying to enter the ministry."

Harry's eyes grew wide and his mouth dropped. He looked at me and smiled. He put his hand on my shoulder and he pushed me gently backwards. Even a gentle push from Harry contained significant strength. He still was a big, strong man!

"Sky told me you would be a minister someday after hockey. She said you had a leader's heart, and that God guided you where he needed you. Sky knew things, Paul, which other people could not see. You and I know that she was so special in what she knew and could see! I knew it, man, I knew it!"

He shouted and now everyone looked at us.

"I love this! This is what I am talking about!" Harry was beside himself with excitement, he was like the Harry of old, when he was getting in the Trans Whizzer to go cruising, or he spotted some young lady in tight pants wiggling along, shaking her assets.

The women came rushing out of the kitchen to see what the shouting was about in the living room. Harry moved towards the center of the living room and started to speak aloud.

"Father Mark, Father Mark, please over here, please, father." Father Mark shuffled over with some assistance from Ronzo. The old priest stood by Harry, and Harry put his arm around him. Harry then motioned for me to stand on his other side. When I did, he also put his arm around me and the three of us stood there.

He shouted, "Here in the whole, entire world are the only two people who could stand me and my wacky and occasionally insulting ways, since I was just a little boy who did not honestly want to at one time or another, sock me right in the mouth! My two most favorite men of God!"

Father Mark looked at Harry and smiled, "God forgive me, Harry. I do not want to speak for Paul, but you may want to count me out, since I sure wanted to belt you one right in the kisser, after you tried to run me off the road that day!"

I thought about that same day and the ride on the flipper and the now famous water slide incident, so I guess in my heart, Harry was out of people left in the world who did not want to knock him out at least once.

I raised my hand slowly, "Count me out too buddy, that day on the flipper at Seashore Heights put me over the edge."

Unsolicited, Rose raised her hand, "Ditto for me, Harry, remember the water slide?"

Mr. Redmond cleared his throat and his hand went up, "Every day, from let's see, when you were about two years old, until right now."

Binky stepped in and raised her hand, "That night at the Black Bear Club when you lit up that wretched cigar and proceeded to blow it in my hair and face." Binky fluffed her hair up, dug her left foot into the floor, and said to Harry, "It took me three washings and a special shampoo to rid my hair of that awful smell!"

On and on it went, around the room, as each of Harry's loved ones, confessed their individual moment of truth, when all they wanted to do was give him a good, solid, knockout punch.

The Big Spike raised his hand, "When you shot the hockey puck clean through the windshield of my two-day-old Rhino Model 10 Super Glide."

The old man raised his hand, "When you came over to my house and helped me change the oil in the Putter Classic model 200. Do remember that one, Harry? When you forgot to screw the oil pan, plug in until after you refilled the oil. I had to yell, what the hell is this bullshit while the oil ran down the driveway." Harry frowned and shook his head up and down in sad reflection of the now famous, "oil event."

Mr. Hobnobber, ever the politician and attorney, cleared his throat and spoke up, "Well, we hardly know you, Harry, but speaking for Mrs. Hobnobber and me, I have heard enough testimony to make up my mind. Since we stole our laws from the English . . . ahem . . . sorry Mum, and we base our laws, as they do, upon precedence, and since the overwhelming majority opinion is that you needed a few good belts in the noggin' here and there, we vote with the majority."

Mrs. Hobnobber shook her head just as her daughter does, in a vigorous up and down motion, in agreement while saying, "You are a big, strong, good-looking guy, and a legendary figure, but I am afraid that my husband is indeed correct." Harry was now standing and smiling as we all started to break into laughter at his expense.

Tinky came out of the crowd and growled, "I only just met you, but I saw the look on your face when I spoke my name, so you can count me in."

My mother was the last person left. Harry looked at my kind, loving mother and smiled.

"Now Mum, please, kind, loving, Mum, surely you never wanted. . .." His voice trailed off because he saw my mother was shaking her head back and forth.

"You do remember when you kicked the football into my clothes line of fresh, washed white linens and then you laughed, as the entire line crashed down into the dirt and mud."

"Oh yeah, I still regret that one, sorry Mum."

We then eased up on poor Harry, gathered around him, shook him and we all laughed and hollered at the top of our lungs.

He raised his hands above his head, "I am still a legend! I love this! Now, this is what I am talking about!"

There was no doubt; Harry M. Redmond Jr. was back.

As good old Howard Pailet would say, "It was another magical moment."

I walked into the kitchen to see if I could help with the food, stopped by my mother, gave her a quick hug and said to her, "Rwy'n Dy Garu Di."

She smiled at me and answered, "Innau."

As I continued into the kitchen, Mr. Hobnobber followed me.

"Say Paul, this is all heartwarming and such, and I regretfully must thank you for the invitation to such a wonderful time."

"You're welcome, sir, it sure has been great."

"I can see that as usual—you have left my poor daughter to slave away in the kitchen while you lounge around, but I could not help but overhear you speaking to your dear mother in some kind of gibberish. I wondered what that was all about, Paul. I followed you in here to see if I could obtain an explanation about it."

I laughed at his curiosity.

"That was Welsh, sir, I speak a little Welsh. My mum's father, my grandfather, spent quite a bit of time in Wales working in the lace and silk mills over there before he came to Paterson after the war. My mother and my aunt picked up a good bit of the language through him. He could speak it rather fluently. When I was a little boy, I would hang around him when he played cards and drank beer on Saturday nights with his brother-in-law, who was of Welsh descent. He was over here in America for a while, working with my grandfather in the mills. I picked up a working knowledge of the language then and I study it now, so I am pretty good at speaking some Welsh."

"Hmm, I see, what did you say to Mum?"

"That I loved her and Mum agreed."

Mr. Hobnobber whistled and stared at me.

"Nice to appreciate your mother, even as self-centered as you are, I am impressed. Sometimes, it really pains me to learn of and to realize some of your talents."

I laughed and gave him a pat on the back. "Be careful, sir, I may say some nasty things about you in front of you that you will not understand." I left him with something to think about. I chuckled, as I knew that he would stay up all night researching the language. It came time to eat, and we broke out some beer, wine, soda and a little Scotch here and there for Mr. Hobnobber. We all gathered around the table as Binky, Rose, and the other ladies brought out the food and we prepared to eat.

"Father Mark, could I ask you to say a prayer for all of this wonderful food, and for all of us gathered here together once more?" The old priest shuffled over to the table as the Big Spike helped him over.

He stood next to me and put his arm around me.

"You know for many, many years, I have been a priest to the Redmond family, and I have been lucky to not only be a family priest but also to have grown to know all of these wonderful friends of the Redmond family. I count you all amongst my closest friends, and you have been kind enough to let me be a part of your lives for so many years as a friend, as well as a priest. I love all of you and pray for every one of you every night. I know that I have been very blessed to know all of you, and in a very sincere manner, I must tell you all that I consider you to be my family. I have blessed Christmas feasts, time bomb bottles hidden in cupboards of Ronzo's, cookout meals, Thanksgiving turkeys, Mum's plum puddings and many other meals over the years, but I must say that this one is very special.

Harry's return to the family and the fold is indeed a wish and prayer that I have dreamt of coming true, as all of you have also dreamt for many years. This one is special, and I know that there is joy in Heaven as well as here in this house at this event. With that in mind, I must tell you though, that the time has come for me to share in my duties and allow Paul here to bless the food this time around, and say a word or two. After all, I am retired now, this is his house, and he is just starting out. But first, I have to tell you a story of the first time that I allowed Paul to perform these duties."

Father Mark turned towards me, moved his arm down, and put his hand upon my shoulder, while he told me, "Forgive me Paul, but I have to tell of the beginnings of your career in the service of our Lord."

I did not really remember the incident of what Father Mark was speaking of now. Harry looked at me and shrugged his shoulders.

"Paul was over, as usual, at some Redmond family gathering. You and Harry were about ten years old at the most, and it came time to serve the food just as it is now. Harry's mom, God rest her soul, came over, and asked me to say grace. Paul tugged at my pants and asked me, Father Mark, could I say it this time? I looked down and saw this little, long-haired kid, and said, sure go-ahead, son. Paul stood up proud and tall with Harry right next to him and spoke loud and clear, rub a dub, dub, thank you, God for the grub!"

Oh, boy, now I remembered, as did Linda, Patty, Harry, and Mr. Redmond. After a good laugh and of course, my mother, Mrs. Hobnobber, Rose, and Binky saying how cute I must have been, I was ready to reconsider my new career choice.

"I doubt he has any new material yet, Father Mark!" My father-in-law had jumped in and offered his usual support.

"Thank you, Father Mark, but I think I can do a little

better this time. Let's join hands and pray."

I began, "Rub, a dub." I stopped to see if anyone was moving, but everyone kept their heads down with some snickers . . . they had already guessed what was coming. I restarted, "Lord bless this food to us and us to thy service and thank you for bringing Harry back home safe to us after his long journey. Thank you, Lord, for these wonderful people who are gathered around this table, all of these people whom we love and hold dear to us every day. We also remember all the special saints from our families that have passed from this world and are living with you in your kingdom. No space can ever separate us all, no void is too great that we cannot overcome, no sadness, or evil can harm us, for we are always together forever in your service and in your hands. In Jesus' name, we pray. Thanks, be to God, Amen."

Father Mark looked at me and smiled, as he told me, "A little better Paul, just a little better than the first shot at it."

Binky had outdone herself with the food. She was an incredible cook and everyone let her know it. She had made pasta dishes, salads, chicken and beef dishes, meatballs, some sandwiches and desserts. We cut the cake and Tinky and Linda worked out a little welcome home song for Harry as the big guy cut the cake up into slices for all of us.

After serving the cake, Binky raised her hands and clapped them together hard to get everyone's attention.

Binky spoke loudly as all of our guests gathered around the table, "In lieu of a special drink toast for Harry's return, Paul, and I have decided to skip over that formality. Instead, we have a special treat for the one and only Harry M. Redmond Junior. I do need to warn everyone that you would most likely not want to partake in this special treat, but instead just yell out, here, here, when Harry takes his first bite."

Binky turned towards me and signaled for me to bring

the treat out from the kitchen. I carried out a small, silver platter covered with a towel and set it upon the table. Harry circled in and stared at it. Binky reached down and pulled the towel off the platter, revealing the famous Harry "special biscuits!"

"Here you go, Harry, straight from the dog food aisle, your special biscuits!" Binky proclaimed, as she waved at the display of biscuits stacked up on the table.

Harry dove into the treats while yelling out, "Binky, I love you! My special biscuits!"

We all yelled, "Here! Here!" Harry popped one in his mouth and crunched them, while he smiled as if he was a Halloween pumpkin.

It was a wild scene from the one and only Harry!

After a lot of food, (special biscuits) drink, laughs, and fun, we finished eating dinner. We all helped clean up and put the kitchen back in order.

It finally came to the time that I think we all were secretly waiting for. Until now, not one person wanted to bring up the subject and spoil the welcome home celebration. The question that was on everyone's mind was simple and logical. What exactly happened to Harry during his long sojourn away from all of us, for all of these years?

Harry must have sensed this. He knew that he owed all of us an explanation for the lost time, because when Binky announced that it was time for us to have some coffee and tea, Harry raised his hand and motioned for us to gather around. I knew that we were all about to gather around to hear Harry's story of where he had been for the last five years. I was curious to learn all the details, and to hear of what his incredible journey had been like. I also wondered what had finally brought him back home, where he really belonged.

"I certainly owe everyone an explanation as to where I have been and what I have done, and I would like to share it with you. Please, if we can grab tea and coffee or ya might want sumthin' stronger and gather around, I feel I owe everyone that I love, the story of my journey."

I brought a chair from the dining room table and carried it into the living room for Harry to sit on. We all carried our drinks into the room and gathered around Harry in the living room as he began his tale. Binky sat on the floor right at my feet and the other couples paired off with their spouses. Father Mark sat in a chair next to Harry on his one side, with Mr. Redmond on the other. Tinky and Rose sat on the floor in front of the both of them. As I glanced around the room, and studied the faces of my family and dear friends, I could see the anticipation as well as the pain.

This was going to bring up some very difficult memories for all of us, but it was a time that was long overdue.

I knew that this was going to be one of those tear-jerking moments as Harry cleared his throat and he began his tale.

"I imagine this is going to be a long story. I do feel I need to tell it to everyone, not only do I owe you an explanation but also I need to bring some closure to my own story."

Harry looked down and breathed deeply, as though he was gathering strength for the discussion.

"Now that I am home, I need to begin a new journey, a new life, and start all over once more. After I left Paul, I just drove and drove. I had told him that I was heading for a distant relative in Michigan, but that was not exactly true. Clearly, I didn't really have an actual destination. It was just an all-out effort to flee everything and everyone. While we certainly do have some relatives, up that way, I didn't really intend upon finding them. I just needed to run away as fast and as hard as I could. No one could console me, not even Paul. The pain was too intense for me to stay. I learned how powerful a pain that grief really is."

Harry stopped speaking for a brief moment as he gathered himself; this was going to be a lot harder for him to get through than he had originally thought.

"Grief and shock, as I experienced, are something that physically tears you apart, and it then eats away at you and rips at your very inner being. I look back now and see just how terrible it really was, and I wonder about many things. I wonder why people search all their lives to own materialistic things, you know, as I did. I always wanted fast sports cars, the best hats, ice skates, clothes, boots, tools, and all kinds of other stuff. I always had to have the best of everything all the time. When something like this happens to you, then you realize all that junk means nothing, all that really matters is in your heart. I think that character in that famous movie, you know, that Tin Guy, who did not have a heart, he was actually very lucky. I think if they made a follow up movie to it, then they all went back and talked with him now, the Tin Guy may give it back. Once your heart is broken as mine was, then nothing is ever the same. Yup, I bet that Tin Guy would give his heart back, if he ever had it broken as I did."

Harry shook his head and dwelled upon the thought for a time.

"No doubt, he would have turned it in and given anything to be empty and hollow inside, if he had lost someone he loved." Harry stopped speaking for a few seconds and he was working very hard to compose himself. We all looked around at one another in the room. In the strange Harry sort of way, his analogy was very profound, and he was indeed correct. I know that both Binky and I would agree after our time apart from one another, that was for sure.

After a brief interlude, Harry spoke once more, "Cocoa and I only stopped driving to go to the restroom. We did not eat for days. He was such a smart dog, he knew what had happened, and it tore him up. Unbelievably, I could tell that his love for Sky was as deep as mine was. I knew he missed Paul and all of you too, but he knew that his duty was with me, he was so special. I do not know if I would have survived if not for Cocoa, we often curled up in the back of the bus together, my body shaking and trembling, with him right next to me, he was my only comfort."

The tears started to flow amongst the group, as Harry grew more intense. Binky held my hand tighter, and I watched as Rose started to break up a little. Tinky reached over, put his arm around her, and he grabbed her hand.

"After days of driving, I landed in a small town in Ohio and found a bank. I set up an account that I could access from anywhere and I moved all my money royalties from the song and my savings to this bank."

Harry smiled a little and looked at his sister and Ronzo, breaking the tension just a little.

"As Linda and Ronzo can also testify, the song did so well for so long, it kept us all going for a while. Between that money and the savings, I did not have to work or worry about cash flow. I stayed there for a while in a rented room, but it was a dead-end town that just depressed us even more, so we saddled back up and rode into Michigan. Cocoa and I just explored and checked things out along the way. It was escapism, and we felt better about ourselves as long as we were in a new place and we were moving. I am sure all of us have felt the need and desire to just run away and hide, so you can relate to what I had to do. We rode and rode, until I found this pretty little town up near Canada, called Harbor Springs. It was on the big lake, it was peaceful, and it was perfect. Cocoa loved it, so I rented a one-room cabin, right on the lake, from some old guy who had an ad in a local coffee shop. At first, he thought I was some New Jersey hippie guy, whom he did not trust."

Harry looked at me and smiled.

"I now know what twenty-seven, has faced all of his life."

I nodded my head. I did indeed know that feeling of a

predisposition all too well.

"I swung a deal and gave him one year's rent in advance and he was all of a sudden, my best buddy."

Harry chuckled, keeping his wonderful sense of humor through this very difficult speech.

"Cold, hard, cash has a way of making people ignore certain appearances! We stayed there, every day by the lake, even in the cold, and when the spring came, we walked and fished, we cried, and we both mourned. I set up the little Christmas tree in a corner of the cabin, along with a little box that had Sky's picture in it and her favorite peace necklace. I had no telephone, no television, no music, and no radio. We had nothing, and I did not want anything. Most of the time, we just sat and stared, or we slept. The depression came after the grief, and some days, I didn't even want to go on. The only thing I bought was some pots and pans, a little chair and a sleeping cot, a coffee maker, a fishing pole, and a little refrigerator. I rented a post office box in town and sent out those postcards to everyone, but I just could not bring myself to speak or talk to anyone. Please forgive me for that, but the pain was very intense, and it made me feel that any contact with anyone would have caused me to go over the edge. I had to be alone. It just had to be. I loved Sky so much. I just could not even bring myself to imagine how God had taken her from all of us. It was a pain and an anger that I could not describe. All our dreams, all of our hope, gone in such a short amount of time." Harry began to move uneasily in his chair and his eyes welled up with tears.

He sighed deeply and then continued, "After the first year, the pain grew less intense and I often debated to contact everyone, but I was still not ready. The anniversary of the day Sky died was rough, but we made it. I was down in the center of the town one day when I saw an advertisement in the local paper for a welder in a little shop a town or so away. I went over and spoke with the owner, who gave me a welding test and hired me on the spot. It was a small shop of about ten guys or so, and it was perfect. It was just what I needed, not so much for the money, but it kept me busy and occupied. Slowly, I came back to life, and I would go to the library on Saturdays and try to get news of where Paul was in the hockey world and what was going on back here in New Jersey. I was thrilled when I heard he made it to the next level, and I even saw him listed in the Bear's farm system as the goalie heir apparent in the big time."

Harry had brought up a painful memory for me, but I did not allow my mind to dwell upon it, hockey was in a past life for me now, and I needed to focus on the future.

"It was fantastic to hear of his success, and I would brag to all the guys in the shop about how Paul was my best buddy in the world, as well as the best goalie of all time. This was hockey country way up near Canada, so they treated me as if I was some type of celebrity for knowing, Paul. When I heard about the knee injury and your retirement—it was crushing. It was a huge shock. I kept up to date through telephone books and newspapers with everything I could. I saw when Dad and Father Mark retired, the house at 20 John Street sold, and when my sisters moved. One day, I found a listing for Mr. and Mrs. Paul John Henson. I knew in my heart that Paul had finally found, Binky. Sky had predicted it a long time ago, and we all knew how Sky knew of things that the rest of us did not know or understand."

Binky looked at me and smiled as she squeezed my hand tightly.

"Please forgive me for all that I missed, but it really was for the best. Even though I regret not being here for everyone, I needed the time. I was not the same person then, so it was best that everyone did not see or know me. I was angry, hurt, and mean. At the welding shop, I had a guy who we all worked with who was a real jerk, he was always on my nerves, he had a bad attitude, and he complained about everything. One day, he really got on my nerves. On my lunch break, I tinkered around with some old metal, some parts and pieces, and I made this little box thing with a needle on it. I wrote some markings on it like a temperature gauge. I put it on the wall in the back of me in my welding booth and put this guy's name on it on a little piece of paper."

I sat forward quickly in my seat as I was amazed at what I heard. I glanced over at Mr. Hobnobber, whose mouth was open and he was staring ahead in shock!

Harry continued with what was going to turn out to be just another, simply amazing Redmond phenomenon in a long history of weirdness.

"I called it my Annoy-O-Meter, and I turned the needle all the way up to the top of the markings, to indicate how this guy was on all of our nerves."

I still could not believe my ears, and I looked again at my father-in-law, whose eyes had widened like saucers.

Harry continued, "Well, it got so many laughs and attention that the owner of the shop told me that I should patent it and then manufacture them. So, that is what I did, I took some of my money, found a lawyer, and I was eventually awarded a patent. The owner of the shop and I found a little tool, die and casting shop who produced them and the rest is history. I have sold more of them than we are able to produce, and the money and orders just roll in. It is kinda unreal! I actually have made a ton of money from this little gadget!"

Well, once more, nothing really changes in the world of Harry and Paul. It is the eternal cloud of weirdness and it floats above my head, about ten to fifteen feet above me and follows me wherever I go.

Why should I be surprised?

After all, this is the same guy who wrote a hit song along with his sister that stayed on the charts for five weeks and almost won the song of the year award.

Mr. Hobnobber could no longer hold back, "I cannot believe it, Harry! It is amazing that you invented it, I have one, and it is the most fantastic stress reliever that I have ever had! You are a genius! I keep Paul on it twenty-four hours a day, except for a brief interlude the other day, when Senator Riggs beat him out."

"Father!" Binky yelled out.

Harry pointed at Mr. Hobnobber and laughed, "I love this! That is what I am talking about! Thank you, sir, and I understand about Paul. All sons-in-laws deserve to be on a father-in-law's Annoy-O-Meter! After all, he stole your little girl!"

Mr. Hobnobber clapped his hands in agreement and then pointed his finger back towards Harry, "I like the way you think there, Redmond!"

After a few laughs at my expense and amazed comments at Harry and his peculiar invention, he continued.

Harry once more grew serious, and in fact, his tone became somber, "One day, about a month or so ago, I came home from work and I found Cocoa really sick and lying on the kitchen floor. I was going to get him in the Wagon Bus and take him into town to a vet, but when I picked him up, he just looked at me with his eyes and then he went limp, took one last breath, shuddered, and he was gone. I think he knew, and he waited to die until I made it home." Harry now shook a little as he recalled the incident, and the chuckles about his quirky invention faded from us all.

Cocoa was indeed very special to all of us, especially to me. Many memories of the "world's smartest dog" and all that the three of us had shared ran through my mind. It was, however, painful for all of us in the room to hear of his passing. He was a special dog.

"I took him down near the lake where he loved to sit and watch the water all the time. He had been so old now that he did not get around so well, and he could no longer see very well, so sitting there on the side of the lake was his favorite pastime. I picked a wonderful spot under a tree and I buried him with Piggy, which was, as all of you know, his favorite toy. I knew that Sky was waiting for him on the other side. I knew that they were finally reunited and there was joy in Heaven. He was not only the world's smartest dog, but he was also the best. I cried and cried, and it was more pain, more sorrow, and tears. I could not stand it anymore."

There were not many dry eyes now in our little group as the sobs and tears were now really flowing. Harry was also close to losing it now, but he hung in there and continued, "But as my life has gone on, I realized that I really did have so much to be thankful for, all of you, my family and friends, and all that I have. I would meet people who were lonely and had no one who cared, or who needed someone to talk to about their pain. I realized that while I had suffered, I still had so much to be thankful for in my life. I just needed to stop and realize it. I had to look past the pain to rediscover it. For that, like a lot of things, I have to thank, Paul."

Binky looked at me and smiled.

Harry looked straight at me.

"I only hope and pray that someday, somehow, I can only do just a small amount of good for you to pay you back for all you have done for me and all of us. Of all the people, I have ever known, Paul can weave a tapestry of words that can hold you in place, heal your soul, and hit the nail always on the head. He teaches through his words. God has picked the right person to be a pastor. I can assure you all of that. Of all the things that Paul has taught me, one of the most important was to love and appreciate music."

Harry's eyes wandered to the ceiling as though he was searching for a memory in his mind. He in fact was, as he suddenly said, "Often times, music is the thread that binds our memories, the melodies can invoke past times that are both good and bad, the lyrics can parallel times in our own lives, and it can define your feelings, relax your mind and inspire your soul." He chuckled a little, almost as if he was surprised that he did indeed remember that sentence.

"Do you remember telling me that, Paul? Do you recall being on top of High Mountain while we shared a bottle of bourbon, blaring out a Crystal Zirconium cassette tape? It was that awful night when the Trans Whizzer was in the accident and wrecked. For some reason, those words stuck in my mind forever. Sometimes, I cannot remember my own telephone number but I can never forget those words, it is very strange."

It was a long time ago, but I did remember saying that. I nodded my head in acknowledgement.

"I had acquired a few more things in the cabin as time went on. I now had a telephone, although I seldom, if ever, called anyone. I did purchase a record player, and I had a little collection of music going. The day after Cocoa had passed away, the morning broke clear, cold, and fantastic. I had prayed all night as I sobbed for the good Lord to help me and clear my mind of all this sadness and pain. It was really more than I could take. I opened the window shade early in the morning when I first awoke after crying and being restless all night. I looked out to see this unreal, picture postcard, sunrise over the lake. The sky was perfect, just a few little wisps here and there of puffy white clouds. For some reason, I remembered what Paul had said that night. His words were clear in my head, just like he was right next to me."

Harry was now shaking his head as the memory of that morning had brought on a unique and strange experience. I could see that the incident had been very real in his mind, but I knew that it was very simple; an answer to his prayers had finally come and the healing process had now begun.

"I could hear Paul's voice, I could see him speaking, leaning up next to his old jeep there on the top of the mountain. It was a freezing cold night that night and as usual, all that Paul wore was a light vest, his No Way tee shirt and his old sneakers. He was there, leaning on the jeep, his long hair around him in the nighttime, and it was absolutely real! It was quite startling, as it seemed so genuine, so strange that Paul was right there with me! I could have reached out and touched him . . . it was so real. When I recovered, it was as if a small voice inside of me was guiding me."

Father Mark reached over and placed his hand on Harry's shoulder. He spoke in a low voice, as he struggled to fight off his own emotions, "It was not a small voice, Harry, but it was the voice of God as he did answer your prayers. You had suffered enough, and God does not give us more pain than we can handle. His healing blessings are never far away, even in times of such sorrow."

Harry smiled at Father Mark and grasped his hand, while he agreed, "I think you are right on, Father Mark. It was as if I had suddenly woken up from a dream that had gone on for years. My dulled senses came back to life. I knew what I had to do. I had to hear a special song. I just had to hear it! I ran away from the window, and grabbed my Electronic Transistor Orchestra records and thumbed through them, until I found the recording, *The Big World Record.* I put it on the player and dropped the needle on the song, Mr. Clear Sky. I am not sure if any of you has ever heard the song, but it starts with a weather report and the announcement that the weatherman makes. The weatherman predicts in a loud, clear voice on the records that today's weather forecast is for clear, blue skies. As the song played, I stood in front of the window watching the sun come up over the big lake. It is such a happy and upbeat song that from there, it stirred my spirit and it made me finally realize that it was going to be all right. Sky and Cocoa had each other, and I needed to move on, get back to the people I love, and go on with my life."

Harry could no longer hold back the tears, he lost his voice, and the tears rolled down both of his cheeks.

"The sky was blue in front of me from horizon to horizon, because she was there opening up Heaven to the Earth, and it was all going to be better from here on in. I knew I would still have pain, sorrow and miss them both, but I knew it was going to be different."

Harry pointed at his own face.

"These are tears of joy, folks. They are no longer tears of sorrow."

Harry wiped his cheeks and his mouth with his hand until Father Mark handed him a tissue.

"For I now know that the world goes on, no matter who we lose, or what we gain, or what pitfalls of life fall in our path. Life goes on, and it is up to us to follow it. Loved ones such as Sky and Cocoa move on as part of the great plan and mystery of life, but there are always signs that they never leave us. Heaven opens up clear skies for us all, we just need to pay attention and follow the signs. I was renewed, right then and there, I was renewed."

Father Mark looked at me through teary eyes and winked. I smiled at him, because we both knew that God had taught Harry the same thing that he and I knew on that night so very long ago. Binky was hugging me now around the neck and sobbing her eyes out, along with the rest of the room. Mr. Redmond stood up and hugged his son; he could no longer hold back the emotions. I held Binky as tightly as I could; it was up to me to absorb some of her pain.

Choking on his words, Harry sat back down after embracing his father and he went on, "I went straight to my writing table, found Paul and Binky's address and filled out the postcard, right then and there. I prayed that he and Binky still cared enough to call me, and the rest as they say is . . . history."

Harry finished, sighed deeply, and he was silent for a few moments. He then stood back up from his chair as he told us, "I want to say, thank you to you all, for all you have done for me, for sticking with me, for loving me, and I promise that I am here to stay. I will make it up to you all for the worry that I caused as well as the pain and the suffering. I love all of you with all of my heart."

A remarkable story, from the pain, to the incredible invention of his little money-making gizmo, to the utter joy and sorrow of the journey of one man from despair to a renewal. Family and friends rushed in to hug the big man, who truly was a legend. I can say that at that point in my life, I was thankful to God for just letting me call Harry M. Redmond Junior, my best friend.

It had been quite a day, and it had such a range of emotions that it exhausted you. After Harry finished his story, we all surrounded him to assure him that he was in a safe place, with lots of support, and it was all going to be all right.

Harry shook my father-in-law's hand and smiled at him. "Mr. Hobnobber, I need your help, sir, as I need a larger place to manufacture my products."

Harry had grabbed Mr. Hobnobber's ear and his full attention now. Harry was his hero now anyway, for his little invention that he loved to use so much to proclaim his love of me to the world.

"I want to acquire a little factory here, in and around Paterson, bring some jobs back home to where my roots are and build these gizmos by the millions!"

Mr. Hobnobber was now in his glory as he spouted, "Harry, my boy, you are my kind of guy, once you get settled and get away from the influence of my constantly being educated, thickheaded, hippie, weirdo son-in-law, then please make an appointment with my office. You know that boy never has a job, Harry, unlike you and your obvious high ambitions!"

Harry came to my defense, in a vain effort to defend my honor, "Sounds good, Mr. Hobnobber, but you know Paul did play professional hockey for many years."

"That is not a job! That is just a bunch of street hooligans, bashing each other over the head with sticks, while hiding under the disguise of a sport! But forget twenty-seven and his endless flaws, I happen to serve on an urban renewal business development committee in the senate and we can help you with location, business plans, employment recruiting, and the whole ball of wax."

Mrs. Hobnobber moved into the discussion, "Dear Harry, once you get settled, please come over with Binky and Paul to our home, we would love to have a dinner party or an afternoon of tennis on our courts to get to know you better. Do you play tennis?"

"I never did, but Paul and I played a lot of sports in our time, so I would be willing to give it a try. Besides, please forgive me in front of your husband, but old Harry calls it as he sees it. I bet you look really good in a tennis outfit there, Mrs. Hobnobber!"

Mrs. Hobnobber grabbed Harry. She planted a big lip lock Hobnobber kiss on old Harry, as Mr. Hobnobber laughed and yelled out, "Now that's what I am talking about, Harry! I love this!"

Mr. Hobnobber had adopted one of Harry's most famous war cries! Harry was a big hit with my in-laws and as usual, he had not lost his famous skills at saying all the correct things to the ladies, even the married ones!

I was helping Binky in the kitchen, and I noticed Rose and Harry gather over in the corner of our dining room. They pulled two chairs up close to each other and began to speak quietly with one another. Binky also noticed, and we smiled at one another. In the other rooms, the party was still going on as everyone now was in a great big party mood. We had some music going now, some more drinks, and the discussion and atmosphere remained lively. Harry was home again, and the reunion was complete. It was time to move on and to begin anew.

Ronzo came into the kitchen along with Tinky and he asked, "Hey twenty-seven, do you have a book of matches?"

"Sure, Ronzo, here." I tossed him a book from the kitchen drawer.

"Thanks! Mr. Hobnobber has some fancy cigars and we are going to each try them out on the front porch."

As soon as the word, "cigar" had been muttered, Binky turned, looked, and put her hands on her hips. "Outside, outside, outside, dear Ronzo and my dear brother!"

Ronzo laughed, "So I guess a few kisses with you later when Paul is not around will be also out of the question!" Ronzo was now kidding with Binky and he smiled, grabbed some Dingleberry beers from the fridge, and ran with Tinky out to the front of the house.

Binky shouted to them, "If I smell one little puff from one of those wretched things in my house, you both will be in big trouble! Make sure both outside doors are closed!"

I did not say a word, but I smiled at my wife's disdain for cigars, even though when her father smoked them, it was fine! I reminded myself to look in our kitchen cupboards later, to see if Ronzo may have planted one of his famous time bombs in there when no one was watching!

Binky and I continued to clean up and organize the kitchen. I grabbed a load of trash, pulled out the bag, and took it out the back door. As I walked out the door and over to the side where we kept our trash cans, I heard some shouting from around the front near our porch. I smiled as I realized it was where Ronzo, Tinky, and Mr. Hobnobber were enjoying a few cigars and some drinks outside, and keeping well out of Binky's radar range.

I tossed the trash into the barrel, and I was going to walk back into the house when I realized that the shouting in front was something different.

"You are not welcome here!" I clearly heard Ronzo's voice shout out.

My hockey instincts took over. Years of playing had sharpened me as to when trouble was brewing on the ice and a fight was going to break out to change the tone of the game. Instantly, I ran to the front of the house. As I rounded the corner of the house, I saw Rose's husband, Daniel, push his way past Ronzo and make a break up our front stairs. Ronzo reached for him, but he was too fast for the big man's reach. Mr. Hobnobber stood in front of him and he knocked him over and violently pushed him out of the way.

Tinky then moved over to defend his father, as I heard Daniel scream, "Get the hell out of my damn way, you little punk!"

Tinky grabbed him around the waist and he held on for the ride, as Tinky and his small, little body was doing his best to prevent him from making it to the front door. Daniel turned around, raised his closed fist and arm high in the air over Tinky's face. Just as he was going to let his arm and fists fly and crush poor Tinky, I made it there, jumped the porch railing, and latched onto Daniel's arm in mid-punch.

My grip was strong, and I clamped down on him with all of my strength to stop the punch. Daniel was shocked to see me arrive and I am sure it hurt his arm and wrist. I clamped down with all my strength and he moved back with the pain.

"I don't think so, Daniel."

His eyes grew wide, "Well, if it is not the former, rugged, tough, hippie goalie with the freaky wife. She is so weird, but with a body like she has, I am sure there are a few things she is good at." We locked up with one another.

We were struggling as he laughed out loudly at me, "You now have found God, and are a wimpy little follower of the Lord. If you know what is good for you, you will let go of me, I am going in there to pull my stupid, witch of a wife out by her hair and drag her home so I can beat her ass silly! Anyone who is in my way will know it as I will take them out just like I did these clowns here!"

Daniel was a big man, he was a few inches shorter than I was, but he outweighed me by quite a bit. We wrestled and struggled for a bit until I was able to overpower him with my arm's strength and gain control of his direction.

I could smell the booze on his breath. He was bombed out of his mind, and I knew from Rose's testimony that he was a nasty drunk.

Upon hearing his cruel words, I felt that fire inside of me, that old fire that never left me. It was erupting. It was as if I was back in the net again and I was in the flow. O'Malley was taunting me, along with the big center from the team in Maine from so long ago. The puck was heading straight at my head and I was about to grab it right out of the air. The flame grew high, it burned bright and strong, and I was in the flow.

I increased the grip on his arm and I could feel his pain as I kept my eyes on his other free hand to see if he would swing at me with it. I turned him and forced him to buckle and stumble in my grip.

"One more step, Daniel, one more step," I dared the drunken bum and felt as if I was giving him a fair enough warning. He took me up on my challenge, moved towards the porch front door and cracked open the handle with his free hand.

It was over for him. I was not going to toy with him any longer! I instantly grabbed him by the throat and picked him up in the air.

"Ronnie, close the door, so no one sees us!"

Ronnie jumped around us and pulled the door closed.

"Now, you drunken idiot, I will give you a very short Bible lesson. Peter cut the ear off the Roman soldier, and Jesus healed it. Being a Christian does not make you a wimp. Sorry for you, but you misjudged us. If you take one step other than straight down those stairs, then you will be praying that Jesus and all the major prophets show up to save your sorry ass."

I squeezed him even harder until I could see him really suffering badly, so I eased back a bit.

"This is my house and you hurt my family, insulted my wife, and threatened my friends. Now, you will face the wrath of this long-haired hippie, follower of the Lord. I hate to inform you that I do not need legions of angels to back me up. I am going to take care of you all by myself. I will slice you and dice you into little pieces right here on this porch, you drunken bum. No one on this Earth hurts my family and friends and gets away with it."

I knew he was in deep trouble now as he was really struggling with the pain. I still had him with one hand on his throat, but I also had him on his arm with my other hand. I could feel my anger swelling, but I was aware of my strength and under control.

"Apologize to these men, and apologize for what you said about my wife, or I swear, you will wish that you were never born. There will not be enough doctors in the world or prayers to save you, so make your choice really quick, tough guy."

"I am sorry, I have been drinking, I am very sorry. I am drunk, I am out of my mind," he struggled to speak as I eased up my grip.

I let him go. He dropped to the ground, rubbed his throat where I had held him, and he looked at me.

"Now go and think really long and hard about where you are in your life. Even in a drunken stupor, you need to be accountable that you would do such a thing or say such evil things. I will pray for you, I do not know the demons that you have right now, but you need to run as far away from them as you can, Daniel."

I pointed at him and pushed all of my hair from out of the front of my face.

I was a big, strong man, and I was now red faced and my muscles pumped up. I imagined that I was now a little frightening in my appearance. I am sure no one here, even Ronzo, who had known me forever, had seen this wild side of me.

"I swear if you hurt Rose, or come around here ever again, then it will really be ugly." He bounded down the steps, staggered in his drunkenness and turned back towards us.

Safely out of range, he once more became a little braver, "So now, what will stop me from calling the police and filing an assault report on you?" Now I was pumped up once again, and any sympathy that I had for him quickly disappeared. I walked down a few steps towards him and watched as he backed up.

"Do it, Daniel! Do it, you wife beating, drunken, coward! In fact, I will go inside and call them myself."

I was furious now, and Tinky put his hand on my shoulder to calm me. I think he was afraid now that my shouting would alert the folks inside the house as to what was going on outside on the front porch.

"Let me ask you, what will you say? That you are drunk out of your mind, you assaulted three men, and you threatened us all. Top it all off, with the fact that you trespassed on private property to try to beat your own wife, silly. Sure, do it, call! I will sit right here on the front stoop and steps and wait for them."

I sat on the steps, folded my hands calmly on my lap, and waited for his answer.

Daniel pondered it for a moment, felt his throat again where I had grabbed him, then turned and staggered down the street and disappeared into the night.

Tinky and I picked up the stunned Mr. Hobnobber, who had stayed on the porch floor after Daniel knocked him over.

"Are you all right, sir?"

"Dad! Are you okay?" Tinky pulled him by his arm as he pulled his father to his feet.

Ronzo was still watching and guarding the front door to make sure that no one inside heard, or was aware of the ruckus that had occurred.

Mr. Hobnobber rubbed at his knees and asked, "Who on Earth was that madman?"

"It was, Daniel. He is Rose's estranged husband, and he was very drunk. It is over. Are you sure you are, okay?"

"I was just about to let him have it, Paul, when you showed up," Tinky said as he smiled at me.

Ronzo came over and put his hand on my back, "Thank you, Paulie. I was a little too slow to stop him. I tried, but he slipped by me. If I had caught him, it would have been Vietnam or the old neighborhood all over again."

I smiled at Ronzo and gave him a pat back as we all turned towards Mr. Hobnobber. I brushed off Mr. Hobnobber's pants and Ronzo picked up his cigar.

"Thank you, Ronzo. I would hate to waste a fine cigar because of some drunken, wild, barbarian. I must confess that I never saw him coming. He pushed past Ronzo in a flash, and all of a sudden, I was on the ground. It was very disturbing."

Mr. Hobnobber turned towards me and asked, "Where the devil did you come from?"

"Around the corner, sir, I heard some shouting as I was putting out the trash."

Mr. Hobnobber shook his head gently from side to side.

"I must admit, that you do always seem to show up at the right moment, it is very strange. I think we all must keep this incident amongst us men, it could greatly disturb the wonderful time we have had today. Our dear, little,

Rose would be an emotional catastrophe if she heard of this. Ronzo, did anyone inside notice or hear us?"

Ronzo waved his hand in the air to indicate it was all clear, and he said, "No one heard, Bill. I closed the porch door in time."

"Good, then no harm, no foul, do we all agree?"

Mr. Hobnobber was indeed correct. Rose and the other ladies would be a wreck, and if Harry or my old man got wind of it, then there would be no safe place on planet Earth for Daniel to hide. That would be a deadly combination. Dear Rose was too precious to us all.

We all agreed.

"Are you sure you are ok, sir?"

Mr. Hobnobber looked at me, but he did not answer the question.

"Thank you, Paul. Your father once told me that you are fearless and that you will defend your family and friends to the end. He was right. He was also correct, when he told me that God help the person whoever hurts or tries to hurt our dear Binky. You are indeed a guardian of us all, in body and in a very strange sort of way, in our spirits as well."

He smiled at me and patted me on the shoulder.

"Please do not try to shake my hand there, Henson, but I am sure that wild eyed, maniacal, drunken, slob knows what it is like to face one of your death grips. I bet he did see Jesus for a second or two!"

Mr. Hobnobber was now standing up straight and tall. He dusted off his shirt and stuck his cigar in his mouth.

"And one more thing, please stop calling me sir, will you, just call me, Dad. It is really annoying, all that sir' stuff. I am running out of little papers to put on my Annoy-O-Meter with your name on them. It is costing me a fortune in paper replenishment."

"I will do that, Dad."

"Good, it is a shame that you cannot enjoy a cigar after

all that testosterone you worked up there, twenty-seven. My sharp and keen-sensed, daughter, would detect it on you in a second and exile you to the basement. Moreover, it is not good for an almost man of the cloth to be seen smoking, big, old, cigars. But that is your tough luck, now, isn't it?"

"You are correct again, Dad."

"I am always correct. Right, men?"

All three of us answered, "Yes, Dad," as we walked back into the house.

It was becoming late now, and the party broke up as folks started to leave. We shared some pleasant goodbyes, and we all made plans for us to get together again really soon. Tinky stayed a while speaking with Harry about getting together with him and Linny to work on some music together; they had really hit it off. Tinky said goodnight and soon it was just the four of us left.

Harry caught Binky and me in the kitchen, "I will find a hotel close by, youse guys have your hands full with Rose, and you do not need me hanging around too."

Binky put her left foot down hard on the floor as she usually does when she needed to make a point, "Nonsense, Harry, you will stay right here with us."

Binky was not going to accept that plan, "Paul will make sure the pull-out sofa is all set. I have extra linens, and we have a bathroom downstairs, as well as up, so you will have your privacy. I would never allow such a thing after your long journey."

Harry smiled and put both of his hands up in front of him. "Ok, there, Bink-a-roo-ski, I know not to mess with you." Harry knew of Binky and her, "forceful ways."

"Is it all right if I bring in Sky's little Christmas tree and put it in the corner of the dining room? I do not want to leave it out in the Wagon Bus, if ya know what I mean there, twenty-seven."

Harry had been true to the words that he had told me

long ago in his driveway, as he loaded what was left of his life into the Wagon Bus, to begin his journey. He did indeed; carry the little tree wherever he went. They had decorated the same tree right before she passed away before Christmas in 1980.

Rose had now joined us in the doorway of the kitchen and she was leaning on the frame listening to the conversation. I felt that she did not want to intrude, and that she right now, was feeling just a little awkward at the reunion, and the four of us being together once again. Binky gave me a quick look with her eyes when Rose had appeared, and I knew how to read my wife's sharp mind. She also knew that we needed to include our dear Rose and pull her into the fold. I walked over to Rose, put my arm around her, and pulled her close to me. Rose hugged me and smiled as she appreciated the gesture.

I then turned towards Harry, "Of course Harry, we will all give you a hand."

The four of us went outside and grabbed Harry's gear and he carried the little tree and put it in the corner of the dining room, along with a little picture of Sky in a small wooden box that contained some of her peace necklaces. He handled the emotional moment well. I could sense he was growing stronger, as he plugged in the lights and the four of us stood in the darkness, watching it twinkle for what seemed as if it was hours and hours. We all reached out for one another's hands and joined them together, but we did not say a word.

Time, tears, and memories had passed, but the bond the four of us shared still remained.

We gathered in the living room, we sat there, and we talked and talked. We shared old stories of past times as well as new ones. Harry wanted to hear of how Binky and I had gotten back together as well as my adventures of playing hockey. Binky even dared to show Harry the little heart tattoo on her shoulder with the twenty-seven inside, which turned her red and amazed Harry.

Rose was quieter than usual, but she was enjoying it all, I could tell she was thrilled that the four of us had reunited again, as we had been so long ago; it was just awkward for her under her present situation. We were very careful in some of our conversations not to dwell too much on a situation or recanting of some adventure that would be painful for her, as well as for Harry, but it was inevitable that something would come up.

Surprisingly, Harry dug up an old memory.

"Hey . . . I brought something along that I thought we could all share in."

He walked over to his luggage and tried to open it up, and then he burst out laughing.

"I still always have trouble with zippers, twenty-seven. Not very much ever changes!" I got up and helped him with the troublesome barrier that was one of the few things that could defeat the great and powerful Harry in this world! I opened one of the luggage cases and then Harry dug around in it.

He returned while carrying an envelope.

"I know that Paul got one of these, so I suspect Rose and Binky did as well. I never opened mine and I think Paul did not open his either."

We all recognized the envelopes as the pictures mailed from Howard Pailet, which captured some of our magnificent Black Bear Club weekend adventure.

"I never opened mine, even after Paul and I got back together," Binky confessed.

We all looked at Rose. "I could never face the thought of it," Rose said as she shook her head. "I do have it with me, though! It was one of the things I grabbed before I left the house. I could never leave it or toss it away, so I packed it in one of my bags."

Harry looked at Binky and me.

"We both have ours," I said. Binky then stared in at

Harry with one of her famous stares, waiting for what he had on his mind.

"What do you say that we open them together? We can do it tonight! We are all here together!" Harry stated the obvious. "You do all realize that this is the first time that we are all in the same place together since that special weekend?"

Ouch! I sat back and waited for the reaction.

Binky smiled, as did Rose, so in seeing their reactions, I agreed. I went upstairs with Rose and grabbed Binky's as well as my envelope. I knew right where we kept them, and Rose pulled her envelope out of one of her bags. We came downstairs, and I handed Binky her envelope.

"Now, on the count of three, tear it open," Harry instructed us.

"One, two, three!"

The sound of paper tearing confirmed that after all these years the long wait was over! All of us pulled out the pictures and gazed at them in wonder. Rose, of course, started to cry, but Harry, Binky, and I laughed. They were fantastic pictures; you could tell a professional photographer took them. We all then commented on them, which was our favorite. Look how we were dressed; check this one out, and so on and so forth. The consensus was that the picture of the four of us together was the favorite, although Harry and I voted for the picture with the two girls kissing opposite cheeks of a red-faced Howard. I commented on how the girls looked, of course, stunning in all the pictures. Harry added that it was a shame that Harry and I were in a lot of them to spoil the effect! Even though it stirred up some old memories, it was a good choice to make. We had finally remembered together a time in our lives that we had shared, which was so special to the four of us.

I sensed that old feeling returning, as if it was normal for us to be together, as we had been for so long. I looked at

Rose as she stared at Harry, and she studied his every move. I knew what was deep in her heart. I just wondered what was going on within my best friend's mind.

The day drew to a close, and it was now very late.

It was way past the time to get some sleep. Everyone was exhausted and weary. Binky and I made sure Harry had all that he needed downstairs. We said our goodnights, hugged each other, and all headed off to our bedrooms to get some sleep. As I was lying there next to Binky, I heard her drift off to sleep right away, as she gently started to breathe as she did when she was sleeping soundly. All the emotions and hard work of the past few days had caught up with her.

I stared at the ceiling for a while and felt like I needed to steal Howard Pailet's words once more.

I knew that all of us had received the blessing of another magical time.

I finally drifted off to sleep, after sometime making saves in my head, riding in the Trans Whizzer with Harry, walking up the path to Christmas Tree Mountain, fishing his choppers out of my beer, and countless other memories that wandered through my head.

Harry was back, and we all needed to hold on tight.

5

Be Careful What You Wish For!

I was up very early and I dressed in my workout clothes for a run. I crept down the stairs and slipped out the front door, being very careful not to disturb anyone. The rest of the gang was still sound asleep, but I needed the workout to clear my mind and keep me feeling as if I still could get in that net and take on the world. I did the same routine, ran the same streets, up the same hills, wore some leg weights and arm weights as I ran, and then did my flexibility drills over at the local playground.

I passed one or two of the other locals who worked out early and we greeted each other. Most folks still waved and called me, "twenty-seven," even after all these years.

I always walked home. It was very hard to break the ritual I had started. When I walked in the back door, I was surprised that everyone was up and sitting around the kitchen table enjoying coffee.

"Good morning, twenty-seven! Running around out there like a maniac . . . as usual!" Harry beamed. "Still slow on the stick side . . . low to the ice, I bet!"

I punched him gently in the arm, gave Binky a kiss, and said hello to Rose. Binky smiled and remembering my father's ravishing appetite, she said to me, "We were waiting for you, Paul. Now that your father has left, you may actually be able to have some French toast. Do you want to have some French toast?"

"I would love that! Let me take a shower and I will be right down."

We enjoyed breakfast together. Harry had the newspaper out and he was studying the real estate section pages.

"Hey Paul, I know it is Sunday and all that, so I thought we could all go to your church together. I think that they would allow two wayward Catholics over there in Lutheran land, wouldn't they?"

"They will. Binky and I would enjoy that, Harry. That would be great."

Harry looked over the top of the newspaper at me, "Great, then maybe we can check some of these rental houses out here that I see in the paper, I would like to land in and around Manchester Borough if I could. We can go straight from church, all dressed up to fool the landlord into thinking we are all nice, church going folks."

Harry seemed to be recovering nicely; he was back to his usual conniving ways.

"I can research it all for you, Harry. I did some preliminary scouting of the area for you already," Binky offered, while pulling a bunch of papers out of a small leather case that she now always kept nearby for carrying her constant research.

Harry looked over the top of the newspaper again and smiled, "Of course you did, Binky, I knew that. I bet you already have narrowed down the selections too."

Binky fluffed her long hair proudly and nodded quickly to indicate the affirmative answer to Harry's response. Some interactions were exactly as if the four of us had never missed a beat. It seemed as if the five or so years between us did not matter, it was as if it had only been a day or two of separation!

Off we all went to a pleasant worship service together, a quick lunch, and then we jumped into the Wagon Bus to hit the roads and turn our attention to finding Harry a house to rent. He wanted a house; he was quite adamant that he did not want an apartment. Binky provided a lot of her, detailed, in-depth type investigation results, and information, and she was in her glory pointing out any flaws, the location benefits, as well as various advantages and disadvantages on these homes. How she had known that Harry was interested in Manchester Borough remained a mystery, but there were not many details that ever escaped my wife, and her research-detailed-mind.

I moved into the back seat with Rose so that Binky could direct the house hunting operation from the front seat. From there, Binky could provide information to Harry as he cruised up and down the streets checking out the homes on the list. Rose and I settled in the back seat. We were enjoying observing the interaction of Harry and Binky, as my wife directed the command of the mission. She was in charge and clearly in control. Poor Harry mostly nodded his head as Binky went on and on with conveying even the smallest detail of her research on the local real estate scene.

After quite a bit of cruising up and down neighborhoods and streets, Harry and Binky settled upon a nice Cape Cod home with two bedrooms, with a small backyard that was located on a side street, off the main drag of Union Boulevard.

Harry found a pay phone, called the number in the ad, and spoke to the landlord who agreed to meet us out at the home. We pulled up to the home, and the owner was waiting out in front. He was a short, round, older man with very little hair, a big beer belly and a little frown on his face. He wore a New York Comets' tee shirt, dungarees, and an old pair of work boots. He frowned when he saw Harry and me, but perked up considerably, when he spotted the two young ladies.

"Hey, there, Comet man! I am, Harry M. Redmond Jr.," Harry said as he reached out to shake the owner's hand.

The man did not extend his hand out, but instead, he stared right at me and asked, "Are youse guys a bunch of hippies who live together, because if you are then the house isn't for rent anymore."

Harry laughed and shifted gears, "Hey are you, a hockey fan? You must recognize one of the greatest goalies whoever played and who just happened to be from Paterson!"

Oh boy, Harry was going to beat this poor guy like a drum.

"That's him, right there, Paul John Henson, the famous professional goalie." Harry pointed at me.

"I hate hockey, I am a football guy," The owner said as he looked down and pointed at his beloved Comets' tee shirt, proudly proclaiming his love for his team.

He then pointed at me.

"Ha! That, there, long-haired hippie, there played hockey. He just looks like some dressed up, polished up hippie. He is pretty tall and big though."

I loved it; nowhere on Earth will you find more openly honest, frank speaking people than in northern New Jersey. A visitor from Georgia or the Deep South who was used to, "southern hospitality" would have a hard time understanding the native northern New Jersey male species. They would last about two hours and be on a red eye back to Atlanta. Luckily, we all spoke the native language and understood the culture.

Harry turned up the blabber knob to work a deal, "Yes, well, he is retired now, and he is studying to be a minister."

The owner laughed even louder now, "Ha! Now, I know he is some kind of hippie! Maybe a minister, in one of those commune churches in someone's garage over on Bogart Street. I bet it is right next to that whacko with the big, yearly, Christmas display. What are you people, a bunch of jokers and clowns? Are youse guys wasting my time here or what? I would not rent a garden shed to a hippie like that guy there, minister, hockey player or whatever else youse say he is or was!"

The owner frowned and crossed his arms in front of

him.

We all looked at each other, since this was not going so well, to say the least. Harry was in trouble. Making headway with this hard-core crabapple was a little tough, so he shifted gears and appealed to the big, bellied guy's male instincts. This called for a change in Harry's strategy. Obviously, sports and religion were not going to cut the mustard!

Shifting focus away from me, Harry now directed his attention to the ladies. Harry produced a couple of fake laughs to cover up the fact that he really wanted to deck the insulting homeowner.

He then launched into his redirection, "Next to Paul, the lady with the great legs and figure is his wife Binky, and this other fabulous looking young lady here with the perfect smile is my friend, Rose."

Glancing over to the ladies, he checked them out up and down and suddenly there was a slight change of attitude.

Oh yeah! Harry had hit pay dirt!

The owner smoothed out what little hair he had left, sucked in his big beer gut, tugged at his belt and smiled.

"Nice to meet youse ladies!"

Of course, he ignored me.

Rose and Binky smiled but they did not say a word. Binky was holding off, transforming into attack mode from prim and proper mode, for the sake of Harry. She knew he really liked the house, but deep inside, she wanted to punch this big bag of wind lights out. I doubt that at this point, this guy was making much in the way of favor points with either of them.

After his hormone levels had settled out, the homeowner suddenly piped up with a thought, "Hey wait, you are sure youse guys all don't plan on living here together in one of those big hippie communes, do you?"

"No, no, I live by myself. I am a widower, my wife passed away about five years ago."

The owner's face changed a little; maybe he was not such a jerk after all, as he said, "Oh, I am sorry to hear that, do you want to see the house?"

Harry had broken through! I was not surprised. Harry still could sell ice to an Eskimo.

The owner opened the front door, and he held it open as he explained, "I live right across the street, so I keep a close eye on this place. It used to be my uncle's home."

When the ladies heard that, they knew they had the angle to work! Both of them turned up the eye appeal as they swayed by the owner, swinging their hips, exposing a little cleavage and batting their eyes at him as they walked by. They were about to play him like a fine violin.

"Good afternoon, ladies." He gawked and drooled as they walked by. "Do your friends come by often, Mr. Redmond?"

Harry, of course, knew the drill; we had all hung around together way too long. Making and working deals was in Harry's blood, it was to him, a normal part of everyday life. To Harry it was the same as breathing.

"Oh sure, sure they do, but no wild parties!"

The owner smiled. His little baldhead was thinking that he could often check out the sexy, female, laden scenery from his front porch.

He stuck his hand out now, "Steve, Steve McDonald."

Harry shook his hand. Harry had him in the bag now; he just had to work the deal. We looked around as the owner stood by.

"I like it is a nice house, but," Harry proclaimed since he was now closing in for the kill. The owner folded his arms across his chest. After all, great legs, pretty gals, perfume and hairdos, would only get us so far. Working a deal in northern New Jersey is a way of life. For years, New Jersey public school teachers taught deal making as a separate lesson in elementary school, right between a game of, "seven up" and mathematics!

"Can you afford three hundred and fifty bucks a month though, pal? I need references, other than the long-haired guy there, and I need to know where you work, so I can check you out. I deal with deadbeats from Paterson really hard, you know. This is the suburbs, after all, no street deals here."

Harry stared him down now, as the owner with his beady, little eyes, stuck out his big, beer barrel belly, in a vain effort to make his appearance to be more important. He had no idea with whom he was dealing with here. Harry M. Redmond Junior, inventor of the world famous, Annoy-O-Meter, roller skating marathon champion, race car driving champion, boardwalk game champion, welder par excellence, award winning, songwriter and banjo player.

What a resume!

Harry then circled in for the final approach, "I will give you three hundred a month. There is a little smaller joint over on St. James, I have my eye on, and he is only looking for two hundred and ninety bucks a month."

Harry turned towards the three of us and waved his hands in the air.

"You know what, youse guys? I really do not need all this space, just for me."

Mr. McDonald shifted his feet uneasily, and his eyes darted back and forth in his head. Harry had called his bluff!

"No way, will I take three hundred, I don't even know if you can afford it."

Harry laughed, "You do not understand there, old McDonald, if we work a deal, you do not need to check on my employment or anything like that."

Harry waved his hands in the air and stepped back casually. "I will bring you cash tomorrow, when the banks open, and pay you an entire year's rent in one shot."

It was obvious that Harry was making a lot of money

between his gizmo meter, welding, and his song royalties! He had struck up a deal of a lifetime, and it stunned poor Steve McDonald.

Harry then put the icing on the deal cake, "I will even take you over to Puppy's Grill for a hot Texas Weiner."

Steve's eyes lit up! He looked like he could down more than one Puppy's dog, that was for sure!

He asked, "All the way?"

"Sure, all the way there, old McDonald-a-roo-ski. Mustard, onions, and sauce."

"Well, three hundred a month it is then, Mr. Redmond! Welcome to the neighborhood!"

"Please call me Harry, just call me, Harry."

Another deal completed for the world-famous, Harry! Mr. McDonald had just met Mr. Deal Maker himself, and old McDonald had folded his tent quicker than campers do in a thunderstorm. The two men shook hands. They worked out a time for the settlement of the money tomorrow, and we all parted, as if we were best friends. He even shook my hand, and I was firm, but in relative terms, I backed off from squeezing the bones out of his hand for his hippie comments about me.

After all, he did come around to be a good guy.

The deal was over and Harry was thrilled. We took off in the Wagon Bus and went off to grab some dinner.

Harry was spouting off now, "I love the house! It is in a great spot. Thank you so much Bink-a-roo-ski for all of your help!"

"No trouble at all, dear Harry, it was an easy research, as my initial information quickly narrowed down what I knew you would like and what you would discount." Binky was on top of her game today!

"I plan on working a deal with Binky's dad next week for a place close by here and getting it together. I am thinking of opening a little factory for my gizmos and gadgets as well as a custom welding and fabrication shop. I have hardly any gear, mostly what is here in the back of the Wagon Bus and my luggage. I can buy some nice furniture to fill the place up. Maybe, youse gals can help me with that. Twenty-seven and I would not know what to buy."

The women agreed, and it looked like the plan had come together. It was nice to see Harry so happy and occupied. He was back, and we had all better be careful of what we had wished for.

He had that same old look back in his eye! Harry had a nice dinner planned at a local casual restaurant. The establishment served nothing fancy, just some beer, wine, and some standard dinner and lunch fare. I did have to admit that it seemed very normal for us all to be together. Harry, of course, in keeping with his standard operating procedure, flirted with the waitress when she came over. He also had some fun with the manager of the place when he circled around. The poor manager was a nervous, little fellow with big, bulging, eyes that popped out of his head. Harry was pretty much, just being plain old Harry!

Harry had ordered a hamburger and when it was set in front of him, he looked at it for a while and then asked the waitress, "Say there, cutie, what do you think of this hamburger? Do you see anything strange about it?"

The waitress looked quizzically back at Harry and then looked at the hamburger, "Well no, it looks like a hamburger usually looks like, sir."

"Well, c'mon now! Zoom on in there with those big, pretty, green eyes there and check it out a little more careful."

You could tell that the poor waitress was quite puzzled while she studied the hamburger on Harry's plate.

All three of us also looked at it and I had to admit, I also did not see what the trouble was. I studied it hard, thinking that perhaps Harry had dropped his famous, false choppers in the meal.

Harry stood up, and we all held on tight as he bellowed

out, "Mr. Manager, Mr. Manager. Come on over here, please."

The poor manager hustled over to the table. The perplexed waitress did not know if she should run and hide, or help in some manner, and she stood on the side nervously thinking she had done something wrong.

Harry was bellowing out as he looked over all the restaurant patrons seated at their tables, who were looking at him as if he was a nutcase. The three of us glanced at each other and I shrugged my shoulders.

Yes, Harry was back.

"Relax, everyone, this is a great place, no trouble with the food, I love this joint! I did not find a mouse in my food or anything like that."

The manager came over, "Please sir, please! How can I help you? This is a disturbance to the other patrons."

"Disturbance!"

Harry laughed and shouted aloud while shaking his head at the suggestion.

"No. I do not think so. We have caused some disturbances over the years, and this one does not make the cut. Take a look at that burger there, my good man! Use those big eyeballs of yours! I think we have invented a new sensation."

Now, all six of us gazed in, as Harry picked up his burger and we all checked it out. A man from the next table and his wife also stood up and came over to look at it too.

Finally, Binky pointed at it and she said, "It has two lids, Harry. The burger has two tops, but no bottom to the bun. They made a mistake in the kitchen and must have put two tops on it and missed the bottom."

Sure enough, we all saw it now. The burger had two lids, you could see the sesame seeds on both of the buns, and it had lettuce, tomato and mayo, on both the top of the burger, and the bottom.

"Exactly! Good eyes as usual, Bink-a-roo-ski! You are

not researching hamburger buns currently, are you, Binky?"

My wife shook her head back and forth rapidly, to indicate that she was not currently involved in any type of hamburger bun research.

"Now, watch as I taste it."

We now had a large crowd of other fascinated diners around as Harry opened wide and took a bite of the two-lidded burger.

"Fantastic! The toppings on each side are awesome! Add this to the menu right now, bug eyes, and call it the Harry Burger!" Harry turned around and shouted to the rest of the patrons, "Anyone who wants to try a free Harry Burger, raise their hands right now!"

About fifteen people raised their hands.

Harry leaned into the manager and spoke softly to him, "You charge two bucks for a regular burger, make the Harry Burger four bucks, I will pay for all of these burgers that the people eat here tonight. Add it to the menu, and I will take fifty cents on every burger you sell from this point forward. I will retain the rights to the name and reserve the right to market them on my own. I will be by in the morning to get you to sign some papers and finish working the deal. Is it a deal there, bug eyes?"

The manager looked around and smiled when he saw all the people who were ordering the newly created Harry Burgers.

"Deal and my name is, Charlie."

The two men shook hands.

"Sounds good, Chuck-a-roo-ski, nice work."

The pretty waitress smiled at Harry. "Wow, you are quite the guy, Harry. So, handsome too!"

She was smitten.

"Here you go, cutie. You are on the payroll now, too. Did anyone ever tell you that you have a great backside, and that you look great in those tight, black pants?" Harry handed her twenty dollars.

I sat there thinking. Amazing, it is simply amazing. Now, we could add this to the Annoy-O-Meter, the famous song, his various alter egos, the Black Bear Club, his special biscuits and countless other strange, unusual, and incredible Harry incidents. Harry is the only guy I ever knew who could turn a cook's mistake into a money-making deal named after him. The legend continued! Harry sat down and smiled. The three of us just shook our heads.

"What? Do youse guys want to try a bite?" Harry held the burger up. "It is really good."

Binky and I had to go to work and school in New York City in the morning, and Rose wanted to take the day off to go and check out some ideas that Father Mark had given her with her marital situation. Harry was going to stay tonight and then he would be off in the morning to finalize his house rental, his hamburger deal, and who knows what else he would cram into one day.

We arrived back to our house in one piece, without any more deals with difficult homeowners or Harry inventing anything new or unusual. We sat around enjoying a few beers and a few glasses of wine, but for the most part, we all had quite the weekend and we retired early.

When Binky and I left early in the morning, Harry was already up and had his bags, Sky's tree, and his other gear in the Wagon Bus.

"Hey youse two, thanks for everything. It was quite a weekend," Harry said as we met in the driveway.

I encouraged him, "It is all going to work out fine, Harry. Good luck at the new place, we will check in with you later."

"Paul, I am a little concerned about Rose, is she doing all right?"

"I think she has some tough decisions to make Harry, and she may have made them already. We as her friends, just need to support her and that is all we can do at this point."

Harry nodded his head, "I understand, it is just a little awkward for me and I am sure for her as well, with us having one time been an item and all. She is still married, so you know that I will play it cool. I will not deny that I still care about her, I just am not really sure in what way. It is very conflicting for me right now. I just need to be careful . . . you know."

Binky took Harry by his hand as she told him, "We know, and you are doing the right thing. Harry, just see how it all develops. There is not much else you can do."

"Does she need any dough?"

"Thank you, but we took care of that for her. She can stay with us for as long as she needs to until she can get on her feet. I would rather her be with us right now, anyway. With her folks, so old now and in Florida, the three of us and our family circles, are all she really has here right now."

Harry nodded his head. We shook hands, and Binky hugged him goodbye. We all took off, we had to catch the train, and Harry had a big day ahead of him. I had a long day of classes scheduled, so I asked Binky to take an earlier train out of the city and pick me up later at the station back home in Great Falls.

Binky and Rose circled back to the station to pick me up, but it was already almost eight at night by the time I arrived back in New Jersey.

After greeting my wife with a kiss, and saying hello to Rose, I sank in the seat of the jeep and sighed. I was tired.

"If it is all right with you, Paul, I thought we would go over to the Town Tavern for dinner. You are so late tonight. You must be beat."

"I am, the Town Tavern sounds great, I had no idea this would be so exhausting, it is worse than playing hockey or I am just getting old."

"I think this past weekend wore us all out, it was so emotional, and then we all stayed up so late that one night. It caught up with us all."

Of course, my wife was correct. It had been quite a weekend.

"Harry called, he has a telephone already, and he is setting up the house. He worked all the deals with no trouble, even with his new Harry Burger. Rose and I will go over on the weekend and help him. Linny and Ronzo said they would be coming down from the Poconos on Friday night to help too."

I chuckled as Binky pulled into the parking lot. Harry was quickly wasting no time at all in getting it together. We sat in the tavern, ordered some drinks, and checked out the menu.

Rose put down her menu, looked at me and explained, "Paul, I spoke with Binky about this already. I had a sad but productive day." Rose was gathering her thoughts, so I also put down my menu and I politely listened while she spoke.

"I spoke with the priest at the parish that Father Mark had sent me to, and there is no reason to continue with this marriage. I am going to file divorce papers tomorrow and move on with my life. As a Catholic, this is a major decision and a painful situation for me."

I knew in my heart that this was coming, but I did not really think it would occur as quickly as it had.

"I am sorry, Rose, but I understand."

I felt stupid, but that was all that I could think of to say. For sure, I needed to work on my counseling skills.

Rose continued, "I just want you both to know that this has nothing to do with Harry returning, I would have done the same thing any way."

Binky looked at me, she was waiting for me to say something first. I cleared my throat and told her, "We understand. Rose, you and Harry have a history together, and that may or may not mean anything to the both of you. Time will tell, it has been so long and so much has happened. Please, you have to just be very careful and go slow. This is going to be very difficult for you, and we are both here to support you in any way that you will need."

I did believe that Rose would have ended the marriage regardless of Harry returning or not, but I found the timing of all of this to be anything but ordinary.

Rose was upset, but she was very confident and composed. It was obvious that she now had a purpose.

"You two are the best. I do not know what I would have done without the both of you. I will just need a week or so, until I can get my act together, find an apartment, and get settled."

Binky fluffed her hair up, so I knew she was going to take control of the situation, "I have it all under control, dear Rose. I have researched all the available apartments, and convenient rentals in the area, keeping a travel circle within Great Falls, Manchester, Paterson, as well as your current place of employment."

Rose smiled, she knew that my wife was amazing, and she did have everything under control.

"Until then, you will stay with us, and then we all will assist you, as well as Harry, become settled in your new places, as well as a new direction."

I thought to myself, this is why I love this woman!

I begged out of the weekend work at Harry's new house and let the ladies, Linny, and Ronzo help Harry. They all understood, but I think Binky was becoming a little worried about me now. I reassured her that I was all right, I just needed to concentrate, and these studies were very difficult. Lately, the course work from the seminary had overwhelmed me, and I could use the peace and quiet to catch up and dive into it all. I have no idea why Martin Luther had to write such long catechisms and so many dissertations, but I found myself wishing that maybe I had been a Methodist.

Maybe the Wesley brothers were a little less prolific.

I heard from the gals that Tinky was also over at Harry's new place every day, as those two had hit it off well. I knew they would. As I had told Harry, my little red haired, bass playing, brother-in-law was our kind of guy. I was sorry to miss out on all the excitement, but Rose, Tinky, Harry, and Binky, would give me a daily wrap up, and they would come over to our house to check in with me, make sure I was eating, and hanging in there. I had set up a small study on a desk in the corner of our dining room, and I was knee deep in papers, books, Bibles, and pencils. I guess I had now fully transformed from a long-haired, hippie goalie into a long-haired, hippie student.

I sure was a long, long way from the Kansas City Hawks, the Long Island Roosters, and the Albany Flying Dutchman now.

Once in a while, no, not once in a while, it was more than occasionally. As of late, I needed to be honest with myself, because recently, the feelings returned quite often.

I now had to admit that I missed hockey.

I missed the excitement; I missed the sweat running off the edge of my mask like a river, even though I was standing in the middle of an ice rink, I missed my teammates and the special bond that you form with them, as you all blend in as a team. There is something to say about the extraordinary relationship that you form with your teammates as you fight and claw your way together. It is unique, very special, and unlike anything that I had found in ordinary "civilian" life. I missed transforming into a mental zone that no one could reach me and getting in that blessed zone, I called the flow. That was where I was so deep in my concentration and in my focus; there was no beating number twenty-seven. I was at my mental and physical peak. It was very hard to describe, but I knew that I missed that feeling the most.

Sometimes, I wondered if I would ever feel that way again.

Not a day went by that I did not hear in my mind, the sound of a hard slap shot hitting a wooden blade, or the sound of a skate cutting the ice hard in front of me. I missed that loud dead "clunk" noise that a puck would make when it hit the boards behind the net. I reached up and fingered that little scar over the top of my right eye, and I smiled. I did not miss some of it, that was for sure.

My life was so much different now; my life was calmer and more settled now. Even with Harry back here!

In the next few weeks, life finally settled out, as Binky found Rose a really nice, small, apartment to live in that she could afford, (and was close to all of us) she filed her divorce papers, and it seemed as though Rose was on track to rebound from this catastrophe in her life.

Harry met with Mr. Hobnobber and found a site for his little factory and welding shop. Binky and I settled into our married life once more. I had mentioned to her one night that with all our friends so close now, our fondness for Great Falls and our little house, that maybe we should just call up our landlord and make him an offer on this home and buy it. Binky made a good point, because while she initially agreed with me, there was no clear direction as to where I would end up after seminary. Once I graduated, I had to apply for ordination and that could be an adventure in itself. There was no telling where I would end up for a job after that, so it was best for now, if we stayed loose and kept our options open.

Binky was correct, the future for us was very uncertain.

Binky picked me up from the train station on one Friday night, months after Harry had returned, and she was very excited. It was now late summer, and we had not really had the time to go away or spend any sort of vacation time at all this entire summer.

"Oh, please tell me that you do not have a lot of course

work this weekend, and you can free up some time."

"As a matter of fact, I am in very good shape this weekend as far as my studies go. I am looking forward to having some relaxation time. I have a feeling my lovely wife has something planned!"

Binky was intense now, so I knew she had a plan.

"I do, I have been so worried about you and all of this course work, therefore, Harry, Rose, Tinky, and my parents have planned this huge dinner party, with cocktails, some wine tasting for Rose and my mother, music with Tinky and Harry, tennis, and all kinds of fun this weekend, for all of us at my parent's house. My father misses you! After all, he is so fond of you, twenty-seven."

Oh no, I thought, a weekend with my father-in-law! At least I have Harry and the gang this time around to run interference for me. I actually had to admit it that despite my father-in-law's well-concealed fondness for me, it sounded like a relaxing and attractive time. I needed a break, and I was curious as to how Rose and Harry were interacting and getting along. In addition, my father-in-law was always good for a journey or two up Mount Weirdness. I had not heard too much of Harry and Rose even being together, so perhaps this would be the first time in a long time that I would be brought up to speed on what was going on between them. I had been so busy that I had to confess to not keeping up with the situation.

"I received some of your favorite English cooking recipes from Mum, so I thought I would lock myself down in my parent's gourmet kitchen, while you are off playing tennis and see how I do on preparing them. I do not care for tennis much, and Father is such a sore loser that I would rather stay away from the courts. You deserve some special cooking for all the hard studying you have been doing, and my parent's kitchen is perfect for me to try them. Plus, my parents have been really hinting around for me to try them too, so I thought this would be the perfect weekend."

"Wow, this will be a treat, I am certainly a lucky guy this weekend, thank you!"

Now, this was a little more than just some special incentive. Let's see now, authentic homemade English cooking from my own Mum's secret recipes, a beautiful wife, friends, and family. My wife sure knew how to take good care of me.

Oh yes, and add a dash of Senator William T. Hobnobber too.

I swung the old jeep out into traffic and rolled on up Main Street.

"In case, I do not tell you enough Binky, Rwy'n Dy Garu Di. Thank you for planning this, I know I have been buried in books for months now and it has been a little difficult for you."

"I love you too, my dear Paul. Those are the only words I know in Welsh, so please do not say any more, until I have had additional time to research the language. And no, you never tell me enough, twenty-seven, never." She smiled at me. No stares, just that smile that always melts me away.

"Hello, dear Father and Mother, it is so nice to be here."

My wife ran up and kissed her father and then her mother. They were dressed perfectly, with Mrs. Hobnobber in a stunning, form-fitting black evening dress, decked out in all of her expensive jewelry and Mr. Hobnobber in a dinner jacket.

I looked down at my No Way tee shirt, dungarees and my old canvas sneakers. Oh, well. You never actually fit in now, do you, Paul?

Harry, Rose, and Tinky were there already having some drinks and chatting. They waved to us from the living room when they saw us arrive.

Mr. Hobnobber hugged Binky, and then he looked at me and frowned. That was his usual greeting and reaction when he saw me.

"Wonderful to see you, my beloved daughter and I see that as usual—your husband felt the need to overdress for this evening."

I ignored the greeting and decided to play the happy son-in-law routine.

"Hello, Mom and Dad. How are you?"

Mrs. Hobnobber shook her head and reached out for me, "Oh dear Paul, come over and give me a kiss and a hug, you look so tired. You are becoming so worn out."

I hugged my mother-in-law who, of course, had to give me her famous lip lock kiss. I was used to her by now.

She smiled after kissing me and looked at Binky with a giant smile on her face, exposing her gleaming choppers. Mrs. Hobnobber stood back and said, "Oh how, I love that beard and hair!"

"Tired, tired from what? The guy has never worked a day in his life. For years, he stood in front of a hockey net raking in big bucks for doing nothing. Now, all he does is push pencils around and endlessly study! Dear Binky, has to slave away to support him all the time while he lounges around studying Bible verses. What a racket! He is not anything at all like his best buddy Harry here, who is a true ambitious, independent, entrepreneur. Why, his newest idea is the latest craze! The Harry Burger is now going to a line of frozen foods, the man is a genius!" Mr. Hobnobber was in topnotch insult form today, and hitting the bull's eye of his favorite target, which of course, was me.

I smiled, went over, and patted Mr. Hobnobber on the shoulder.

"Hello, Dad."

He hid his hand behind his back when I approached him. I never, ever shook his hand since that fateful first meeting.

Binky and I greeted Tinky, Rose, and Harry in the living room while the Hobnobbers headed for the kitchen to prepare dinner.

Harry studied me up and down and spoke, "Hey, twenty-seven, I thought we lost you forever there, buddy."

"Sorry guys, it has been a bit rough, but I think I am through the worst of it. Everyone tells me the first eight months are the worst. I imagine they try to weed out the non-academic types. I am achieving good, solid grades. I think that I will make it. In fact, I doubled up these credits and carried over a lot from college, to push through quicker. For a little while, I had some doubts, but now, I think I will make it.

Harry looked at me. "C'mon twenty-seven, after all the O'Malley's of the world that you faced, this should be a walk in the park."

"I hope so, guys. I met the bishop of this district last week. He toured through school, speaking with students and meeting people. He seemed uptight, and he was not overly impressed with me, with all my hair, the beard and such. I could tell that I did not fit the mold, you know."

Tinky piped in, "Well, you never really fit the mold, Paul. Even on the hockey rink, but that never stopped you before and I have a feeling, it is not going to stop you now either."

"You are correct, Tinky. It looks as if I am an outcast, since I could not find an internship, or a church to sponsor me, or an ordination committee. It looks as though the bishop is the one person that could approve my ordination. I need a job, and he is the big boss."

Tinky shook his head and his face turned a little redder than usual as he said, "We are all with you, Paul. We have no doubt in your brainpower. My sister always told me, when she would describe you to me, as the smartest man that she ever met. I was always amazed that she would describe you that way first and then mention the hair, the hockey, music, and so on and so forth."

"Thanks, Tinky, I appreciate the kind words, even more

so when they come from a male side of the Hobnobber bloodline."

"Yeah, Dad sure beats you like a drum, but that is because he loves you. He loves you to death. He talks about you all the time when you are not around. You are actually his hero. He just will never let you know it."

Binky piped up now, "Of course, dear Father loves, Paul! You know that he has to put up his big front." Binky grabbed my arm and put her arm through mine while she looked at Harry. "Harry, now are you really doing something with the Harry Burgers?"

Harry laughed and took a long sip of his drink as he answered, "Sure I am Binky, and more than that, the three of us have a big announcement to make."

Harry put his drink down and put his arms up.

"Gather around everyone, Mom and Dad Hobnobber! Come on in here! We have some big news! Get your parents, will you Tinky?"

Harry was bellowing while Tinky ran off to find his parents. He returned shortly with them as they walked in with a puzzled look on their faces.

"What is going on here, Harry? You are not running for political office in this year's elections, are you?" Mr. Hobnobber was curious as to the nature of the announcement, as were both Binky and I.

It was obvious from the look on Tinky as well as Rose's face that they already knew about this.

Harry laughed, "No, no, not yet! Not only did I work a deal to market frozen Harry Burgers last week, but I also went down to Chuck-a-roo-ski's place yesterday and bought his restaurant. I had some extra, cold, hard, cash due to another half million-piece order of Annoy-O-Meters that my accountant said I had to invest, or pay taxes on this year. I went down to see Chuck, and I plunked the cash down on the counter in front of him in a big, brown, paper bag. His big, bug eyes bugged out even more. He could not refuse my offer, so we made the deal happen."

Harry moved over, pulled Rose in on his one side and Tinky on his other side, and put his big arms around them both.

"Tinky and Rose here are going to run the joint for me. I plan to turn it into a dinner, dancing, drinks, and live music place. I will have live sports on those new, big screen televisions and we can even let everyone meet the famous, goalkeeper number twenty-seven one night, on a hockey appreciation night! Harry Burgers, of course, will be the leader on the menu, promoting my fame and fortune. Tink-a-roo-ski will run the entertainment side for me, and Rose is going to run the business end. They are on my payroll now as co-managers."

Harry cleared his throat, lowered his voice a little, and then he continued with his announcement, "I also kept that cute, little waitress with the great smile and amazing ass."

"Atta boy, Redmond! Way to identify your marketing assets!" Mr. Hobnobber shouted and pointed at Harry.

Rose frowned at Harry and gave him her patented punch in the arm.

"Harry, that is fantastic, how exciting!" Binky was thrilled.

Despite the continued presence of the pretty waitress, Rose was beaming, "I am so excited everyone, I never did anything like this, but Harry thinks I can do it, so Tinky and I are going to give it a try in the management end."

Mr. Hobnobber shouted in excitement, "I love this! That is what I am talking about! Tinky actually now has a real job, instead of strumming his guitar and mooching off me! A job by gracious! Tinky has an actual job! Now, if my son-in-law would get to work, the entire family would be employed!"

Mr. Hobnobber was congratulating all of us. Lately, Mr. Hobnobber had adopted Harry's favorite war cry, and he shouted it quite often.

"The man is remarkable! Of course, I will take credit for this during my reelection campaign. You know . . . inner city renewal, helping the poor and downtrodden man to become a successful businessman, but that is all part of our politics of course!"

Harry put his big arm back around Rose and pulled her close to him, as he spoke to Rose, "Onward and upward dear Rose, time to get out of that dead-end job and make your way as part of the Harry M. Redmond Jr. Empire! Big things, gang, big things! I renamed the joint, 'The Lovely Rose.' With Rose working the crowds every night with her smile, great figure, dressed to the hilt, with her charismatic personality, and Tinky working the patrons into a frenzy with the right music, the place will be a gold mine!"

I looked at Binky; she smiled at me and gave me a wink of her eye. She and I were on the same page, Harry had made the first move in the romantic chess match that was going to be up to both Harry and Rose to play.

After the excitement of the announcement, Binky and I excused ourselves to prepare for cocktails and dinner. Binky and I went upstairs to one of the spare rooms and we changed for dinner. The Hobnobber mansion had about ten bedrooms, but we always stayed in this same room when we visited.

I sat on the end of the bed, tying my shoes as Binky finished changing.

"Harry sure is happy, but he seems like a man on a mission to always be doing something."

"I think he stays so busy jumping from one thing to another, to keep his mind from wandering."

"I think you are right, Paul. That does make sense. But did you see how he looked at Rose when he was explaining about the new night club?"

"I did, this is certainly going to get really interesting," Binky looked at me as she spoke, fluffed her hair up, and winked provocatively. She stood in front of me and said, "I have that same look when I stare at you. Paul, do you think they would miss us if we were a little late arriving downstairs for cocktails?"

"They might, but with an invitation like that, I really don't care."

I reached down and untied my shoes. . . ..

"What a glorious morning, team! We are all going to have a grand time here exercising, enjoying life, as well as the sport of tennis," my father-in-law said, while he breathed in deeply and then exhaled as he stood on the side of his prized tennis courts.

Harry, Rose, Tinky, and my mother-in-law joined him as we now all stood together outside the fence, next to the tennis courts in the rear of the Hobnobber mansion. Mr. and Mrs. Hobnobber were dressed in expensive, perfectly matched, tennis attire with the finest sneakers, hats, wristbands, headbands, and tennis racquets.

They looked like a marketing snapshot for the cover of a tennis magazine.

Rose, Tinky, Harry, and I were standing there like a bunch of bums. I wore an old Albany Flying Dutchman practice shirt and my canvas sneakers. Harry, Tinky and Rose, wore some old, cut-off dungarees made into shorts with tee shirts on and any old pairs of sneakers that they could find. Binky was already in the kitchen immersed in research and her English cuisine-cooking mission, so we were on our own.

Team oddball versus the professional Hobnobbers.

"Now, Mrs. Hobnobber and I, of course, are seasoned players and we are an unbeatable doubles team. We have won the championship trophy at the country club in our age bracket for five years in a row."

Mr. Hobnobber continued explaining and organizing the matches.

"Tinky has played tennis since he was a little boy, but sports have never been his strong point."

Poor Tinky turned even redder than usual, and he shrugged his shoulders, while saying, "Hey, I am a musician, not an athlete."

"Now, since I have continually been abused, embarrassed and brutally treated by my professional athlete, son-in-law in various sporting outings, I decided to concede defeat and not subject myself to any more of his evil, self-inflating torture," Mr. Hobnobber stated while he broke into a broad smile, while my mother-in-law, frowned at her husband.

"I have done what every good, conniving and evil New Jersey politician would do, and brought in ringers to pummel his huge ego into a submission for once in his life. I was not willing to risk putting our string of victories on the line at his devious hands. Even though Harry and Paul have both stated under some badge of honor that they never played tennis before, I know all too well, how he operates."

Harry raised his hand and spoke, "Dad Hobnobber, tennis was not exactly big on John Street in Paterson. Believe me, when I say that, I think you are safe. It was, as Mum would say, not exactly our cup of tea. We did not have any tennis courts in our neck of the woods, you know."

Mr. Hobnobber shook his head back and forth to show that he did not trust us, as Mrs. Hobnobber smiled, posed, and fluffed her hair at Harry.

The four of us looked at each other. Harry leaned in and whispered, "Why did you not just let him win a few times, Paul? Now he has that O'Malley type look in his eye."

"It is not that easy, Harry, I tried, but he always would catch me going easy on him and get all fired up. He is the ultimate bad sport and a sore loser."

"Oh boy! Did he ever win one thing?"

I shook my head back and forth to show that he had never won.

"Why did you not just play checkers or Warship or something like that? I used to cheat all the time at the board games, that is how I used to beat you. That would have been a better plan, because he now has made it his single mission in life to beat you at something there twenty-seven. Forgive me there, Tink-a-roo-ski, but he is a bit of a whacko. That is why he is such a successful politician."

Tinky answered Harry, "Hey, you will get no argument from me boss!"

Mr. Hobnobber clapped his hands together loudly, and spouted, "All right now gang, time to play a bit! We will start with Mrs. Hobnobber and me warming up with all of you to show off how fantastic we are, and then we will play Rose and Tinky in a match and destroy them very easily. The highlight of the day will be at eleven o'clock when Doris and Walt Mangini arrive. You see, the Manginis are tennis professionals and instructors from our country club. After warm-ups, they will then take on Harry and Paul in a doubles match and it will be my distinct pleasure to watch the destruction, while I sip ice cold lemonade at a table courtside here."

Mr. Hobnobber turned and pointed to a set of tables and chairs set up alongside the courts with a brightly colored red umbrella mounted over it.

"I will be alongside my stunning, gorgeous, wife dressed in her little, tiny, expensive, tennis outfit for full flaunting of her fantastic figure. There, I will enjoy watching the famous, twenty-seven and his longtime, sidekick, be finally beaten, destroyed, and humbled in a sporting event."

Harry shouted out, "You do look hot, Mom Hobnobber! I love that outfit, great legs, man, great legs!"

Mrs. Hobnobber blew Harry a kiss as Rose punched him in the arm.

Tinky whispered to us, "Dad really does love, Paul. It is just that he is a bit of a sore loser at sports. He seems to be harboring a little grudge against Paul for all the defeats that he has suffered in their playful little competitions."

Harry feigned surprise, "Wow, Tink-a-roo-ski, I see that. Could you downplay it a little more, though? Saying that your old man is a bit of a sore loser, is like saying that Jack the Ripper really was not such a bad guy after all, he was just a tad misunderstood."

I decided to jump in here and boost Mr. Hobnobber's confidence, "Sounds like a great day you have planned there, Dad, we are looking forward to it!"

Mr. Hobnobber smiled as he felt as if this was finally the moment, in which he had waited for. He had lured us up here to his tennis lair, and now he was going to enact his revenge. He had plotted our demise completely and thoroughly.

We all picked up some extra tennis racquets that Mr. Hobnobber had pointed out for us to use. Some had torn strings, peeling tape on the handles, and one was missing the top corner of it.

The Hobnobbers, on the other hand, used their custom balanced, hand-fitted, million-dollar racquets, and headed out to the court. Even the handles on their racquets had custom pearl inlays with their initials engraved on the ends of the handles.

Rose, Tinky, Harry, and I stood on one side as Mr. Hobnobber picked up a ball, reached high over his head, and served the ball at us. Rose screamed as the ball rocketed past her. She spun away from it, waving her racquet in the air as the ball bounced to the end of the court.

"Nothing personal, dear Rose, we are just warming up, honey! We love you! We really do!" Mrs. Hobnobber yelled to us from the other side of the court.

I looked at Harry and reasoned a little to him, "Harry, how hard can this be? It is sort of like playing goal, and we just have to stop the ball from getting past us with this racquet thing."

Harry waved the racquet in the air as if he was testing the theory, while he said, "I am not so sure, twenty-seven, this looks like it is a lot harder than we think."

Perhaps we were doomed, even the ever confident, Harry had some elements of doubt in his mind. The Hobnobbers then proceeded to fire off retrorocket tennis balls at us, while Tinky and Rose ran around trying to avoid being blasted and pelted with tennis balls.

Harry and I ran around waving our racquets in the air in a vain attempt to defend them.

Mr. Hobnobber was clearly in his glory, as he had finally found the goose that laid the golden egg and his ego was building.

My father-in-law bellowed out sarcastically, "The point of the game is actually to hit the ball back over to us!"

Harry and I were running around like maniacs, sweating like pigs, but not really figuring anything out. Harry, at one time, actually managed to hit the ball, but it went straight up in the air and did not even come close to going over the net. After about a half an hour of this torture under the false pretense of warming up, Mr. Hobnobber waved and signaled for us to come over to the side of the court. We all held each other up and dragged ourselves over to the side. Harry was breathing like a steam locomotive, Tinky looked like a thermometer ready to blow, Rose had welts on her legs from tennis balls pelting her, and I was sweating from head-to-toe.

The Hobnobbers looked as fresh as daisies on a bright spring day.

I guessed that this was not a Mr. Bluebird on my shoulder day that God had planned for me, so I crossed this one off the list.

My father-in-law was in his glory at our failed performance on the tennis courts, as he shouted with glee, "So this is great, isn't it? Sure, humbled you out there, hotshot twenty-seven, I do not think you even hit the ball once."

Mrs. Hobnobber slipped in there now, turning from her prim and proper mode, into her evil alter ego, as she spoke in glee, "I love when you blast it really hard over the net, William! It gets me all hot and bothered for later on tonight!"

"I know you do, baby doll. It sure is fun for us all to participate in a friendly, family game of tennis."

"Fun, it sure is fun, Dad," I finally caught my breath enough to squeak out an answer. I was in good shape, still ran, and worked out every day, and I was a mess from running around as a lunatic waving my racquet in the air. I could imagine how poorly my three teammates felt!

"Well, come along, Rose and Tinky. Let's have a pleasant tennis match, before the Manginis arrive to annihilate Paul and Harry," Mr. Hobnobber said, as the Hobnobbers strutted out to the court like roosters as poor Tinky and Rose dragged their worn-out bodies out there.

"Good luck there, team Redmond, and win one for the nightclub!" Harry shouted out encouragement and fist pumped in the air. Tinky just waved his racquet at Harry in disgust.

Harry and I sat on chairs next to the court.

"We all have as much chance out there as O'Malley does at following in your footsteps and becoming a minister. Ya know, like you are studying to become," Harry said, as he picked up a glass and poured some water.

"He is one, Harry. Therefore, I guess we have a chance."

Harry spit out the mouthful of water and looked at me in shock.

"Ya gotta be friggin' kiddin' me, Paul?"

"No kidding, Harry, he is really a minister now. He came to our wedding in his collar. I guess I forgot to tell you about that."

Harry smiled, shook his head, and laughed. If Harry

found something surprising, then you know it is strange!

"Well, why should I be surprised? I guess O'Malley had to make up for all the mayhem he caused on the ice. I sure would have loved to sit in on that confession! I bet Heaven had some smoke coming out of the clouds as O'Malley spilled his guts. I wonder if he confessed up about when he taped razor blades to the end of his hockey stick blade."

Harry turned his attention to the tennis courts and pointed at my in-laws.

"Hey, look there, it sure looks as if your in-laws are happy now! I can only imagine how it was, facing them by yourself when you first met them. Nice folks, but they sure are high on the old weirdo meter, now, aren't they?"

This frank analysis was coming from a guy whose own family used to go to the corner supermarket dressed up in full official New York Bugs' baseball uniforms equipped with metal cleated shoes and all.

Harry continued to assess the situation, "The really scary part, is that this guy helps run our state government. I will tell you that Mrs. Hobnobber sure does look good in that outfit, though. I truly wonder how a whack job like Mr. Hobnobber landed a hottie like her! Rose is not too shabby looking today either. She looks incredibly fantastic in those shorts! Whoowee! Her ass looks fantastic today. Despite the fact that she looks as if she is going to have to check into the emergency ward after this game."

I just sipped some water and agreed with Harry while watching Rose and Tinky already behind about ten to nothing. We stood up and cheered when Tinky actually hit the ball back over the net. It was out of bounds, but hey, he hit it! Tinky bowed as we stood and clapped. Rose hit the ball once or twice, as did Tinky, and they actually won a point or two, but for the most part; it was a complete and full defeat for team Redmond nightclub. Rose and Tinky were just thankful for the game to be over and they could now sit down.

Harry and I congratulated them, and the Hobnobbers bounded over the net to thank them for a great match.

Rose walked over to the table, sat down, and sighed deeply.

"Next victims!" Rose yelled out.

I shrugged my shoulders and felt that a happy twist on the situation was in order, "Look on the bright side, Rose . . . at what a great workout you had."

She just looked at me and waved her hand at me. I do not think that Rose was buying what I was selling.

Harry was up dancing around and stretching as if he had gained some confidence. He was bouncing in the air, waving the racquet back-and-forth pretending that he actually knew what he was doing.

He was not fooling us.

"I am into this now! How hard can it be? I think it is a timing and positional game. We have taken on tougher assignments, twenty-seven. This is an easy game, it is just something we never played before, and we have to get into a groove. C'mon Paul, you are a professional goalie, man, still in tip top shape, you are the real deal."

"Hockey, yes. Tennis no, this is the first time I ever picked up a racquet in my life."

Tinky was exhausted, and he sat slumped in a chair sitting next to Rose, and explained, "I hate sports. Hey, good luck with that groove thing, boss. Dad is on a mission. He is bringing in the Manginis to beat you two bozos like drums. You do know and realize that they are tennis pros? He snookered youse dopes."

Harry and I did not say a word, as we knew we had been lured into a trap by my revenge seeking father-in-law, and we were about to be destroyed by tennis professionals.

"I have seen them at the club and they are like some kind of robotic tennis machines. I think Binky was the smartest of us all." Tinky sighed, and he said, "I sure wish that I knew how to cook."

Harry dropped his racquet on the table and said, "What we need here team is an inspirational boost." I could see that street smart, mind of Harry spinning his little wheels around in his mind. All four of us stared down at the other side of the court when we heard Mr. Hobnobber's voice.

"Doris and Walt, it is so nice to see you!"

Mr. Hobnobber was walking over to the side of the court to meet some people, who we now had to presume to be the Manginis. A tall, well built, man with perfectly groomed jet-black hair, a perfect tan, and a big, wide smile revealing perfect, gleaming, white teeth strode over to shake Dad Hobnobber's hand. Behind him was a gorgeous, tall, blonde haired woman, who also had a perfect tan, and perfect white choppers. They both also were wearing very expensive looking tennis outfits, and fancy sneakers, and they were carrying expensive looking bags for their equipment.

"Sarah, Bill, so nice to see you. You are looking so well, thank you for the tennis invitation." The two couples were exchanging hugs, kisses, and greetings.

"That my loser teammates—would be the Manginis," Tinky stood up, pointed towards the other end of the court and announced. "You think that my father is annoying and has a big ego. That is nothing compared to these two birds. There are not enough Annoy-O-Meters in the world to cover them."

Harry whistled while looking over at the meeting of the two couples. He was admiring Mrs. Mangini. "She is some dish, look at that tan and figure, they both cannot be real, they may melt in the sun from all of that plastic. I bet melted breasts are a bitch. Anyway, they look like real-life, Hollywood movie stars."

Rose stood up, and she had to agree with Harry and his observation. Rose replied, "He is like a god and she is like a goddess, they are perfect."

Mrs. Hobnobber smoothed her hair and tennis outfit out

after hugging and lip locking Walt Mangini. She directed the group over towards where we were standing and she explained as they walked over to us, "You know our son, Tinky of course, but please, come over and meet our wonderful, son-in-law and his friends."

Mrs. Hobnobber led the Manginis over.

I could hear Mr. Hobnobber explaining a warning to the Manginis, "Don't shake the long-haired guy's hand, whatever you do, it is a trick he pulls to wound you ahead of time." Mr. Hobnobber was running over behind them, waving his hands over his head as an additional warning.

"Tinky, it is so nice to see you again!" Mr. Mangini reached out his hand to shake Tinky's hand. "We were so hoping to see you out at the club to take some more lessons and improve your horrible physical condition."

Tinky just stood there after shaking his hand, glaring back at Mr. Mangini while trying as hard as he could not to explode at the comment. He finally answered, "I have better things to do then hang around that club with a bunch of pompous jerks."

Harry, Rose, and I glanced at one another and smiled. As I had stated many times before, Tinky was our kind of guy. The smiles faded from both of the Mangini's faces rather quickly when they heard Tinky's comment.

Mom Hobnobber moved in for damage control, "Please meet our son-in-law, Paul John Henson. Paul, please meet our good friends, Walter and Doris Mangini."

The Manginis moved over to face me as I walked over, smiled, and then greeted them.

Mr. Mangini glanced at me and reported, "Forgive me, but I will not shake your hand out of a special request from your father-in-law."

Mrs. Mangini stopped, looked at me, and her eyes went up and down my entire body. She turned back to my mother-in-law and smiled as she spoke slyly, "So Binky found herself quite a hunk here! Where did she find you, young man? Perhaps over at one of the clubs? Henson, Henson, hmm, I do not recognize the name. Is your father a member? What does your father do for a living there, handsome?"

I laughed a bit. The outward advances and observations of Mrs. Mangini did not offend me at all. It seemed to be the way these types of folks acted.

I decided to answer her with the facts, "No. I am from the north side of the city of Paterson, Mrs. Mangini. My dad is not a member of any country clubs, except maybe the club of hard knocks and wrench swinging. He is a retired machinist."

Well, both Mr. and Mrs. Mangini frowned at my words. In fact, as soon as I had finished stating that my father was a machinist, and I was from Paterson, that was it! It was as if I had suddenly announced that I am sorry, but I have just contracted a bad case of Bubonic Plague. They both just stopped, the smiles faded from their faces, and they took a few steps backwards.

I knew the drill, as did Harry and Rose. I looked over at Harry and I knew that he had grown weary already of their pompous act.

Harry was not happy, so I shifted gears, "These are my two closest friends in the whole world, Mr. Harry M. Redmond Jr. and Ms. Rose Graziano."

Harry was going to play it as close to the cuff as he could without ripping off Mr. Mangini's head.

"How are you doing there big, white, choppers?" Harry said as he moved over and shook Walt's hand vigorously. He was, however, the outrageous Mr. Harry M. Redmond Jr.! Walt frowned as Harry moved over to Doris. "So, Doris, it is my pleasure, say, you are a hot little number, maybe we can chat a bit later. I am an old hockey player and I need the phone number for your dentist."

Doris weakly shook Harry's hand and forced a smile as she now studied our rag-tag group. The Manginis then politely greeted Rose. Harry stood there smiling with his hands on his hips, but I knew inside that he was burning up. I was very proud of him since the old Harry would have spit out his false choppers and pummeled old man Mangini into submission, right then and there.

"So, who are we playing today, Bill? Surely you did not bring us out here to play tennis with Paul and his motley collection of rag tag friends?

Mr. Hobnobber cleared his throat. He was feeling just a little uncomfortable at how this all was shaking out.

"Well, I did Walt, you see, it is a little hard to detect from his outward appearance, but Paul is a retired professional athlete. He was a professional ice hockey goaltender for many years for a number of different clubs. He really came very close to playing in the big league for the Boston Bears. You will be competing with Harry and Paul, out on the court. They have never really played tennis before, but we thought it would be a nice introduction for them."

Doris and Walt looked at Harry and me and then back at Mr. Hobnobber. They both started to laugh aloud.

Walt spoke between laughs, "Ice hockey, oh my, a brutish, sport of wild men out there beating each other over the head with sticks. I see by his jersey there, the Flying Dutchman, very scary! Never really played tennis before, this should be an interesting time of it. Perhaps, we should start with a nice game of badminton."

The two of them had a nice laugh as we all stood there looking at them.

Tinky leaned in and whispered to me, "I told you, Paul."

Rose was turning red, and I saw Harry just glaring back at them. Rose was now fired up at the overly, obnoxious behavior of these two pretentious snobs and she smiled through a forced grin and told us, "I would love to knock those white teeth right out of both of their faces, just hold me back guys!"

Walt smiled and looked at me and wagged his right index finger back and forth in the air to me. "I am afraid that playing ice hockey is not going to qualify you for a productive day of tennis with us, Paul, but we can take it easy on you and show you how to play the game. Let's warm up a little."

I could tell by his body language that Mr. Hobnobber was now a little uncomfortable with his ringer's attitude and he looked at the four of us, forced a smile, and then watched them as they walked out onto the court. Mrs. Hobnobber was not very happy now with the behavior of her guests, and she crossed her arms in front of her and watched from the side of the court.

Mr. Mangini walked out towards the court waving his golden racquet in the air and he proudly proclaimed, "All right now, let's warm up and have a nice little match here, I am sure it will be a lot of fun!"

Mrs. Mangini arrogantly wiggled her plastic enhanced body over to pick up her gear, as she chuckled and laughed, while joining her husband out on the court.

The Hobnobbers went and sat at a table on the side of the court as we watched the Manginis gather themselves in the middle of the court, then they split up on opposite sides of the net and they began to tap the ball back and forth to one another. After some mild warm-ups, Walt reached high over his head and served up a rocket ship of a shot that dropped just within the boundary of the end line of the court. Then he looked over at us, smiled a little smirk, and hit another, and then another that was even harder. It was similar to a bunch of slap shots in hockey warm-ups, and I watched and plotted in my head as to what the goal of this game was going to be. I stood on the side watching as they were obviously sending us a message of what they intended to do to us once the match started.

They did not intend to "take it easy" on us.

Harry turned and looked at me and he spoke angrily,

"You know, these folks are really super-arrogant, in fact, they take it to a new level. The great team of Harry and Paul could suffer a major loss to these two bananas. They are playing us as if we are a bunch of fools! I still say we need some inspiration. We cannot let these two take us apart. I mean, geez . . . you faced worse than this, I am sure. It is time for one of our famous Harry and Paul's action plans."

I shrugged my shoulders and studied the ball's speed as Walt knocked ball after ball over the net at a speed that seemed a little slower than most shots I faced. I could easily pick up the flight of the ball; it was just a matter of adjusting to the strategy of the game.

Rose was angry; she came over, put her arm around my shoulders, and looked right at me.

"C'mon, twenty-seven, you two can do it! You are still twenty-seven, go in there, and shut them up. I would give anything right now, to see you two shut these two, horrible people up!"

Harry and Tinky walked over to my side and now they were all working hard to get me into the flow, but I did not feel it yet, I was just studying the shots as I flashed it repeatedly in my mind. I smiled at them, as the ball became easier for me to follow, and I felt as if I was following it pretty well. Harry and I walked out onto the court as I heard Mr. Hobnobber clapping from his table. He had a huge smile on his face as he felt his redemption was very near.

Harry and I looked at each other, as Walt yelled over to us, "So, are you two young men from that wonderful, clean, shining, slum city of Paterson ready? Or perhaps, you have to go pick up your monetary assistance checks from the government early this month and want to call it quits now?"

The Manginis laughed and smiled at one another, and they were getting quite a charge out of their overly inflated egos.

"I always knew that Binky had a rough and loose side to her, but to cross over the railroad tracks and pick out some long-haired, hippie, from the other side is a little surprising. I guess she felt that she had to settle for someone, after our little Walter Junior had his chance with Binky, and was not interested in her. She just was not up to our standards!"

Bang! Bang! Bang! They had crossed the Rubicon!

Harry looked at me and he saw the look on my face change. That old fire had ignited when they crossed the line, and it was burning higher and higher. I felt it rising, and the flow came over me. I reached into my pocket, grabbed a hair tie, and bundled all my hair up in the back of my head, and tied it all off.

Harry looked at me and smiled. He had the eye of the tiger on and the two of us came together and tapped our racquets into each other's at the center of the court. We had fought many wars together on the ice, in bar rooms, on hockey rinks, and on the streets.

Harry knew the drill!

"That's it now! We are not going to take any more of this bullshit! You are in the flow, Paul, I can tell!"

I didn't even answer him, but turned to face the Manginis and I stared them down.

"Oh yeah! Oh yeah!" Harry yelled out. "You should not have insulted Binky there, big choppers, because you just gave us the inspiration that I was looking for!"

I heard Mrs. Hobnobber yell out now, because she too had heard the comment about Binky, "Kick their asses, Harry, kick their asses, twenty-seven!" My mother-in-law had turned from the prim and proper perfect host into a wild woman cheering on her family. She had left her husband alone at his table, and moved over to sit with Rose and Tinky, as she was obviously miffed at her husband, as well as the attitudes and comments of the Manginis.

I stood there and simply said, "Serve it over here, big mouth." This was a flow that I had not felt in a long time, and it was something I needed right now in my life. These two buffoons had no idea of what intensity they had ignited inside the two of us. Walt smiled and reached high over his head and bashed the ball as hard as he could right at me. I saw it clearly. It was much slower than a hard or even a mediocre slap shot, and the ball was spinning and easy to see. I set my feet and stared it down just like a puck at my head. I reached up with the racquet and knocked the ball squarely back and it dropped right inside the line, between the two of them.

I heard Rose, Tinky, and Mrs. Hobnobber cheer from the sideline as Harry came over and shook my hand.

"I love this! Now this is what I am talking about!"

The Manginis were stunned as I looked over at them and said, "Our serve."

"You say that you two have never played tennis before?"

I looked back at them, "Not until today, but we seem to be picking it up rather quickly, eh? But then again, we need to get this game over rather quickly, so that we can pick up our assistance checks!"

I threw the tennis ball over to Harry, who caught it in the air. "You serve it, Harry! Aim it right at them like a slap shot. Think like the Big Spike would do in a volleyball game and just nail that ball at them as hard as you possibly can."

Harry nodded, and he reached high in the air with his big, giant arm and beer barrel chest and swung his racquet. He nailed the tennis ball like a rocket ship.

The ball screamed at Doris, who tracked it and returned it to the far-right-hand corner of the court along the sideline. I had watched her eyes, and I knew it was just as a shooter would do in hockey. She had looked for a second, at a spot on our side of the court, where she must have thought she could drop the shot. She must have felt that location was a spot that I would not be able to reach. Just as I would follow the eyes of the shooters, I had watched for years on the ice, I did the same for her eyes. She had tipped her hand, and I had caught it, revealing to me what her strategy was.

I was off in a flash to that spot on the court; I gently tapped the ball with a backhand and watched as it dropped easily over the net for another point for us. I felt really good now; I was loose and gaining confidence. This game was position, speed, and strategy; it was a piece of cake.

Harry was worked up now, and he yelled over the net, "I guess you will need to take it easier on us there, big choppers, because you see, you have just met the famous, long-haired, hippie goalie, twenty-seven, and old Harry, and we are about to wipe those smug smirks off of both of your faces."

The Manginis looked at each other and dug their heels in.

"Bring it!" Walter yelled.

I knew right away that they did not stand a chance. I could feel it.

Harry served another rocket, which Walter returned hard and fast to Harry. I dove to my right and nailed it back before the shot even reached Harry and it dropped in for another point. This was just like playing goal; I just had to stop it from getting behind me or to Harry.

Mr. Hobnobber was now standing up and yelling towards his hired guns, "You should not have brought my daughter into the discussion Walter, you fired him up now! I warned you that he was a professional athlete, he just looks like a hippie weirdo!"

I was sweating, bouncing back and forth across the court. I dove right and left, front to back, chasing down shots. Harry would knock one or two shots back, if I was way out of position, and he would yell instructions to me and insults over at the Manginis.

We were a team, just as we always were, in both sports and in life. We always knew how to back each other up.

I was in a serious flow and it felt really good. Right then and there, I knew we had them. There was no way they could get the ball past us. Serve after serve, with the same result. Harry knocked it over like a missile, they returned it, and I would track it back. Harry had picked up strength, as well as skills in serving as the game went on, and his superior strength was too much for them. Once or twice, he hit it so hard that they could not even see it to return it.

Rose, Tinky, and Mrs. Hobnobber were beside themselves cheering for us. It was a shutout, and in actuality, the Manginis never really stood a chance. They never scored a point, or even won back the serve.

When we scored the final winning point, they were stunned, as was Mr. Hobnobber.

His dream was dead as team Redmond ran out on the court to hug and congratulate us. The Manginis stomped off the court, gathered their gear, and headed off, as Mr. Hobnobber followed behind them in an effort to provide damage control.

"Walter, Doris, please, come back, we have a nice lunch planned and some cocktails. Please! Where are you going?"

Harry bounded over to them and got right up in front of the Manginis.

"Say, thanks a lot for such an enjoyable game. Please send me the number and information for your plastic surgeon, would you? I have this tricky nose here and I sure could use a recommendation."

Needless to say, they left without another word.

Harry turned to Mr. Hobnobber, and told him, "Say, Dad Hobnobber, I would not count on getting a Christmas card, any votes in the next election and a box of chocolates from the Manginis this year." Harry stood there smiling and sweating as he pointed at the Manginis' quick exit.

Mr. Hobnobber stood there and watched as they left. He shook his head and put his hands on his hips.

"I am ashamed of myself to have brought those pretentious people here. You know, they deserved for you two to whip their backsides after the way they acted."

"You should be ashamed, dear William. Their behavior and insults were quite atrocious. I came close to knocking those big, fake, white teeth out of both of their heads myself!" Mrs. Hobnobber clenched her fists, and I knew that if she had a right hook as good as her daughter's, then it would have been a sure trip to the dentist for the Manginis.

We all gathered around Mr. Hobnobber. He spoke softly with an air of repentance in his voice, "That comment about you two boys and your heritage was bad enough, but when they made that comment about our beloved Binky, they got what they deserved."

"They did dear, and you should be very proud of Paul and Harry. They defended our honor," Mrs. Hobnobber was now smiling widely at the two of us.

Mr. Hobnobber looked at us and smiled. He said, "You two men are amazing! You never play a game before, take on two professional players, and shut them out without a point. I am very proud, I could not ask for anything more from my son-in-law, my son, and their friends. I have learned a serious lesson here."

Harry walked over and put his hand on Dad Hobnobber's shoulder. "It is all right there, Senator Hobnobber, we still love you! They crossed the line with twenty-seven. And you just do not do that and get away from it without some type of serious repercussions. I have seen it all of my life. He is the greatest natural athlete that I have ever seen. He is the nicest guy in the world, but if you cross the line, then you will have to deal with it."

Harry put his other arm around Tinky, who was standing next to him.

"You see, Mr. Hobnobber, we are a team. All of us, we always have been, even when we were all apart, scattered around the country, we never stopped rooting for, caring for, and loving each other. Before it was Rose, Binky, twenty-seven, and me. Now we have added Tink-a-roo-ski. Never, ever underestimate, what the right team can do, Mr. Hobnobber, you can take on anything if you all set your mind to it and work together."

Harry took his arms off the shoulders of the two men and he pointed at me with his finger, smiled, and continued with his speech.

"A long time ago, twenty-seven's old man and my old man taught us what the right team could do if you just work together. We built swimming pools in backyards with hand tools, roller-skated forty hours for charities, fought and beat men when we were outnumbered, beat seasoned hockey players on real hockey clubs when we were only teenagers, climbed up mountains to drag down Christmas trees, changed car engines in our driveways with ropes, chains and sheer muscle, and shoveled snow from the main streets, so that we could get to work in blizzards. It was what you did in the neighborhood that we grew up in together. We called it working together, and our folks taught us valuable lessons that have lasted a lifetime. Now, with Paul all hooked up with God and all, we have the ultimate team. No one can stop us! It sort of makes you want to go to church, now, doesn't it?"

Mr. Hobnobber smiled and looked at us. His spirit softened, and he was humbled. That did not happen very often! He motioned for us to all get together in a circle. We put our hands together in the middle, and we clasped them as one.

"You are a very wise man, dear Harry, and I have learned what it means to be a teammate and to join forces together for a just cause and a mission. It is an important lesson in life for all of us, but mostly for me. I love this!" He shouted.

Then we all cheered and yelled together in unison, "Now, that is what I am talking about!"

Never again, did my father-in-law challenge me in a sporting duel of any kind; in fact, he never mentioned it ever again.

We all made our way back to the house, sweaty, smelly, and a little worn out, but in great spirits. It had been, in a roundabout sort of way, a very exhilarating and uplifting morning. I needed to see my beautiful wife, so I headed directly for the kitchen.

I missed her!

The aroma of what she was creating floated throughout the house like some tantalizing aroma from Heaven. I could not place all the smells, but it did bring me back to my childhood and the smells that came out of my mum's kitchen.

I walked in and Binky was in the midst of pots, pans, mixing bowls and a counter full of ingredients as well as recipes and papers. She was standing there with an apron on over top of a tight, form-fitting, blue dress, with her blonde hair flowing down all around her. I stood in the kitchen, just inside the doorway of the kitchen from the dining room, and leaned up on the wall.

I just stood there admiring her and smiling. She was still the most striking woman that I have ever seen.

The rest of the gang followed me into the kitchen. The smells were too much for them too.

I walked over to her and Binky held her hand up in the air. I noticed that Binky was holding a large wooden spoon. Binky had been using the spoon to stir some concoction in a mixing bowl in front of her on the counter.

"Stop right there, twenty-seven, you need a shower, and as much as I would like to kiss or hug you, there is no way you will hug me or come any closer."

I stopped in my tracks and laughed.

"I did not prepare enough food for the Manginis, because I knew that they would not stay for lunch or for dinner. I anticipated that they would lose to Paul and Harry in the tennis match. I had little doubt that it would not take twenty-seven very long at all to get the hang of the game, and their smug remarks most likely set him off into one of his more famous flows. Despite their experience as so-called professional players and instructors, I am quite sure they never ran into anyone quite as strong as Harry could perform while he served the ball. My research and some additional calculations put the potential for his serve, to be upwards of ninety miles per hour or so. Being even worse losers than my dear Father, I am sure they left in a huff."

Binky then took her spoon and continued working and mixing some ingredients rapidly around and around in the mixing bowl as we all gathered around to listen to her.

"They are really, awful, snobbish folks and for such supposedly refined persons, they have appalling attitudes. That does explain why they raised such a dreadful and vulgar son."

She stopped mixing the ingredients and left the spoon in the bowl while she turned to look at all of us now staring at her and listening.

"I had to knock that horrible son of theirs, in the mouth one afternoon at the club a few years back, when he decided to make a lewd remark about the large size of my breasts, and then continued to attempt to take liberties with an exploring hand or two on my posterior, while I walked by to escape him."

Binky quickly shifted from her prim and proper mode into the hidden alter ego of her super strength, adept prowess with her fists and her toughness. She clenched her fists and you could see on her face, the memory of the incident still fresh in her mind. She then reverted to the prim and proper Binky, and went back to vigorously mixing the ingredients in the bowl.

We all stood there amazed at the incredible accuracy of Binky's prediction, results of her research, her deadly right hook, and her long dissertation. I leaned back on the counter and just stared at her. She still took my breath away whenever I looked at her. I thought in my mind, thank you, Lord Jesus for this woman, thank you for how much I love her, and thank you for what I have in this life.

I am indeed a very lucky man.

Binky stopped mixing her ingredients and moved the bowl around on the counter, and she smiled at me.

"How close am I to being correct?" She then leaned in with that famous Binky wide-eyed stare as she awaited my answer.

"Right on, my dear Binky, you are right on."

Harry added, "That was incredible Bink-a-roo-ski, it was dead on!"

"I knew it."

She had cleanly shifted from intense Binky to the prim and proper, coy, shy, happy Binky in mere seconds. She was now elated at her accuracy, wiped her hands on her apron, fluffed her hair, and dashed over to a pile of pastries that Binky had piled up under a towel on the counter.

"I have been on the telephone with Mum all morning and I made these. She told me that these were your favorite treats from the time that you were a little boy. She told me, she could never quite get them correct, as you loved your grandmother's recipe the best. I researched it and tweaked the recipe a bit. Try one please." Binky handed me what was indeed, my favorite snack in the whole world, traditional English lemon tarts in a small, pastry crust.

Everyone gathered in and stared as I took one, smiled, and took a big bite. It was beyond fantastic!

I was instantly and magically transported to standing in my grandmother's little apartment in Paterson, while my sister and I sampled a hot tart out of the oven as she stood, smiled, and called us, her, "little ma'ducks."

Everyone stood and watched while I chewed and swallowed it.

"Heaven, Binky, pure heaven, positively perfect, just like you! Now, I am going to hug and kiss you even if you don't want to."

Binky screamed and laughed as she ran away from me as I made a false start towards her.

"Stop right there, dear husband! You will never even survive to try the Shepherd's Pie for lunch and you will surely meet your demise before the roast dinner with beef and Yorkshire pudding." She then stopped, smiled and held out her arms for me, as I rushed in any way.

"Roo een dee garry dee," Binky said to me as we embraced.

Mr. Hobnobber yelled aloud, "We know, we all love you too, Binky!"

Suddenly everyone was learning Welsh. It was that kind of day.

6

A Lot of Round Pegs in Very Square Holes

Time passed quickly, school had churned on, and in my efforts to overload myself as usual—I had doubled and tripled credits and course work. I had also carried over additional course credits that were accepted from my previous academic efforts, so before I knew it, I had the required credits for graduation with a master's in theology degree. I did not make a big deal about reaching my goal. For one reason, I didn't really have a job lined up! I planned to graduate without a lot of fanfare, but I knew with Harry and the Redmond family always lurking, that would be nearly impossible!

The Lovely Rose was a huge success for Harry, Rose, and Tinky. The place was jammed every night. True to his word, he had a "meet twenty-seven" hockey night that Harry heavily promoted on Long Island and I suspect there were some "ringer" type invitations, sent out to Kansas City, Norfolk, and Albany.

Harry must have wanted to ensure a turnout; he also was worried about my spirit being broken from the spotty job prospects on my horizon. I think he wanted to remind me of the good times that I had on the ice. He flew people in from those locations and paid their way and expenses to make me feel important and boost my spirits. I knew that my wife and my best friends, Rose and Harry, as well as Tinky, knew that deep in my heart, hockey was something that I sorely missed. I think they felt if they could inspire me and bring back old memories, I would start to feel better about the new profession that I had chosen for my career and life path. I know they were all worried about me and that they could sense the apprehension that I had about graduating and not having any solid job on the horizon.

Hockey was difficult to replace in my heart and soul, and I wondered if I was doing the right thing now, by pursuing this crazy idea to become a clergyman, after having such an unusual career before this.

I was quite amazed when so many folks turned out for the special event. Some of them actually wore my old hockey jerseys and seemed to be genuine in recognizing me after all these years. I did recognize the desk clerk from the hotel that I stayed at so long ago in Kansas City, who came all the way to Paterson to meet me once more. That was very genuine, and I made sure that she took many pictures and that she went away very happy. The rest of them may or may have not been setups by that tricky old Harry.

My old man has a saying, "All the actors aren't in Hollywood," but I did greatly enjoy the night, anyway. I had to admit, it brought up some mixed feelings and once or twice, I almost thought about calling up some of my old contacts and asking around if there might be some hockey coaching opportunities on the horizon, but I shelved that idea rather quickly.

All of Harry's other ventures were also rolling along very successfully. It sure seemed as though he had a Midas touch. His Harry Burgers were all over the place, I went into the local Foodworld supermarket and ran into a giant, life-sized, cardboard cutout of Harry in the frozen food aisle. He was there, grinning in full color cardboard in front of me, while holding a Harry Burger in his hands. It was unreal. The welding shop had tons of work and of course, with people like the Manginis out there, the demand for the Annoy-O-Meters was still very huge.

Harry had built an empire, but he remained the same

guy. He drove his old Wagon Bus, helped people whenever he could, and lived in the same rented house over in Manchester. You would never have known that he had become a wealthy and successful man. Through it all, we sensed that he and Rose grew closer and while they did not actually date yet, they had some bond growing all the time that was very hard to put your finger on. Rose was not yet divorced because the process still required a few more weeks, but Binky and I felt that Harry was just waiting for the appropriate time.

Binky left her full-time research job to be her father's campaign manager for his reelection. Having learned his lesson about teams and teammates from the now famous, "Mangini" incident, he proudly announced that he was, "building his team" and he was paying his beloved daughter an outrageous amount of money to ensure her assistance in his bid for reelection.

He, of course, won in a landslide vote!

Binky then decided to find a new position in New Jersey rather than take the train into New York City anymore. I was very happy about that, as we would no longer be going into the city together any way, with school ending for me.

I graduated from seminary and Harry closed The Lovely Rose to the public and despite my wishes for a quiet, low-key time, they threw me a famous humdinger of a Redmond party. The words, quiet and Redmond, just will not mix. As usual, everyone came, even Father Mark, who was now really getting on in the years, but was still getting around.

I will save you the details, but of course, it was the same drill; pictures taken; many tears were shed, people laughed, people hugged, and people cried. It was a great time, and just another notch in the Redmond tradition of the world's greatest shindigs!

Now, it was time to get to work. It was on to my next

step in life. I faced a cold, stark, bleak reality.

I now needed a job.

"You know, Henson. I always knew that it would come down to this. From the day that I first met you in seminary class one day on a tour, and I asked the professors who the long-haired, bearded, hippie guy was, I just knew it."

Bishop Werner Beck Clodhopper Von Houten, shuffled some papers around on his desk, then sat back in his chair, and sighed. He put his glasses on top of his head and looked at me as I sat opposite him across his big, wooden desk in his office.

"I knew that I would have to face the day when I would have to deal with you and your unique situation. I asked the professor that day, and he told me, Henson, Paul John Henson. I made a mental note of that name. I made a mental note because I was not quite sure what it was about you Henson, but I knew you were different, and that our paths would somehow cross someday or at some time."

I continued to stare back at the bishop and I did not say a word.

Bishop Von Houten stared at me and he asked loudly, "Do you know what the professor told me, Henson?"

"No . . . Bishop Von Houten, I do remember the visit, but I was not privy to any discussions, so I would not want to venture into any guessing as to a discussion subject."

Bishop Von Houten frowned at me and answered his own question, "He told me that you were a brilliant student, very tippy top of the class, long hair, and beard, wore rock-and-roll tee shirts, old sneakers, never spoke of the Lord aloud to anyone, and stayed very much within your own world. He told me that you were absolutely brilliant, but you had an unusual career path that had brought you to where you were sitting in the class at that very moment. He told me of your past career as a professional ice hockey player, but he could not really tell what was leading you to a career in the ministry. The trouble was that you did not fit in. You were the round peg in the square hole. Now, here you are in my office, and I have your application here to request ordination. You, my long-haired, hippie friend, are a conundrum that I do not want to deal with."

I shifted uncomfortably in my chair. The tie, and suit that I had on suddenly seemed ten sizes too small. The bishop was about sixty-five years old. He was tall, with a thick head of white hair. He wore a traditional black suit with a white collar, and he seemed to be a very uptight individual. He remarkably reminded me of my father-in-law. It seemed as if the two of them were brothers, or related in some way.

I could not even in my wildest imagination, think that on the face of this good, old Earth there would be two William T. Hobnobbers, but this is, after all, the life of Paul John Henson!

My hockey sense was really on full alert here now. I was in deep trouble. This was not going to be one of those long sought after, "Mr. Bluebird chirping in my ear type days" that was for sure.

"So now, I have all your papers in front of me as you come in here looking for a job, and make no bones about it, this is a job interview, and I hold the keys to your future. Let me see here," the bishop said while he picked up my paperwork. The papers included a resume, essays on my life and ambitions, school transcripts, and an information sheet that I had recently completed as part of the application process. The information sheet had asked me just about every question about me that could have possibly come up, including my shoe size!

He looked at me quickly to gauge my initial reaction, and then back to the papers, and he began to read from them aloud to me as I sat in silence.

"A poor kid who grew up hard on the tough streets of the northern section of Paterson. Your mother is English and your father is a retired machinist. You tug at my heartstrings, Henson. Played hockey on the streets and then on the ice and slowly rose up from an unlikely background to become a professional ice hockey player. Quite a success story if it actually applied to what you want me to believe that you would like to do now."

Ouch! The bishop did not really pull too many punches!

"Now, you are a retired professional ice hockey goaltender, who went to school after an injury ended your career. You missed being called up to the Boston Bears in the big time by one week."

He looked at me and put his glasses back on top of his head and frowned.

"Do you really expect me to consider a retired ice hockey goalie for ordination? There has only ever been one other in the entire Lutheran church, and he renounced his former evil ways before he was ordained."

I started to answer the question, but I stopped in mid-voice when the bishop, while still frowning, held his hand up to indicate for me not to speak.

The bishop seemed to frown an awful lot.

He began speaking once more, and I sat back in the chair and did not say a word.

"Let's see, a sport full of violence, cussing, fist fights, yes, indeed, a wonderful breeding ground for the ministry. Bishops like I am, always scout the local hockey leagues for future ministry candidates."

I faintly remember my father-in-law telling me the same thing a few years back.

"Worked as an electrician and then an electrical project manager for a contracting company."

He looked at me over the top of the papers. I did not react, but sat up straight and true in my chair, with my feet flat on the floor.

"You indeed, held your grades at the highest level, despite a terrible course load to finish ahead of time and graduated number one in your entire seminary graduating class. Number one! Do you realize how difficult that is?"

The bishop stood up with his hands on his desk, leaned over, and he was now screaming at me. I nodded my head in agreement.

"Of course, you do. You did it! I was about fifty or sixty in my class, and now, I am a bishop!" Bishop Von Houten had some whacko tendencies very close in intensity to my father-in-law! He sat back down in his chair, lowered his voice, and continued to read from my papers.

"You speak almost fluent Welsh. Of course, it would be something strange like Welsh, not German, Swedish, or Dutch, or another language that I could actually use in the Lutheran church, but Welsh. Welsh with a hard, New Jersey accent, how productive."

Wow! He was beating me worse than Mr. Hobnobber did after a few strong cocktails!

"Married for six years or so, no children yet, and your wife's name is Binky and your brother-in-law is Tinky. Is this stuff for real Henson, or is this some kind of sad, distorted, fairy tale?"

I shook my head back and forth and managed to say, "No sir, that is all correct." This meeting had doom written all over it.

"Now, I have all kinds of letters of recommendations here. One from some big shot, blowhard, local business owner, named Harry M. Redmond Junior, who just happens to be your best, boyhood buddy, another letter from a retired Catholic priest, who writes a sob story about how God steers you here and there, and he thinks that you have been called from since you were a little boy. A Catholic priest who is vouching for a young man to become a Lutheran pastor! This stuff is unreal Henson, unreal. I wish I were making all of this up. It gets even better, with a big, long, letter full of big words and political nonsense from a New Jersey State Senator and attorney who also happens to be your father-in-law. This is all nice, well and good, but no sponsorship from a local Lutheran church, no ordination committee backing you, no internship, no one in the Lutheran church is going out on a limb for you, son."

As much as he was beating me up, I did have to agree, as this was my fear from the middle of seminary.

Bishop Von Houten had nailed it.

"There is nothing concrete for me to hang my hat on. Do you know why? Because you do not fit in, you are the odd ball out here, you have long hair, a beard, and you listen to Close to The Crevice by the rock band No Way instead of Lutheran hymns. Basically, you are a hippie who thinks he wants to be a Lutheran pastor!"

Bishop Von Houten pointed his finger at me as if he was predicting what I was going to say, and he needed to stop me in my tracks before I said it.

"Now, before you even try it, don't give me that song and dance about Jesus and his apostles having long hair and beards, because it will not work."

His voice grew a little softer, and the tone of his voice changed to a less aggressive delivery.

"Why not rethink your plan Henson and try to give me something to go on? Go home and shave, cut off all of your hair, dress in nice suits, smile, and hold doors open for old ladies, tell them to go in peace, then smile, and kiss some babies. Try to fit in somewhere before you request this ordination. Get in with a church, wear the Lord on your sleeve, pray aloud, quote scripture, and act as if you have a sincere calling to the ministry. With your good looks, all trimmed up, the ladies will be screaming for you to be in the pulpit every Sunday, so they can stare at you and drool. You could preach about lust every week and convert them in droves. The collection plates would be full every week."

He stopped speaking, put his head down, and turned back towards me. I knew he was going to continue with his painful advice and analysis, and he did as he said, "But no, you want to stay the same as you were when you were seventeen, prowling the streets of Paterson! Why?"

The bishop was red-faced and angry with me now, and I could now tell that he had said his piece and that he was finally going to allow me to speak.

I gathered my thoughts and made my first attempt at an answer to his question.

"Because that is not who I am, Bishop Von Houten, I am only who the Lord makes me to be, so I come as I am, rather than be a fraud."

"Oh please, I am not buying that at all, Henson! Why do you even want to serve, Henson? Once more, I ask you . . . why?"

"Because, I know that is what I have been called to do, I need to share what I have been through to teach people how much God cares and how he works in our lives every day. I have a lot of unique life experiences to share."

The bishop stood up from his chair and pushed it out of his way. He then walked to the window in his office and turned his back to me. He was a very intense, and to be honest, a slightly rude, and straightforward individual. He did not say anything at all, for quite a long time and neither did I. He then started to speak with his back still turned to me.

"I have to tell you, Henson . . . the Lutheran Church is a business, just like any other business. I know you do not want to hear that, as you think Jesus himself will come down from Heaven and fill up our collection plates, but that is not how it works. The church has an image, and I have a duty to uphold so that the business of the gospel continues on and on forever. Henson, you seem as if you are a tough person, so I am going to lay it all out here face up on the table, I do not think it is fair to you to mince words at this point. You just do not fit in with that image. I know that is not what you want to accept, Paul, but it is the truth. I just do not feel that you love the church enough to do this job, to fit in, to become what I need to advance the Lutheran Church and lead souls to our Lord. You do not give me anything I need, and without an ordination committee pushing you, I am afraid that I am the only one who can ordain you right now."

He turned back around to face me. I still sat upright in the chair and did not move.

The bishop sat back down in his chair, looked once more at my papers, and he sighed. His eyes were quieter and his voice was calm and low as he spoke, "Yet, I have a young man sitting in front of me who is no doubt brilliant in his studies, diligent, and dedicated. Your background check is clean as a whistle, not even a parking ticket. You are like some kind of old lady or something."

I held back a smile as Harry's description of me came to mind.

"I hear you did not even cheat at that Warship board game when you were a kid. I cheated my older brother all the time at that game. When we played it, we would always end up rolling on the floor punching the living daylights out of each other, until our father broke the battle up. I used to move my ships all over the game board myself. Everyone cheats at that game. You finished schooling in half the time, ahead of all those other students who are sure bets to be ordained by next week and may have half of the brains or life experience that you have, Henson. That is because they fit in. Despite the hair and all, you look like an athlete, not a pastor. You stand tall and strong and are built like a rock. You are very handsome, and my goodness, you almost broke my hand in two when you shook it and I am six feet five and still strong as a bull. You are indeed, an unusual situation, Henson, and I feel bad for you, I really do."

Bishop Von Houten seemed sincere, his tone had changed from his previous aggression, and I sensed just a bit of sympathy for me now.

"I bet you think I am not acting like a man of the cloth and that this is a tough situation, Henson, like I am abusing you and handing you off a really bad deal."

When I heard his words, I felt inspired.

I felt calm and peaceful. I was not yet moving into a flow, but I knew I had the perfect answer to his statement. The feeling had come over me, when he had said that it was a, "really bad deal."

I knew that he had no idea of what a "really bad deal" was, and that he really did not know what had brought me to his office this afternoon.

I smiled, leaned in close over his desk, and told him, "Oh no sir, this is not tough nor is it abusive, you are just telling me the facts that you see from your side of that desk."

Bishop Von Houten frowned at my statement.

"So, you have been in tougher spots, Henson? All that time studying, all that money spent on education and now you are being rejected for a job?"

"This is not tough, sir. This is all just part of God's plans to mold me and make me stronger."

I continued to lean in towards him. I now needed to make my point, "You see, in my opinion, tough is breaking two toes playing goal in a game on a wicked, hard slap shot, and then having them set at a hospital. When you finally limp home that night, the phone rings in your little apartment in some strange place that you now live, and it is the wife of your best buddy in the whole world, telling you how she is sick, and dying in a hospital and the family needs you right away. Then you drive four hours through the night to make it in time to the hospital as you stand next to her deathbed. For six horrible hours, you stand next to your friend and watch his beautiful, vibrant, young wife die in front of your eyes. Tough is dragging your best buddy up a hill following her casket, while you hold him up, because he is now a twisted, sobbing, wreckage of a human soul. Then you carry him back down the hill, holding him up, and supporting him as what seems as if all the tears on Earth and in Heaven rain down upon all of you. All the while, you are asking yourself, why a loving God would take from this world, such a wonderful, fantastic, young woman. Why would she be taken in such pain, in such sorrow, from such a wonderful, young man as my best buddy is?"

I remained calm, but intense, while I still leaned in close over the edge of his desk. My favorite music recording was very accurate today, because I was indeed close to a crevice.

"All of his life, he was seeking that kind of love, that kind of companionship, and then when he finally found what he had been seeking, it was taken from him. The pain was immense, almost beyond description, as they were just starting out in their life together . . . stolen from his arms with all of life ahead of them. Tough, is that all those dreams were now shattered, all those plans were gone, all that love that they shared, all of it lost. Gone forever, from what I always believed was under control of a loving, caring God! Bishop, I came out of this all with the answers that I needed and sought. I came out of that horrid situation with faith, hope, peace, and joy. I did not come out of it despondent, or in despair. I had learned, and now I knew the real reason God allowed it to happen. I was at peace with the explanation, sir. Which was that it all is under God's control, it is part of a plan which we might never understand, and that simple truth is what gave me the strength to go on and the joy, peace, and hope of a lifetime."

I leaned back in my chair now and lowered my voice a little.

"That is tough sir, this is not tough. You see, I may only look like a long-haired, hippie freak, weirdo, but God has already used me as he had planned, if this is part of the plan, then it will be, if it is not, then I will be moved onto whatever the plan is for me. I understand, sir, your situation, but I can tell you only the truth, and who I am, and what I know I can do. I know my abilities, sir, and I know that if you give me a chance, I can make you and the Lord proud of me. I know what to do. I am fearless, I do not back down from anyone, or any challenge, not even bishops who think I am a long-haired weirdo. I solve problems, bishop, I always have, and I always will."

I could tell that Bishop Von Houten was stunned at my very long answer to his question and statements. He was now uncomfortable, where before, he had been confident, and aggressive.

A moment had changed everything.

He had stared intently at me, while I had made my long speech, and during my speech, he had not moved or even said a word. His face showed no emotion at all. He now stared back down at his papers and then he looked up at me.

"You are a powerful speaker, Henson."

He seemed to be thinking as he picked up a paper from the far corner of his desk and he studied it for a few seconds.

"I bet you were one helluva goaltender, Henson. I can picture that in my mind. I never played ice hockey, but I did play an awful lot of football, and I can pick out a great competitor. You must have been something else."

"Thank you, sir. I always tried to do my best."

"You loved playing. Did you not love it, Henson? It is still a huge part of your soul. I can read a man's soul."

"I did, Bishop Von Houten. It was my life during a period when I needed it most."

"I bet you had many tryouts in hockey, Henson. Did you have a lot of tryouts to show coaches what you could do and try to make a team?"

I was not sure where this was leading, but I answered

him factually by saying, "Yes, bishop, many of them."

"I bet you did not fit in then either, let me guess, long hair, beard, rock-and-roll tee shirts, old canvas sneakers, hard New Jersey accent amongst Canadians and New Englanders."

"Yes, that is correct, sir."

"How many times did you fail to make a team, Henson?"

"Never sir, I always made the cut."

"Never? Why, Henson?"

"Because, I knew that I was the best goalie that was out there, and I played fearless, hard, and the best I could every time. I never failed, ever. I always left all I had, every time out on the ice, because that is where I always fit in, no matter what anyone else tried to tell me."

The bishop stared long and hard at me.

"You never failed to make a team ever, Henson?"

"Never, sir."

I could tell that was not the answer that the bishop had wanted to hear.

"You know, Henson, there is something about you, I am not quite sure what it is, but it is an edge, a look in your eye. You have a fire burning deep down somewhere, I am not sure why or what it is for, but there is something about you."

He paused for just one moment and then he continued, "I have a special situation this Sunday, a church with a pastor who is away for an emergency and I have no one to fill in. My roving pastor is already booked, and I could not find a retiree or a pastor from another district to fill in. Therefore, I will have to fill in myself and I will have to miss my golf game. I am willing to give you a tryout Henson, one shot to change my mind, one chance to prove you fit in. I will perform communion and the entire liturgy, and you will handle the sermon. I will warn you, Henson, this congregation is the pits. Snobbish, stuffy, uptight, and wealthy, they dislike everyone. The sad part is that they pretend they all are perfect Christians. It is in an affluent Bergen County town, fancy, wealthy folks a long way from Paterson, so they are sure to stick their noses up to you. One chance, Henson. That is what I am willing to offer. What do you say?"

I had hit pay dirt! It was hard to curtail my excitement as I jumped up out of my chair and cried out, "Thank you! I am your man. I will say it one more time. I never failed in a tryout, sir."

I stood up, stuck out my hand to the bishop, and smiled. He ignored my hand, reached down on his desk, and instead, he held up a piece of paper.

"Here is the address, early service, be there by seven in the morning. I am not going to shake your hand, Henson. I need it to serve communion."

I only smiled and nodded to him. There was not much else to say.

I went straight home and filled Binky in on all the details of the meeting and job interview. She had been waiting patiently at home, and I knew that she was very anxious to hear the outcome of my interview. As we shared some tea together in our kitchen, I explained the entire afternoon and details of my meeting, while Binky listened very closely. While it was not exactly what we both were hoping for, she was, of course, in my corner. I had been knocked down, then stood back up, and had been given a chance.

That was all I or anyone else could ask for. Binky was supportive, loving, and hopeful. She was, after all, Binky Henson and as soon as she heard all the details of my assignment, she immediately was going to head for her books to research the material that I would require to be successful! I stopped her in her tracks, kissed her, and then held her, while I explained that I really felt the need to go have a few beers, relax and have something to eat. It had been quite a meeting, and we both were hungry, so Binky agreed to table her research until later.

We both jumped in the jeep and drove over to The Lovely Rose, where we knew the gang was also anxiously waiting to hear of the results of my job interview.

We all gathered in a quiet table in the back of the restaurant as I related to Harry, Rose, and Tinky, the details of how my meeting went with the bishop, and the details of the "tryout" situation Bishop Von Houten offered me.

Harry was a little upset when he heard the details and he would not sit down. He paced the floor in front of us.

"So, what did you do to this bishop windbag guy that has him gunning for you, twenty-seven?"

"Nothing, nothing at all, Harry. I only met him very briefly one day at school, and that was it. He does not think I have what it takes and that I fit in. He does not like my hair and appearance, but he finally did come around to at least give me a shot."

"There must be something other than that." Harry stopped pacing and put his hands over his head while he was thinking and stared at me. "Did you shake his hand?"

"Well, once yes, but I do not think I broke it."

Harry started pacing once more.

"I mean, this is ridiculous. Of all the honest, trustworthy, and perfect people in the world to be a pastor, you are it. I mean, geez, you have been a victim of Old Lady and Mr. Nice Guy syndrome since you were born! What more can he want?"

Harry stopped pacing once more and faced the table.

"Paul is the only guy I ever met who would not even cheat at playing Warship when we were kids. I even caught Father Mark moving his ships around once when we played a game."

Tinky growled, "I used to cheat all the time, until Binky caught me. Getting socked by her, it was just not worth it."

Harry's emotions were on fire, he rattled on, and on, "I mean geez, after all this, the bum gives you one shot and one shot only. Seems like a raw deal, twenty-seven, it really does."

"Well, Harry, I did not go the traditional route. I have to admit that I came from a very convoluted background to get where I am now. I never had the support of our church, even after Binky and I were married there. They all looked at me as if I was some long-haired stranger. I was the outsider. I could not come up with any internship, it was one rejection after another, and as soon as the decision makers took one look at me as well as my resume . . . they dumped me. Hockey players do not make good ministers, or at least that is the stigma of what everyone thinks!"

Rose looked concerned; she had been sitting silently until now when she said, "Well, that crazy O'Malley did it! However, I guess he did not go into a mainstream denomination, and went the independent route. Twenty-seven, we are all with you. You know that we will all be there, sitting in the congregation and supporting you."

Rose was now smiling at us, and I knew that she was doing her best to root me on and encourage me.

"Now, that I am divorced, I guess I need to think long and hard about where I will attend church. I have only been to a few of your services, but I was very comfortable in the Lutheran church. I would enjoy going more often."

"That will be great, Rose. Maybe someday, I actually will have a church for us to all attend together. Thank you, guys, I know you will be there, and that is very important to Binky and to me too."

It was nice to have the support of all of your friends, but this one was going to be on me. I knew I had to come up with something big or it was over.

Binky spoke up as Harry had a few drinks delivered to our table. While taking a sip of her Martini, (shaken not stirred) she offered what sounded as if it was preliminary research results, "We can always move to another area and Paul could apply for ordination with another district or synod in another location in the country. That would be a last resort, of course, as our wish is to stay here with everyone, or at least close to here."

Harry shook his head back and forth, "No, we don't even want to think about that, I would buy twenty-seven his own church before I would allow that!"

He pulled a chair out and finally sat down next to Rose. I think Harry was more nervous than any of us were.

"Rose is right, of course. We will send in the entire battalion of support troops for this battle. I hope that crabby, old, bishop guy, realizes who he is dealing with here. Youse guys need to know that I even plan to pick up Father Mark and bring him over, collar and all. You know I meant what I said the day that I returned to New Jersey that I owe you so much, Paul, for all you have done for all of us, and I will find a way to make it up to you someday. We will all be there for you, all of us."

I smiled at him and reached across the table as all of us put our hands together in the middle of the table and held them for a while. Harry was very upset, and he was serious about this turn of events for me.

I thanked them all once more for being such wonderful friends, "Thank you. I know I have all of your support."

Tinky had not said anything right away, but I could tell that he was thinking. Eventually, he did ask the question that I had in the back of my own mind since I had left the meeting with Bishop Von Houten.

"So, my famous brother-in-law, what subject do you have planned for this sermon?"

"I don't have anything right now, Tinky. Nothing, complete writer's block. I have two days to come up with the sermon of a lifetime, and right now, the idea well is dry."

Everyone at the table seemed a little shocked that I did not have a plan or even an idea for the sermon. You would have thought that I would have been working on this for quite a long time, in preparation and anticipation for this moment. However, the truth was, I had not even given it one thought until this afternoon. I did not really know why, I guess I thought that I could just whip a great sermon up spontaneously.

"The sermon cannot be a rehash of one of our adventures, or some crazy situation that happened to us that I can adapt to the gospel. It has to be different. It will come to me, I just have to settle in, pray, and be confident. I have been in tough spots before and I always do well under pressure, so I just have to dig in, pull my goalie mask down, tighten the straps on my pads, and do the best I can. Of course, having everyone there will be a huge morale boost for me, but this is going to be a tough crowd, and I only have one shot."

Harry had brought some more beers and drinks over for all of us and I took a sip of my beer while I explained, "You know it is kind of ironic that the bishop feels my background is of no help to me in this new career at all, but in many ways, there are so many parallels. Big pressure, crowds, being a leader, in many ways he is wrong. When I am up there on Sunday in the pulpit, if I turn around there is no one in back of me, it is just like standing in the net."

Binky looked at me and winked. That wink always knocked me over with its allure. She leaned back, now displaying confidence in her husband while she said, "You just need to get in the flow twenty-seven, and I know something will come along and you will get there. I know you will."

One day and night went by and no sermon came to me. Nothing at all, not a single word. I sat at my little desk in our dining room and stared at a blank piece of paper for hours. I started and stopped, wrote a few words and crossed them out. I thought how this was bad because my mind was completely empty. Binky was busy; she had taken a day off her work and had been out with Rose all day. She had left me alone in my thoughts, so it was not as if I was distracted at all.

Saturday morning came, and Binky cooked up a large breakfast for us. She was really working hard to keep me upbeat and in focus, but I could tell that she was not relaxed. Binky was worried about tomorrow. Strangely, I was not worried at all; I just had no ideas for my sermon. It was a major problem, but I was treating it as if it was nothing at all, as though I knew I would make a save at the last instant. It was strange, even to me.

"Thank you for a fantastic breakfast. I have come up with a little opening note and a framework in my mind for this sermon. I am going to my desk and I am going to write this." Binky looked elated at the news, but the truth was that I only had a very vague idea in my head.

"Oh good, Paul, that is great news! I plan to go out with Rose. She wanted to pick up a special dress for tomorrow. I will leave you to your thoughts and peace and quiet."

I smiled and then stopped to think. Deep in my mind, Binky going out for the day had set off a red flag in my head, but I ignored it for just a moment.

"That is great, do you think Rose is trying to impress or put some moves on Harry?"

Binky gave me her patented fast up and down head nod to indicate that was indeed the case. For some reason, something in my mind clicked. I had ignored it a moment ago, but now it was back. I gently reached for Binky, pulled her close to me, and hugged her. I just felt her warmth and held her for a long time.

I whispered in her ear, "Please stay. Does Rose need you to help her, or can you stay home today?"

Binky pulled away, and she looked at me as if she was surprised at my request.

"Of course, I will stay, but I do not want you to be bothered as I go around the house doing my weekend things."

"No, no, no, please do, I need you to do all the normal things that you do." I did not really know why, but I wanted Binky to stay home. I gave her a kiss on her forehead and walked over to the desk. She came over and hugged me around my neck.

"Are you sure?"

"I am sure. I need you around today, Binky."

"Then I will stay." Binky went over to the phone to call Rose.

For some reason, when Binky said that she was leaving for the day, it made me lose all of my thoughts. She had to stay, and I did not know exactly why.

Despite the current haziness in my mind, I offered, "I am happy to hear that Rose is trying to impress Harry, I really am."

Binky smiled and nodded as she dialed the phone.

I then sat down at the desk, took my pencil, and wrote exactly four words down on my pad, and then I stopped. Nothing more came, other than those four lonely words.

Binky went about her day, cleaning, dusting, and doing laundry and other than a time or two, to make some general chit chat; she left me at the desk. Nothing came to mind, just a blank, empty mind, as I just stared at a paper, while writing down . . . nothing. I went for a quick run, to see if that would shake out some ideas, I showered, put on some No Way music on the record player, I ate a sandwich for lunch with Binky and still nothing. I picked up my Bible, read different chapters, and passages, hoping for some type of inspiration.

Still empty, nothing but a deep void in my brain.

I could tell that my wife was concerned because I saw her glance at the paper a few times and she saw that it was empty of any writing. Still, she remained upbeat, and she did not mention anything about it.

It was around three in the afternoon, and now I found myself pacing the bottom floor of our home. I went from the living room to the dining room and back and forth. I could not stand it anymore. I thought I would go find my wife and see what she was doing. I found her in our bedroom sitting on the bed with her back propped up with pillows on the headboard. She was intently watching the television with a pad and pencil on her lap. She smiled at me as I flopped down on the bed next to her and sighed.

"I have nothing, Binky. I have not come up with a bloomin' thing."

I slid over and looked at her pad.

"Something for your research?"

Binky nodded, while still watching the show. I looked at the television screen and it seemed to be some kind of boring documentary on some type of construction project. I did not want to be rude and interrupt her show, so I waited for a break in the program and looked over at her.

"A little unusual show for you to enjoy, Binky. What is it all about?" I leaned back on the bed pillow next to her as she lit up with a huge smile.

"Oh no, it is fascinating, I have been taking notes, it may be something that dear Father could help with. It is about a group of disabled persons who came together to work on a large construction project, and despite their disabilities, they were a great success. People never believed that they could do it, but these amazing people built this apartment house by themselves, people with no arms, some with no legs or hands, deaf, dumb, and blind people, all working as a team. It is fascinating. By hard work and teamwork, they proved everyone wrong who doubted them just because of how they looked, or because they were disabled. The folks came from all over to accomplish the mission and build the building. They wired it up, plumbed it, ran the excavation vehicles. It is really a wonderful story."

Binky wiggled over closer to me and showed me some of her notes that she had written on the pad.

"The one sub-story was really wonderful about a Jewish

gentleman who was wheelchair bound with no legs. He had lost them in World War Two. He was a civil engineer from the Bronx, New York, who became best friends during the project, with a heavy equipment operator who only had one arm, and who had an excavating business and lived in Kansas. The Jewish man was saying how his friend had accepted him just the way he was and how they became such wonderful friends. It is very touching to see folks from all types of religions, and walks of life, who came together for such a cause. Now, they have built and finished the apartment house. They use it only for the housing of disabled people, so it has a very special meaning to everyone."

I jumped up from the bed and startled poor, Binky. She dropped her pad and pencil at my strange reaction.

"That's it!"

I reached over, pushed her gently down, and gave her one of the longest, most passionate kisses that I ever had given her.

"I knew that I needed you around! I knew that God, for some reason, was telling me to have you stay here today. You were the key! I will be back, in about one hour. I will have this written in one hour."

I was jumping around now, babbling in front of my wife.

"We will go to dinner tonight, you and me, a date night, just us!"

Poor Binky was thinking that I had lost my mind. I ran out into the hallway, stopped, and I returned.

"I promise that I will be back to pick up where we left off."

She now smiled and looked at me. "After that kiss, you better." Binky jumped up from the bed and she ran after me a little.

"Paul, are you feeling it? Are you in the flow? Please tell me that there is not even a marble that could roll by you and make it into the net behind you. That is what you would always say when you were at the top of your game, twenty-seven!" She stopped at the top of the top of the stairs, stared in with the Binky stare, and waited for my answer.

"Oh yeah, yeah, yeah, dear Binky. I am feeling it. I have this game in the bag. Not even a marble, dear Binky!"

She smiled, gave me the rapid Binky head nod, and went back into our bedroom.

I sat back in front of my desk and the flow was strong. I wrote feverishly, and in less than one hour, I had completed the sermon. It came so quickly and so strongly that I knew that I did not even need to write it down. I would be able to remember it word-for-word tomorrow. It was coming from deep within me, there was no doubt that it was coming from within my soul. I felt just as I did when I was under a scoring attack in the net. I was back there in my mind, diving around, making saves, tracking the shooter's eyes, feeling the flow of the game. It felt fantastic. It was what I had been missing until now, and it was that passion for my new career that I needed to discover. I wrote "Amen" on the end of the paper and put my pencil down.

I smiled and bowed my head for a quick prayer.

"They did not stand a chance, not even a marble got by me," I said to myself.

I then headed back upstairs. I was hoping that the show Binky was watching was over by now; if it was not, then I had a feeling she would have to catch the end of it on a repeat.

Sunday arrived, and it was bright and clear. It was now late summer in 1987. I really loved to see the fall of the year and cold weather coming.

Oh, how I love that cold weather!

I dressed in a black suit, white shirt, black tie and a black jacket. I also packed in a little bag, my canvas sneakers, an old No Way tee shirt, and a pair of black dungarees. Binky looked at me a little strangely when she saw my bag's contents, but she did not say a word. My hair was long, but trimmed, my beard was trimmed, and Binky pronounced me good to go. She, of course, looked fabulous, in a fantastic, black dress with a delicate, gold Luther's rose cross around her neck, which I had given her for her birthday a year or so ago.

I put on a wooden cross on a braided lanyard that Binky had given me when I graduated seminary. She said it fit me because I reminded her of a rugged cross.

I was confident, I felt better than any other day ever, as if I was getting in the net to face the best shooters. I knew I was at the top of my game today. I could just feel the flow was ready to take over when I needed it.

I folded up my sermon and put it in my jacket pocket.

We arrived at the church early and met everyone outside. All the gang had gathered around me on the front lawn of the church to wish me luck. My parents, my sister and her family, Ronzo, Linny, Harry, and Rose, my in-laws, and Tinky were all there. One by one, they came by, shook my hand, (except for Mr. Hobnobber) hugged me, and wished me all the best. I knew I had to go right down the list of my entire emotional support team, as they gathered in line to wish me well. Rose and Tinky stood hand-in-hand, and both of them had tears rolling down their cheeks. I guess the both of them were having an emotional contest this morning.

"Well, Paul, the odds are highly stacked against you, my boy, but I have learned not to bet against you."

"Thank you, Dad Hobnobber . . . for the support."

"I would not thank me. My research indicates that you do not have even a remote shot of success, and as you know, I only have the facts to go on."

"I understand that, yes, I do, Dad."

"You might as well get in there and go down in a

blazing pillar of smoke and fire. After wasting all that time and money on a useless education, it is worth one shot."

I always enjoyed these heartfelt chats with my father-in-law. They were such confidence boosters.

Mrs. Hobnobber, of course, lip-locked my face right there in front of the church and she squeezed me until my eyeballs almost burst out of my head.

I was thrilled, as well as shocked, when Mr. Redmond, Patty, and the Big Spike arrived!

All the way from Florida and California on only three days of notice! That was really a huge, unexpected surprise. Let me tell you, it was extremely touching. There were no better friends on the entire face of the Earth than these folks were. All of our years together had only increased my heartfelt admiration for them. From climbing mountains to cut down Christmas trees, to dancing on the patio at 20 John Street, to Mr. Bug on their front porch, they were the best.

After greeting them all, Mr. Redmond spoke up, "Harry sounded the alarm, Paul. He told us you were in trouble and when we heard that, we knew that we all had to come. After all that, you have done for us. The least we can do is come and cheer you on."

I was deeply touched, but I was starting to hope that my support group did not think I was playing in a hockey game and I needed actual cheers for motivation. I would not put anything past them, and that was my fear.

The Big Spike spoke up now, "Hey Paul, if by chance, the church has a summer picnic, I can always come over and pick that crabapple bishop off with a power volleyball serve. That will even the score, you know."

"Thank you, George, I will certainly keep that in mind, but let's see how this all turns out first." George nodded and gave me a little fist pump. I was hoping Patty did not catch me for one of her famous jealousy inducing hugs, but she remained under control.

Next in line was Father Mark. He was dressed in his black priest's attire with his collar on and a gold crucifix hung around his neck. The old priest wobbled a bit and Harry steadied him as he reached over and patted me on the back. He reached down and took the wooden cross from around my neck, kissed it, and then put it back over my head. He then took a little piece of paper and put it in my jacket pocket. His hands were shaking and trembling as he struggled to place it inside of my pocket.

"Just before you get in the pulpit, Paul, please read it. God be with you, Paul."

"And also, with you, Father Mark," I said, as we shook hands.

Harry grabbed me and spun me around. He gave me one of his famous bear hugs. "Go get them, twenty-seven! If you had pads on, I would tap them! I know how badly you want this and we are all with you. Together forever, twenty-seven, we are all together forever."

"I appreciate that, Harry." He and I embraced once more, and I was ready. My mum and sister and her gang came over along with the old man and they all had tears in their eyes. I hugged them all and kissed my mother. I turned to the entire group and then looked straight at Rose and my wife, smiled and told them, "This will go along quite well everyone, believe it and it will happen."

Binky hugged me, kissed me, and whispered in my ear how much she loved me.

With the entire dramatic family and friend scene behind me, I now focused on my mission. I turned, waved to them all, went in the rear door of the church, and looked for the pastor's study. I had arrived earlier than Bishop Von Houten, which I was glad for, as I quickly changed into my No Way tee shirt, my black dungarees, and exchanged my dress shoes for my sneakers. Then, I put on a long pastor's robe and my wooden cross over the top of it, so no one could tell what I was wearing underneath it. I picked out a robe with a high neckline so you could not see that I did not have a necktie on. I took the papers with my sermon on it and stuck it in my robe pocket. I then took the paper that Father Mark had given me and stuck it in the front pocket of my pants.

I just finished with my preparation when the door to the study opened and the bishop came in. He nodded at me.

"Good morning, Henson."

"Good morning, sir."

"Decided to stay with the hair, beard, and hippie look I see."

"Yes sir, no reason to change now."

"Nervous, Henson?"

"No, I am not, sir, I never really get nervous. I played many big hockey games in difficult situations in front of big crowds. I have no real emotions as far as nerves go."

Bishop Von Houten looked at me and shook his head. He pulled a black robe over his head, sat down behind the desk, pulled out a small Bible, and opened it up on the desk in the study. He read a passage or two, then closed it and bowed his head to pray.

When he had finished, he looked up and asked me, "Have you prayed today, Henson?"

"Yes sir, many times, earlier when I went for my early morning run and workout. I prayed a lot when I played goal. When you make your living standing in front of hockey pucks, you tend to pray an awful lot, sir."

The bishop did not answer me, but he stood up, looked at me, and nodded his head, almost as if he suddenly understood that prayer could have been a big factor in my past success.

"This boorish bunch will take one look at you and reject you, Henson. They will see that hair and beard and then moan and groan, so please be ready for it. Follow my lead. I will nod to you when I need you to interject. I am not going to ask if you need prompting on the order of worship. After we met the other day, I spoke on the telephone with one of your professors, who assured me that you could perform an entire service for any season of the church year from memory. Can you really do a Tenebrae service from memory?"

"Yes sir, I can."

"Honestly, I really would rather not be here, Henson. I have long since given up conducting worship services, and I had a nice golf game planned with a rabbi friend of mine."

"I see, sir. Well, maybe we can get through this rather quickly and get you out there on the course any way. I will try not to hold us up by speaking too long in the pulpit, sir."

The bishop looked at me, he frowned a bit and said, "You really are fearless, Henson. You are a man of your word, that is for sure. Ready?"

"I am, sir."

We stepped out of the pastor's study and walked down the main hallway together towards the sanctuary. I could see the choir gathering as well as the acolytes and the crucifer. The church organist had started the opening bars of the processional hymn. I hoped that the congregation did not notice my old sneakers under my robe! The bishop and I gathered into the line behind the entrance processional and he looked over at me and noticed the wooden cross around my neck.

"Nice cross there, Henson . . . very rugged looking. It fits you."

"Thank you. My wife gave it to me."

We walked in and followed the choir into the front of the church. I passed my family and friends and I could hear the occasional gasps of horror that the bishop had warned me about as the congregation spotted the long-haired, hippie, want-to-be pastor, who had just invaded their church. I just smiled, and it did not bother me in the least.

Where, oh where, is O'Malley now that I needed him?

The bishop performed the opening announcements and introduced me as Mr. Henson, his assistant for today and that I was a recent graduate from seminary. I announced the opening hymn, and we were under way. As I stood there in front of the congregation, I could see the intense stares and demeaning looks from the parishioners. The bishop was right, I had not made the cut, and all I was getting were many, "What is he doing here?" type looks.

I looked at my wife, who was beaming at me. I winked at her; she smiled and gave me a little wave. She was next to my mum, the old man and my sister and her family. Then in the same row, it was the entire Redmond gang, along with Harry and Rose, Father Mark, my in-laws, and Tinky.

It was quite the cheering section. We sat down while the lay leader made some comments to the congregation and of course, the bishop received a very honorable and warm greeting from the entire congregation.

I then received a very brief mention, and the lay leader even stumbled over my name, as he looked at the bulletin a number of times and still got it wrong. I heard a couple of cheers and comments from my support group, but luckily, they all remained fairly restrained. Bishop Von Houten looked over at me, frowned, and then he spotted my old sneakers that had peeked out from under my robe.

He shook his head. "I see it took you a long time to polish up your shoes for a nice, mirror shine today there, Henson."

"I need them for my message today, sir," I whispered back.

"I think I will come to regret this day, Henson. I really do." The service progressed and the moment of truth rapidly approached as the sermon was right around the corner. The church bulletin did not have any information other than my sermon was listed as simply, "today's message." There had not been enough time to provide a title because I had not completed it in time.

Bishop Von Houten addressed the congregation after the choir finished their hymn of the day, "Today's message from the pulpit, will be provided by a recent graduate of seminary, Mr. Paul John Henson."

I could hear the moans and groans of the congregation because they were disappointed that the bishop was bailing on the message and they were stuck with the hippie bum.

I clearly heard an older man in one of the front rows say to his wife, "Is that the hairy guy? How do they allow a guy who looks like that to preach?"

I smiled and chuckled a little. This is just like a hockey game it really is. I even have doubting fans in the stands!

The bishop walked back to the pastor's bench, and he whispered to me, "You are on Henson, keep my golf game in mind, will you?"

It was time to strap on the pads, smooth the ice in front of the net and get in there. I was not nervous at all, but I had to admit the flow had not yet kicked in, but I knew it would. I stood up and started to walk to the pulpit. I reached down into my robe pocket, took out my sermon papers, then reached, and pulled out from the pocket of my pants, the paper that Father Mark had handed me. As he instructed me to do, I read it just before I stepped into the pulpit.

"Blue skies are all around you now, Paul, blue skies with rays of sunshine peeking out amongst the clouds."

I smiled and looked at Father Mark, who made the sign of the cross to me. I stepped up into the pulpit, crossed myself, and looked at my wife, family, and friends.

The whispers, moans and groans continued from the now disappointed group of parishioners.

I raised my hands and arms up in a blessing and bowed my head, "Grace, and peace to you from our Lord and

Savior Jesus Christ. Amen."

Now it was time, all that preparation, all that studying, all the efforts, and it all came down to this. I guess it really had to be this way. For me it seemed like it had to be unusual or it was just not worth it.

"Croeso. Bore Da."

Mum and Binky instantly answered, as well as to my utter shock, a man in the far back pews of the sanctuary, "Good day to you as well."

I had spoken welcome and good day in Welsh and apparently, there was an older gentleman who also spoke the language in attendance.

I looked at him and he perked up, smiled, and now studied me from afar.

I thought . . . okay, here goes. Now, for a real shocker. I took off my wooden cross and carefully laid it on the pulpit desk. I reached over my head and pulled off my robe, revealing my No Way tee shirt and attire underneath. I neatly folded the robe and placed it inside the pulpit.

I heard the gasps; shocks and surprise ripple through the sanctuary like a tidal wave. I heard the bishop exhale loudly and cough behind me. I could only imagine what his face looked like!

I did not allow them any time to recover, as I started to speak, "I am sure if we all examine our hearts and minds today, we can admit that there was a time when we felt that we just did not fit in. Maybe, it was in sports when you were younger and never picked to participate on a team, until some coach or manager assigned you to a group. Maybe, it was for a job interview when the hiring person told you that you did not obtain the position because you just were not the right fit for the job. I am sure that no matter how successful, or confident you are right now, while sitting in these pews, that at one time or another you were an outcast, a person who was told you are too short, or too tall, not smart enough, or too fast, or just not quite fast enough."

I needed to exaggerate a point here, so I made sure that I had pulled all of my hair out from behind my head, and that it had not stuck inside of my tee shirt. I wanted it to be all hanging in front of me and hanging down straight and long. I reached behind me, grabbed the lengths of hair, and made sure that it was straight and obvious.

I continued with my sermon, "Maybe, they told you that you did not have enough hair, or that you had too much hair, or that you sang poorly or your accent was different or strange. Many people are told they are too round, or too skinny, or their names sounded funny or were different. I know a lot of folks who have been sent away crushed in spirit, after being told they just flat out did not have what it took to get a job done, without even being given a fair chance, because of what they looked like or what they may have believed in. All of us have faced that moment at times in our lives. I know I have. People generally take one look at me and judge me as being different, or non-conforming. They judge me instantly, upon how I look or how I speak, before they even know anything about me, my family, who I really am, or how I arrived at where I am at this very moment in time."

The congregation leaned in now and I could tell that I had made a large majority of them uncomfortable with my statements. I saw some frowns disappear from some faces of the congregation.

"I am proud to say that my grandfather was the toughest and most fearless man that I have ever met. I know that some of you will find it hard to believe by where I am standing right now, and by how I look, but I played professional ice hockey for many years. I faced, on the hockey rink, many men who were tough guys. In fact, brutally tough, who would laugh as their own teeth tumbled out of their mouths and blood poured out of their wounds. They would skate to the player's bench and allow the trainer to stitch up a cut with the same needle and thread that he used to repair socks and then get right back out there for another shift of play. They thought nothing about going toe-to-toe, in some all-out fistfight with an opposing player, for the sake of possession of a little, black, piece of rubber that glides on the ice. No matter how tough and rough the toughest of them were, none of them could hold a candle to my grandfather. He was born in rural England on the edge of Sherwood Forest. He lived to be almost one hundred years old, and I am confident that he would have, at the age of ninety, been able to demolish the toughest of those tough, guy hockey players that I knew. You see, when he was a little boy in England, he was playing on a garden wall, he tumbled off it, and broke his right shoulder and arm very badly. A horse doctor, or what we would perhaps consider, to be a veterinarian, operated on him with primitive surgery in the rural countryside. He was the only doctor around, and he had little or no painkillers to use during the operation. The pain must have been beyond horrific."

I noticed just a few of the parishioners nod their heads in agreement with my description of the pain. At least some of them were listening! In seminary, when performing our practice sermons, the instructors gave us all types of tips for breaking up your sermon, making eye contact and throwing a few lighthearted moments into your words to keep the congregation interested in the message. I sure made a lot of eye contact because most of the text I knew from memory. I did not really require my notes. As for the rest of those tips, I threw them into the wind. I was going to hit this hard, no jokes, or levity here, I needed to win this congregation over, as well as the bishop with a knockout sermon, so I continued right back into the message with only a very short pause between thoughts.

"As a result of the operation, he kept his arm, but it never grew much past the length of where it was when he was a ten-year-old boy. He had a little short arm that hung on his side, looking weak and useless. However, weak and useless, was not what my grandfather was. Folks classified my grandfather as a disabled person, but my grandfather sure did not consider himself disabled. His left arm grew stronger than ten men's arms would be. His chest became huge and powerful and was the size of a beer barrel. As is the case so often, with a person with a severe disability, the other parts of your body grow stronger to compensate for the weakness. When the big war broke out in England, he tried to join the military, but the military doctors rejected him due to his arm. So instead, he joined the Queen's Forestry Service, and amazed people by climbing trees with one arm to clear the forests for the RAF to hide planes from the enemy, in and amongst the trees. Very often, he and his fellow workers would be hanging in the trees, when the enemy planes would come overhead and strife the forest with gunfire, trying hard to kill the defenseless tree climbers. Every once in a while, the enemy would hit pay dirt and kill one of the tree climbers. Still, day after day, they continued with their work, they were not afraid. He told me stories of how during their time of working in the forests, people of all ages, races, religions, and beliefs who were rejected from the military for one reason or another, joined together to defend their homeland. He told me how no one really cared how tall they were, or how they spoke, what they looked like, or what was wrong with them. They all bonded together to fight for what they believed in. No one ever mentioned his little arm. They accepted him as God had formed him."

I noticed some of the congregation looking around at each other out of the corners of their eyes. I had now struck a little chord with people here and there.

"After the war was over, my grandfather became a tradesman. He was trained how to repair silk and lace making machines in England and in Wales. When the mills closed up in England after the war, due to the rebuilding of the damage from the horrific attacks and bombing, he needed to find work and decided to come across the pond for work. When he came to America, he brought his young family to Paterson, New Jersey, the silk city where the lace trades and silk trades of his homeland now thrived. Despite his knowledge of these same machines, he was rejected for jobs, as the decision makers for these positions, told him that he spoke strangely, and besides, he could never lift with his one arm, the parts to repair the machines that made silk and lace in the city of Paterson where I grew up."

I was feeling it now and as I spoke, I demonstrated lifting up a heavy part in the air with my arm. Now, I did not have a big, thick arm like my grandfather had, but I was strong and in great shape! My short sleeve tee shirt revealed some authentic muscles in my arms. Looking back on the scene, I think it added just an element of realism to my message!

"My grandfather amazed them, by lifting up very heavy machine parts with one arm. Parts that usually required multiple men to lift. They gave him the jobs. He also amazed people by reciting from memory, Bible passages, and great works of literature that he had learned in England by reading. He spoke word for word from memory, passage after passage, of the classics like Dickens, Shakespeare, Kipling, even though he never went past, what we would have considered here in the states, an eighth-grade education. He spoke fluent King's English and some Welsh despite, once more, his supposed lack of education."

I spotted the Welsh speaking gentleman, smiled a little smile in his pew, he now knew why I was able to speak his language.

"When he encountered a man in a public house one afternoon that had, as he would say, one, two, three, too many beers and decided to taunt him about the size of his arm, he picked the rude man up by his neck with his good arm until the man begged for mercy. I am sure that man never poked fun at a disabled person again for the rest of his life! When I was a little boy, he told me in his strongest English accent, never allow people to judge you, Paulie boy, for how you look, or how you talk, or how you walk. Make them judge you for what you do, how you treat others, and for the person whom you really are. Never change for anyone, Paulie boy. Always be who you are. If they think you are different, or you do not fit in, then prove them wrong, for you will be the better man for it. God made all of us the way he decided to make us. So be who you are and always be proud of it. God does not hand out tickets to Heaven so that only the perfect people will be allowed in."

I stopped for a moment and breathed deeply, I needed to gather my own emotions, as I felt very strongly in my heart about what I was about to convey.

"My grandfather was brave and fearless, he was proud of who he was, where he came from, and what he looked like. My grandfather was a really cool guy, and I loved him. Short, little arm and all. He was a great man."

There were now very few dry eyes in the formally hardened and standoffish congregation. I could hear tissues opening and noses honking and blowing. I looked over at my wife and she sat there smiling at me with tears running down her cheeks. Harry held Father Mark's hand on one side and Rose's hand with his other, while Rose did her best to control her sobs. The old man was holding my poor mum as she dabbed her eyes with a tissue.

"You see, I believe that with God there are no tickets to Heaven, or boundaries, or rules and regulations, as to if you are qualified or not. It really doesn't matter who you are, or what you look like, or how long or short your arms are in order for you to achieve acceptance to the Kingdom.

No matter where you came from, how much money you earn, how long your hair is, or what music you enjoy, God always moves the obstacles so that we all belong. It is the greatest comfort of all to know, that even if you are an outcast, or feel that you never quite fit in, you do always fit in with God. All God asks, is for the faith to make it happen, and pledge to him every day . . . Lord, I will do my best today to live as you would want me to. You will then be justified by your faith alone."

I waved my arms around above my head and pointed out the grandeur of the inside of the sanctuary.

"You see, it really is so simple, all of this, all of these hymns, choirs, worship services, fantastic buildings, candles, and all the other things all around us here today. All of it actually, comes down to a very simple thing. It comes down to a sort of blind faith that leads us to follow a light, a guide, a way, and a purpose. A faith that comes from within each of us. It is no different from love, kindness, joy, and hope. Faith in the Holy Trinity is really not very different at all. To understand and to have it make sense, all each one of us has to do, is believe it, and it will happen."

I folded my notes together and said, "Amen."

I reached back down and grabbed my robe from the pulpit shelf. I pulled off the wooden cross and put my robe back on. I pulled all my hair out from under it and then put the cross back over my neck.

Turning my back to the congregation to leave the pulpit, I suddenly heard Harry yell out at the top of his lungs, "I love this! Now that's what I am talking about, Lord!" I quickly turned around and smiled, as Harry was standing up with both of his arms in the air, fist pumping the air!

Father Mark was tugging at Harry for assistance in climbing to his feet. Harry helped Father Mark up out of the pew as he feebly wobbled to his feet. The old priest turned and faced the congregation. He held his arms up over his head and bowed his head in a blessing.

Father Mark then spoke as loudly and clearly as he did when he was a younger man, "And all of God's people said!"

The entire congregation now stood up. Even I could not really believe that this was happening, but a Lutheran congregation was following the direction of a Catholic priest!

Everyone including Bishop Von Houten was now standing as one, and they all shouted in unison in answer to Father Mark's request, "AMEN!"

A moment had changed everything once more!

My cheering section had come through; I knew they would never let me down!

After the congregation recovered, and they all sat back down in the pews, I looked at Bishop Von Houten and he was not reacting to the next step in the order of worship. He had taken out a handkerchief and was dabbing his eyes, so I stepped out in front of the congregation and spoke.

"Please stand as we join in singing our closing hymn, number 560, 'A Mighty Fortress is Our God.'"

I walked back to the side of Bishop Von Houten, as the organ started to play the introduction to the song, and the congregation, as well as the choir, stood up.

"Thank you, Henson . . . I was distracted."

"No trouble, sir."

We stood next to one another as the song began.

"Henson . . . I need you to pretend that we are singing. I want to make that golf game so I will ask you some questions now."

"I understand, sir."

"I just need yes or no answers here, Henson, no big, long, explanations. Thirty-five years of watching a congregation has provided me with a special insight, Henson. The big guy who stood up and started the disruption. He is your best buddy who lost his wife that you told me about."

"Yes sir, he is."

"I see his spirit is now renewed because of your efforts and influence. He has almost recovered from his profound grief and he is now a successful businessman."

"Yes, Bishop Von Houten."

"The very pretty, obviously Catholic, short, gal next to him staring at him with goo-goo eyes is in love with your buddy, but they are not together as yet. That gal loves you too, Henson. Please keep that in mind. Those two are about to look to you for guidance. You do know that, don't you, Henson?"

"I will keep it all in mind. Yes, I do think that will be coming up shortly, sir."

"The tall, blonde, gorgeous, woman with the black dress smiling at you who spoke Welsh and is all teary eyed is your wife, Binky."

"Yes, sir."

"The old priest who stood up with the blessing is the same priest who wrote me the weepy-eyed letter and the tall, bald, guy shaking everyone's hand and kissing the baby in back of him, is the state senator who happens to be your father-in-law."

"Correct."

"The beautiful woman next to him is your mother-in-law and the little, short, red-haired guy next to her, growling like a criminal while he sings, is your brother-in-law."

"Correct, sir."

"The pretty, older woman who spoke Welsh is your mother and the man next to her, is your father."

"Yes, sir."

"Then we have your sister and her family, you can tell your sister, you, and her look alike. I think your hair is just a little longer than hers is, though. The rest of the people in that pew are your entire best friend's family. The family has all known you forever."

"Yes sir, that is correct again."

"Do you realize how much these people all love and care about you, Henson? I was closely studying them during the sermon."

"I do, sir."

"You are the leader of them all, somehow Henson, you have been a pastor all of this time, you just did not realize it, nor do you require some stupid-ass official papers to declare it. You are the spirit who has nurtured them and guided them all, even to some extent, the old priest."

"I am not quite sure of that sir, but if you say so, I will defer to your experience over mine."

"I was mostly wrong about you, Henson, but I was right about one thing."

"What is that, sir?"

"There is something unusual about you, I still cannot put my finger on it, but someday, I will. There is even another person here in the congregation today who speaks Welsh. I mean, what are the odds of that? Do you not find that really strange, Henson?"

"I imagine it is a little strange sir, but strange things always have happened around me. There is no question about that." The song was now entering into the final verse, and we both looked up at the congregation.

"Smile a little Henson, pretend you know what verse we are on. I will ordain you next Sunday at my own home church in Newark. The early morning service, Henson. That way, I may be able to make my golf date and a beer drinking appointment with the rabbi in the afternoon."

"Thank you, sir, I really appreciate it."

"I suppose this same group will be there, and most likely will cause the same, or a similar disruption."

"I think that is a very safe bet, Bishop Von Houten."

The bishop frowned a little, and then realizing the congregation may have seen it, he forced a fake smile.

"You know, Henson. Your record is still perfect. You still have never blown a tryout."

"I did mention, Bishop Von Houten, that I always leave it all out there on the ice."

The song had just about ended and it was time for the final blessing and dismissal.

"Henson, you finish it up, will you, and remember when you shake these people's hands as they leave and want to greet you, please don't hurt any of them. Watch out for the young, pretty, brunette haired gal in the third pew on your left. She has stars in her eyes as she stares at you. She does not realize you are married and that your wife is here."

"I will do that, sir."

I moved out to the front of the sanctuary and raised my arms in a blessing.

"May the Lord bless you and keep you, may the Lord shine his countenance upon you, and give you peace."

I smiled at my pew of support and said, "Amen. Go in peace and serve the Lord."

I think my pew of support was the first to answer, "Thanks be to God!"

7

An Impossible Assignment

The ordination ceremony was very formal and surprisingly short, in fact, it was actually over within a matter of minutes. I had my cheering section in attendance, and as had been predicted, they did jump in there for a celebration moment or two. Bishop Von Houten prepared for the worse situation though, so he happily conceded that it was not as bad as he had anticipated.

Harry closed The Lovely Rose to the public, and we had one of our famous parties there. I was not going to argue with him about this party, not this time; it would not have mattered, anyway! It was another one of our magical times.

I had to admit that I was very surprised at my wife and her reaction to my new employment. She was beside herself with joy and excitement, and exuberance at my success with landing the new position. Looking back, I think Binky was very upset and stressed that after all of our hard work, I would not be able to fulfill my dream and it would all have been for naught. I was concerned initially that she would not want to be the wife of a minister, but I was indeed very wrong. I did not wear it often, but she loved when I wore my black suit and white collar. She said it was the most handsome that I ever looked, and she said it drove her wild!

Binky was always happy in our life and marriage, but now it seemed as though she had also moved to being very content and settled. I think she was happy to have a direction and a sense of comfort. She loved her job; it was close to our house, and the position paid Binky a very nice wage for her hard work. I have to say that Binky was really the perfect wife and companion. Our love grew every day, and it was a very special love.

I still worked out and kept up with my training as much as I could, but now, I felt some more little aches and pains here and there. My old hockey wounds stayed close to me for reminders of a now long gone way of life.

Harry was well, very typical Harry. He also was thrilled at my new career, as he gradually shifted his gears and introduced me now as, "His best buddy, hippie, pastor who used to be the famous, hippie, goalie twenty-seven."

Harry had to describe everything!

Harry, Rose, and Tinky, still worked together every day at the restaurant and club, but I could not really sense where Rose and Harry were in their relationship. In fact, other than a business relationship as well as a friendship, I am not sure Rose and Harry had a relationship. I was fairly certain of where Rose's heart was, but Harry kept his distance, and I could not quite get a feel for where he was in all of this. I knew one day, he would come to me, and I needed to be ready when he finally did.

I worked directly for Bishop Von Houten in his Newark, New Jersey offices, and that is where I reported for work every day. He kept me occupied with busy work and had me substitute for some vacationing pastors here and there, but the first months or so of my employment had been relatively uneventful.

I sat outside my boss's office, early one Monday in the spring of 1988. He had asked me to report there early in the morning and I waited for him to arrive.

"Come in Henson, will you? Booorrra daw or whatever it is that you say in the morning, Henson."

The bishop unlocked his door, and we stepped into his office together.

"Good day to you also, sir."

"Sit down, Henson, I had a good weekend, no one bothered me so I enjoyed it."

I sat down in the guest chair in front of his desk.

"That is good, sir. It is always nice to relax."

"I had a nice visit in my office here with your father-in-law, while you were out in the field goofing off last Friday. He stopped by to give me a political push for some things he felt he could help the church with this year. I like him a lot, Henson . . . he . . . and I think alike."

"I do notice quite a few similarities in you and him, sir, yes, I really do."

Bishop Von Houten smiled at me. It was obvious that he enjoyed the suggestion that he was the same congenial and easygoing type person as good, old, Dad Hobnobber. I suddenly felt that this was not going to be one of those long sought after, "Mr. Bluebird chirping in my ear type days" either.

"He gave me this stress reliever gizmo as a gift, and I have to say that it is fantastic."

The bishop opened his desk drawer, and of course, he pulled out the latest version of the famous, Annoy-O-Meter, while he got up from his desk. He removed a picture from the wall behind his desk of him winning some kind of big golfing trophy and proudly placed the meter on the nail in place of the picture. He then reached down, filled out the little paper tag and slipped it into the slot, while setting the needle to eighty percent.

I did not even have to look at it to know that my name was on the tag.

Bishop Von Houten smiled and put his hands on his hips in deep satisfaction as he gazed at his new prize. As he stared at it, he said to me, "I love this thing, that buddy of yours is a genius, pure genius." He then sat back down in his big leather chair. "I love this picture! This is a picture of me winning the golf tournament two years ago, at the club, when I finally beat that pesky, Rabbi Goldberg."

I glanced over to view a picture displaying Bishop Von Houten with a wide smile, standing on the golf greens, with a large silver trophy in his hands.

I felt a compliment was in order, so I delivered one for his ego, "It is a great picture, bishop, it really is. You should find a new spot for it in your office."

"I will, Henson. Maybe you can take care of that for me, maybe over there, next to the picture of me winning the bishop of the year award."

He pointed to a spot on the wall on the right side of his desk. I nodded that I agreed with his selection. Covering all of the bishop's walls were awards, plaques, or pictures of him winning something, or an actual presentation to Bishop Von Houten of some type of trophy, award, or certificate.

"Henson, you will notice that I put your name on my new little gizmo there because to be honest, you are annoying the living stuffing out of me."

"I am sorry sir, what have I done wrong?"

"Nothing! That is the trouble, Henson. I just am growing tired of sending you out on these substitution assignments."

I was puzzled, so I dared to ask, "But . . . isn't that my job for now?

Bishop Von Houten frowned at me for asking, so I guess I had, of course, blown it by not reading his mind.

"I know what your job is, Henson, I am your boss! The trouble is, after you substitute at a church on a Sunday, I am then haunted and brow beaten by the congregation's leaders on Monday morning, with endless phone calls and messages. You see, it is the same thing over and over Henson, after you show up with all those wonderful sermons and long flowing hair. The leaders of the churches call me up and harass me to kick out their own pastor and have you assume the pastoral duties. I still get calls from the church that you preached at in your tryout, inquiring if they can install you as their regular pastor. They all drive me nuts for days and days, and I have to avoid their phone calls and messages. I am too busy for all of this unneeded clamoring for your services, Henson! Way too busy! I missed two golf dates with Rabbi Goldberg last week alone! Besides that, now all the pastors in our district are getting gun shy to have you around the district. I spoke with Pastor Stueben last week about a day he wanted off, and the first thing he asked me was if the long-haired, hippie, guy was coming or not. I need you to preach a few lousy sermons on purpose to take the pressure off, will you, Henson?"

"I will work on a couple of bombs today, sir, to keep on standby."

My boss smiled at me, because it was clear that he enjoyed my answer that time.

"Good! Perfect! Be sure to make them real snoozers, will you Henson, no more of those heartfelt, clearly worded, biblical sermons, make them mixed up, deep and convoluted!"

"I can do that, Bishop Von Houten. That should be a piece of cake."

"I wish we could put a fake plastic nose on you also and one of those bald-headed plastic caps. Even the old battle axes love all that hair, big muscles, and facial mess you have going on there. Those old biddies and all the young hot ones have bouncing hormones and are all hot and bothered over you. Do you ever preach on or read from any of the Old Testament Henson?"

"Sure, on occasion, Bishop Von Houten."

"Well, stay away from the Song of Solomon, Henson. If you read any of those words then, you better have an ambulance stand by to resuscitate some of those old crows and have your track shoes on to run away from the younger ones!"

"I will take that advice, sir."

"It is a shame. You are so annoying and appealing, Henson. You bring in a fortune in the collection plates wherever you preach! The extra money turns my accounting upside down, and I have more work to do on the budget projections, and my financial books!"

"I am sorry about that sir, I will wear some robes that are really big on me, and try my best to look and act a little goofy."

"Good idea! I now have a plan Henson to resolve this situation. I came up with it over the weekend while talking with Rabbi Goldberg about you. Therefore, like any good conniving boss, I came up with a brilliant plan to get rid of you for a while, Henson. I am sending you into exile to a church out in Morris County. This church has been a thorn in my backside for two or three years now, so it is a nice, impossible, task for you to fail at, so I can yell at you about it. After this, I should be able to give you a really poor work review, and keep you at your presently low salary for a while so my budget looks good. All these requests for your service, and glowing praise about your performance, will undoubtedly put the ridiculous idea in your head of some kind of huge, salary increase. My plan will work to provide a massive failure on your record, and that should keep any silly notions of a salary increase out of your mind."

"It sounds great, Bishop Von Houten. I am looking forward to that."

Bishop Von Houten stood up from his chair and walked over to where he mounted his prized Annoy-O-Meter on the wall. He stared at it, smiled, and then turned back towards me to provide some more details of my "impossible" assignment.

"The congregation is down to about thirty members or so, they have not had a regular pastor in about four years, and are just about out of funds. I think there, may be two or three board or even a few charter members left there now, we support them financially, and they are a huge hit on my budget. The building and the little parsonage both require complete renovation and overhaul; it is really a mess, Henson. The roof leaks, they have buckets in the sanctuary to catch the rain, the heat only works occasionally, so they freeze and burst pipes all the time. Last month, they blew out all the lights in the sanctuary with some kind of major electrical trouble. I tell you, Henson, the place is one-step away from a bulldozer. They do not need a pastor. They need a wrecking ball."

"Sounds like the perfect spot for me to start off at, sir, it really does."

The bishop smiled broadly, as he clearly was enjoying the fruition of his plan.

"The church had a mountain of trouble that contributed to the decline, including some old guard members who are, or were, real sticks in the mud. I do not have time to recap all of the history, but the main trouble is that the State of New Jersey cut right through in front of the church about ten years ago, with the interstate highway. The state had promised to provide access with a little ramp and roadway to the church, but then they never came through. The only way to get to the church is to get off the highway, wind along about ten miles of country roads, and enter the property through the back way. It is a major pain in the neck, so people just gave up. There is a brand-new Lutheran church about ten miles away or so, and it is right on a main drag, so people grew tired of this old church, crabby members, and the confusing road."

"I see, bishop. That does sound as if it was a bad break."

"Well, it was, but I have no time for all that weepy eyed stuff. I will send you out there to ride it into the final phase before we can close it and move what is left of the members over to a real church. That is, it, Henson, wrap all that hair up and get out of here."

Bishop Von Houten waved with his right hand at me in

a motion for me to get up and leave. He then reached for a paper on his desk as I stood up from my chair.

"Here is the name, address, and information you need, get yourself out there as soon as you can, and see what you can do. There is a telephone number for a maintenance man there at the church. He will be your contact, Henson. The guy has been there for years, the poor fellow. He can let you in and tour you around the wreckage."

I reached out to shake the bishop's hand, and said, "Thank you, Bishop Von Houten."

"No way, Henson, I am leaving early today to play golf and I need my hand to kick Goldberg all over the course. Besides, someday, I will wipe that eternal optimism off your face, Henson. I think one look at this place will do it!"

I thanked the bishop once more, cleaned a few things out of my desk, returned to Von Houten's office with a hammer and a picture hook to hang his picture up for him, and headed out of the district office to find my jeep. I looked down at the paper and saw the name of the church. "Reunion Lutheran Church, Hibernian, New Jersey." I put the jeep in gear and headed for Broad Street. I wondered what I had gotten myself into this time.

I drove straight home and changed into my usual casual attire of a No Way tee shirt, black dungarees and my faithful canvas sneakers. I then called Binky at work and told her the latest news.

"Oh, Paul, that is wonderful news! Your own church!"

My wife was very excited.

"But what do you mean that it is only until they close down the church? I did not even realize that such a thing could happen to a church. I will check into that right away with some research and see how that may be avoided."

I chuckled, as I knew the wheels of my wife's research-oriented mind were spinning, so I explained a little to her, "The church has been struggling for years, something about being isolated from access due to some sort of road construction, a bunch of uncooperative, old time, members and now it is down to only a few remaining members. We have to go out and check it all out Binky, can you scoot out of the office this afternoon or are you jammed up?"

"I am already heading for the door. I have wrapped everything up for the day and I can make up the hours another day. I will be waiting at the curb in front of the building."

I had called the number for the maintenance man that Bishop Von Houten had given me, but I only received a tape machine, so I left a message in hope that he would be there to let us in. I picked Binky up, and she immediately took the map and began to study it in order to guide me in. Binky's excitement was very contagious at this point. I did not want her to be bitterly disappointed, so once more, I warned her with all the information that Bishop Von Houten had provided me. I told her again about the condition of the facility as well as the longer-term plan for the eventual closing down of the church.

Nothing deterred Binky, or her enthusiasm, and she was a chatterbox during the entire ride up to Morris County. I could tell she was very anxious to see what the church was like.

In the spirit of the moment, I left out explaining to Binky the part where the bishop had exiled me to this assignment in hopes of my imminent failure.

"Oh, I know what that cantankerous old boss of yours told you, but you are a problem solver and I know that you will figure out a solution to the declining condition of the church," my wife proudly proclaimed, as she smiled and stared out the window of the jeep.

I loved her for many things, but I think I was most proud of her support and confidence in me. But from the description of the situation that I had received from the bishop, it sounded like an impossible task. I sometimes felt that I did not deserve her rather high opinion of me since the victories in my new career had been very limited and not overly impressive, but my wife nonetheless was quite thrilled.

She was indeed a breathtaking woman. I think she had grown even more beautiful in the last year. She seemed very content with the future as well as the events occurring in our life together. I watched her out of the corner of my eye as we rolled up Route 80 towards Rockaway from Paterson on this clear, early spring day. Her long, blonde hair was tumbling around her shoulders and her clear, blue eyes focused upon the landscape as it passed by her window. I was impressed by the calm look on her face. It was as if she did not have any doubts that her husband was going to succeed.

"Turn at this exit, twenty-seven," Binky instructed me as we rolled off an exit ramp. "There it is, back there, can you see it?" Binky was pointing to a church, nestled in a small wooded setting about one hundred feet, or so off the ramp. I worked hard at keeping my eye on the road, while I also tried to catch a glimpse of the church, but there was not too much to see as we continued down the ramp.

"Oh my, I see what the bishop meant now. The ramp and highway cut off the road that used to lead to the church. There is no way to get to it directly."

My wife then picked up the little map as well as the directions that Bishop Von Houten had given me. She guided me in with a left turn here, a right turn there, straight down this road for a few miles, and soon we were wandering through a residential area of homes.

"This is indeed, unfortunate twenty-seven, as there is no way to get there without all of this driving."

After what seemed like an awful lot of turns and many miles of going nowhere, with Binky guiding me in, we finally came to a turnaround. We noticed a small dirt road in the curb in the middle of the turnaround. There at the base of the dirt road, we spotted an old, weathered, and barely readable wooden sign cut into an arrow shape that someone had nailed on a tree. The sign was simply marked with, "Reunion L.C." in faded black paint.

"Turn up this road here by the sign," Binky was pointing up at the tree.

I pulled the jeep up the road, passed one older home on the right side and another home on the left side of the dirt road, and sure enough, it led us to a parking lot with the church sanctuary right in front of us. To the right of that was a large building that seemed to be a fellowship or education hall. Set off to the side, all alone, was a small house set on a little hill behind the other two buildings. It was a lovely, idyllic setting, full of natural beauty, a sprawling landscape framed by tall trees, and fantastic views of the horizon to the east and to the west. The tragedy of it was right away, very apparent to us both. To hide such a beautiful property away from the world seemed like a major injustice. The property truly did have inconvenient if not nearly impossible access that made it a driving adventure to even find out how to get here.

We pulled the jeep up into the lot and parked it close to the back of the church sanctuary.

"This is wonderful, Paul. It is so beautiful here!" Binky said while she stepped out of the jeep as I stepped out of the driver's side. She was right. It was similar to a little, natural park tucked away and hidden from the world amongst the tall trees and natural landscape.

"It sure is Binky, what a view there over to the west."

We looked out past the buildings and observed that the rear door of the church faced directly into the western sky. From how high we were, it was a clear, wide-open shot to the horizon. I grabbed Binky's hand, and we walked together towards the church. The only other vehicle in the lot was an old pickup truck that we were hoping belonged to the maintenance man and he was somewhere on the property.

"We do not have any money, so whatever you are interested in selling me, I am not buying anything!" We heard a voice shouting behind us from the other end of the parking lot near a side door of the larger building. We turned and saw a tall, lanky man with a thick, black beard striding across the lot towards us. We stopped and waited for him.

"I am sure you are selling something! Let me guess, toilet paper, hand cleaner or some kind of light bulbs that last for twenty years without ever burning out! I have an important guest coming shortly and I do not have any time for a sales pitch, from some long-haired, hippie, guy peddling stuff, so beat it! Will you?"

The tall man finally reached us and he stopped in his tracks about three feet in front of us. He took off his hat and stared at the two of us. He was a light-skinned black man, who looked to be in his early fifties or so. In addition to his black beard, he had short hair with just some touches of grey along the sides and edges. He was dressed in work clothes and a light jacket.

He frowned at me, and spoke, "I must admit that it is unusual to see such a gorgeous woman selling things, so forgive me for saying that she would do a lot better without having you come along. I still would not buy anything, even from you, young lady, because the church really does not have any money, so goodbye!"

He put his hat back on his head, spun around quickly, and he started to walk abruptly away.

I smiled, laughed at his protective nature and impatience. I then decided to have a bit of fun with him.

I shouted out to his back, "So, this important guest that you are expecting, sir, would not happen to be a chap named Paul Henson, would it?"

The man stopped in his retreat, turned around and looked back at us.

"Why yes, that is right, Reverend Paul John Henson,

how would you know?" his voice trailed off and his face turned red. He suddenly had a look of horror on his face. "Oh wow. I am so very sorry! Are you really, Reverend Henson? It is just that, you do not look, well, you do not look like a minister. I am really sorry, sir. I am always very careful about strangers that come around here. We are so isolated."

The poor man was obviously embarrassed at his error.

"Please don't worry about it. Everyone I meet at first seems to have a very similar reaction. Let me guess that I look like a professional ice hockey goaltender?"

"No, that would be even a farther reach of the truth than you resembling a minister, I see you have a great sense of humor." The tall man was smiling, and he laughed.

"Nice to meet you. I am Paul John Henson, and this is my wife, Binky Henson."

The man took his hat off and held it in his hand as he smiled and shook our hands. "I am really sorry, Reverend Henson, it is just that you do not look like, well, to be honest . . . like I expected. It is nice to meet you both, I am Dave Sharp, and I maintain all of the property."

He turned to Binky, and he was still very embarrassed.

"I am very sorry, Mrs. Henson, for the gorgeous comment, I did not realize, of course, who you were. That is not a very nice thing to say to the wife of a minister, or in fact, any man's wife. It makes me seem like some kind of womanizer or something."

It was obvious that Mr. Sharp was a very kind and humble man who was quite sincere in his approach and apology.

Binky smiled at him and said, "No need to apologize, Mr. Sharp, I actually appreciate the compliment from such a humble gentleman."

"She is gorgeous, isn't she, Mr. Sharp? I see that you are a man who calls it as he sees it!" I decided to loosen up the moment and reassure him, so I patted him on the back.

"Say, let's take a look around here and see what we have going on."

The three of us walked towards the sanctuary as Dave Sharp explained, "I have to be very honest. It is not a very good or pleasant situation to look at Reverend Henson."

"Please call me Paul, Mr. Sharp."

He stopped walking and looked at me.

"Okay. Please call me Dave, but I need to address your position, so can I call you, Pastor Paul?"

I remembered how pleasant that sounded when Rose first called me that title a while back. That sounded good, so I said, "Sure that will work, Dave."

"I have been here for more than twenty-five years, in fact, this very day, it is exactly twenty-seven years."

Binky squeezed my hand, and I felt that cold shiver that every once in a while, go up and down my spine ever since the day I met Sky Blu. On occasion, these things just happen to me; it is part of the great mysteries of my life.

"Did you say twenty-seven years, Dave?"

"Why yes, Pastor Paul, that is a long time isn't it?" Dave was looking at Binky and me, and he must have noticed the shocked look on our faces. He asked, "Are you, both all right?"

We both recovered ourselves, I saw Binky smiling and her bright blue eyes sparkled as she answered Dave, "That is a long time. We are fine, Dave. My husband and I are just very happy to be here."

"Well, okay, but when you take a look around here, you may get back in that jeep and take off as quickly as you can."

Dave opened the door to the sanctuary and revealed a typical, dark, oak trimmed, Lutheran architecture interior, with a low altar, in front of rows of about seventy-five pews on each side. The narthex was at the rear of the church, with two side doors off the center of the sanctuary. The sanctuary had a high roof, trimmed out in impressive oak slats that carried straight up to a high peak. The altar had areas on each side of it for the choirs, and an organ off to the side on a small, flat perch. Above the altar was a flat roof that projected out as if there could be a bell tower mounted directly above the structure.

Binky had stopped in the center of the sanctuary, and she was looking around in wonder, as she said, "It is wonderful. I love how the roof goes up like that, how unique a design!"

It was a dated structure, but it was apparent that upon the original conception, design, and construction of the church, that it was quite an impressive piece of architecture. Once the awe of the majestic, original design was over, and you started to focus on the lack of maintenance, then you realized the building had some major repair issues pending that required immediate attention.

"I do the best I can, but only when Bishop Von Houten gives me money to fix something. I do not have to tell you that does not happen very often! This is a fantastic sanctuary, let me tell you how wonderful it was years ago! The design is something special, but now it is so sad. Everything is falling apart right in front of my eyes. We have four or five roof leaks along the edges and one at the top."

Dave kicked his foot at four or five buckets sitting on the floor that captured the runoff, testing them to see if they had any water in them. Dave then began to explain the condition of the church in detail.

"The main sanctuary lights all blew out here two weeks ago. It looks like a big problem in the main electrical panel that I cannot repair. Our carpet is a mess. I clean it, but it is shot. The carpet is paper thin in spots. The wood all needs polishing, we need paint, the heat works sometimes, and then it cuts off with no real reason. It cut off in the winter in the middle of the night. Then the plumbing froze, and it burst a bunch of pipes. It was an awful mess over all of that side of the building. The bishop would not approve any money for the repairs, so I just cut off that section of the building. Now, we have no restrooms over there."

Dave pointed in a corner of the building towards a small hallway. He was now becoming quite melancholy, and I could tell that this man loved this property like his own. He had a passion for it, and he was very upset by what had happened to what he perceived to be his life's work.

Dave sat down on the back of a pew in the rear of the church and sighed. He looked around and his face showed an element of despair.

"I do not want anyone to think that I have not been doing my job around here, it is just without any money or supplies, it is an impossible task to maintain such a large facility. I fix what I can, keep it clean, cut the grass, and stay busy. Sometimes, I fix things with donated materials or used things, you know, things that I find free or I am able to barter for. I wish you both could have seen this place before it all went downhill. It was spectacular."

Dave looked around at the inside of the sanctuary as he continued to speak, "I hang in here, because I love this place, I am a member as well as an employee. I was married here, my kids both had their baptisms here, and they all went through confirmation classes here. It was a church full of pride, joy, and the gospel message was loud and clear at Reunion Lutheran Church."

His eyes filled with tears and his voice cracked with emotion.

"Then, the highway went through and cut off the road to the church."

He turned and pointed out towards the front of the sanctuary.

"You can still see it on the other side of the highway. The state never did provide the access road they told the church board they would. You know, it is about fifty feet, a lousy, fifty feet of road and they would not do it. I would be dishonest to say that it was all about the access road. We also had some issues with our leadership, both from the pulpit, and with a handful of nasty and stubborn members that are still here. They do not help with anything, but just hang around to complain and rise up to cause trouble once in a while. After all of that, and the highway coming through, it all went downhill from there."

"Dave, I understand, I know a little about maintaining buildings and no one is going to say that you were not doing your job here." I put my hand on his shoulder to show him some support.

He smiled a halfhearted smile and took a deep breath, "Thank you, but it has been a terrible three or four years, Pastor Paul. We have not had a full-time pastor for years now. We might have ten or fifteen members at the most, who come to a worship service on a regular basis. There is no Sunday school, no organist, no choir, and we only have substitute pastors on rare occasions. Some weeks, we just conduct services the best we can on our own with our elders, when the bishop does not send anyone. We only have two elders left and they cannot even serve communion, so we often do not even administer sacraments at our services. It is so sad. It has almost regressed to being pitiful, to be honest with the both of you. We have to use a tape recorder to play the hymns during the worship service."

Binky looked at me and I could see in her eyes the sympathy she was feeling for poor Mr. Sharp.

"They cut my hours down to twenty a week and I now report to the bishop. I know that you also share the same fun that I do, working directly for ole Von Houten! Luckily, Mrs. Sharp works or we would be in a very difficult financial situation."

"How are the conditions of the other buildings on the campus?"

"Not good, pastor, about the same really. The parsonage is a great house. It still has great bones and style. I love that little house. It used to be so nice. It needs a roof now, painting and updating, but it is still a great place. No pastor has lived there for years now . . . it is such a shame. It is really very cozy and quaint, just tucked up on that little hill on the side of the property. At one time, it had a young family living there, with kids running all around the yard. It all seems like such a long, lost, time now."

Dave was very upset now, and you could see how much that the church meant to him in his life, both spiritually and in his work. His eyes filled with tears again and he hid his face from my wife and me.

"I have prayed for something to change, or someone to come along and help us. However, I never receive an answer to my prayers. All I wish for is for this wonderful place to be restored back to what it was back then. It was so vibrant, growing, and a holy place where you could see the influence it had in people's lives." Dave walked towards the rear doors on the west side of the church and opened them up.

Binky and I followed him as we listened. You could not help but feel the man's pain.

He took a deep breath and sighed. His eyes were wide as he was thinking of another time and place.

"You need to see this place in the fall of the year, when the leaves are changing. It is so breathtaking, Pastor Henson, and Mrs. Henson, especially out to the west that you can see the hand of God in the trees and in the sky."

Binky and I smiled at how strong Dave's faith was.

He turned back and closed the doors.

"I have to admit how surprised that I was to hear your message on the telephone tape, not that I mean any offense, but I am actually very surprised that the bishop sent you here. I can see that you are young, just starting out, and he feels we are just about down for the count now anyway, so

I guess he sent you here to close us down. With him, it is all about the money that is all it is about, Pastor Paul."

Mr. Dave Sharp was a very smart man.

"I need to show you this. It is the most troublesome of all the repairs for me."

He waved for us to follow him to the center of the sanctuary, which we did. He then pointed straight up to where the roof went up in a dramatic rise to the peak of the building. Binky and I followed him to a spot where there sat a large bucket sitting in the middle of the floor, and we both looked up.

While he pointed, Dave explained, "It is hard to see without any lights in here, but this water leak has gone on so long, it has rusted that one large steel support truss way at the top there."

Dave continued to point up towards the roof as Binky and I strained to see what he was indicating to us.

"I received one proposal for the repair, to fix it and weld it. It was shocking because they wanted about fifteen thousand dollars to repair it. No way, could I get that kind of money from Von Houten. I have a tough enough time getting him to fork over twenty dollars."

Binky looked up. When she saw how high it was, and what a difficult situation it was, she simply shook her head and said, "Oh my, that does seem like an awful spot to get into for the repairs, Dave. It is so high!"

"Mrs. Henson, I am afraid for the structural support of the roof. This is very serious if I cannot get it welded."

I was looking up, studying the steel beam when I felt it suddenly come over me. When I heard Dave say, "If I cannot get it welded" and he was speaking of the repairs, it came over me like a sudden rush of adrenaline. It was the same flow that came over me in the final minute of a game, and I was holding a shutout in my back pocket. It was a stronger flow than I had felt in years and years. It was even stronger than when that special idea for a sermon came upon me.

There I was in my mind, in my Long Island Roosters uniform, standing in front of the pipes. The crowd was going crazy, and the stands packed with screaming fans. I could hear the skates on the ice, and the knock of the puck on the wooden blades. I heard the shouts of instructions from my defensemen in front of me, and I felt my eyes watching the opponent's faces for clues as to where the next pass or shot was going. I was standing there once more in front of the net, sweat dripping off the end of my goalie mask like a river, all of my muscles were loose, I was bent over in a crouch following the puck as it traveled around the ice in front of me, there was no way I could ever let in a goal.

I was unbeatable. Not even a marble could roll by me.

My mind brought me back to the church, and I almost fell over because the flow was so strong. This moment had changed everything in such a way that I had never experienced before.

It was very clear to me now . . . why God had led us here. I knew why I had played hockey at such a high level. I also knew why I was injured and never reached the big league. I knew why I always reverted in my mind back to my time in the net, how I faced and approached the game and all of its challenges. It was because my fate now was for God to use me in another fashion. My time had come, I had learned how to face challenges in the net, in life, and now, I was ready for God's plan to use those skills for the greater good of the Kingdom.

I smiled and reached for my wife's hand and I felt a calm peace come over me.

Binky looked puzzled until she saw my face, and she took my hand while she said, "I see that the flow came over you, didn't it? You know what to do now, don't you?"

I smiled at my wife. Binky knew what had happened.

I looked at Dave and I could see that he was studying

my face.

I needed to share my flow, so I stated, "Dave, I think it is all going to be just fine, all of this is going to work out just fine." I reached out for his hand and I motioned for us all to gather around each other. He seemed puzzled, but he took my hand and with his other hand, he took Binky's hand. In our little circle, we bowed our heads. I did not pray aloud, but I focused on the flow, and what it was steering me towards in my mind.

I finished and said, "Show me the road trouble. I need to see that location now. Please, Dave, I need to see the issue with the access road."

Poor Dave must have thought I had lost my mind. As much as Binky trusted my instincts, I think my poor wife may also have shared some of his same doubts.

He led Binky and me to the side door and out to the front of the church facing the highway. Dave pointed out, showed us all the details of the road situation, and explained it in great detail.

I remained confident, even after seeing the trouble from a closer view.

"Dave, today we plan and relax, because with God there is always a plan. Tomorrow, we begin to restore Reunion Lutheran Church to full glory. I know in your heart that you were not expecting a long-haired, hippie for a pastor, and that you were disappointed. You see, God steers me where God requires me to go, God always has, and God always will. I have faith, so I go along with all of the plans. Often, it is not exactly what I would have wanted or desired, but who am I to argue. The best news is that I come with a team, not only do you get me, but you also get a team. My lovely wife here you have already met, but there are a few more and you will meet them all. Some are here, and some are saints with us in Heaven, their individual glory shining down on us all, steering us, loving us, and supporting us, through all of these trials and tribulations."

Dave seemed uncomfortable, and a little puzzled, but Binky was now in the same flow as I was. She was beaming at me, her beauty shining around her like a beacon.

"I know I do not look the part, but at one time I was an electrician, and I also know a little about heating and cooling. Tomorrow, I will get to work on those lights, the broken pipes, the heat that goes on and off, and all the other things that you need repaired. You see, I just tie all of this hair up, grab my tools, and get to work. I have a friend, no, let me rephrase that, I have a brother who is the best welder in the entire world, and I have a feeling we can get that beam taken care of. Another part of our team plays a mean church organ and I know a gal who sings so clear it is as if she is an angel." I smiled at Dave, as he seemed to relax a little more.

"Her husband is also an electrician, and I know that with one phone call, he will be here with me, dragging his tools and voltmeters, with him. I promise you here and now, Dave, that you will not need that tape recorder this Sunday, you will have a choir, and you will have an organist."

Dave smiled and the look in his eyes changed from cloudy to clear. It was as he was having a great burden lifted off his shoulders. I pulled Binky close to me and I put my arm around her shoulders.

"The best part of all is what came to me as I stared at that access road that never was built. You see, this gorgeous lady works hard every four or so years, to reelect a particular New Jersey state senator that despite his hard-core approach has a heart of gold. I know that he can have the fifty feet of road taken care of in no time flat, in fact, since this is a reelection year, I suspect you will see paving trucks out there by next week."

"Oh, twenty-seven, I never thought of that, I will start on the research that will be required, first thing in the morning. Dear Father, will be thrilled! That is why you were in the flow because it all came to you. You really are the smartest person in the entire world."

Dave was flabbergasted and I could tell he did not know what we were talking about or what to say.

He finally asked Binky, "Did you say, twenty-seven?"

I put my arm around his shoulders, "She sure did Dave, it is a long story, but the part I was kidding about when we first met, about me being a professional, ice hockey goaltender was actually true. I wore the number twenty-seven as a uniform number for years and years. My number is more than a nickname—it is an alternate identity."

"Really? Hockey player, pastor, electrician, heating repairman, wow, you really run the gamut. You sure are different, Pastor Paul. I am not quite sure what it is about you, but I know that whatever it is, I am with you!"

His face brightened as though something suddenly came to him. "Hey, your number twenty-seven is the same as the number of years I have worked here as of today! My goodness, I can see that God has answered my prayers. I see what you meant pastor when you said that God sends you where he feels he needs you. I wondered why you and Mrs. Henson were so startled when I mentioned the years of service I have here."

He looked at us both and shook his head.

"You both are very special people. I can see that now."

I smiled, thanked him, and we shook hands.

"Wow, strong handshake!"

"I will be back early tomorrow with my tools, until then, grace and peace."

Binky went up to him and gave him a kiss on the cheek. She smiled at him and simply said, "Thank you, Mr. Dave Sharp, for all you have done here."

Poor Dave's eyes became teary once more and you could see how touched he was. We waved goodbye, and we headed for the jeep.

Mr. Dave Sharp was in my former world of hockey, and now in promoting the Gospel, as Harry and I would say, "Our kind of guy." He held the defense up just long enough, until help arrived, and for that, I would always be eternally grateful.

Bishop Von Houten was in for a surprise. He may have once more underestimated Paul John Henson and his merry band of helpers. He might just have to cough up a raise after all.

Thank you, God, for finally sending me a, "Mr. Bluebird chirping in my ear day."

I had been waiting for a little while.

We arrived at the side of the jeep when Binky came close to me, hugged me, and kissed me. I could feel how happy she was without even speaking, just by her body language in holding me.

"I cannot believe it, Paul, but I knew you had the flow come over you and that the ideas flowed into you. I felt the flow also, I think I might have been feeling exactly what you were thinking and going to do."

"Of course, you did, Binky. We are one, you and I, and you know what I feel now. You know my thoughts, my dreams, my hopes, and feelings. I love how you are so happy since I was ordained and started this new job. Your eyes are always twinkling now. It is something different that I am fascinated with, Binky. You have a glow to you now, like I have never seen before."

"That is because I love you, more than I can ever really convey or describe. I know you now have a mission. I was worried about you for a long time. All the hard work that you put into your education, I could tell how hard you were working to replace what you once had in your life when you played goal. I knew that you needed something that made you feel the same way and challenged you just as hard."

The breeze had picked up a bit now as the afternoon was waning. Some of Binky's long hair blew over in front of her face. I gently moved it away from her face, while my wife continued to speak, "Despite what you said, sometimes, I could see the sadness in your eyes when you mentioned hockey. I would watch you studying the game on television, your body swaying and following the puck, as if you were still in the net. I watch you from the windows when you do your little, goalie workout drill in our backyard, following the same routine that you have done for years. I hoped and prayed that something would bring you back to those same feelings and flow. I saw it in your eyes there at the church, and I am so happy for you."

Binky reached up and gently touched my cheek, right underneath my eye with her finger, "Paul, I can always tell what is going on with you by your eyes. Everyone, who knows and loves you, can see inside of you through your eyes. Mum told me to watch your eyes years ago when she and I first met. They are the windows into your soul, Paul."

Once more, in fact, that was twice today, that I felt that cold shiver going up and down my spine. Those were the same words that Sky had told me on the porch at 20 John Street on the first night I met her.

"I thank God every day, for your love and what you bring to me and the rest of us."

We both climbed into the jeep, I started it up and put it in gear. Binky was so excited and she insisted on holding my hand as we drove. When I had to shift the gears, she took her hand off and then grabbed it right after I finished. I was euphoric at her wonder, love, and enthusiasm.

"Tinky called me at work right before you called and wanted us to go over to, The Lovely Rose for dinner. He was very excited about someone he wants us to meet."

I nodded my head and told her, "We can head straight there, I am starving. Maybe we can get a plan with Harry, Rose, and Tinky to head out to the church and get this work underway. I also need to call Linny and Ronzo. I will never be half the electrician that Ronzo is. I am sure between the two of us, we can knock those electrical repairs right out."

We arrived at The Lovely Rose, and Rose and Harry greeted us. They were very excited as well as they were very happy to see us. Harry explained that Tinky would be along shortly, and that he wanted to introduce Binky, and me to his new girlfriend.

Harry caught me on the side and whispered to me, "Be prepared. She is pretty unusual, let's just say there is a lot of her to love. But I know you, and you will not judge her for how she looks. There is more here than meets the eye. Old Harry can tell." I nodded my head and while I thought that I understood what Harry was implying that Tinky's girlfriend was a large person, I also knew Harry well enough to know that there was a little more to it than just that.

"I have great news for everyone. Binky and I really need your help."

Rose stopped in her tracks and she grabbed my hand, as though she sensed this was something very special. Her instincts were strong, and we all had been together so long that she could read our body language.

Rose was looking beautiful these days. No, in fact, as she grew a little older, Rose had turned into a fantastically stunning woman. She was always dressed in fine clothes, she had grown her hair a little longer, and she had gained such an air of confidence. She was quite the catch for someone. I just hoped in my heart that someday, it would be Harry.

"Whatever the two of you need, we have got you covered," Rose said. "Harry was just saying to me today, Rose, I think we need a new adventure. I am not surprised, knowing our history together, that it appears as though one has come by!"

Harry led us to our favorite table in the back of the restaurant and we all sat down. We shared with them the day's events, meeting Dave, the bishop's plan, and some of the conditions of the facilities. Rose and Harry were amazed when we told them about the number twenty-seven coincidence. I know Binky and I were very excited, as we must have been talking fast, and I could tell Harry was a little lost.

"Slow down there, Paul, slow down there, Bink-a-roo-ski, you mean this place is really in that bad a condition?"

Binky and I both nodded our heads in agreement.

"Wow, this bishop of yours really does stack the deck against you whenever he gets the chance now, doesn't he? I think that the bishop might have single-handedly raised my company profits with Annoy-O-Meter purchases to put your name on them. How many does he have now?"

"No doubt, he does love them, and yes, they all have my name on them. With regard to stacking the deck, I do not know. Harry, on one side of the coin, I agree with you, and on the other hand, I choose to be optimistic. I prefer to think he is testing me to see what I am capable of."

Harry sat back, pushed his hair back from his forehead and his face lit up. He clearly was thrilled as he replied, "Well now, let's just show him who he is messing with here! He does not realize the resources that we as a team can provide." He jumped up from his seat and was fist pumping in the air while pacing back and forth on the side of our table.

Old Harry fired up the emotions now, and his face was flush with the rush of a challenge.

"It is time for one of our famous action plans there, Paul! You know that I will pull out all the Harry M. Redmond Jr. stops for you. I will climb up and weld that stupid-ass beam myself! I will bring the big lift out there tomorrow, we may have to move some pews to get to it, but you know that I will fix it all for you."

Harry stopped pacing, and he walked over to the side of the table, put both of his hands on it, and leaned over. He faced us and you could tell how intense he was now.

"It is a done deal, guys! I will provide all the materials. After all, my accountant is always after me to make charitable donations, anyway. I guess God was telling me, no, until today for a reason. I will pull all my men from the shop, load up the big truck, hook up the aerial lift, and head out there early tomorrow. You call Ronzo and Linny tonight and youse two guys fix those lights, pipes, and electrical and get that heat working. I am sure that Linny will start to work on a plan with Rose to organize everything. Linny will be happy to work with Tink-a-roo-ski on a choir. Leave the rest to old Harry and my crew. Rose, I will need you for logistical support. Tinky can run both sides of this joint for a few days."

Harry was obviously now looking forward to the work. He waved for the wait staff. "I love this! Are youse two guys hungry?"

"Starving Harry. Binky and I have not eaten a thing since breakfast."

Harry happily announced, "I have a new Harry Burger on the menu. It was Rose's idea. She has taken over from me now as a marketing genius, and I am about to promote her to the chief executive in charge of everything for me."

Rose smiled and blushed at the praise.

"It is the double Harry Burger. It is lifted in by a helicopter and lowered on your plate it is so big!"

The young waitress that Harry kept on the staff came over.

"Yes, boss," she smiled and wiggled her hips as she came over. She still had stars in her eyes for the big guy.

"Hey darling," Harry said to her. Harry ordered two double Harry burgers for us and some beers and drinks. I watched Harry very carefully around the young waitress, as did Rose. I was very impressed as he did not flinch or check her out at all, despite a pair of pants that she was wearing that appeared as though an artist painted them upon her body. I knew deep down now that there was clearly another woman on his mind. I knew Harry, as well as I knew myself, and this was a very good sign.

Our order arrived and Harry showed us the new burgers. "I love this! Now that is what I am talking about, a double Harry Burger air lifted in by a helicopter it is so big! Rose is a genius, a pure genius!"

Rose deflected the praise by changing the subject, "What can I do to help out other than what my boss here needs?"

"Rose, I have a vision for this big, church dinner. Very special, very social, almost a rededication dinner. We will need you to run this event. It needs to be huge and very special. I can see you handling the entire thing, from planning to the actual event. We need your marketing talents, Rose. I will need to fill this church quickly in order to save it."

"I can handle that, Paul. It will be right up my alley."

"Binky is already on the road access. She will research it and be on it with her father in the morning. I have a feeling that he is going to be all over this one because it will be a chance for some huge exposure for him. After all, it is a reelection year."

"This is fantastic, the whole team together on an adventure, just like old times!" Harry was ecstatic with the thought of the challenge, and whether or not it was an old instinct, or just the strength of his emotions, it was difficult to tell, but he reached out and grabbed Rose's hand. Rose seemed surprised at first; she looked at Harry and obviously enjoyed the affection. Harry held her hand tightly in his hand and you could see how animated he was. We waited for it to progress to the next step when Harry suddenly stood up from the table.

"Here is Tink-a-roo-ski and his gal!"

Walking toward us was Tinky and alongside of him was

a young lady. A large, young lady. They both had big smiles on their faces as they approached the table. Tinky was waving to us, as he walked closer, making their way through the crowd, across the restaurant floor.

The restaurant was already crowded, and it was just a little before dinnertime. The place was a gold mine. I could see that Tinky and Rose really had done quite a fine job here.

Binky looked at me and I shrugged my shoulders. She then looked back at Tinky and I heard her say in a low whisper, "Oh my."

Tinky approached the table, and he seemed happier than I have seen him in a very long time. "Hey guys, hey, dear sister," Tinky growled in his best gangster voice. "I really want you to meet someone!"

Next to little Tinky was a large woman. In fact, let me please be factual here; she was huge. She had to be at least six feet tall, and she was as wide sideways as she was tall. She wore an old, worn, dirty pair of dungaree coveralls, carried a hard hat under her left arm, and she wore a pair of muddy work boots. Her brown hair was tied up behind her head, but it seemed as though it was perhaps shoulder length when it was let down.

She smiled from ear-to-ear. She and Tinky held hands as they walked over to the table. It truly was a stark contrast. Here is this large and overwhelming woman standing next to little, Tinky with his broad smile, red face and red hair.

Tinky stood next to us all and proudly spoke in his classic growl, "I want you to all meet my girlfriend, Miss Betty Anne Schmidt!"

We all stood up to greet Betty Anne.

"Betty Anne, this is my co-worker and friend, Ms. Rose Rose."

Rose stood up, shook her hand, and said, "It is my pleasure, Betty Anne."

"I think you may have already met my boss, the world-famous Mr. Harry M. Redmond Junior. In fact, there are very few people, who do not know Harry or have at least heard of him!"

"I think we met very quickly the other day there, Betty Anne. It sure is nice to meet you. I have not seen Tinky smile so much, since the morning I slipped a little Old Post Mortem bourbon in his Big Bob's, Sugar, Fizzly Whizzly cereal, after one of our famous nights out prowling the streets."

Tinky looked at Harry, and then he seemed to remember the event. "I wondered why they were so soggy that day, and I had a wicked headache later in the afternoon. Is that what that was?"

Harry nodded, "Sure was."

Tinky turned to my wife, and me and introduced us, "This is my dear sister Binky, and I think you can guess that the tall guy, with all of that hair next to her is my brother-in-law, Paul John Henson."

Betty Anne stomped over to us, and it felt like the very foundation of the restaurant was shaking. She took one look at Binky and said, "I have heard so much about you, it is really nice to meet you. Finally."

Binky smiled and reached out her hand, "It is nice to meet you too, Betty Anne. Have you had a chance to meet our parents yet?"

I looked at Betty Anne's face and at her still positive facial expression; I knew she had not yet met the famous Mom and Dad Hobnobber.

"No, but I sure hope to meet them in a few days. It is going to be wonderful."

I thought to myself, be careful what you wish for, Betty Anne.

"We should all plan to have a wonderful dinner together over at our parent's home. My brother and I will make the arrangements. It will be quite the time."

I tried hard to shake the image of Betty Anne meeting

Mom and Dad Hobnobber for the first time from my mind. Yes, quite the time, should be a fairly accurate description of that event.

"I would love that, Binky. I look forward to us all enjoying an evening together over at the Hobnobber family home."

Hmmm, enjoying. That word, in this case, is indeed a very optimistic word.

"Reverend Henson! Please no offense to meeting everyone else, but I have been so looking forward to meeting you!" Betty Anne moved away from Binky and started stomping her giant body over in my direction. I planted my feet firmly in case of a collision. She smiled broadly at me, and I could not help but notice how pretty her face was, that she really had perfect facial features and pearly white, giant teeth. She could certainly give the Manginis a run for their money in a white tooth contest.

"It is also very nice to meet you, Betty Anne, but please call me, Paul."

"Oh no, Reverend Henson, out of respect for you, I could never do that."

I must confess that in defense of a potential hug, I made a rather quick suggestion, "Please, let's all sit down."

I motioned for Harry to push chairs over to us. Betty Anne and Tinky sat down between Harry and me. She lowered herself into the chair, and I hoped that she would make it past the arms of the chair without being stuck. She squeezed past the arms and like a giant cork in a bottle; she landed successfully with a little thud.

Betty Anne placed her hard hat on the floor next to her chair and started to speak, "I have to tell you what a thrill it is to meet the man who really changed my life. I have to call you reverend out of the great honor I have, in finally meeting you tonight."

"I do appreciate that Betty Anne, but I am not quite sure what I have done that could have been such a significant event. How about just calling me, Pastor Paul? Will that work for you?"

I really could not get used to the reverend's title; it seemed excessively formal for a long-haired, hippie, pastor.

The big gal smiled and tapped the top of my hand very gently, "Perfect, I love that! Pastor Paul."

Tinky joined the conversation and started to explain, "Paul, please listen, I gave Betty Anne a tape-recorded copy of that first sermon you preached when you won over the bishop and he agreed to ordain you. You know the one about fitting in with God?"

I nodded my head.

"Oh pastor, that sermon touched me in such a way that I have never felt before. You can all see what a large person that I am, and that, along with my job, gave me a terrible complex about me. I had no self-confidence at all. Tinky here was trying hard to boost my self-esteem and honestly, he wanted to date me, but I firmly resisted. I never felt as if I was good enough."

"What kind of work do you do, Betty Anne?" I asked as my curiosity was getting the best of me.

"I work with my dad in our excavating and paving company. My dad is also a large person, so we call it Big Dad and Big Daughter Excavating and Paving. I love it! Out there all day digging in the dirt and running the big machines, it is fantastic!" Betty Anne was a very excitable and enthusiastic person and she was very likable; she really was contagious.

Tinky cleared his throat and growled, "She never felt good enough, hey look at me, my name is Tinky, I am red like a fire engine, my hair sticks out of my head like a rooster, you need a microscope to find me and she feels inadequate?"

"But you play a mean bass guitar there, Tink-a-roo-ski!" After the compliment, Harry reached over and shook hands with Tinky.

"I love that nickname, Mr. Redmond—that is so cute for my little Tinky!" Betty Anne laughed aloud and the table shook with her volume. I held onto my beer mug and grabbed Binky's Martini glass (shaken, not stirred) so it did not topple over. Rose picked her mug in the air and Harry helped her steady it.

"I listened to you preach that wonderful sermon, and Tinky told me how people perceived you to be just some long-haired hippie. When I heard your words, it touched me in a way I can never describe. I realized that no matter how I looked or what people thought of me, that God loved me and sent his grace upon me. I remember listening to your sermon and the story of your grandfather and the obstacles that he faced. I felt this great understanding and warmth come over me. After I cried my eyes out from tears of joy, I then felt so different. I was renewed and reunited with whom I used to be. It gave me the self-esteem I needed, to know that all of us fit in."

Betty Anne giggled a little, "It is so true that God does remove obstacles for us. In fact, even those who may be too large in order to squeeze into the tighter spots. Thank you, Pastor Paul, for your wonderful words. Thank you for hope for all of us, who do not quite fit in."

She had tears in her eyes and I did not really know what to say. I did think to myself how almost everyone around me was always so emotional, all this crying of tears of joy, as well as, at times, some tears of sadness We all hug, smile and were so close. I guess it was just a part of our lives.

Binky put her arm around my shoulders and pulled me close to her. "Thank you, Betty Anne, I am quite humbled, but I think all of the credit belongs to a much higher authority than Pastor Paul John Henson."

Betty Anne dabbed at her eyes with a tissue and she composed herself. "I then recovered my voice, my confidence, and I started to sing again. You made me believe in myself again. Let me show you!"

She suddenly pulled herself out of the chair and popped up. We all grabbed our drinks and held them in our hands as it felt like that section of the city of Paterson tilted just a little bit. Betty Anne stood up, untied her hair, and let it tumble down to her shoulder length. She smoothed it all out and you could see that she was indeed a beautiful woman, both on the exterior, and on her interior.

She then started to belt out in a loud, crystal clear voice, the first verse of, "Beautiful Savior." Her volume was so intense, it seemed like she had swallowed a microphone and had an internal amplification system. She sang as if she were an entire choir of singers! We all sat there in shock as this giant, young lady belted out the song. The rest of the people in the restaurant stopped, looked over, and when she was done, she received a standing ovation from us, as well as the patrons.

She sang wonderfully, as if she was a professional, and she had belted it out without even taking a breath. Right there in the restaurant, she had sung her heart out, and to us, it did not even seem as if it was a strange event. Strange and unusual events were actually normal to all of us! There was no question that Betty Anne was amazing, and we were stunned and in awe of her singing ability.

Tinky sat there glowing with his admiration for Betty Anne's talent clearly displayed on his little red face. "Can she sing, or what guys? I have it all planned for her and Linny to get together! Can you imagine what a band I have been forming here with this kind of singing talent?"

"Wow, that was really wonderful singing Betty Anne, and I must say your timing is also right on the spot. Binky and I were just over here discussing with Rose and Harry, a little church assignment that we stumbled upon today. We are in need of an organ player and some choir singers."

"Oh, Pastor Paul, I would be thrilled to sing for your church. It would be a way to pay you back for what you did for me."

"You do not owe me anything, you give me way too much credit, it sounds as if you did it all yourself."

Betty Anne smiled, and she shook her head, "No, Pastor Paul, everything that I have heard about you is true. You are exactly as I knew you would be. Forgive me for saying, but you and Mrs. Henson make a stunning couple. You are amazing together, as are Mr. Redmond and Ms. Rose. It is as if the four of you are all as one."

Betty Anne had made the observation of Rose and Harry out of innocence as well as upon their interaction and body language. I saw Harry's face light up with the idea. Rose had an aura of hope around her, as I had not seen in quite a long time.

My wife spoke up and asked, "Excavating and Paving. Betty Anne, is that what you said that you did?"

Betty Anne said, "Yes, that is correct, excavation, site work and all kinds of paving, stone work, and grading." Binky was staring at Betty Anne with one of her patented stares, and I could see her mind working the angles for the road in front of the church.

"Oh my, Betty Anne, I need to speak with you tomorrow. I will be researching some important points first thing in the morning, and I may have an immediate need for your services."

I then filled Betty Anne and Tinky in on all the details of the church, the condition of the facilities, and our plan for the work and restoration.

Tinky took a sip of his drink and looked over the edge of his glass at me. "I am on the choir mission, Paul. I will also call Linny and Ronzo and get them over there, for you. I will tell Ronzo about the electrical situation, and I need to speak with Linny about my musical ideas for the choir, as well as my new band that I would like to form. What else do you have cooking that I can help with?"

"I need an organist for this Sunday, and there is only one person that I trust with the job. Can you get a substitute for the Methodist Church?"

"Sure thing, to be honest, hanging around all you Lutherans, has made me want to look for a job with you guys. I am tired of playing the same old Wesley penned hymns. I like those death dirges that youse guys play. It brings out the power of the organ and makes me more red-faced."

Harry glanced over at me, winked, and gave me one of our positive hand signals to indicate that it was going as planned. I knew now that he had known in advance a little bit more about Tinky and his new gal, and that our plan was coming together.

Betty Anne was speaking with Rose over a subject that I had not been paying attention to, when something struck her funny, and she burst out into a loud, belly shaking round of laughter. We all grabbed our mugs and glasses as they all shook and danced upon the table. The table rocked as if there was an earth tremor. Harry made a quick grab of his Wall Crawler and Rose's Purple Pirate beer. I just managed to pick up Binky's Martini glass before it toppled over from the ground, shaking tumult of her laughter.

Perhaps, up in old Sussex County, Mum's teacups rattled in her cupboards, and over in Pennsylvania, I pictured Ronzo making a mad dash to his cupboards to check the status of his sacred bottle of booze hidden deep in the recess of his cupboards! Good thing I still had those old goalie reactions and made the critical save of my wife's drink!

Amazing, it was really amazing. We had just added another player to the team. It was the end to another perfect day. . .. Well, there now were so many of us—let us just say that it was the end to another perfect day.

8

Renewal and Remembrance

It was raining the next day, but that did not dampen our spirit or enthusiasm for our mission. Harry and his crew, along with tools, trucks, welders and the aerial lift showed up. Rose came along in her car and followed them. Binky had been up very late after we had returned home from dinner; she was already working on the research required for the road. I checked on her before I went to sleep and she was a knee and elbow deep into newspapers and some books. She then went into her regular workplace very early to utilize some of their resources. I knew by now; she was already burning up the research avenues, working with her father to make sure the road finally became a reality. Harry and I were at the church very early before sunrise and Dave Sharp arrived early too.

"This is unreal, Pastor Paul, how much is this all going to cost?"

Harry laughed. "Nice to meet you, Dave, old boy! Cost? Why, it will cost you a sore elbow and a stiff back, but as far as money, it will cost nothing!"

I introduced Dave Sharp to the world-famous Harry, "Dave Sharp, please meet, Harry M. Redmond Junior. He is the brother that I told you about yesterday. I also would like you to meet Ms. Rose Rose, who is my other dearest friend in the whole world."

Dave shook both of their hands. "This is unreal. It is like a dream come true to see all of this." The introductions were not over yet as the door to the sanctuary opened up and in walked Linda and Ronnie. Ronzo was carrying his tool bags, filled to the brim with tools, voltmeters, amp probes, other electrical tools, and troubleshooting aids. Ronzo had semi-retired about a year or two ago, and I could tell he was anxious to dive back into the trade and keep his skills sharp. After greeting our old friends and introducing them to Dave Sharp, it was time to get to work.

"Well, we can stand around and pat ourselves on the back all day, but I hear this place is in rough shape there, Sharpie. I think it is time to stop talking and get to work. If you start unbolting those pews from the floor, I will see about getting this lift in here to check out that steel way up there."

"Dave, once you have finished helping Harry, if you can get Rose and Linny pointed to the fellowship hall and the kitchen, I would appreciate it."

"I am on it, Pastor Paul."

Ronzo and I grabbed our electrical tools. We headed towards the main electrical room, in order to check out the lighting panel that fed the power to the sanctuary light fixtures. We placed our tools in front of the main panel and checked it out.

"It sure has been a long time since we worked on a job together there, twenty-seven. I hope I still have what it takes to get this going, Paul. I promise I will do a better job on this than I did on that pool splice plate!"

We stood together for a moment, in the midst of some ghosts of the past, as we both remembered that now famous exploding pool incident from the legendary Harry's resort.

"Ronzo, you are still the best in the business, so I will defer to you on this one."

"Thanks, but that is a bunch of hooey, because you are a pretty, dog gone, good electrician yourself, but thank you, anyway, Pastor Paul. This place looks a little rough. I think praying may suit us well before we tackle this mess. After all, this is high voltage here."

"I can do that, Ronzo." I put my hand on his back. We both bowed our heads, while I said a short prayer aloud, to guide us and protect us as we tackled the electrical trouble. After we had both prayed, Ronzo stood in front of the panel and held his hands on the front cover, while feeling it for warmth. He then put his nose over the vents on the cover and sniffed a few times.

"She is a burner, twenty-seven. Two seventy-seven-volt lighting, with a four-eighty feeder. There are some three phase four eighty-volt feeds in here for the heating and air equipment. She has cooked. I can smell it. We need to kill the power to this puppy. We could have been arcing in there and I do not think we want to even take the cover off with the power on."

Ronzo was still the best in the business; he was just like an old hound dog sniffing around for the trouble. I agreed as I thought he was dead on; I could smell the ozone in the air too.

We found the main switch in the electrical bucket and shut off the power to the panel. Now that it was safe and void of power, Ronzo and I pulled the front cover off the panel. Sure enough, there it was, a massive burn out of wires right in front of us. Ronzo had been dead on, and we had avoided a catastrophe. It reminded us both of the same situation that had earned Ronzo a free ride to the Black Bear Club so long ago! This was a burning and arcing situation and certainly could have led to a fire. It did not take us very long to identify the exact bundle of bad wires as well as some arcing on the buss bars and circuit breakers.

A few hours of labor, some new parts and some cleaning up, and we knew that we could get this back into shape.

Soon, the property was buzzing with tradesmen and repair activity. I leaned out of the electrical room to see Harry riding the aerial lift to the top of the sanctuary. The crew had managed to maneuver the big lift into the sanctuary, and they now were preparing to address the steel issues high up at the top of the roof. Soon afterwards, I heard the familiar arcing of his welding machines, as Harry worked on repairing the steel. I realized that it had been a very long time since I had heard that sound. Boy, oh, boy, did it bring me back to some very old memories! Mr. Redmond, Ronzo, Taylor Industries, my old man, tools from Substantial Industries, boat trailers, and the old bomb of a truck from the shop . . . wow . . . it was so long ago!

True to his word, he was up there himself, welding in the sections of new steel. Harry also reported that he had found the source of the roof leak and that he could repair it from the inside once he completed the welding. It was something about a crack in a seam on a skylight up at the top of the roof.

Rose and Linny worked on the ground, taking orders for parts and supplies and arranging delivery of materials, making coffee, working in the fellowship hall, and the kitchen, and making snacks for the work crew. Rose helped us with locating some new circuit breakers and wire that we needed for the repairs to the lighting load center. I gave her all the contacts from my memory for all my old supply houses from my days of working in the electrical business.

She returned happily in a few minutes to report after speaking in a flirtatious voice, mentioning the famous number twenty-seven, and working the men over the phone like a fine fiddle, they agreed to donate the new parts and even deliver them to us for free!

Ah yes, the lovely Rose was so true in more ways than one.

By the time lunch break came around, we had already accomplished a lot of work. A young deliveryman from the electrical supply house dropped off the wire and the circuit breakers to the church. We began the repairs to the panel right away, as we were anxious to wrap the work all up and have the lights back on, when we heard some chatting outside of the electrical room.

The young man, who had delivered the electrical supplies, drooled over Rose for a while and she had flirted with him just enough to keep him interested, but she held him at bay. Ronzo and I stood outside the door to the electrical room listening when we heard the conversation between Rose and the delivery man. We then both watched Harry's reaction when he spotted the man and his interaction with Rose.

"Looks as if there are some sparks from the past that just will not go away," Ronzo said to me, as he elbowed me in the side.

We watched together as the situation evolved before our eyes. I turned to Ronzo and said, "It is a ton of hope and dreams, my old friend, that they both harbor within their hearts. Dreams that were shattered and dreams that just will not go away."

Ronzo did not say a word, but I knew he agreed.

Harry was on the lift and he was not happy. I saw him once reach for the lever to bring the lift down, but he caught himself and returned to his welding. He kept lifting his helmet up and checking in on the situation, and I could tell he was very uncomfortable. I now knew what the magic formula might be to bring Harry to making the first move, but it had to be the perfect situation. I knew that the moment that will change everything would happen. I was confident now; it was just a matter of time. Something was holding Harry back from making the first move, and I could not quite get a handle on what it was. I would figure it out, eventually. I knew that I would.

Ronzo and I returned to our work; we replaced the burnt sections of wire and the circuit breakers in the panel. We then all took a break and sat around enjoying some coffee and we rested. It was still raining out, and that proved advantageous as Harry and his crews were able to discover the sources of the roof leaks and repaired most of them. Two of the other leaks along the lower edge would need to wait until the rain stopped, but at least we had them in our sights now.

Dave Sharp was still a tad bit on the negative side. He would need a strong dose of our interaction to bring him around to being more positive.

He displayed his cautious approach by saying, "This is all well and good, Pastor Paul, and I am thrilled that all of this work is being accomplished, but until we get that road situation corrected, we still will have a major problem on our hands." Dave was a cautious individual, and I imagine that years of adverse situations had dulled his optimism.

I worked on giving him the first dose, "Hold on, Dave, please know that Binky has that under control right now. She is an expert at research and organization, and I have no doubt that she already has all the background information as to the original trouble. She has the solutions to the obstacles detailed, categorized, and laid out. The real ace in the deck, though, is her relationship with that attorney and New Jersey State Senator that I mentioned. You see, he is her father. Senator William T. Hobnobber is my father-in-law."

Dave Sharp took his hat off and whistled. "My, you sure have quite the team behind you, Pastor Paul!

Harry stood up and pointed at Dave.

"Now, you get it there, Sharpie, I love this!" Harry picked the poor maintenance man up, gave him a huge Harry-like bear hug, and almost broke him in half.

"This is what I am talking about! You are our kind of guy Sharpie, are you signing up for the team, or are you going to stand on the sidelines with all the doubters?"

Dave answered, "No, I am with all of you, I really am." I think poor Dave was afraid to answer the question in any other manner!

"Then you need to come down to our club one night.

Grab Mrs. Sharpie and bring her down to The Lovely Rose in Paterson for a night of dancing, jumping around, and howling at the moon. Do it, Sharpie! I will cover it all for you, all of it on me! Have one or two of my famous Harry Burgers and a bunch of ice cold, Big Boulders or Dingleberry beers."

"Harry Burgers! My wife and I love those! We buy them frozen all the time! I like Big Boulder beer, but those Dingleberries are way too sweet." Dave Sharp was now clearly impressed with the bombastic, world famous, Harry M. Redmond Jr., just as is everyone else who meets him.

"You mean to tell me that you invented, Harry Burgers?"

"Sure did, as well as the famous Annoy-O-Meter that you see advertised on all those commercials on channel eleven in the middle of the night."

Dave now was really on his heels. He grabbed Harry by the shoulder and laughed aloud while telling Harry, "I have one of those too! I have it on the wall in my maintenance shop! I keep Bishop Von Houten on it, set at about ninety percent all of the time!"

We all could relate to his choice of people.

"Sounds like a plan there, Sharpie, with us it is one adventure after another, so come along for the ride and let's see where it all takes us."

We finished lunch and Ronzo and I checked the repairs on the electrical panel. I called out to the work crew in the sanctuary, "Well, it is the moment of truth here folks, we need to see if we can make like a little section of Genesis here or not."

Ronzo and I put the cover on, turned the main power back on, and flipped a few of the circuits back on. I gave the signal, and Harry and Dave went over and turned on the wall switches.

Ronzo and I stood in the doorway, watching out into the sanctuary to see if we had successfully repaired the circuits or if we had failed. The switches were now on and the sanctuary lights slowly flickered to life. Soon, we had a glow of heavenly ambiance. The fixtures were very nice; they cast a soft, golden glow of light that bathed the entire sanctuary in a wonderful and peaceful atmosphere.

Rose and Linny cheered and clapped, and Dave took his hat off and smiled, as if he had just won the lottery while he said, "Pastor Paul, you sure are a long-haired, hippie, electrician too! You and Mr. Ronzo are quite the team!"

Ronzo and I patted each other on the back for a job well done, and we gathered up our tools. The sanctuary glowed with the lights and all of a sudden, it all started to look like it was all coming together. Now that Harry had repaired both the steel and the leak, Harry and his crew removed the lift out of the sanctuary, and started to put the pews back. I went to work on the heating system and checked out the broken pipes, while Ronzo followed along to assist me. The afternoon waned on and before you knew it, the day was drawing to a close. Tomorrow would be another day. I thanked Linda and Ronnie for all of their hard work and they packed up and headed back to Pennsylvania. They had a long ride ahead of them, so we wanted to make sure they set out before it became too dark.

Harry's crew packed up and left to bring all the tools, truck, and lift back to his shop in Paterson.

Soon it was just Dave, Harry, Rose, and I left at the church.

"I need a fire eye sensor for the boiler, Dave. I will obtain that in the morning and buy that part myself. That is why the heat keeps tripping out due to flame failure. They are expensive, but I will cover that one on my own."

Binky and I never touched our savings account, therefore we sure could afford to jump in here and help the church.

I looked out the rear door and I could see the sky was clearing and the rain had stopped. "It looks like tomorrow will be clear, so we should be able to fix the leaks on the lower edge of the roof. I think by Sunday's worship, we will have gotten rid of all the buckets and we should be in good shape."

Harry agreed and pulled off his little welding cover from his head that he wore under his helmet. He wiped all the sweat off his hair and head. It had been hot welding all day up at the top of the roof.

"I think you are correct there, twenty-seven, it is looking good."

Rose walked over and handed me a paper, "Here is the information on some supplies that I will need to get the kitchen squared away for that big dinner you have planned. I will take care of ordering all of this. I just wanted you to see what my plan is, Paul. Tinky called into the church phone and he told me that Binky would like you to head home for dinner. She has prepared a special meal. I think the rest of us will all head for dinner at the club. Tinky planned on coming out tomorrow to turn on and check out the organ for Sunday. If you do not need me, I can switch places with him and I can then cover the club tomorrow."

"I think dinner sounds good, Rose! That plan sounds as if it will work for all of us. It sounds as if Binky may have some things on her mind. I am sure that Tinky has whipped up something special for you at the club too. It has been a long day."

Dave thanked us all, and we made plans to meet in the morning.

Harry moved in close to Dave Sharp and caught his ear, "You know there, Sharpie, I heard they cut your hours here at the church and that you could use some extra jingle. I am sure once twenty-seven gets this rolling and packs this joint once more with people praising and shouting, then we can get you back to forty hours. Until then, I could use a man down at my shop with all-around talents like yours. There is always something broken, and that needs fixing at the restaurant or at my factory or shop. I pitched in here and it sure felt good, but after all, I am the big shot around these parts. I cannot be swinging tools all the time. I have to play the part of the big blowhard, you know. I have an image to uphold! I am sure you and Mrs. Sharpie could use the extra dough. So, what do you say, how about twenty hours here? If you do not mind the ride into the city of Paterson, then I can give you twenty hours there."

Dave's face lit up, as he said, "My prayers sure have been answered. I cannot even believe all that has happened since yesterday afternoon when I spotted Pastor and Mrs. Henson! Why sure Mr. Redmond, it would be my pleasure!"

"Call me, Harry, Sharpie. Just call me, Harry. Done deal Sharpie, Rose will take care of all that pesky paperwork for you. See ya in the morning!"

Rose was thrilled. I could see the passion, love, and caring in her face for Harry. She recognized that the big guy had a heart of gold and he never, ever, forgot where he and I came from. Harry was always looking to help people who might be down on their luck, or whoever needed a break and a second chance at life. He was always appreciative of how, at one time, someone believed in both of us enough to give two poor trade school boys from good old Paterson, a chance to make something of ourselves.

"Are you riding back with me, Harry?" Rose asked.

"Say Rose, I have just a little more to do here, so if you do not mind, I will hitch a ride with twenty-seven, he can drop me off and I will meet up with you at the club."

Rose nodded, she seemed a little disappointed, but off she went towards her car.

"Paul, I will call your wife when I get back, and tell her you will be home soon. The phone here does not seem to work all the time. I think we have to put a service call in on that as well."

"Thank you, dear Rose. We will see you in a bit, drive careful now. Go in peace, Rose." I kissed her cheek, she gave me a kiss back, and I thanked her for all of her hard work.

"I love you, Pastor Paul."

"I love you too, Rose."

"I love that title, Pastor Paul. It fits you so well. Hey, don't forget to pull the hair tie out of your hair, we do not want to get Binky all worked up."

I had forgotten it, so I reached up and pulled it out now, while thanking her, "Yes. Thank you, Rose."

She waved a little wave and headed for her car. Harry and I watched her walk to the car, and he shook his head. Her body swayed and wiggled, and I could tell by his facial expression that he certainly did not mind checking out Rose from a safe distance.

"Fine looking, woman there, Paul, she sure is a fine-looking woman. She is even better looking now, as she has gotten older, than she was years ago. Ahem . . . certain parts of her developed a bit more . . . if ya know what I mean."

I now could tell that Harry stayed behind for a reason. I had known him for a long, long time. There were a few tools around to clean up, but it was nothing that could not wait until the morning.

He had something else on his mind.

"Yes, Harry, she sure is, big guy, she sure is."

He picked up his welding helmet and his gloves and he fingered the little special plaque on top of it that said, "Big Harry." Underneath that Harry had added the words, "Sky Blu." He then pulled the peace necklace out from under his welding shirt and held it in his hand.

"Hey, thanks Harry for everything, I really cannot thank you, enough buddy. I think that by week's end, we may have this thing licked. There are a few issues with the other buildings, but we can tackle them as well. What do you think?"

"Sure, sure, Paul, we got it, we always get it, I really enjoyed working with you again, and it brought back an awful lot of memories. An awful lot of memories."

I walked over to where he was picking up his tools and said, "Like building a pool in your backyard with half of the neighborhood helping?"

Harry chuckled, "Yeah that sure was something, Paul. How about pulling an engine out of a Takajunky model 10 with a rope over a tree branch? Hey, if it is all right with you, I will bring a smudge stick and smudge-a-dub-dub the church tomorrow."

"Great idea, please do it, Harry."

He tossed his tools and equipment into his tool bag and knelt down in front of it while he was gathering up odds and ends.

I could tell he wanted to talk, so I walked over to him and put my hand on his back. "Are you all right, do you need to talk, Harry?"

He stood up, sighed deeply, and I could see his face and mouth shudder as he fought back the emotions.

"You know me so well, Paul. I am sure you already know that I am in love with Rose."

"I do, Harry, and I am sure that she feels the same way. I hope you do also realize that, Harry. She never stopped, even from years ago, Harry. It just all fell apart for many reasons. Then Sky came, and it all changed, but Harry, she never stopped caring."

He looked up at me as he stopped throwing tools into his bag and he answered, "I think you are right, twenty-seven. I hold back telling her how I feel and I do not know why. I keep it straight business and I am not really sure why. I just keep my distance. For some reason, Paul, I just cannot bring myself to pull the love trigger. I somehow always go back in my mind to Sky. For some strange reason, I think that if I allow myself to be with Rose, then I am betraying Sky and our marriage. I think I am crazy, but I will never, ever stop loving Sky, ever."

His eyes grew wide and clear, as he asked me, "Do you ever forget, Paul? Do you ever cry or forget? How do you remain so strong all the time? All that has happened to us, and all the time that has passed, it eats away at me all of the time. It seems as if you can shut it all out and remain so steady and strong. To me, it is just all a blur in time."

I had nothing to offer Harry, except the heartfelt truth, so that is what I delivered to my best friend, "I have a strength that does not come from me, Harry. It comes from a fire that God put inside of me, but believe me, I feel hurt and pain and I know how much you hurt at times, I really do. When I was alone on the road, playing hockey game after game, in one strange place after another, it was the toughest time of my life. I felt as much as I was in the spotlight and a supposed hero on the ice that I was a failure in the things that were the most important to me. Binky was gone for what seemed like the rest of all time, Sky had passed, and you had fled from the grief. I had a pain so deep inside of me that it never went away. All I could think about was what had happened with Sky passing, and some people that I cared most about in the world were gone, shattered or in trouble. You know all too well the pain of grief, but loneliness is not a lot of fun either."

I saw Harry's body shudder with pain at the mention of that dark, painful time in both of our lives.

"It stayed inside of me every day. A dull ache that nearly drove me crazy. It went away when I skated into the net and then when the game was over, it was back, as strong and powerful as it always was. Harry, I swear that I prayed every night for God to allow me to cry, or to get rid of that pain, but he just kept feeding me strength and faith. God would not allow it because he was molding me for a mission. A mission that now is clear and bright, it is a mission of hope, joy, reunion, and renewal. It is for us to carry on what wonderful people such as Sky Blu Redmond already knew in their hearts. Do I ever forget? No, Harry . . . never. I still do not really ever cry, but I never forget. Not a day goes by that I do not think of Sky, or that terrible hospital room, or that terrible night."

I walked over to him as he knelt in front of his tools, listening to me. He was working hard to fight back tears now and wiping his eyes with an old rag.

"But I also never forget the good times, like riding in the Trans Whizzer or the Sonic Mobile, with the music blasting in our ears and the wind in our faces. How could you ever forget the parties at 20 John Street, street hockey games on Geyer Street, the Black Bear Club or High Mountain, or dancing through the night? How I wish I could be on top of Christmas Tree Mountain one more time, cutting down a tree, with Patty dreaming of 'Dinky the Orange Teddy Bear' lights! Could you ever forget when the night would come and you and I were out there doing all the things we always did and taking on the world together. No, my dear friend, I never forget, ever. The ghosts of the past follow me forever, and they are ghosts of joy and of sorrow, but they never allow me to forget."

His eyes filled with tears and he looked away for a moment. I touched his shoulder to let him know I felt his sorrow and that I would help to absorb his pain.

"You need to put an end to this, Harry, or it will drive you crazy. I understand how much you love Sky, but she wants you to move on too. I assure you, Harry, that she will never leave you ever. You are not betraying her or her memory by falling in love again. My goodness you are a man. That is a normal feeling, Harry. It is not that you are crazy, it is normal. I think in this world, we all need to realize that, perhaps, we do have multiple soul mates. There is nothing wrong with that fact. Memories are wonderful, Harry. Please hold them as I do, near to your heart and mind. Someday, the present days will be the days that you talk about fondly, not the days of old memories."

He stood up now, looked me square in the eye, and said, "I believe you, Paul, I really do, but it is tearing me up."

"But you cannot allow memories to tear you apart. As great as some of those times were, and as painful as some of them are, they are gone. Sky is now a voice, a strong guide for you in your own book of time, Harry."

He looked at me and wiped his eyes and face with his rag. I needed to work fast for Harry now and seize this moment. I continued with my counseling of him, "Sky was too special to all of us ever to forget. You know that. However, you need to seize the moment, Harry, before it passes. It is sometimes strange how fast time goes by, and now you cannot allow this time to escape you. Rose may not wait forever, my friend. She is, after all, a young, vibrant woman. Now, you have a chance at joy that God is giving you once more. What you have right here and now in the present is real . . . it is very real, Harry. I know a really smart guy who once told me a long time ago, that some of the greatest lessons that life had taught him, came out of the worst times that he had lived through."

Harry looked at me. He had now remembered that he had said that, and he seemed surprised that he actually had. It was as if he found some confidence or I had really struck a nerve or an old way of life inside of him.

"The good Lord wants you to be happy, and you deserve it."

"I know that, Paul. I am for the most part happy, but for some reason, I cannot ever approach Rose or tell her the truth."

"Something will come along and trigger it for you. You will know when the time is right. However, you need closure, my friend, you need to close that chapter in your life, not forget it, but you need to close it and move on. It will just happen, until then, keep an open mind and heart.

Just allow it to come to you. If it is meant to be then it will happen, it will be a plan from God that you will not really have any control over, Harry."

He looked at me and a faint smile came to his face.

"Believe it and it will happen, isn't that the way you say it, Pastor Paul John Henson?"

"Ah, something like that thirty-five, something like that, hey check that out, I told you Sky is always around."

I pointed to the sunset off to the west that we could see out the door of the church. Harry and I stepped out, and we stood there in awe. The sky was clearing out and the rain clouds were being chased away now at the end of the day. You could see the sun setting and the peeks of blue sky working hard to make a last-minute appearance between the dark clouds. He and I stood side-by-side for a long time, while we were staring out at the sunset. We did not say a word, but then again, Sky was saying it all for us.

We rode back home together, and I dropped Harry back over at the club, and then continued on to my house. Binky had made a wonderful dinner, and I had filled her in on the details of the day. Binky also had made a lot of headway on the road situation, so we had shared in each other's success. It was obvious that despite our intense friendships with the rest of the gang, that tonight, Binky wanted the night to be about us. She wanted to share in her research and hear all about the progress that we had made at the church. She and I were sitting in the living room, relaxing, listening to some music, when the telephone rang. I motioned to my wife that I would pick it up and I reached for the receiver.

"Hello."

"Hey, twenty-seven."

It was Harry on the other end.

"Say, I need to take care of something tomorrow and I was hoping that you and Binky were both available to go with me."

I knew right away based upon our discussion today where it was that we were going to go.

"Sure, thing Harry, no sweat, I will ask Binky and see if she can go into the office a little later."

"Are you not going to ask me where we are going? Or do you already know?"

I hesitated for just a moment, but I knew that Harry was way too smart not to realize that I had already known where he wanted to go.

"No, Harry. I understand, and I think it is a good idea to seek some closure. I imagine that you have never been back since the funeral and burial, now, have you?"

"No, not since that awful day, Paul. Have you?"

"Yes, I have Harry. I go once or twice a year to place a flower and a peace sign there."

"I think you are right that I need some type of closure, Paul. It is what I need to do so that I can finally move on. You may not be my priest, but you are my pastor. I will also admit that I just cannot go back there unless you and Binky are with me. Paul, I may not be able to stand the pain without you two with me. It is not going to be easy, but it is what I need to do. Does that make any sense to you?"

"I understand, I agree, and being honest, I knew it would come to this someday. Binky and I will be there for you, say, around eight in the morning out in front of our house. I think we need to drive there in the Wagon Bus. It would only be appropriate."

"I agree, Paul, see you then."

Click, the line went dead.

I filled Binky in on the details of the day with regard to my discussion with Harry. She sighed deeply when she realized how difficult the morning would be for all of us. Binky had never met Sky, but I am sure she felt as if she had. Binky and I would visit her grave tomorrow along with Harry. We would all join in an effort to bring closure to a memory in our friend's life that had clung to him every day for a very long time. Our goal was not to make him forget, but to bring him some acceptance and a level of understanding. We knew that we wanted him to create a little book of memories that he could keep close to his heart forever. My wife was there to support us both. She was strong, and she understood.

I called and left a message for Dave Sharp, telling him that we would be a little later in the morning than we had initially planned, but that Harry's crew and Tinky would be out there on time. He could get the crews started and run the show until we arrived.

The day broke bright and clear and picture perfect. It was unlike the rain and gloom of the weather of the previous day. The sunset that Harry and I had watched at the church late in the day had given us a prelude as to the beauty of the morning.

It did not disappoint us.

I dressed in my black suit and collar because as Harry had told me; I was not Harry's priest, but I sure was going to do my best to be his pastor. Binky selected a black dress and her Lutheran Rose necklace. We stood in front of the house and sure enough, right at the stroke of eight in the morning, the old Wagon Bus pulled up.

We climbed up into the Wagon Bus and after some greetings, Harry put the vehicle into gear and we pulled away. He was wearing a suit and tie and he had a small bag and some flowers next to him on the engine cover.

"You may need to direct me, Paul. I think I have purged the directions of how to get there, out of my mind forever. It is a blur. It really is."

"I can do that, Harry. Would you do better if I drove? I can drive if you would feel better."

"No, I am fine, Paul, I really am. I just will need some help once we arrive at the cemetery."

We drove the distance and along the way, we mostly remained silent. Binky was in the back seat, but she reached her hand out to me as I sat in the passenger's seat and I held it as we drove. It was about a one-hour drive from Great Falls to the cemetery. Once we arrived at the cemetery, we pulled inside the gate; Harry pushed the clutch in and shifted the old bus into neutral.

He turned around to face us and spoke, "I want you both to know how much I love youse guys. I want to thank you for coming here with me, I know that this is not going to be easy for any of us, but we have stood together for so many years, that I knew we needed to stand as one here today. Binky, you never met Sky, but I will tell you that she was special, more special, than I could ever describe. She deeply loved Paul. She told me he would do many great things in his life, touch many people with his efforts, and that he was a great man. She told me things about him that have come true. You need to know that she told me that you would come back because you loved him more than life itself. Somehow, she knew that. Sky knew things that other people did not know. She really did."

Binky reached over to Harry, held his hand and she told him, "Harry, I know that she was special, and she was right about all of those things. We will go joyfully with you. I know there will be joy in Heaven today, there really will be."

Binky looked under the headliner and out the windshield; her eyes followed the clear, blue sky.

"Ironic, how perfect the sky is today, a clear blue. But from the stories that I have heard about Sky, perhaps it is not ironic at all."

Harry put the bus in gear and I directed him as we worked our way through the narrow roads and passages of the cemetery.

"Stop here, Harry. Sky's grave is up that hill there on the left."

Harry stopped the bus and cut off the engine. We all climbed out of the vehicle and I met Binky on the side of the bus and held her hand. I then reached out for Harry's hand and the three of us held onto each other, while we climbed the hill towards the burial site. Harry held the flowers and the little bag in his other hand, as we walked together to the grave which was perched up on the side of the hill.

I remembered walking this same route with Harry on that terrible day, of what seemed like so long ago, dragging him along, with Father Mark helping me, as that dark, bitter wind blew at us with such ferocity. The weather was much different today.

"It is right here, Harry . . . near the base of that tree. It is a wonderful spot, it really is."

We stopped and looked down to where I had led us and the three of us stared at a simple, white, grave marker that read, "Sky Blu Redmond, Peace, Love, Hope."

I then remembered that Harry and Sky's family were much too broken up to make any grave marker selections. Together, Patty, Linda, and I had picked out the marker. It was simple, but it was majestic.

Harry gently reached down and placed the flowers at the base of the marker, and then he reached in the bag, pulled out a peace necklace, and lovingly draped it over the stone.

The sun was strong and bright, and it was warm on our backs as it rose in the eastern sky. We all stood together and crossed ourselves as we reverently stood, staring at the gravesite. Then suddenly, Harry fell to his knees in front of the marker, held his head in his hands, and he started to sob violently. Binky and I held him by his shoulders as she also began to cry. I started to pray aloud from scripture.

I stopped after a few verses and I changed course. Instead, I decided upon a verse from The Gospel of John.

I simply said, "Jesus wept."

My wife and I stood there in silence as Harry poured out all the pain and sorrow from within his inner soul. He came to grips with what he needed to face for so many years. The tears ran out of Harry M. Redmond Jr. as if they were a river that morning, as the tears purged his pain and grief from deep inside of him.

I truly believe God sent him healing blessings, and I think he was strengthened and renewed, I really do. It was there on that gravesite, on that bright sunny morning, that Harry M. Redmond Jr. closed a chapter in his life. Perhaps his renewal did occur in Michigan, on the morning he watched the sunrise over the lake, today, however, he reunited with Sky as well as a part of Harry that he had lost for a long time.

Harry M. Redmond Jr. was back in full, all of him.

He slowly became more composed and wiped his face of the spent sorrow. Harry stood up and said to us, "It is done, I understand now what has happened and how I need to go on."

He held out his hands for Binky and she gently took them. We stood there together.

"I will never forget, but I will go on."

The big guy moved all of his hair away from his forehead and shook his head gently back and forth. He was recovering.

He then tilted his head towards me, and with just the slightest hint of mischief in his eye, he said, "Twenty-seven, let's just pray the Lord's Prayer together really loud. When we end the prayer, instead of saying amen, let's give it the famous Harry war cry. You know, I love it . . . that is what I am talking about as loud as we can. Right here, on this hillside, in this graveyard! The Lord's Prayer sums it all up for me Paul, you know, I always thought that was the only prayer that you ever had to pray. Those last three verses always send cold shivers down my spine. Can we do that here? Is that not appropriate? I think Sky will be laughing at that, she really will. I think she knows now that I am back to being the man I always was, and who she wants me to be. I may even go out tomorrow and see if I can find a used 1979 Trans Whizzer and put on my black cowboy hat!"

I fist pumped a little in the air, as Binky laughed at my display of enthusiasm and I told him, "It is fine, we will do it. Heaven is about joy, not sorrow, Harry. It is more than appropriate!"

That is exactly what the three of us did, right there on the hillside, and our voices echoed out across the hillside, along the little valley, down through the trees next to the cemetery, and I have no doubt they reached all the way to Heaven.

There was indeed joy in Heaven on this day, there really was.

"So, this is it, Reunion Lutheran Church!" Tinky stood in the center of the pews, looking up and admiring the architecture. "Fantastic, what a shame that they were going to close this church up. It is awe inspiring, like a hole to Heaven right up there." Tinky pointed to the little sky light at the top of the roof, right at the spot where Harry had fixed the steel and the water leak.

Tinky turned towards Harry, "You mean to tell me boss, you went all the way up there on that big lift? No way is my little, red, ass going up there! It reminds me of when Binky tried to get me on that terrible ride down at the New Jersey shore. You know that horrible, Flipper thing."

Ah yes, the Flipper, everyone's favorite amusement ride. Amusement ride! That sure is an oxymoron.

"That is nothing there, Tink-a-roo-ski, someday over some drinks, I will tell you the story of when I lowered Paul with a rope around his waist, over the side of the slate roof on the convent in West Paterson to put up a television antenna. I know God was watching over us that day!"

Tinky shook his head, looked at me and then at Harry. "Youse guys are crazy. Hey, let me see what I can do with this organ. There is a piano too, very cool. I have a nice little choir for this Sunday, Paul. So far, I have Betty Anne, Linny, Ronzo, Binky, and Rose, so we should sound really good for a first go of it. Small numbers, but please be assured, I have some great voices. Even though you cannot sing a lick, Paul, I will ask you to join us, but please do not sing, just make believe you are."

I acknowledged Tinky's very accurate assessment of my singing abilities and assured him that I would only lip sync the songs. I only spoke liturgies. My professors and fellow students in seminary would cover their ears in horror and self-defense, when I would attempt to sing communion liturgies. I received the message loud and clear.

Tinky strode up to the choir loft in front of the sanctuary and checked out the organ. Dave showed him where all the power switches were and before long, he had it all turned on and warmed up. The three of us sat down in the front pew and before you knew it, Tinky was belting out, "Go my Children with my Blessing." It sounded wonderful, and Dave Sharp was very exuberant to hear once again the sound of the organ playing in the church.

"Go ahead and cheer a little there, Sharpie, you deserve it, after holding the line here for so long." Harry elbowed Dave Sharp.

Dave was clearly thrilled and commented to all of us, "That little, red guy, sure can play the organ. I never heard it sound so good."

Tinky finished, stood up, and we all clapped for him.

"It needs some work here and there, but we will get by. Maybe once we have some money coming in, we can get it checked out, tuned up, and back into top notch shape, but it sure will work for now." Tinky seemed very pleased.

I jumped up, excused myself, and headed for the church office to call Binky. I wanted to check and make sure she was okay after our emotional morning, as well as tell her the good news that her brother had just delivered. Harry and I had dropped her off at her workplace after the cemetery visit and we had come straight to the church. I went to the church office and hoped that the telephone line would work. I was relieved when it did. I dialed and my wife answered on the first ring.

She was doing well; in fact, she was very excited, as she told me, "Oh, Paul! Great news! I have successfully cleared the last obstacle for the road. It was some silly paperwork snafu that I uncovered, and once I brought it to everyone's attention, it was only a matter of time before it could be cleared up."

I could hear, even over the telephone, Binky tapping her long fingernails on her desk surface as she was making a point.

"It was some silly nonsense, about a stalled permit to remove the clean fill to cut the road. I told the authority that I was speaking with, how that was ridiculous. What possibly could have stalled the process for all of these years? I had Father become involved, and, in a few hours, it was all set to go!"

"Binky, I love you more and more. As each hour goes on, this is fantastic news." I could picture her on the other side of the phone, fluffing out her long hair, crossing her legs, and sitting confidently behind her desk.

"It was very easy research, Paul. I was able to weed through this very quickly. The caveat is that dear Father is thrilled. He found out that one of his greatest political adversaries and opponents dropped the ball on this one. He is going to hold a big press conference out on the site on Friday. I spoke with Betty Anne and her father, and they agreed to do the work at their cost for the materials, with no markup and donate the labor. Father's office told me that factor has eliminated the need for a bid package to go out, which could have dragged the whole process down. I think if the weather holds out, then by the middle of next week, we should have a road from the highway right into the lot for the church!"

My wife was really amazing. Once she had the details and her research uncovered what she needed, she was virtually unstoppable.

"This is wonderful, dear Binky. I cannot thank you and Dad Hobnobber enough."

"Oh, you can thank me later when it will be more appropriate."

I had to laugh at my wife and her sometimes forthright candidness.

"And you do know my Father. Please be prepared, as he will now make sure you will be in debt to him forever, twenty-seven. This is going to be huge publicity for him. Since it is a reelection year, he is riding this one out to the maximum. He has even named the roadway after himself!"

I love it! Now this is what we are talking about! Well, he did tell me once that he had an ego the size of Manhattan Island.

"Can you come out to the church today? I would love for you to see all the work that we have accomplished."

Binky promised me that she would do her best to duck out early, and we exchanged some more details and hung up. What a woman, she had pulled it all together! That may have been the final obstacle for the entire puzzle. Now, it was just up to me to bring people back into Reunion Lutheran Church. I minimized that task, as it was going to be certainly hard bringing folks back, even if they would now be able to drive directly in off the state highway. There was a lot more to it than just that. I thought about how I am going to be the most unpopular pastor in the world to a certain grouchy bishop. Secretly, I knew that I was really going to love seeing the look on his face when he sees what we have all completed here.

I shared the news of the road with the rest of the gang.

After some backslapping and discussion, we all went back to work. There still were many work assignments to finish up, but we had made a major dent in them now. The team now had all the roof leaks fixed; I installed the new fire eye in the boiler so that the heat was back on. The pipes and lights were complete; the wing of the sanctuary that Dave needed to shut down when the pipes had broken, was now clean and returned to service. Harry, Dave, and the crew were now in the fellowship hall and kitchen, working through a number of issues there.

I planned to have a huge rededication dinner there, in a few weeks, so it would be important to have that building in good shape very quickly.

Tinky was working on his music for Sunday and he was busy in the music hall, glancing through a plethora of old sheet music that had been stored in there. He was very pleased, and, in his glory, checking it all out. I stopped in and poked my head at him through the door.

"How's it looking there, brother-in-law?"

"Oh cool, twenty-seven, just awesome, this place is unreal! I found some music here that has some special arrangements on traditional hymns that I just know I can have the ladies sing perfectly. What a shame this has all sat for so long, Paul. I can eat this up and knock them out of the pews." Tinky was as red as a just picked beet.

"Hey, I know we are family and all, but once you have some dough coming in, and you can afford it, can I maybe be the music director here? Part-time, of course, I could never leave Harry."

He tilted his head to the side and then waved his hands in the air as if he was simulating a banner board in the air. "Tinky W. Hobnobber, Director of Music, Reunion Lutheran Church!"

"The job is yours. I can think of no better man for the job, family or not."

He smiled widely, followed me out the door, and yelled

out as I headed down the hallway, "Could I have business cards, Paul?" I stuck my thumb up in the air as I walked away to indicate that we could do that. "Hey, should I put Tink-a-roo-ski or Tinky on them?"

"Stick with, Tinky!" I yelled back.

Dave had given me the keys to the old pastor's office and now that I had completed most of my repair work, I focused on getting in there and setting the office up, as I would like to have it. Much to the chagrin of my boss, my plan was to stay here; I had no thoughts at all now of failure and closing this magnificent church down.

It was a wonderful office, with a large, old oak desk and a nice view out of a large window of the eastern sky. It had a number of large built-in bookcases, all filled with many old books that I would need to go through. Even though the office had been vacant and closed for quite some time, Dave had kept it nice and clean. It was going to work out just fine.

Sitting behind the desk, I really felt like it was home. I put out some of my personal items that I had gathered up from my desk in the district office in Newark. A picture of Binky went right on my desk in front of me, as well as some small hockey memorabilia and other collectibles here and there. I was sitting at the desk, feeling as if it was all finally coming together, when the telephone on the desk rang and made me jump almost to the roof.

It was the last thing that I ever expected to hear. I reached for it and answered it without hesitation by saying, "Pastor Paul Henson."

It was the telephone line repairman reporting that he repaired the intermittent line failures. We should be back in full telephone service now. I thanked him and hung up. I realized that was the first time I had ever addressed myself by that title. I had to admit that it felt very good, and for the first time in a long time, I no longer felt like I was a retired, former professional, ice hockey goaltender. I was now a Lutheran pastor with my own church. I was now really enjoying the new title that Rose had come up with for me; it was growing on me now.

How about that!

Harry, Dave, Tinky, and the work crews left for the day. I promised to meet them back here in the morning, and I gave them advance warnings of the imminent arrival of, "Hurricane Dad Hobnobber" in a few days.

I realized that I had to come up with some kind of bulletin for Sunday, as well as a sermon of some sort. I had not realized the time when I suddenly heard a gentle tap at the door of my office. I looked up and there was Binky standing in the doorway. She was smiling. She looked as stunning and radiant as ever. Her clear blue eyes flickered at me and her long blonde hair fell all around her as she stood in the doorway. She must have been watching me for a little while and I had not noticed. I had lost track of the time and now remembered that she said she was on her way here.

"I thought I may find you here, I was looking around for a while with no twenty-seven to be found, so I decided to head to the pastor's office. It took me quite a bit longer than I thought it would. This church is a lot larger than I had thought. My dear husband, you look so handsome sitting there behind your desk, you look quite the part now!" She was beaming ear-to-ear as she walked into my office.

I greeted her in Welsh and she answered me in the same language. I was impressed by how much she had picked up through speaking and listening to me, along with her studies. My wife would always proudly proclaim to the world that I was the smartest person she ever met, but I knew in my heart that she was a lot smarter than I would ever be. I noticed she was carrying a very large bag, which she carefully placed inside the door. I came out from behind the desk to assist her.

"Let me help you, Binky."

"No, no, no, now please do not touch. I have it all under control here. This is a surprise for you, so I will just set it here until I see what you have done with your office."

Binky looked around and I could tell she was clearly impressed.

"I love it, Paul, this is perfect for you, so rugged looking. All this dark, oak wood and trim, it really is the décor that I would have picked out for you!"

Binky was delighted with my new office.

"How anyone could ever have allowed this wonderful church to close, or fall into such a sad state of disrepair is a tragedy, Paul. However, you have renewed it. Bishop Von Houten is going to be clearly impressed with your efforts."

"We, my darling, we all have renewed it." I corrected Binky. "It has been such a collective effort of all of us that it is simply a phenomenal success at this point. Of course, without Dave Sharp and his love of the property, I am afraid Von Houten would have shuttered it a long time ago. The repairs are only one part of it, dear wife. Now, I have to figure out how to get some people back in the pews on Sundays."

We shared a kiss and an embrace. She smelled so good; my wife always smelled so good to me.

"I hope my boss is impressed, I need to check in with him, I have not heard from him in a few days, since he sent me out here. Now that we have the telephones fixed, I will give him a call in the next few days."

Binky sat down in a large guest chair in front of my desk and I sat on the edge of the desk.

"Say, do you want to take a look and see what we have finished up around here? I think you will really be impressed."

Binky nodded a rapid Binky head nod, but then she got that coy, little smile that comes over her every once in a while. Her eyes went back and forth and then she jumped out of the chair.

"I do, but first I have to give you this!" She was obviously looking forward to giving me whatever it was that she had carried into the office.

"Sit there in that chair, please!" Binky pointed at the chair she had just vacated and I sat down.

She went over to where she had set down the package when she entered the office, grabbed the package, and handed it to me with a smile.

"I just knew that you would eventually find the pastor's office and that you would settle in. I brought this along because I knew it would be the right time to give it to you today. Please, open it."

I looked at her; I was puzzled because it was a large package and a little heavy. Of course, my wife has superhuman strength and nothing is really too heavy for her.

I opened it carefully under her watchful eye. It was as if it was a Christmas present because Binky was so excited for me to see what was in there. Inside was another package wrapped in brown packing paper and I could smell the strong odor of oil paint.

"Careful now, dear Paul," Binky warned me, as I lifted it out. I then carefully lifted the edges of the paper to reveal a large oil painting in an ornate, dark, wooden frame. Binky was now nearly jumping up and down in her excitement as I pulled out the picture, stood up, and set it upon the edge of my desk.

It was breathtaking. It was a hand-painted oil painting of me; well, to be accurate, it was a painting of number twenty-seven! The painting was of me, crouched down in my goaltending position in front of the net, following a shooter. I was wearing my Long Island Rooster uniform and my old, faithful goalie mask. I recognized the depiction in the painting, from a picture that Ronzo had taken of me a long time ago. It was a picture from the era of when the Redmonds had immersed themselves in the famous photography phase of their lives.

It had been a great picture. In fact, my parents, Harry, and many other folks, have copies of the same picture hanging around in one place or another.

I studied the portrait and noticed something different, as faded and blended on top of the hockey depiction, extending into the remaining canvas, was a much smaller picture of me standing in the pulpit preaching. I was wearing the black suit and collar that Binky prefers me to wear as opposed to a robe.

Someone of great talent painted the portrait. Someone who obviously is a highly skilled professional.

The beauty of it overcame me.

"Do you like it?"

"Binky, I do not know what to say. It is fabulous, but how on Earth did you come upon it? I just do not know what to say."

My wife was beside herself with excitement, because this was something she obviously must have planned for a while. I was awestruck. I really was.

"I had the idea for a long time, Paul. I knew if you ever had your own office that it would be so nice to show all of your unusual careers in a single portrait. That way, when visitors would come to see you, they would know so much more about you and your special background. I had the pictures that I wanted to use, but I needed to find a painter to portray and then paint what I had in my head."

I looked down at the portrait and I could faintly see the initials of the painter in the corner. I read them to Binky, "B-A-S."

"Yes, Paul, I found my painter. It is, Betty Anne."

I was shocked.

"Tinky's girlfriend?"

Binky nodded with her famous stare as well as her fast up and down nod.

"Yes! Tinky mentioned that she now was back to singing

as well as painting. I was intrigued when my brother and then Harry told me how talented she was, so I went to look at her work. As you can tell, she is wonderfully talented. She has painted some incredible paintings, Paul. It is remarkable how a woman who works on site excavation, operating huge earth-moving machines, has also the delicate skill to paint so magnificently. There is so much more than meets the eye with, Miss Betty Anne Schmidt."

I looked from my wife back to the painting and remembered that Harry had told me the same thing on the night when we first met her. Indeed, he was correct, because she has some extraordinary God-given talents. How true, that beauty was only skin-deep. The lessons that my grandfather had taught me long ago, were certainly true. Human beings can be so shallow and cold, if we only stopped to get to know folks that we easily discount based upon appearance, prejudice, conceit, and our own shallowness, then how it would greatly enhance all of our lives.

"She admires you so much that when I asked her to do this, she started on it right away and finished it in a matter of days. She must have worked on it day and night. It was a mission for her. She named it, 'The Many Faces of Paul John Henson.'"

Binky came over and pointed to the painting, down into a far bottom corner, "Look down in the corner there, did you see this?"

I looked where she was pointing down low, into one corner of the painting, was a much smaller rendition of me working on an electrical system, fading into the rest of the portrait depictions.

"Well, I'll be. I did miss that at first. What a complex, and intricate tapestry, she has created here."

I sat down in the chair and held the painting in my hands. I was very touched by the obvious pride that my wife felt for me. She really felt it was important for people to know of my unusual background, as well as where I was now in my career, and in my life. The painting was truly incredible, and the skill of Betty Anne was very apparent.

"We must insist on paying her for it, Paul. She refused to take any money from me for her work. I think if you offer though, she will take some money."

"I agree. I will speak to her on Sunday when she comes to sing in the choir. Let's find a hook and a nail and put it up right away. Binky, you pick the spot. I will go to Dave's shop and pick up the supplies."

I stood up, hugged, and kissed Binky.

"Thank you for the wonderful present, Binky. It is really something special."

"I picked you in the Roosters uniform, because I always loved that picture. You are so intense there. It is a classic pose from the famous twenty-seven. I also think in your heart, they were your favorite team that you ever played for."

Binky was correct, she knew me so well. No matter how many teams I ever played for, I always considered myself a Long Island Rooster. They were a special group of teammates, coaches, and fans. It was a special time in my life. They were the team that first gave me a chance, took me from the streets of the famous, "Geyer Street Gardens," around the corner from Jeff and Harry's home, and believed in the long-haired kid from Paterson, New Jersey. We rode that first season out as underdogs, all the way to a championship together. Finally, the Roosters defeated Jim O'Malley and the Colonials in that now famous seventh game, right before we went into overtime. It was quite a memory for all of us.

As time, has passed, even memories of sour, fierce opponents such as Jim O'Malley, have mellowed, and he seems as if he was just not that bad of a guy, maybe he had some slight anger issues, or he was as they say these days, he was, "just a little misunderstood."

It now seemed as if it was so long ago.

"I wanted you depicted in that black suit and collar, no robes. That black suit and all of your blonde hair in that picture just drives me crazy!"

My wife turned, and she winked at me.

"I will go get the hammer, hooks and nails."

As I spun around to leave, Binky grabbed me gently by my arm and she clasped it. I was puzzled as I turned back towards her.

"I have to confess, Paul. I have a twofold reason for this portrait. You as Pastor Paul also need to practice what you preach. You also need closure now on your past, and what you loved the most about being a goaltender, which I believe, was simply the challenge that it presented to you. I know how much you miss it, and I hope this helps you, as Harry said today, never to forget, but to move on. Now, you can always look up from your desk and see number twenty-seven. Put all those hockey memories in your own little book of time, and place them on a shelf, dear husband. You can open it and glance at it whenever you would want, but you cannot allow it to tear at you forever. You were indeed, a great player and I know deep inside, despite your words, that it grinds and gnaws at you. I know how much it hurts that you were so close, only moments away when you were injured. You knew how you could have made it to the top in the big leagues. That is a fact that everyone who saw you play all knew, but God had a different plan for you, Paul John Henson, I think you now know that."

I held Binky's hand, as I knew how correct she was. I also knew in my heart how I have felt as of late. I was now confident of where we were in our lives.

"Look at my eyes, dear Binky. You say that you can see what is inside of me from my eyes. I will not say a word, just look in there, and they will tell the story."

Binky stared deeply into my eyes and smiled. She saw

the answer that she was seeking.

I returned, and I hung the painting on the sidewall of the office right where Binky had placed a small pencil mark. We stood back, admiring the painting together. It was certainly going to be a conversation piece for me.

"Hey, it is getting late. Do you want to take a quick tour around and then head to meet Harry and the gang for dinner?"

Binky took her purse, and I put her jacket on over her shoulders. She was shaking her head back and forth.

"I want to see what work has been performed here, but I called Rose and told her that you and I had a date night planned for us. I thought we could go to the Town Tavern, just you and me tonight. Then we need to head back home and I think you owe me a thank you, Paul."

She winked at me coyly and this time, it was my turn to nod my head up and down really fast.

"First, we need to stop at home so you can take a shower and get cleaned up. You are all messy from working all day here on repairs, and you smell as if you are either a pipe or some unknown hunk of wire. I cannot quite place the odor . . . it may be copper. I am sure I will obtain the required information to place the smell once I have seen what you have worked on. I also need to obtain data during my tour to research how much longer it will take to bring the facilities up to speed, and to put a dollar amount to all the money that you saved the bishop for his budget. You then will have a much better bargaining angle when it comes time for a salary increase and he wants to low-ball the numbers. Would you wear your black suit and collar out tonight for me, twenty-seven?" She swooped in on me with the Binky stare. I once again nodded and smiled at my wife. There was no way that I could ever refuse that request.

"Good, let's go then, Paul. Show me what you and your merry band of workers have accomplished."

She put her arm in mine, proudly walked out and down the hall with me, as I shut off the light, and closed the door to my office.

What a woman! I thought to myself, thank you Lord, for sending me this lovely gal to be my wife. I am sure I did not deserve it, but thank you anyway!

"I am proud to correct this gross injustice due to the negligence of a few past predecessors of mine! Once the church leadership informed my office of this inequitable situation, I immediately and personally, took the bull by the horns to correct the situation! It took countless hours of research on my part, as well as my staff, to track down what had happened here to prevent the building of this road for all of these years! Now, I am very proud to construct for this small, struggling, congregation, the access road that was promised to them so many years ago!"

New Jersey State Senator William T. Hobnobber was in his element, standing in front of reporters and cameras out along a state highway, waving his arms in the air and proclaiming his success at correcting, "This gross injustice!"

"This should have been done years ago, when the poor, downtrodden church initially cooperated with the state in allowing them the frontage that was requested to build the highway! Nevertheless, somehow, their pleas for assistance went unheard and this poor church suffered alone and in despair! Senator William T. Hobnobber stays true to his word as an elected official for all these years. I always remain loyal to the people whom I serve, and it is with great pride that we will have this road built by next week to allow this church to once more have the proper access to their own property!"

My father-in-law was expounding his heart out here, and he had turned his political blowhard knob up to the maximum setting. The drama and exaggeration of the situation were beyond even Mr. Hobnobber's normal boundaries!

Rose, Dave, Harry, Binky, Mom, Hobnobber, Tinky, and I stood on the front lawn of the church and watched as Dad Hobnobber worked the crowd of reporters as if they were fine violins. The recording cameras rolled for his press conference and announcement of the building of the access road. He was laying it on extra thick even for him; I had never actually seen him in finer form than he was today. His arms were waving above his head. He pointed at where the road was going, wrung his hands together, and whipped up sad facial expressions at all the right moments.

It was a dynamic performance.

Harry leaned in and whispered to me, "Man, oh man, Paul, he is really on top of the old flim-flam game today. What is it your old man always says? Not all the actors are in Hollywood."

I nodded and smiled a little. My dear father-in-law was one of a kind. In addition, to think, he told me a while back he was thinking of semi-retirement. That would never happen. He loved the spotlight way too much.

Tinky growled to the both of us, "My old man is taking credit for all of my sister's work. He sure is a piece of work."

I did not say a word as I could see Binky watching us out of the corner of her eye. She was still very much Mr. Hobnobber's little girl, and I was not going there at all.

"Once more, my longtime opponent in the senate, Senator Wilber Riggs, stalled and mishandled this matter. When I contacted him for mutual assistance on clearing this up, he chose to play the party lines, while these poor people continued to suffer at the church. I was able, with incredibly long hours and due diligence, working the phones for days on end, to clear it all up without Senator Riggs' help! On top of all of this, I worked a deal with a local contractor to donate the labor, and provide the materials for the road at cost with no markup!"

Our instructions from Dad Hobnobber's assistants had been to clap wildly and cheer loudly at their cue, and right on time, we all clapped and cheered so the camera and microphones caught us in the background.

Binky grabbed my arm, "Isn't Father wonderful, for all he has done here!"

"Yes dear, wonderful."

After waving his hands in a motion to calm the staged and phony cheers and claps, Senator William T. Hobnobber continued, "Despite my best wishes to remain far in the background on this, I finally had to concede a small matter under intense pressure from my staff and the people whom I humbly serve. Despite my humble wishes and approach, I finally conceded that the new roadway would be named, Senator William T. Hobnobber Way."

Dad Hobnobber bowed a little and worked his best humble face while he acknowledged the claps and cheers that once more, we had received very clear instructions to provide. Oh, brother, is this one too much or what, I thought. Binky and Mom Hobnobber beamed at his performance. Once more, my old man's famous saying of all the actors are not in Hollywood came to mind. This was an award-winning performance for sure.

"Thank you, for attending, folks. Thank you all."

A reporter rushed in with his microphone and rudely stuck it in Dad Hobnobber's face. He then quickly asked, "Is it not true that your son-in-law has recently been appointed as the pastor of this church, Senator Hobnobber?"

We all stopped to listen. This reporter had dug a little deeper into the situation and had done a little homework.

Senator Hobnobber stopped and turned into his ruthless courtroom alter ego. His voice became deep and rather intimidating.

"Very true, he is the pastor here. So, does that make the situation change at all? Exactly what does that matter? The fact is, the state never built the road, and now, they will build it! I ask you to check the facts! Am I not, correct? The road was never built and it should have been. Am I, correct? Of course, I am!"

He then leaned in with the famous, Hobnobber stare and the reporter backed down. I had to admit Mr. Hobnobber was right on target. His facts were the facts, and we all know that Senator Hobnobber worked on facts. Nevertheless, he was indeed correct. It really did not matter. He strutted back to us like a rooster walking into the henhouse.

Mom Hobnobber grabbed him and planted a huge, lip-lock kiss on him. "I am so proud of you, honey, you were exquisite!"

Harry cleared his throat, "Say, Mom Hobnobber, I think I cheered pretty loud over here, can I have one of those kisses too?"

"Sure, Harry!" Mom Hobnobber exclaimed, walked over and lip-locked Harry, while she forcibly grabbed him by the cheeks of his backside to steady him. Harry was dizzy from the celebration.

"Father, you were wonderful," Binky said, as she kissed her father on his cheek.

"Well, thank you all, I did the best I could. Binky does deserve a little credit here also, for her slight efforts at clearing this all up."

I learned a long time ago that sometimes I was better off not saying a word in these types of strange situations. This reaction has served me well over the years.

I greeted Dad Hobnobber, extended my hand out to shake his, which he, of course, refused.

"No way there, Paul. I refuse to be subjected to your brutal torture even though, you are now indebted to me forever, for this amazing coup that I pulled off on the church's behalf. I keep waiting for you to get old, fat, and soft, sucking down my gorgeous daughter's cooking that you make her slave away in the kitchen preparing for you every day, while you lie around composing boring sermons. Instead, you seem to grow stronger and more physically fit with age. I am, however, too smart to be lured into your tricks and have my afternoon interrupted by a trip to the emergency room."

"Well, thank you, Dad. I do owe you a tremendous, thank you and on behalf of Reunion Lutheran Church, we all thank you."

"Well, make sure they say it with votes there, Paul, votes mean a lot more than thank you!"

"I understand."

"Good, well, we must be off, I have to get back to the office to watch all the news rooms as they rebroadcast my press conference over and over this entire afternoon. My head was not really shiny, in all of those bright lights, was it, my dear Sarah?"

"No, no, no, dear William, you looked just as you always do . . . my big, raging, sexy husband."

Harry elbowed me in the side. This was even more than he could stand, and Harry sure could lay it on thick himself. Dad Hobnobber made Harry look like an unranked amateur in the horn blower genre.

"Say, ah, Paul, when you have a free moment from lounging around here doing nothing, please waltz on over to the Hobnobber family estate."

"Sure, it would be my pleasure Dad, what did you have in mind?" I noticed that little competitive lick in his eye, which I had not seen in quite a long time. I had hoped our sports and athletic competitions were not going to begin once again.

"Well, I heard from your boss, the bishop, that you do not cheat when playing Warship and I recently took up the game. We could share a few drinks, and some quality family time. I would like to play a few rounds with you."

"I would like that, Dad. Once I clear up a few matters

here, I will stop by."

"I will look forward to it."

Harry walked over and put his arm around Dad Hobnobber. "Good call there, Dad Hobnobber, board games are the way to go with, twenty-seven. He is too honest to cheat, and you can move your ships around and destroy him! That is the only way I could beat him at anything when we were kids. You will feel great, to beat him at something and watch him lose."

Dad Hobnobber was smiling widely, already plotting his strategy.

"One more thing Dad, I have this for you, I have finally finished it after a very long time of promising it to you. I thought it was the least that I could give you today for all of your efforts," I said while handing him an envelope.

Dad Hobnobber looked puzzled.

"Well, thank you, Paul, what is it? Is it the long overdue, written, heartfelt, apology for marrying my beloved daughter without my prior permission?"

"Dear Father! Paul is not overdue on anything," Binky jumped in when she heard her father winding it up.

"No Dad, almost as overdue though, it is my dissertation on the interpretation of the lyrics to 'Close to the Crevice.' I finally finished it last week."

The senator spun the paper in his hand while glancing at it. He almost smiled, as he said, "No, kidding. You know, you do keep your promise. It sure took you long enough. Despite the fact that you are a long-haired, hippie pastor, who has spent the best part of the last ten years, doing nothing, while raking in major money, you do eventually come through. I have to say, rather regretfully, that I am impressed that you actually had the diligence to buckle down and perform some quality research, instead of pawning it all off on Binky, and then taking the credit for it."

"I apologize for how long it took, Dad. Those are some

difficult lyrics to figure out, but I think I found some clues of where it all is coming from. I hope that you enjoy it."

"I look forward to reading it. We will see you here on Sunday as we all suffer through another one of your long, drawn out, boring sermons."

"Thank you, Dad. That will be nice."

He waved, kissed all the women goodbye, and he was off, with Mom Hobnobber wiggling alongside of him.

Harry stood there admiring the view of Mom Hobnobber as she headed for the Hobnobber's big Galaxy 3000.

He shook his head, and he whistled.

"That sure is one fine-looking lady from the rear. Her lips are magical, and man, she can grab my, ass any day."

Binky and Rose both punched him in the opposite shoulders as Harry laughed and tried in vain to escape.

"Hey! Big Harry calls it as he sees it!"

We all had our own work to do in the afternoon. Rose and Tinky went back to the restaurant, and Binky had to return to her job, so off we all went on our individual assignments. Harry and Dave were in the kitchen now, working on the last few repairs in there. At one point, I spotted Harry dragging his small welder in there for some type of mission, so I knew they were working on a major repair there. I had to finish the bulletin and my sermon for Sunday, so I returned to my office to complete that task.

I was sitting at my desk when the telephone rang.

"Pastor Paul Henson speaking."

"Henson! What the hell are you doing out there?"

Oh no, it was my boss! I had meant to call him the last few days, but I just never got around to it.

"Well, hello, Bishop Von Houten. How are you?"

"Lousy, Henson! Lousy as usual because of you!"

He was now screaming loudly into the phone, so I held it away from my ear.

"I was sitting here with Goldberg, enjoying my lunch, all

set to hit the golf course with the rabbi this afternoon, when the television over the bar that is broadcasting the afternoon news comes on with a press conference. Of course, what is this news about, but the church that I sent you out to close down! There on the screen is that big, blowhard, senator father-in-law of yours, proclaiming that he, along with help from Jesus, Moses and all the other major prophets, have contracted to build the long, lost road to Jericho that no one else has been able to have built. I sent back our sodas and ordered double shots for Goldberg and me. Five days out there and you have a road built that no one has been able to do for years, Henson!"

I decided to sit on the sideline and let him rant and rave.

"I am going broke buying Annoy-O-Meters to put your name on! I am running out of wall space to hang them. Even Goldberg bought one because he needed to put your name on it because he was tired of hearing about you."

"I see, sir. I am sure my buddy Harry appreciates the business and revenue."

"What else have you meddled in out there, Henson?"

"Well, Bishop Von Houten, we now have many of the repairs completed. The roof no longer leaks, the lights all work, the boiler provides heat, the broken pipes are replaced, and we have made great strides."

"WHAT, THE HELL, HENSON? HOW MUCH DID THIS ALL COST? MY BUDGET HENSON! DID THEY NOT TEACH YOU THE SLIGHTEST BIT ABOUT ECONOMICS IN SCHOOL? MONEY, HENSON! MONEY!"

I placed the phone down on the desk so I could hear him clearly. I thought I would just let him go on and on for a little while until he calmed down. I could hear him carrying on and on about money and his budget. When it finally sounded like he was running out of breath and the volume of his screaming lowered, I picked up the receiver once more.

"So, Henson, how on Earth do you think we will fund this little, unauthorized, ill advised, adventure of yours? Perhaps, you intend to sell autographed pictures of you from your old hockey days on Sundays during worship."

"Well, no sir, you see we do not have to raise any money at all, because I obtained all the materials, labor for the repairs, and renovations for free. I would never have spent any of your money without your prior approval, Bishop Von Houten."

There was silence on the other end of the telephone for a few moments.

"Free . . . Henson, as in no cost to us? Zippo, zilch, nothing?"

"Why, yes sir, not one penny from your budget."

There was another long silence on the other end of the telephone. I almost thought for a moment that the line had gone dead again until I heard a long sigh and some papers rustling on the other end.

"I know that I will regret asking this. Once I hear the answer to the question that I am about to ask, an answer that I most likely already know, we will have to skip golf and Goldberg and I will head back to the bar, but how did you manage to pull this off, Henson?"

"Well, bishop, as you may remember from my previous background that I did work as an electrician for many years, as well as I was trained on heating and cooling systems, when I was in the trade school, therefore. . .."

"Yes, Henson. That was right before playing professional ice hockey and before deciding to become a pastor, in between flying around above the city of Paterson in your superhero cape."

I paused to allow the bishop to enjoy his comment on my background.

"Well, sort of sir, but without the cape part. We were able to perform most of the technical repairs ourselves, along with the help of one of my best friends from the old neighborhood, Mr. Ronzo Boatmann. Ronzo is the best electrician that I have ever seen or worked with."

"I see, Henson, Ronzo. Every old neighborhood in America has a Ronzo. Let me guess Binky, Tinky, and 'Dinky the Orange Teddy Bear' also came along to help."

"Well, yes, my wife and my brother-in-law did help. I cannot vouch for the bear though, except perhaps in spirit. I also repaired all the broken pipes that froze."

"Of course, you did, Henson."

"Some of the old supply houses that I dealt with years ago were willing to help when they heard I needed some materials, but it also took some assistance from our lovely friend Rose, who flirted with them a little, and then managed to have them agree to donate all the materials for free to us."

"I see, Henson, but much-too-much information. Learn to spin it into something that sounds better for a man of the cloth to be involved in, such as utilizing your available resources. Go on."

"Binky and I purchased the expensive, fire eye part for the boiler repair and donated that to the church. Mr. Harry Redmond Jr., whom you have met, and do admire for his great invention of the Annoy-O-Meter, took care of the majority of the large repairs and troubles. Harry donated his entire shop of labor, tools, time, materials, trucks, welders, and an aerial lift to repair the steel beams as well as all the roof leaks. He is right now working in the kitchen on some last repairs. We still have painting and some general repairs to finish up, but for the most part, by the middle of next week, all the serious repairs will have been completed."

"I knew it, Henson. I just knew that it would be a team effort of your entire entourage that follows you all over the planet. You are like some long-haired, Pied Piper of hippie adventure Henson, you really are."

"Thank you, sir."

"I hire one hippie pastor and I also receive free of charge, this whole team of people who come along with him. Amazing Henson, it really is. All of this has happened in five days, Henson, it is really incredible."

I heard the bishop breathe deeply over the telephone, and then he exhaled.

"Please, not another word! I can finish the rest of the story for you, Henson. Your lovely and talented wife, researches the snafu that stopped the road from being built years ago, clears the roadblocks, alerts her big-mouth senator father, and whoopee! The long, lost road is built!"

"Well, yes, bishop. That is indeed correct."

There was another long pause on the other end of the phone.

"And what happened to Darryl, the maintenance guy? Is he now also inspired to become a minister and has run off to join missions in Africa?"

"Dave, bishop . . . his name is Dave."

"That's what I said, Henson. Dave."

"He is here working with Harry in the kitchen, but since he was down on his luck and needed money since his hours were cut here at the church, he now works for Harry part-time as a maintenance man."

"Okay. I understand, Henson. Yes, you are once more flying around in your cape, saving the downtrodden. You know, I sent you out there to close that church down and this is what I get. A pastor who repairs complex electrical systems, repairs pipes, boilers, and his team of friends who do everything from pave roads, to flirt with supply house workers, to climb to the top of church rooftops, welding steel beams, and repairing roof leaks. That is not what I instructed you to do, Henson. I told you to ride it out until we closed it."

"Well, sir, with all due respect, the exact words that you told me, were to come out here and see what I could do, so that is what I did."

Bishop Von Houten paused and then said, "I did say that, didn't I, Henson? You are such a pain in my ass. Well, that is not what I really meant."

"However, bishop, isn't the point to grow our church families and expand in the name of the gospel, not to close down churches?"

"Yeah, yeah, yeah, Henson, I know what our mission is! After all, I am the bishop around here! You know, there are not enough Annoy-O-Meters in the entire world to put your name on, you are so annoyingly correct and efficient."

"Thank you, sir, I appreciate the compliment."

"So now that you have accomplished all this, how do you intend to put asses in the seats and fill the collection plates?"

"I will begin to work on that this Sunday. I have a solid sermon and worship service planned, we have a newly formed choir, the organ is working now, and I have my brother-in-law Tinky all set to play it on Sunday."

"Of course, you have all of that already, Henson. Let me guess, you also will have professional singers in the choir, and spaceships will land from outer space on the back lawn, bringing visitors from Heaven to your service."

"No, not exactly, but it should be a great service sir, please come out, and join me."

"No way, Henson. I will be home putting your name on my Annoy-O-Meter and then after extensive prayer, I will head out to play golf and drink beer with Rabbi Goldberg."

"I see, sir. That sounds like an enjoyable day."

"Any day, I am far away from you and your circle of strange and unusual weirdness is a good day, Henson."

"Well sir, I do need to tell you, how I wrote in the church bulletin of your outstanding support, leadership, and guidance during this difficult period for Reunion Lutheran Church. I wrote a lengthy report, thanking you, for what you had done here, to keep this afloat long enough to see the road built and all the other wonderful things that you have overseen. I also included details on how the repairs came about due to your assigning me here in a fabulous, management maneuver, to utilize your available resources."

His voice suddenly changed, "Hmm, I like that Henson, now I like what I heard. Please send me multiple copies of that will you! I have some extra frames here in my office."

A moment once more changed everything, as all of a sudden, the bishop was a different person.

"I plan to have a rededication dinner and service planned for a week from this upcoming Saturday, at the church in the fellowship hall. I would love to have you there to give you further credit for all you have accomplished. I plan on inviting the entire community and also will work hard to have some press coverage here."

"Is your buddy donating all the food for the dinner from his restaurant?"

"Yes, as a matter of fact, he is doing that, Bishop Von Houten."

"Will you serve free, Harry Burgers? Will your wife and that pretty gal, Rose, be there?"

"Yes, sir."

"I will be there! Great work, Henson, especially on the recognition of my invaluable contributions, of which without, you would have certainly failed. Great work, please keep it all up."

"Thank you, sir."

"Click."

The line went dead. I hung up the telephone. I think that my boss may actually like me.

He just has a difficult time showing it.

A really, really, really difficult time.

9

Reunion

The Sunday service went well, but I was a bit disappointed in the attendance. Despite many folks, seeing the news broadcasts, and the fact that the long sought-after road was under construction, not many of the locals came out. The membership list had shown only about thirty people left in the congregation, so I am not quite sure what I was expecting. I thought it was very unusual that other than Dave and his wife, and one older gentleman, who explained that he was a long-time member, no other church members even came by during the week to visit the church. I imagined that the remaining congregation suffered from a depleted spirit and were down to the final, last gasps when I arrived. We only had about thirty-five people in total who attended Sunday worship, but that included Mom and Dad Hobnobber, my parents, Binky, Rose, Harry, Tinky, and Betty Anne as well as Linny and Ronzo.

I had invited Father Mark, but he could not attend, as he was having a difficult time getting around now. I did call him and speak with him on that Saturday, and although he sounded weak; he remained in good spirits. We prayed together over the telephone, and it meant a lot to each of us to share in the moment together.

When you omitted our group from the total attendance numbers, then it was a very sad turnout. However, I did not let it discourage me, as I did have the opportunity to meet what seemed to be the nucleus of the remaining members, as well as the only two remaining elders serving the church. I think initially; the members were, of course, taken back by my appearance, but it seemed like Dave had done much behind-the-scenes work in paving the way for me. All the folks that we met were thrilled at the progress that had been made on the repairs of the church, and of course, the news of the road was something they all had waited a very long time to see finally come to fruition.

The two remaining elders, as well as a number of other members, made appointments to come and see me during the week. I felt as if that was an encouraging sign. They wanted to get to know me and to learn more of what my plans were for the future of the church. Tinky played magnificently, and our little choir led by Linda and Betty Anne was a huge hit. They sang wonderfully together. I could see that Tinky had his wheels already spinning, on how he had the makings of quite a potential band in the secular world with these two singers.

Mom and Dad Hobnobber met Betty Anne for the first time and in retrospect, having this first meeting at church really softened the impact of that meeting considerably! My father-in-law was on his best behavior; after all, this *was* a church service.

I preached a "middle of the road" sermon that I had carefully planned. Not too much emotion, I kept it very upbeat, with a theme of renewal related to the repairs of the church that I then tied to a Bible verse or two. It seemed to go over well enough, but then again, a large majority of the congregation in attendance consisted of my friends and family. During the announcements period in the order of worship, I did take the time to introduce Senator William T. Hobnobber and thank him for the success of the road. Despite the small audience, he took the opportunity to seize the moment and as always, he remained the consummate politician. He was always on the campaign trail, looking for votes.

After the service, I did have the chance to thank Betty

Anne for the painting. After some considerable persuasion, she did agree to allow Binky and me to pay her for her work.

Overall, my first week at Reunion Lutheran was a huge success. The work that we had accomplished working together as a team in a very short time was truly remarkable. I just needed to figure out a way to increase attendance.

Betty Anne felt that if the weather cooperated, it would take their company about four days to complete the road. That meant we would have it in place for the dinner planned for next Saturday. I told her that I would pray for some sunny skies and clear weather. I was truly thankful for my wonderful friends and family and for all of their hard work and support. Without them, nothing would have happened and Reunion Lutheran Church would be well on the way to being a sad part of history.

Monday arrived, and it was very peaceful at Reunion Lutheran Church. Harry and his crew had completed most of the major repairs now, and the rest would be up to us. Once I had filled the ranks of the church, I knew that I could utilize church monies, as well as volunteer labor, for a majority of the other work that remained outstanding. Work such as painting, decorating projects, as well as general spruce up, was perfect for internal church projects. The trick was now getting the volunteers along with that money!

Dave was off on Mondays. He was down in Paterson working for Harry at his shop, factory, and the restaurant. I had the church to myself and I had to admit that it felt really good after all the emotion, hard work, and hectic pace of the previous week. I hunkered down in my office, determined to work on a new sermon and some fresh ideas. I had some rare quiet time, and I was feeling productive. I had some appointments for later in the week, with some church members and a few worship committee members, but today was free.

Sitting at my desk, I heard a faint knock on the wood in the open doorway of my office and I looked up.

In the doorway of my office stood Ms. Rose Rose.

She smiled at me and said, "Sorry to disturb you, Pastor Paul, but can I have some time alone with my favorite pastor in the entire world?"

I stood up and smiled back, "Rose, what a nice surprise, of course you can, my dear Rose, the door is never closed to you. Of all people, you know that."

These days, Rose still always had that soft element of sadness deep in her eyes that never left. I did have to agree with Harry. As Rose had grown older, she turned from being pretty, to being dazzling. She was a radiant, vibrant, young lady, who had matured into a successful, professional, career-oriented woman. Rose had now settled into her professional life, but I knew this visit was not going to be about her career, it was going to be about a much deeper subject.

Bishop Von Houten might be an old crabapple, but he does know his profession. He had told me on the day when he first met Harry and Rose at my now famous, "tryout," that they both would be seeking my counsel and guidance. I had already managed to make it through the Harry phase of this process, and I had a strange feeling I was now going to be undertaking phase two.

I walked from behind my desk, met Rose, leaned over, and hugged her.

I heard her laugh, "I swear you are bigger and taller than you ever were, you are still so far up there!"

Her eye caught the portrait on the wall of my office and she walked over towards where it hung on the wall.

"This painting is amazing. The talent that Betty Anne has is really something else." Rose was standing in front of the portrait on the wall admiring the painting.

"I agree, Rose. No doubt that it is quite the focal point

for anyone who comes in my office."

Rose turned back to me and said, "I had to come right over, and I am very excited at what I have come up with today. Paul, I have to tell you that I have worked out this great idea for the marketing of the big dinner this Saturday. It should be here tomorrow. Harry said his crew would put it up for me."

I was intrigued. "It will be here? Put it up as in put up a sign or something?"

Rose walked over to the guest chair and she sat down in front of my desk while I stood over on the wall near the painting.

She was excited, and a little animated now, "Well sort of, it is actually a very large banner. I took the same picture that is in your new portrait here of you playing goal and had it put on the banner. I then added the words in large bold print, only God saves more than number twenty-seven. Under that in smaller print, is the invitation to come join us this Saturday, at seven in the evening, for a church rededication dinner at Reunion Lutheran Church."

Her eyes were twinkling now because she was obviously very proud of her idea. Harry was correct; Rose did indeed have a knack for marketing and innovative ideas.

I went and sat down behind my desk and told her, "I love it, Rose, a very nice play on the words there. I am sure my boss is going to throw a fit when he sees it, so that means he secretly will like it too!"

"Oh, that old, grouchy, bishop, he is a real piece of work. I plan to tie it up out there while they are building and paving the new road. It will attract a lot of attention as people look over at the construction work. The fact that there is a major highway out in front of the church makes that spot a fabulous location from which to advertise. The amount of people that will see the banner will be amazing. I have all the other details worked out for the dinner, the food, the soda, the snacks . . . I have everything. It should be quite a nice event."

"Great job, Rose, I cannot thank you enough."

She smiled at me, and then the smile faded a little. Her excitement also had faded. I knew that she was now past the dinner planning, and she had other subjects on her mind. Rose twisted a bit in the chair and then she leaned back.

"You're welcome, Paul. It is like Harry says all the time . . . we could never really pay you back for all you have done for all of us." She sighed deeply; her eyes drifted up to the ceiling and then back down to me again.

I could tell she was searching for the courage to speak openly and honestly. 'Here it comes,' I thought.

"You know, twenty-seven . . . I surely miss . . . how you and I used to talk one-on-one. Those times meant so much to me, Paul. They were very special. I do not know what I would have done without you, Paul, and all of your advice and guidance."

"We did share an awful lot together, Rose, but we still do."

"I know we do, but it is just not the same. I just cannot get that old feeling back. Somehow when we spoke years ago, I always held out hope. I held out hope that you . . . well, Harry would . . . I know you are way too smart not to know how I feel."

I looked at Rose, our eyes met thoughtfully, as I spoke in a low voice, "You mean how much you love, Harry? In fact, how much, you always have, Rose?"

She nodded. I expected her tears to come shortly, but she remained strong and seemed for now to be in control of her emotions.

"I cannot explain it, Paul. I have tried everything. I look pretty for him, we laugh, we share things, he holds my hand once or twice in a conversation, and it sends a shiver down my spine. I wear nice perfume, nice dresses, and every time, I think I have broken down his barriers, nothing happens. It is as if he is holding back, holding back on showing me any affection, other than being an employee or a close friend. He keeps it strictly business all the time. It is tearing me apart. I am working side-by-side with him so closely, and yet, we are so far apart from where I want to be. Occasionally, he moves in and I think this is going to be the moment. I hang on the edge of anticipation, waiting for him to make a move, to tell me that he cares, or something, even more than that! Then, it fades away."

Rose hung her head down a little and her voice choked with some soft emotion.

"I am so sad, Paul. I now know how you must have felt years ago, when you were all alone playing hockey in those strange places, longing for home and for Binky. Loneliness is so bitter, so painful. It is terrible, Paul. It really is." Rose no longer could hold back the tears and her eyes now welled up.

I moved out from behind my desk and sat on the edge of the front of the desk, next to her.

"Rose, it is all right, please do not ever be lonely, you have so many people who care about you."

"I know that Paul, it is the emptiness I feel in my heart that causes loneliness. I go to work, it is busy, it is challenging, and I forget. Then the work ends, the day ends, I go back to my apartment, and it is all over. Then the loneliness hits, the sadness, at what I once had, and I long for those wonderful times to return. I really think they never will. Those times were so special. They were unlike anything that I have ever known in my entire life."

I knew all too well that same feeling. I could feel her pain at the exact description of how it eats away at you, day after day. I needed to comfort her, I needed now to search for the words to help her, and I prayed in my mind for the right words to come along to provide her with guidance and comfort.

"I never really stopped caring for Harry, it was just that I grew so weary of all the drama, the chasing of other women, and of him just not being or acting as himself. Then, when it all fell apart for all of us, I could not handle it and I took the easy way out. Why do people always take the easy way out, Pastor Paul?"

"I do not think you took the easy way out, Rose. You did what you felt was best at the time, no one would find fault in that. Harry was and is, a virtual hurricane of turmoil and emotions. He can be difficult to keep up with."

Rose did not address my answer to her question, but she continued with her explanation, "Sky came along and, of course, you know the rest. I have noticed that Harry is so different now. He still is so funny and makes me laugh. Nowadays, there is a deep caring he has for people, such as an appreciation of where he has been in his life, and what he has learned from all the dark times and pain. He in many ways has calmed down, and he is so steady . . . like you are. He is smart, reliable, honest, generous, and predictable. I love him, Paul, with all of my heart, and I just wish and pray that it all could have been different. All I want is to settle down, for that special train loaded with love and all the other things you told me about that night, to come down the tracks in my life."

Rose leaned forward and put her hands on the edge of my desk as if she was holding onto it to steady herself. She sighed deeply, looked up at the ceiling of my office and then back down to my eyes.

I let her collect her thoughts and strength.

"I know that I would love to have what you and Binky have. I fear it will never be. It is out of reach with Harry now. Maybe, I need to forget and move on with my life, find a new job, and just begin all over."

I had to laugh to myself, as Harry had now become, as he grew older, that typical man that he described in his own theory so many years ago. He himself, the world-famous Harry M. Redmond Jr., was now the type of man who women want to marry, but not date. In his own way, Harry had called his own number so many years ago. As crazy as the Harry Theory was, it actually had mountains of truth associated with it!

I looked at Rose and her tears and I knew she was searching for an answer, for some type of hope. It seemed as if Rose had exhausted her emotions and laid her cards face up.

It was now time to be Pastor Paul. We needed a little change of scene here. I was utilizing some tricks taught to me in seminary to relax people during emotional counseling situations, but in reality, I did not know exactly what I was going to say to Rose.

I motioned for Rose to move over to a guest chair on the other side of my office and she got up, moved over, and sat down. I pulled over the other guest chair from the corner of the office and sat in front of Rose.

I was searching my mind for something to say, to provide comfort to Rose. I felt strongly that Harry had closed a chapter of his life at the cemetery, but I did not know if he was ready to open a new one. As well as I knew Harry, I had no real direction that I was feeling of how this would turn out. I decided that I would just have to go with it on this one.

"Rose, I am not going to give you my standard old clichés, such as believe it and it will happen, or hang in there and have faith, and so on and so forth. The truth is that Harry is struggling himself with his own feelings and direction. I know he cares for you deeply. I think that in the past few days he has made great strides in controlling his emotions and obtaining a new direction in his life. The memory of Sky and their love and relationship still lingers in his very soul. The last thing you want is to live, and share your love with a memory, Rose. Harry knows that . . .

he really does. He now is way too wise and honest, ever to do that to a person whom he loves. You see, that shows how much he cares about you and how he has changed. The old Harry would have not cared, he would have run off somewhere with you, and then run ramshackle over you and life and move on."

Rose was now listening very intently, and she finally said, "Paul, I understand, and I agree that Harry is so different now."

"Rose, I have no great words of advice and wisdom for you on this, but I do know Harry better than anyone. Something will make his mind up. Something will turn for him and trigger his feelings and stir his inner soul. He then will make a move. He in many ways reacts like a trigger to something, so you need to be ready. Now, whether it is the decision that your heart desires, I do not know, but with Harry, always be ready. If and when, you move in and consume his very inner soul, then you will know it."

I reached out, took her hand, and looked at her. The sadness, longing and sorrow in her eyes were very deep. It was difficult for me to see my dear friend feeling so poorly. She had been depressed in her spirits for so long now that I felt she was cheating herself of time and happiness. I searched for the words that she wanted to hear to provide some sort of comfort. I had to be honest with her. This situation did not call for hopes and dreams and words based upon pie in the sky assumptions. That would not be fair to Rose.

"Rose, it may never, ever happen that you and Harry resume your romance. However, you are a young, gorgeous, vibrant, woman who is smart, successful, and has a lot of love to give to a man. Sometimes, as much as we pray, hope, and desire, it is God's plan for us to go on in a different direction than what our heart desires. I learned that. For certain, I truly learned that."

I glanced up at the portrait on my wall.

"You have to realize that remaining positive and charging forward in your life is always the best way to go. Thinking positively will bring positive results, thinking about being defeated, will bring only despair and defeat. I know that from playing goalie. Sometimes, I felt like David marching out to face an army of Goliaths. Even when I felt poorly and felt weak, I skated out there, and once the flow of the game came over me, the confidence came. I then knew that I was not going to be beaten. Rose, put on your own armor of change, skate into your own net and smile, laugh, dance, love, choose your dreams and life will reward you. Turn on the light of hope and joy and shut out the darkness of despair. You are way too special not to do that."

I then remembered the front porch at 182 Belmont Avenue in the old neighborhood, a warm summer night, cold beer, and my grandfather and a conversation we had.

"Just take heart and know that everyone cares about you. You have so many friends and people who love and who respect you. If Harry is in your romantic future, then it will happen, but if he is not, then remember, once you have a circle of support, combined with the correct frame of mind, as well as loving friends and family, you have all the power that you need to succeed at anything in life. Then you and your loved ones and friends can charge off into life's battles with your battle flags unfurled, ready and able, to take on anything that this old world can throw at you. Perhaps, you do need to move on, put all your old memories of our wonderful times together and your love for Harry, inside of a book of time, and place it on a shelf in your mind. Open it at times and remember, but live for you, live for now, not for what once was."

I had a calm approach and the same words I used in speaking with Harry came to my mind once more, "Someday, the present days will be the days that you talk about fondly, not the days of old memories."

Rose opened her purse, took out a tissue, and wiped her eyes. I stood up, went over to my desk, pulled out some more tissues from a tissue box, and handed them to her.

"Thank you, Paul. I can see that you were prepared for a visit from emotional Rose."

One of the first things I learned in seminary in my counseling class was to have a box of tissues available at all times.

Good lesson learned there for sure.

"I think you are right, Paul, your advice is wonderful, as it is also painful. I feel much better, I really do. I knew I missed chatting with you. I just did not realize how much until now."

I did not answer her. I did feel deep inside by her reaction that I had helped her in some way. I just smiled back and nodded my head.

It now seemed as if a million dreams were circling in and around her mind. She was such a caring and genuine person. I do not ever think I had met a person who wore almost every emotion possible on her exterior, more than Rose did. I would begin today to pray fervently for her to find what she was looking for, and for all the help in Heaven to help her find it.

I could not have asked for a more authentic friend; she was very special to me. Rose stood up from her chair and walked over to my desk. She picked up a little hockey stick memento from the edge of my desk and fiddled with it as she laughed at it. I could tell there was something else on her mind.

"I have been thinking about one other thing the last few months or so, Paul. If I am going to move on, then I just made my final decision. I want to convert to Lutheranism and join your church here, Paul."

I must admit that I was shocked, and it must have shown in my face as Rose smiled at me broadly.

"Wow, was that statement that much of a shock to you?"

I recovered rather quickly, but I still was off guard, "Frankly it is, Rose. Are you sure? What brings this on? It cannot be my dynamic preaching. Or now, could it be?"

"Well, of course, pastor!" She joked a bit and then grew serious.

"Honestly, I want to remarry someday and raise a family, you know, move on finally. I love what you said a few minutes ago, to put on the armor of change. If I am to do that, then I need to be brave, and armor is what I will need. You see, if I remain Catholic, then I cannot share in the full sacraments and be a real member, if and when, I remarry."

"I can certainly understand that, Rose."

"In all honesty, I really have connected with the Lutheran services, I am comfortable here, and it is something that I know that I need to do to move on with the healing process. Of course, the fact that you are the most wonderful and handsome pastor in the world, and I enjoy listening to you, is indeed a big influence."

Rose stared at me and paused a bit, then she continued to speak, "In fact, Paul, I am not just saying this because of our relationship, but I could listen to you speak for hours. Talking to you is always like swallowing a big, magic tonic or potion. I do not ever really understand how you have this calming effect on people, but it is very real."

Rose put her head down and she hid her eyes from me a little. This was a difficult choice for her to have made. Rose had reached a crossroads in her life, and now it was time to decide upon the direction in which she was going to take. First, it required a reunion of her soul. She needed to reunite with her own dreams and desires. It was so ironic that this was happening on the heels of Harry visiting Sky's grave, where he also had a reunion with his inner soul, hopes, and dreams. Then again, thinking about Sky and her presence, perhaps it was not irony at all.

I am sure that it was exhausting to Rose, in both her

mind, and her spirit. She was gathering all of her thoughts and feelings before speaking. I knew that this was something that she had thought about for a long time. I was now feeling much better about her choice by interpreting her body language.

Rose looked up and her face was confident and assured now, "I have been thinking of it for a while now. It was not a split-second decision, Paul. You know how deeply I feel about my spiritual beliefs."

"I understand, and I am glad to hear that it was not a quick decision. I will be, of course, happy to assist you, and we can instruct you rather quickly. I hope that once we fill this church back up, then I will have many people in my membership classes, but for now, I am afraid it will be only you and Pastor Paul. If you can stand me one-on-one, then we can get started whenever you would like. It is a simple process, some instruction, some reading. Some of it is actually very similar to your old catechism classes."

I stood up and went to the bookshelf, looking for some pamphlets that I had seen last week.

"I am thrilled, Rose. You will be my first, brand-new member. I can think of no other person in the world that I would rather it be either."

Rose stood up; she gathered her purse and jacket. She came over, hugged me, and kissed my cheek.

We held each other for a while. It was almost as if I could feel the hurt and pain leaving her body. It was very strange, as if I was absorbing it from her. I remembered that night so long ago on the front porch of 20 John Street, where Sky told me that Harry took strength from me, and that was why I felt drained at times. I knew that I would face many challenges in my new career, but I also now knew that the doubts I had about the life I had left behind were all gone. Many reasons had led me to this position. I wondered how many lives I was required to touch as I made my way along the path that I was now venturing upon. Sky had also told me on that very same night that I should be doing exactly what I was now doing. It was all very strange.

Sky really knew an awful lot of things about the mysteries of life that I could only hope someday to understand.

Rose was relaxed, she was no longer tense or on an edge.

"I do love you, Paul. You have always been there for me . . . from the day we first met."

"Rose, I always will be, you know how much Binky, and I love you too. Now, go in peace and serve the Lord."

I heard her whisper very softly, "Thanks, be to God."

The road installation went rather quickly as the weather held out. Betty Anne, her father and their crew were the real deal. There was no messing around with this bunch! In no time at all, the crew had cut the roadway, dug and set curbs, leveled, and graded it, had some stone brought in, and the surface paved smooth and clean. The only remaining item left was the installation of the road sign with my father-in-law's name on it.

I could picture what a huge event that would be in the very near future as I could see it now in my mind. I am sure the front lawn of the church will overflow with reporters, cameras, and television crews, all out there, clamoring over each other, as Dad Hobnobber would, "humbly" accept such an honor, while pointing at a road sign with his name emblazoned upon it!

As the excavating and paving crew worked, I had the pleasure of meeting them all. Dave and I would go out and check on the progress, bring them coffee and snacks, and interact with them, as they worked out in front of the church.

I really enjoyed chatting with Betty Anne's father. He was a big hockey fan, and we shared some stories and hockey opinions. He was amazed at my old career and swore that he saw me play a long time ago at the old Ice

Land rink down in Great Falls. He was as much fun as he was large. He was outgoing, gregarious, honest, and let me tell you, by what I was watching him move and pick up with one hand, he was one strong guy! I greatly enjoyed our time together, and I hoped that I could spend more time with him.

He was, as my old man would say, "A hard hat guy." I loved how my father could define people with a short, quick label that created a picture in your mind's eye that was absolutely perfect. Mr. Schmidt was a hard hat guy, and that truly summed it all up.

Harry and some of his workers came out to the church later in the afternoon. Along with assistance from Dave and me, we installed Rose's promotional banner. It hung down from the front of the church to some stakes that we had tapped into the ground.

It was huge! It covered most of the front of the church and it waved in the wind like some giant advertisement for the Tremont Cup hockey finals. It sure was something that was for sure! I could hear Von Houten screaming at me already. Harry went to his truck, pulled out some stakes and another little, banner sign.

"Here, we need to put this out here also under the large sign. Please give me a hand here, Sharpie. I came up with this one on my own. Rose does not know about it yet."

He unraveled it, and we all gathered around it to see what it said.

Dave read it aloud to all of us, "All you can eat! Serving authentic Harry Burgers, from The Lovely Rose in Paterson, New Jersey. Meet and greet the beautiful Ms. Rose herself in person!"

Harry beamed like a lighthouse as he told me, "Sorry, pastor, but sometimes you have to pull out all the stops in the name of promoting the gospel. Food, beautiful and sexy women. You have to sell it, you know . . . brings them old, tired, worn out souls searching for meaning and maybe a little love-making in their lives, out of their lairs. I wished you had let me serve booze, wine, and beer. I would have packed the joint. Shameless, uninhibited, self-promotion there, Pastor Paul, this is no time for your usual, good guy, conservative approach! But old Harry, can only bring them here. It is up to you, the famous hippie Pastor Paul, to make the saves of their souls!"

The big guy put his arm around me and pointed up at the sign, "But saving is what you always have done there, Paul."

"How much did this all cost, Harry?"

"Oh, you are still such an old lady, Paul, don't worry about that stuff. Old number thirty-five has it all covered."

He stood back admiring the signs and I could see his chest swell with pride. "I told you that Rose is a marketing genius, that gal has almost as beautiful a mind as she is beautiful. I love it!"

Harry ran out towards the roadway. He was now jumping up and down, pointing at the sign while he screamed at the top of his lungs, "I love this! Now that's what I am talking about!"

Harry screamed as passing cars beeped their horns and flashed their headlights. Only in New Jersey did things such as these seem ordinary.

"He sure is quite the character, Pastor Paul," Dave commented as we watched Harry jump up and down and attract attention.

"Yes, he is, Dave. He could sell ice to an Eskimo."

"I know that. I must have ten Annoy-O-Meters already. I am running out of walls to hang them on."

Saturday came and Binky, Rose, Dave, Harry, Tinky, and I spent all day setting up, cleaning, and prepping the fellowship hall of the church, to be ready in time for the big dinner.

The hall was a very large building and could hold quite a few people. It was wide open, with a large tile floor, some rooms that served as classrooms lining the perimeter, and it had a good-sized kitchen on the one end. We all worked hard to whip this large hall into something special for dinner.

Binky agreed with me that I should continue my old ways, so I remained dressed in my usual garb. I wore a No Way tee shirt, canvas sneakers, and dungarees. After all, why change now? We all agreed to keep it casual, some religious music as well as secular, keep it friendly and open. I thought it was a good plan.

Before we left our house, for some reason, I gathered up a lot of old music tapes and threw them in a box. One or two caught my eye that I had not listened to in a very long time. I picked up many of them and placed them back into the box. When I picked up, "The Greatest Hits of the Riding the Range Boys Band," for some reason, I lingered on that one for a while. After some thought, I threw it in the box and took it along, but I didn't really know why.

I had not listened to it in a very long time.

Once we arrived at the fellowship hall, I set the music center up with a cassette player and some speakers on a table in the center of the hall along one side. I placed the box of tapes next to the table for use later. The food arrived, along with my merry band of followers, as Bishop Von Houten would say. My sister and her family came up from southern New Jersey. My parents attended, as did Linda and Ronzo, Dave Sharp and Mrs. Sharp, the Hobnobbers, Betty Anne and her family, in fact, all the crews who were local. Father Mark was missing, as was Mr. Redmond, the Big Spike, and Patty, but they were all with us in spirit.

I actually had the pleasure of a wonderful telephone call with Mr. Redmond earlier in the week, and he sounded wonderful. We shared some of the latest news, and he was thrilled to hear of all the work and repairs that Harry and I had accomplished together.

"Your old man and I taught you boys well, how to use

those tools," he proudly told me. "Only buy those Substantial Industries tools, Paul, the others just do not last as long."

I had to agree with Mr. Redmond on all of his advice and thoughts.

The local reporter for the small-town newspaper, the *Morris County Blabber*, came by and of course, Senator William T. Hobnobber swooped in for the interview. The sheer magnitude of my father-in-law's personality caught the poor newspaper reporter off guard and overwhelmed him. At six o'clock, which was an hour early, the hall was already packed. I would guess the turnout to be well over one hundred persons.

The crowd was a mix of young and old, there were some new people, as well as old parishioners who came out to see what was new at Reunion Lutheran Church. It was fantastic because you could just feel the spirit rapidly building.

Dad Hobnobber was in his glory, working the floor, while meeting, greeting, and stumping for votes for his fall reelection campaign. Luckily, Harry, Tinky, and Rose brought along some of their crew from the restaurant, as it was hard to keep up with all the food and drinks. It appeared that it was a huge success. We were all working hard in the kitchen and Harry was ecstatic.

He praised Rose up and down, "I told you guys, she is a genius, sheer genius! This place is packed! A huge hit, Paul, a huge hit!"

Binky had purchased a large bouquet of red and yellow roses, which she placed in a vase. She then placed the rose display upon a table set on the side of the hall. I placed some pamphlets and information about the church on the same table, as well as some brochures on The Lovely Rose. It was the least we could do for Harry's generous donation as well as Rose and Tinky's hard work and efforts.

As we all worked in the kitchen, I felt a tap on my

shoulder and a familiar voice interrupted me.

"Finely dressed for the occasion, I see, huh, Henson?"

I turned around to see Bishop Von Houten standing behind me. I turned around, smiled, and reached out my hand to welcome my boss.

"Welcome bishop, it is great to see you!"

"Ah, ah, no handshaking Henson, golf tomorrow. I was a little late, but I did manage to meet the young reporter out there from the local newspaper. Recognizing my importance in this entire event, he took my picture as well as promised a full-page article on me, my career, and the overwhelming role that I had here in the success of the restoration of this church."

"Congratulations, Bishop Von Houten, that is really wonderful."

"Yeah, yeah, yeah, well it is. Say, pick me up about fifty copies or so of that paper when it comes out, will you Henson, I need it for my memoirs and to show off to Rabbi Goldberg."

"Will do, sir."

"I know I will regret asking this, but please, Henson, tell me where do you get this unusual behavior from? You suffer from delusions, Henson, and this time, you must really have your head examined from all those knocks on your noggin' while playing goal. Only God saves more than, twenty-seven! Leave it to you to turn the gospel into a sideshow, Henson. I swear you drive me crazier every day!"

Binky and Rose saw that I was in trouble. They quickly mobilized, scrambled, and came to my rescue. The both of them came over to greet and say hello to the bishop. They were dressed to kill. Both of them looked stunning, perfect hair, wide smiles, all perfumed up, and they turned the charm buttons up to maximum settings. Smiling, they greeted the bishop, and he immediately melted into a pile of quivering Bishop Von Houten gelatin.

"Why, Bishop Von Houten, it is wonderful to see you! You are looking so well," Binky leaned in and kissed him on his cheek.

Rose circled in on his defenseless left flank.

"Bishop, is that a tan I see on you? My, how you are looking so handsome. All that time on the golf course, no doubt!" Rose swooped in giving him a maximum dose of perfume and charm.

"Why, Mrs. Henson and Ms. Rose, it is so nice to see you both again! Thank you, yes. I have been out on the course a little here and there, you know, very busy all the time in the office, but I do get out a little now and then."

He sucked in his belly and tried to move the excess to his chest.

"Did I tell you that I won another tournament last week? Beat the yarmulke right off of Rabbi Goldberg's head."

A quick dose of perfume, an innovative and strategic wiggle here and there, a flip of the hairdos, a little attention, and Bishop Von Houten was renewed!

The next round of diversionary tactics came from Harry, who promptly produced a Harry Burger, along with all the sides.

"Here you go there, bishop old boy, a Harry Burger prepared just for you as the guest of honor!"

"Why, thank you, Redmond! I wish Henson had your manners and realized my importance as much as you do. Did you ever consider a career in the ministry, Redmond?"

Bishop Von Houten sat down right there in the kitchen and took a big bite of the burger.

Between his stomach and his mind, the team had now neutralized Bishop Von Houten.

I pointed to the podium and looked at my watch, "I better get out there. It is just about seven."

I walked out to a small podium we had set up and tapped on the microphone. The crowd hushed and gathered around the center of the hall in front of the podium.

"Good evening and welcome to Reunion Lutheran Church and our rededication dinner. I am Pastor Paul John Henson and on behalf of my family and friends, I would like to thank everyone for coming here tonight. I would be remiss in first not welcoming our special guest of honor, Bishop Werner Beck Clodhopper Von Houten."

I turned and pointed towards the kitchen, hoping that my boss could stop eating for long enough to listen to my words.

"Who, without his expert guidance, leadership, and support, we would not be standing here this evening. The bishop is in attendance here tonight. Please join me in thanking him for his efforts."

I knew how to butter my own bread for sure. Bishop Von Houten appeared from inside the kitchen and bowed as the crowd clapped and acknowledged him. He waved to the crowd and smiled broadly.

I could see a little blob of ketchup stuck to the side of his mouth.

"I also would like to thank Senator William T. Hobnobber, who is also here tonight. The senator was the driving force in finally completing the road out in front of the church."

The crowd once more clapped, Dad Hobnobber stood up, and worked the crowd like the expert he is. Bishop Von Houten and Dad Hobnobber were certainly two peas in a pod!

"I also need to thank Mr. Harry M. Redmond Jr., Ms. Rose Rose, and Tinky Hobnobber from The Lovely Rose club and restaurant in my home city of Paterson, for all the wonderful food that they so kindly have donated to us tonight."

The three of them stood and waved together to the crowd.

"Let us all bow our heads and pray. Lord Jesus, we

gather here renewed and reunited, once more to thank you and give you glory and thanks for all you have given to us tonight and always. Amen."

Short and sweet, Henson, keep it short and sweet. This crowd wants to eat and have fun tonight. I could sense it. Get in the net, make the saves, win the game, and go home. No time for big, boring, blabber. My hockey sense still served me well.

"Tonight, is all about reunion and renewal. It is my hope that those of you, who know this church already, will continue to come and support it, and those of you who are searching for a church home will consider this a place to attend, to have fun, share in the gospel, and be renewed. I look forward to meeting and greeting each of you tonight and hope that you will come back tomorrow for the worship service. However, tonight, we will eat together, dance a little, laugh a lot, and share in the moment. I have been so lucky and blessed in my life, to have the greatest wife in the world, to have the love of my parents, and friends and family. Without them, I would be nothing. They are my guiding light and strength, and they are who drive me. This church has been reunited and renewed from the grace of God for his glory. However, each one of us requires reunions of ourselves and renewal of our spirits. On occasion, it is good to retool our lives once in a while. Sometimes, life's twists and turns leave you tired and worn, just as this church was until just a few short weeks ago. It is God's plan for all of us to look around, breathe deeply, and take a long, hard, look at where we are going. Regardless of where you have been, or where you may be right now, if your life has been a difficult one, or if you have all the joys that you could imagine, then tonight pray for reunion with God and renewal for the future. That is really the message of the Gospel. It provides us with reunions in Heaven and renewal for now and evermore. Thanks, be to God, Amen."

Binky met me at the side of the podium and gave me a hug, and Dave Sharp back slapped me as I passed him by. He then turned, hugged me and thanked me.

Bishop Von Houten walked over with his napkin still stuck in his neckline and stood next to me as we watched the reaction of the crowd.

The crowd seemed happy, as though they connected with and enjoyed my message. A few loud claps broke out and then slowly built until the hall was ablaze with claps and cheers.

Their spirits were renewed, or they just were hungry and were very glad I shut up so they could eat.

Time would tell.

"Well done, Henson, well done. You know, for a long-haired hippie, whacko—you do seem to have a handle on things."

"Thank you, sir, I do my best."

"You bunch of bananas sure hug and kiss each other all the time around here. I think you are the most emotional bunch I have ever run into."

"I agree, sir, we are all very close."

The bishop stood next to Binky and me, and looked out at the crowd, as they were all now moving about, eating, and sharing in one another's company. Some people you could clearly see were old friends, reuniting, and some were new acquaintances, but it all seemed to be working. Bishop Von Houten seemed to be taking it all in and gathering his thoughts.

Tinky walked over to the music table, dropped in a tape, and some music from The Beer Caps and Soda Band floated out of the speakers. Tinky grabbed Betty Anne, and they were soon out there, jumping and dancing to, "Twist, Jump Around, and Shout."

I noticed the bishop's foot tapping in time to the music at the same time that Binky also noticed it. Binky grabbed my hand, pointed down at it to me, and smiled.

Bishop Von Houten looked out at Tinky and Betty Anne jumping around and dancing on the hall floor. He leaned over in close to speak with me, "I hope the floor joists are strong here, Henson, you did not have to repair those, did you?"

"No sir, they seemed to be in good condition."

"I sure hope so, with those two pineapples jumping around out there."

Bishop Von Houten stood back up and he almost smiled. He seemed to be enjoying this evening.

"You know something, Henson? I had told you when we were sitting together in that church over in Bergen County, where I gave you a chance to prove yourself that I felt I would come to regret that day. I had spotted those old sneakers under your robe, and I thought to myself that you were hopeless, Henson. Do you remember that statement?"

"I do, Bishop Von Houten. I do remember that."

"It does pain me to admit that I was wrong. In fact, I will go so far as to say that I have joy in my heart over that day, Henson, I really do. I have prayed about it quite often, and even though I am a crusty, old, codger, Henson, I do think you are a gift from God to me, here late in my career. You have renewed me. You know . . . even bishops require renewal and reunion of faith. You will understand that someday, Henson, you really will."

He smiled at me as I placed my hand gently on his shoulder. Binky put her arm around his shoulders and she pulled him closer to her.

Bishop Von Houten had tears in his eyes, and he did not make any attempt to hide them.

He looked at me and stated, "I think I finally know what it is about you! You are a rock, Henson. A big, fearless, giant, rock that will take on anything. You always remain positive, despite all the things that come your way, and it rubs off on everyone around you. It is a quiet optimism. A confidence that it will always turn out right . . . no matter how difficult or strange the situation is. I have no real, accurate, description of you other than that. Not even the strongest hammer or the hardest blow dents you, Henson . . . nothing. I agree with that old priest, Father Mike, you are strong because God gives you something special, an edge, a guiding light, that includes an inner fire that burns bright and strong. God moves you where God needs you, because that is what your mission is, Henson. It really is. You are certainly the most annoying fellow that I have ever met."

"Thank you, sir, I appreciate that. With all due respect, bishop, it is Father Mark, not Mike."

"That is what I said, Henson! Father Mark. All those years of listening to that loud, No Way music has ruined your ears. Get that checked next week along with your head. Will you please do that, Henson?"

"I will do that, sir."

The bishop turned and walked back to the kitchen and I heard him shout, "Hey, Redmond, let me have another one of those fantastic, Harry Burgers!"

"Come on in here, bishop old boy! Sit down, and let me tell you about the time when we were dopey little kids, that Paul and I tied Father Mark's leg to a chair at a picnic in our yard! Well, being perfectly honest, I tied his leg to the chair. Paul was trying to untie it without him noticing. You see, I think old Father Mark had a few too many glasses of the old communion wine and he. . .."

Binky and I mingled together, and we worked the crowd. I introduced Binky and myself to more people than I could ever remember, but we both did our best to place the names and faces for future meetings. We met an awful lot of people. It became hard to keep track of them all, but it was going very well. Having a drop dead, gorgeous wife such as Binky Hobnobber Henson on my arm sure helped me make some headway here! Everyone seemed positive, excited, and happy.

We were about an hour or so into the event when I

spotted Rose off to the side chatting up a storm with a handsome young man. I then recognized him as being the deliveryman who came that day to drop off the parts from the electrical supply house.

Ah ha!

I surmised that he had seen the sign out on the highway and returned tonight, to take us up on what the sign had advertised. After all, it had broadcast to the passers-by, the offering of meeting Rose once more. He had now stepped up his game in the pursuit of the lovely Rose.

I pointed the meeting out to Binky who raised her eyebrows and shrugged her shoulders a bit, as she spoke, "She seems to be enthralled by him, Paul, and he is very handsome too. Perhaps, Rose has finally found herself someone."

Rose had a soda in one hand, and she was laughing and listening intently to the young man as he spoke. She was working him like a fine violin. You could easily see that the man was smitten. Binky and I walked over to the side near the music table when I spotted Harry pop out of the kitchen. He wiped his hands on a towel, and put his hands on his hips, while he stood there surveying the crowd.

As he casually stood there, his eyes scanned over the hall, but they stopped when he spotted Rose and the young man off in the corner. Even from a few feet away, I could see the look on his face change. Then it came over him. As his posture changed, he clapped his hands together, pushed the hair back from his forehead, threw the towel on a nearby table, and he dug at the floor of the hall a little.

I knew that look so well; it was a look I had seen so many times before in our seemingly endless adventures and the sharing of our lives together.

I called it, the eye of the tiger.

I had seen it in hockey games when the action became fast or intense. Harry played defense in front of me for years, from when we were little kids hacking around on

Geyer Street, to playing on the ice together. Harry was a solid defenseman; he knew how to play the game. In the corners and behind the net, there was no better player along the boards. Until Harry hung up his skates after suffering that terrible injury, I really thought the two of us had a chance to play together for many years at a high level. Harry would turn on a dime when the pressure of the game changed. I would make a big save and Harry would skate over to me, tap my pads, and smile. He would then turn into a raging dynamo that made the notorious hockey tough-guy, Jim O'Malley, even in his heyday, look like a cupcake. I would also see it when a job went south, and we were in trouble, and we had parts and pieces all over the floor that just would not go together. I had seen the eye of the tiger, when a big, giant, tattooed guy that was like the side of Mount Everest would challenge him in a fight. I also saw it when Harry roller skated forty hours straight to win back the heart of a young lady and raise a lot of money for a charity, and I saw it a long time ago in an incident involving a famous punch bowl at a dance. Until now, the last time that I saw it was recently on the tennis court when the Manginis insulted us and we defeated them so soundly.

When Harry had the eye of the tiger, then defeat was just not an option.

He had that same look now, as he stared at Rose and her newly found suitor. It was there, rising up in his eye as a thermometer would on a hot July afternoon.

A sudden thought hit me, like a quick blast in my mind, and I went back to another time and place. I then remembered the tapes that I brought from home. I ran over to the box and thumbed through them until I found it. I was a little frantic because I knew what I had to do! I stopped the music and some folks who were dancing looked over at me to see what had happened.

Binky quickly walked over and asked, "Twenty-seven, what are you doing? Those people were dancing."

I waved to the folks out on the dance floor, as I mouthed that I was sorry, and then turned to Binky, "I know, dear Binky, but trust me, please, I just have to do this, I will explain and you will understand in a second. I am so sorry."

I found the tape that I needed, spun it in my hand, and popped in the Riding the Range Boys Band tape! I fast-forwarded it to the selection I wanted and pushed the play button. I smiled as the music started to play the famous song, "I Heard It in My Cowboy Hat," and I turned back towards Harry.

Harry heard the music start. He looked over to me with a surprised look on his face, and he studied me for a little while, because my changing of the music puzzled him for just a moment. I think he was searching the recesses of his mind for the memory, and it puzzled him as to why I had dropped that particular tape. I hoped that we were both on the same wavelength. I was doing my best at guiding him and pushing him for that trigger that he had been searching so badly to find.

Suddenly, Harry received the transmission loud and clear.

He broke into a wide smile, with a spin of his right hand, and a wave of his fingers, he sent me our quick, "Harry and Paul, hand sign of acknowledgement."

Binky was also watching the scene unfold. She now slowly walked back to my side, as she was also not quite sure of what I had done, and what Harry and I were communicating to each other.

I smiled back at him. He looked at Rose, then back towards Binky and me.

"Oh Paul, oh Paul," was all my wife could say as she grabbed my arm and intertwined it in hers. She also had remembered the last time that we heard this song together, such a long time ago. Binky put her hand over her mouth as she often does when she is nervous. We both stood there watching together while the memories stirred in the three of our minds and in our hearts.

When the song reached the verse where the singer belts out, "If I ever married a woman, then it would be you," we watched Harry powerfully stride across the floor of the hall towards Rose and her new would-be beau. He stopped along the way, just for a moment, at the table where Binky had placed the vase of roses, and pulled one long rose out of the vase. After plucking a single rose from the bunch, Harry then continued on his way towards Rose and the man.

When he reached them both, I saw Harry say, "Excuse me" to the young man as he gently moved him out of the way.

Harry grabbed Rose, took the soda glass out of her hand, and gently placed it on a table. He then handed her the rose from his hand, gracefully bowed in front of her, bent her over, and gave her one of his famous, grandstanding, Harry kisses!

Rose was shocked and when the kiss ended, she reached up and hugged Harry around the neck as if she would never let him go.

The poor, young man walked away, I guess that was the last thing that he had ever expected would happen!

Harry then very quickly led Rose by her hand out on the dance floor. He whipped her around like a rag doll once more, just like that night so long ago at Lord Crudley's Bar. All that was missing was Harry's big, ten-gallon hat and those expensive, black cowboy boots.

What a scene! The trigger had finally come! Harry M. Redmond Jr. was back indeed, and Ms. Rose Rose was at his side once more.

I now knew that these days would be the days that we would talk about fondly, not only just the days of all those old memories.

"Bink-a-roo-ski, I reckon old Harry has found himself

one of them, there, pretty gals to dance with now, hasn't he?"

Binky looked up at me with those irresistible blue eyes, "I reckon so, Paul. Now nothing will be impossible for them, not kissing the sun, or touching the stars, or walking barefoot, across some hot desert. Nothing at all."

I recognized my own words and shook my head. My wife was simply amazing. She really was.

Bishop Von Houten wandered over, as it seemed like every person in the entire hall was now watching Rose and Harry.

He placed his hand on my shoulder and softly said, "Henson, you better brush up on your wedding services because I have a strange feeling that you have one coming up."

"Yes sir, I will do that."

I now knew why, I had to take along that tape tonight.

Somewhere, some place, wherever he might be right now, either hidden in the dark recess of a basement, or tied to a porch rail, waving in the wind . . . Mr. Bug shed a tear.

It was a fantastic, crisp, autumn afternoon in early October 1988. The sky was clear and bright, with only a few little white wisps of clouds passing along. It was becoming later in the afternoon now, and the sanctuary at Reunion Lutheran Church had people packed to the rafters.

Everyone was there, friends of ours from far and wide, as well as Mr. Redmond, Linny, Ronzo, Patty, the Big Spike, Betty Anne, Dave and Mrs. Sharp, my parents, my sister, my in-laws, oh my, all of them! Even the man himself; Bishop Werner Beck Clodhopper Von Houten and Mrs. Von Houten attended, along with his best friend, Rabbi Irving Goldberg and Mrs. Goldberg. The church was full of people because it was as if a Hollywood celebrity attended this afternoon.

You see, I was the best man for Harry M. Redmond Jr. at a wedding this afternoon, with just a little twist to it. I also was the pastor that was performing the service, because I was marrying him this day, to the lovely Ms. Rose Rose.

Standing next to Harry was Ronzo, the Big Spike, and Tinky. Next to Rose stood my wife, as well as Linda and Patty.

After waves and waves of words laced with a multitude of emotions, I finally arrived at the part of the ceremony where I said, "I now pronounce you man and wife."

After I made the pronouncement, I reached down to the wheelchair next to me and gently pulled Father Mark to his feet.

He held his hands over his head and said in a loud, clear voice that could have come from a twenty-year-old man, "And all of God's people say!"

"AMEN!" shouted the congregation.

"Give her a kiss, Harry."

It was the perfect ending to another, Harry, Paul, Rose, and Binky, and oh my, there are now so many others . . . perfect day.

After the exit fanfare ended, I headed to the pastor's room off to the side of the sanctuary to change out of my robe. I was changing clothes to hustle off to the reception, where I knew we had to prepare for one more of those famous Redmond shindigs. I had promised Binky that I would wear my black suit and collar, so I needed to change into that quickly.

I exited the pastor's quarters in the rear of the sanctuary and noticed my wife was sitting on the edge of a pew waiting for me. She stood up and smiled. She looked radiant, as usual, in her fabulous maid of honor gown.

"You did well, there twenty-seven, what a great service."

"Thank you, my dear Binky. Indeed, it was a wonderful time, a great time, in fact." I paused for a moment as I thought and then said, "A long time coming, that was for sure. Hey, it was my first wedding!"

She met me and greeted me with a kiss and a hug.

"I suppose we better get off to the reception, you know the drill, pictures have to be taken, and dances need to be danced."

Binky laughed as she put her hand in mine, as we walked side by side up the center aisle of the sanctuary. She asked, "Do you think we will need to dance to, 'Living Love?'" Before I could even answer, my wife said confidently, "You lead, of course."

"Ok dear. I am sure I also will get caught for a fake, jealousy filled, Patty dance as well."

"Thank you for wearing your black suit. Paul, you look like someone I should marry and not just date."

We reached the rear door of the sanctuary and opened it up to see an unbelievable sunset in the western sky right in front of us. Hand-in-hand, we both stopped and stared at the panorama.

It was breathtaking.

Golden rays of sun illuminated the red, gold, and yellow leaves that had created a colorful tapestry on the trees surrounding the church property. Fading sunlight bathed the surreal scene . . . it was as if the sunlight was streaming straight down from Heaven. In light of the day's events and the events of the past, we were indeed witnessing a broadcast of hope, joy, and peace straight from God.

"You know, Paul. We really should look into moving into that little, parsonage house here. Dave is quite correct that this place is one of the loveliest spots on Earth. You can see the hand of God in those trees. You could fix it all up with Harry, Ronzo, and Dave. We all could be very happy there."

"It is very nice, Binky, that is for sure."

"It has such a large backyard that you could build a swing set, and maybe, a little playground for children back there."

"I could indeed. It is a great backyard."

We took a few steps and stopped to look once more at the sunset.

"Do you think that hockey store that you buy items from up on Loudon Road in upstate New York, sells little, tiny, infant hockey jerseys? I am thinking about ordering some little, tiny, Long Island Rooster jerseys with the number twenty-seven on the back."

A bell went off in my thick, puck-hardened head! Swing sets, houses, playgrounds, infant hockey jerseys! Ding! Ding! Ding!

I looked at Binky and she smiled while I saw a little tear roll down her cheek. I grabbed her and hugged her tightly.

"When did you find out?"

"Yesterday, the doctor called. I just had to wait until after the wedding to tell you, I thought it would be so special. The baby will be due according to my research . . . around May, twenty-seventh."

I felt that cold shiver along my spine once more. Thank you, Sky, thank you once more. I knew it would be on the twenty-seventh, I just knew it.

When we pulled away, I felt the tears rolling down my cheeks. Binky saw the tears. She smiled as she reached for a tissue from her purse and dabbed at them on my face.

"Oh my, now, my dear twenty-seven, is that really some tears that I see on your face?"

"I reckon so there, Bink-a-roo-ski, it sure is." I then softly whispered to her, "Rwy'n dy garu di wastad ac am byth."

In front of us as we hugged, the sky was perfectly lit up with the sinking sun, displaying radiant blue skies from one end of the horizon to the other. If you studied the sky carefully, you could just see the last remnants of some white, puffy clouds floating here and there in between the rays of sunlight peeking out from what remained of the now fading day.

THE END

Epilogue

The telephone rang on my desk and it startled me. I shook my head a number of times and came back to reality. I wondered how long I had been staring out that window at the sunset.

I picked up the receiver and before I could even finish saying my greeting, I heard Harry's voice ask, "What are you, Binky, and the kids, doing this weekend after church?"

"Well, I do not know, we had not really planned anything yet, why Harry?"

"Can you get away for the week with Rose, Blue Cloud, and me?"

"I don't know. I need to check. You know how it is, Harry, I need to check with Binky and plan out my work, see what is going on. . .."

"Oh please, you are the big chief guy now, are you kidding me!"

"Well, where are we going? Sometimes Harry, I would just once like to know what you are planning in advance, just once in my lifetime, Harry."

"Oh, geez! Stop being such an old lady, will you, Paul? You of all people know that it is one adventure after another, so come along for the ride and see where it all takes us."

ABOUT THE AUTHOR

If you ask Paul John Hausleben, he will tell you that he is not an author, he is just a storyteller. His mission is to continue to write and tell stories to warm your heart, make you laugh, and sometimes make you cry, just a little. Most of all, he deals in memories, and helps you to remember the good times of your own life, and the special people who touched you along the way. Paul was born and raised in Paterson, and then nearby Haledon, New Jersey, and began writing at an early age. He revisited a writing career later in his life, and he now is the author of a number of novels, compilations, short stories and audio and video works. Most of his work touches upon nostalgic remembrances of simpler times, and tells the stories of heartfelt, humorous, and special human relationships. Other than writing, among many careers both paid and unpaid, he is a former semi-professional hockey goaltender, a music fan and music reviewer, an avid sports fan, photographer and amateur radio operator. He now resides in Somewhere, U.S.A., but his heart always remains along Belmont Avenue in good old Paterson, and Haledon, New Jersey.

Other books by Mr. Hausleben that you also may enjoy

The Time Bomb in The Cupboard and Other Adventures of Harry and Paul.

The Night Always Comes, Another story from the Adventures of Harry and Paul.

The Autumn Collection

The Christmas Tree and Other Christmas Stories. Tales for a Christmas Evening

Crows on a High Wire

The Miracle Tree, Another story from the Adventures of Harry and Paul

Heaven's Gain

The Summer Collection

And many others

Coming Soon?

You may contact us via email at ctte27@gmail.com

www.ingramcontent.com/pod-product-compliance
Lightning Source LLC
LaVergne TN
LVHW020657110826
845149LV00012B/2022

* 9 7 8 0 9 8 8 6 3 3 6 2 9 *